A PLAGUE OF SWORDS

MILES CAMERON

This edition first published in Great Britain in 2017 by Gollancz

First published in Great Britain in 2016 by Gollancz
an imprint of the Orion Publishing Group Ltd
Carmelite House, 50 Victoria Embankment
London EC4Y 0DZ

An Hachette UK Company

1 3 5 7 9 10 8 6 4 2

Copyright © Miles Cameron 2016
Maps copyright © Steven Sandford 2013

A CIP catalogue record for this book is
available from the British Library.

ISBN 978 1 473 20887 2

Printed and bound by CPI Group (UK) Ltd, Croydon, CR0 4YY

www.traitorson.com
www.orionbooks.co.uk
www.gollancz.co.uk

To the members of the Compagnia della Rosa nella Sole
From whom I learn, every day and every event
This book is dedicated

NORTH HURAN

Squash Country

N'Pano

Thorn

ADNACR

INNER SEA

Nigara

Albi
Lissen Carak
S'Hawks

Colocton R.

Ruin hil
Aba du Jour

The Stones

South Colocton

The ALBIN

HARD FELLS

N

ALBA
ENCIRCLED by the WILD

SOUTH HURAN

The Great River →

THRAKE

Green Hills

Middleburg

Lonika

Amfipolis

THRAKE BAY

To Alba

MOREA

LIVIAPOLIS

MOREA BAY

Broget

NORTH

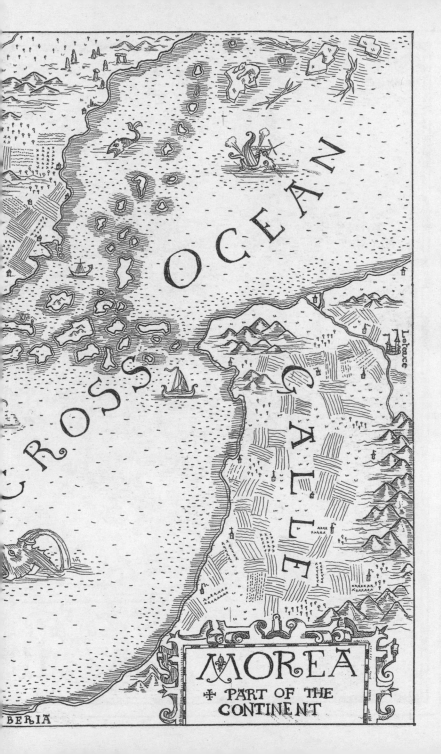

CROSS OCEAN

GALLE

Leitauce

MOREA
✠ PART OF THE
CONTINENT

BERIA

Barracks
Stables

University

Lion's Mouth

Student Quarter

Liu

Prologue

Spring—Southern Galle

This is absurd," the King of Galle said. He looked at his military councilors, who gathered their horses around him.

To the south, the direction in which the Royal Army of Galle was crawling, stretched several miles of armoured men and horses, baggage wagons, pack mules, donkeys, carts full of tents and cookpots and food and wine. They were strung out along a road built in the ancient past and expected, in the present, to support the occasional convoy of merchants into the mountains and a trickle of pilgrims visiting those religious sites still in the hands of man.

They were moving through an empty landscape. Villages were deserted as far abroad as the foragers rode; sheep pens were empty, no cattle lowed, and there was almost nothing for the army to steal, which was making it hungry and surly.

"Nonetheless," Ablemont said. He paused, waiting until the king's temper passed and he had his master's full attention. "Nonetheless, Your Grace, we will have to retreat. In three days we will have no food."

The king shrugged. "Then let us retreat in two days. I find all this shameful." He glanced at Ser Tancred Guisarme, the royal constable. "I told you where I needed to go. Was it too much for you, planning to feed my army?"

The high constable had endured several weeks of marching with the king, and he turned a little redder than the spring sun had burned his unarmoured face, but he was outwardly calm. "Your Grace," he began.

Ablemont raised an eyebrow. "We have kept Your Grace informed as to the`…hmm…difficulties. Of the deserted countryside." He fingered his beard. In the fastness of his mind, Ablemont was not wasting words on his king. He was instead considering how very much he wanted to retreat out of this countryside empty of life, and begin again, with spies and carefully tended scouts. And some contact with his brother in Arles. If there was anyone still alive in Arles. His total ignorance of their foe was the most terrifying aspect of their whole situation.

"I have sworn to relieve Arles," the king said. His voice held a hint of gloating. After all, the Count of Arles begging aid from his king put the stamp of legitimacy on the usurpations of the last generation. And would reverse the contretemps of a year ago, when the king's unsubtle attempt to seize Arles had been frustrated by an unknown foreign sell-sword.

Arles, once an independent kingdom, had been recently annexed to the crown of Galle. Only last fall, the rumours had begun that creatures of the Wild were loose in the mountains of Arles.

The Lord of Ablemont had been born in those mountains. Indeed, his brother was Count of Arles and ruled the rump of the kingdom that their grandfather had ruined and their father had nearly forfeited. He looked at the foothills around them, the deep folds in the earth, the heavy dark forests. Ahead, to the south, the true mountains rose, and there would still be snow in the deep woods and on the mountaintops.

He shivered, despite the miniver that lined his hood and his magnificent white surcoat. The city of Arles—one of the oldest settlements of mankind in the Antica Terra, with a fortress that towered even above the mountains, a fortress that the hill people said had been built not by men, but by God. Or gods. Depending on your point of view and the nearness of a priest of Rhum.

His brother, who hated the king; whose daughter Clarissa had been attacked by the king in one of his predatory moods; who desired nothing more than the restitution of sovereignty that history had denied him—*his brother* had begged the King of Galle to rescue him from the attacks of the Wild. And yet, despite the fact that the army was a mere two or three days' travel from the great fortress city, they had received no word, no messenger.

Only the silence of the woods, and the empty villages.

All this in the passage of a few heartbeats.

"If we wait two days to retreat, we will lose horses to starvation while we move back to our supplies," Ablemont said. He did not say, *and our retreat will be a shambles, a rout, without our ever seeing a single foe.*

The king pursed his lips. "I won't have it," he said. "Make camp here and send for food."

Ablemont opened his mouth to protest, and instead caught the constable's eye—a decision made in a single heartbeat. It was difficult to resist the king's will at the best of times, and harder still when he was in a temper. Court etiquette defined how even a favourite could and could not speak to his king, and Ablemont's position, however secure, was achieved by managing the king, not by confronting him. And besides—as Ablemont scanned the hills around them—this was a good location, with a shallow stream covering their front, and three high hills on which to locate their camp.

Ablemont's thoughts went immediately to the problem of supply. Every ton of food would have to be moved on this spiderweb-like road net, and he needed to move quickly to have food brought from Austergne, to the north.

"I will put my pavilion here," the king said. "See to it." He waved a gloved hand and rode down toward the stream, and his household knights—the largest, best-trained knights in Galle, and thus the world—followed him.

"See to it!" Guisarme spat. *"Ventre Saint Gris!"*

Ablemont didn't allow a flicker of feeling to cross his face. "Will you site the camp while I arrange for some provisions to reach us?" Ablemont asked.

Guisarme shrugged. "I miss Du Corse. I miss all that experience. He knows everything about war. And camps. Why did the king exile him?"

Ablemont was already writing on a wax tablet.

Guisarme gave orders to two of his own household knights, who cantered off toward the column of wagons behind them. He waved to the king's standard-bearer, Ser Geofroi. The knight, who had perhaps the highest repute of any knight in the kingdom, bowed courteously from his saddle.

"Here, good knight," the constable said, and Ser Geofroi bowed again, rode over, and planted the iron ferrule of the great standard deep in the ground with a single thrust. The wind caught the magnificent standard of blue and gold and blew it out straight. Men cheered.

Ser Geofroi dismounted, gave his horse to his page, and stood, fully armoured, by the standard. He drew his great sword, placed the point fastidiously between his armoured feet, and stood like a steel statue by the great flag.

Ablemont, whose mind worked on several problems at once, finished his third set of orders and looked up to find the royal baggage wagons parked in an orderly row behind Ser Geofroi and half a hundred royal servants beginning to lay out the kitchens, the pavilions, and the horse lines for the household.

Guisarme had just dismissed Vasili, master of the king's works, with a bow of thanks; Steilker, the North Etruscan master of crossbows, was less enthusiastic, but eventually agreed, and he dismounted, handed his horse to a page, and began to issue orders to his own mercenary infantrymen. The Etruscans treated war as a science and not an art; they had precise ways to approach every problem. They'd come to Galle when the Duke of Mitla's daughter, the Queen of Flowers, married the King of Galle. De Ribeaumont and most of the old nobles detested them, but Guisarme found them very useful. Du Corse had sworn by them, before his "exile."

"He failed the king," Ablemont said.

"What?" Guisarme asked.

"You asked me, half an hour back, why the king exiled the Sieur Du Corse. I would answer, he failed the king. And he is not in exile. He is on a vital mission for His Grace."

Guisarme smiled knowingly. "Oh, the Alba adventure," he said. He was old enough to know what he knew, and what he didn't; an old warrior who could neither read nor write, he was canny enough to have survived three kings of Galle and a great deal of war. "He failed in one of the king's ridiculous schemes, you mean," Guisarme said. "So now he's been sent on another. I wasn't born yesterday, Ablemont. I know the king tried to seize Arles, and failed. He tried to seize Dar, too, as I remember, allied with the Necromancer."

4

Ablemont frowned. "That is untrue. Ser Hartmut…"

Ser Tancred laughed, his point made.

Ablemont nodded, his mind already elsewhere. Another man might have winced to be reminded how he had directly helped his king plot the downfall of his own brother, but Ablemont didn't work that way. He enjoyed the exercise of power, and he saw means and ends with a clarity that frightened lesser men. Arles had no need of independence. The King of Galle was ideally situated to unite all of the Antica Terra; with the Duke of Mitla astride all Etrusca and the King of Galle sovereign in the north, their heir—for Mitla had no sons—would be king of all. Emperor in fact, and eventually in name.

Ablemont took a deep breath. His busy thoughts raced around his head—timetables, supply lines, stocks of food. Even as he thought, the royal army halted and began to make camp, and even Ablemont's mind of wheels and gears knew a little jolt of joy. The power of the King of Galle was most clearly expressed by the speed with which his army marched up and built their camp. Knights, the kingdom's mailed fist, did not dig, but the others, archers and spearmen and peasant levies and servants, did. A dozen engineers under the master of crossbowmen—all Etruscans—dismounted with mallets and stakes and white linen tape and began to pace off distances, and behind them, men with spades and picks and shovels came to turn the tape lines into ditches and palisades. Men went up the hillsides looking for trees, axes and saws in hand. Horses were picketed and fed.

Ablemont's first messages, sent to the high officers of the army, arrived, and every one of the Lords of the Host, the feudal officers who commanded contingents under the king, was ordered to put his men and horses at half rations. There was grumbling, but it was muted.

Toward sunset, as Steilker handed in his "suggestions" for guard positions and watches, one of his Etruscan officers came to the edge of the circle of men gathered around Ablemont. He had an older man with him, dressed in a plain mail shirt and thigh-high boots and wearing a plain arming sword with a hooked blade.

"You have almost a third of the army standing watch," Ablemont said.

Steilker nodded. "I haf to assume ve are in the very face of the enemy." He looked around. "Although zo var I haf seen nuthink."

Ablemont looked at his secretary. "All of my couriers are away?"

"They rode an hour ago or more," the secretary replied. "My lord."

He saw the Etruscan officer at the edge of the circle, took in his pallor, his posture, and beckoned. The man bowed.

"My lord, we have found..." He paused. He was clearly shaken.

"Out with it!" Ablemont said impatiently.

The Etruscan shook his head. "You should see for yourself, my lord," he said.

"Far?" Ablemont snapped.

"Half a league," the crossbowman said. "My lord."

Ablemont set his face. "Tell me first."

"Corpses," the Etruscan said. He took a breath of air. "Quite a few."

Ablemont took a breath. "Peasants?" he asked. It was almost a relief.

"My lord should see for himself," the crossbow officer said. He glanced at his mate, the older man.

The older one spat something in Etruscan.

"Where is De Ribeaumont?" Ablemont asked. The marshal was, after the king, the most important man in the army.

"With the king," a squire said.

"Playing cards," murmured a voice.

Ablemont made a disgusted sound. "Very well. Fetch me a horse. A *riding* horse," he said. Ablemont wanted a bath and a cup of hot wine and he wanted everyone to *do their fucking jobs* starting with the king. And De Ribeaumont. He and the aged Guisarme were usually adversaries in the War Council. Twenty days in the field and the old man looked like a better ally every day.

"Ser Tancred?" he asked.

Guisarme shrugged. "Oh, very well. Show me some corpses. I'm sure I'll sleep better."

They followed the Etruscan officer through the last light, across a hillside already denuded of trees, covered in tents, and resounding with the din of ten thousand men snoring. There was no reason for soldiers to linger awake; the food, such as it was, was cooked, and most of the fires were already out.

It was growing colder every minute.

Ablemont followed the Etruscan up the hill with a pair of his own squires, both young men of good family in Arles, and Guisarme and his squires behind. They rode up and up the hill, which was quite high, symmetrical, with a round summit crowned by an ancient dry-stone wall.

"Master Vasili ordered some peasants to clear the summit and build a citadel there," the Etruscan said as they halted and picketed their horses.

Ablemont could see why. The hill was central to their position and high enough to command quite a view. He looked south for a long time, and imagined... was he imagining it? That he could see the lights of Arles. If Arles still held. He passed a hand over his eyes and tried to imagine what the hell was happening.

Something moved at the very edge of his vision—a darkness against the darkness, away to the east. He stumbled in shock. Whatever he had seen was flying, but it must have been huge.

"What's that?" he asked, pointing.

The crossbowman officer paused. "A cloud, my lord? I don't see anything. Too dark."

"What is your name, sir?" Ablemont said.

"Sopra Di Bracchio," the man replied. "My lord. This way."

Ablemont spoke enough Etruscan to know a nom de guerre when he heard one. Some penniless exile from one of the great cities—probably Mitla itself. Ablemont was, in the main, in favour of penniless exiles. They were loyal and their motivations were simple, until and unless they attempted restorations.

"*Bastardi*," Di Bracchio spat. "I left men on guard, and they are gone."

Cold moonlight soaked the round hilltop, and the old stone wall looked like rotting teeth in green-grey gums. Ablemont was shaken by whatever had moved in the corner of his eye. It had been far away, and large, and very black. Or that was the impression he'd received in the fraction of a heartbeat.

Guisarme was still in full harness, and when he dismounted, he drew his sword. When his squires made to dismount, he shook his head. "I'm old, and I've seen a lot of dead bodies," he said with a smile. "You are young. Keep your sweet dreams a little longer."

To Ablemont, he said, "I mislike this. It feels foul. I mislike the missing sentries."

Ablemont wanted to deride the old man's fears, but he could not. "When we reach the camp," Ablemont said, "please locate your missing sentries and send me an explanation." He drew his own sword.

"Stay and watch the horses," he told his own young men.

7

De Braccio nodded. "This way, my lords," he said.

They walked up to the circle and the cold seemed to deepen. And there was a smell—of old earth, of roots and trees and…something cold and metallic. And fresh. And dead.

The stone walls were higher than they appeared. Di Bracchio grunted and led the way to the right, toward a dark depression that was revealed as an entrance.

"So glad we waited for darkness," Ablemont said. "Show me the carrion."

But the words no sooner passed his mouth than he saw them— dozens of corpses. The entrance of the old hill fort had blocked his view, but the inside of the ruin was packed with dead men like the inside of a barrel of salt fish.

"So many men," he said. "There must be…hundreds."

"They ain't men," said the old crossbowman at his side. "Di Bracchio's afraid o' the church, but I ain't. Look at yon."

Ablemont frowned in distaste. "You brought me all the way here to see a charnel house?" he asked. His gorge was rising and the smell was terrible. And *wrong*.

"Oh God," Guisarme said. He knelt by one and his whole body shook. "God," he said again. "Christ and all the saints. Blessed Saint Denis be with us." He was moving quickly.

Ablemont made himself move. "What are you talking about?" he asked. He put the corner of his cloak across his nose. The smell was like an assault. A few of the dead men had odd, long, ribbonlike worms coming out of their eyes, like a disgusting mimicry of tears. But the worms were as dead as the men.

"None so blind as those who will not see," the older man said. "By Saint Maurice, my lord. *Look at them.*"

Something in Ablemont's mind snapped, and he *saw*. They were not men at all.

They were *irks*.

The night seemed to last forever. Ablemont slept badly, and the second time he awoke he'd been in the grip of a nightmare. He rose, pulled on boots and a heavy gown, and walked out of his pavilion, scattering sleepy servants and buckling on an arming sword. He walked along the whole front of the camp, and found every post awake, and most of them equally terrified, although he saw many different methods of controlling fear, from loud, fast talk to angry displays of bravado.

At the far eastern end of their camp he found the Etruscan, Di Bracchio, still awake.

"Have you found your missing men?" Ablemont asked.

Di Bracchio shook his head. "No, my lord."

"Deserted, eh?" Ablemont asked.

Di Bracchio shrugged, a distorted shape in the darkness. "Who would desert here?" he asked.

If Ablemont agreed, he didn't advertise the fact. He walked all the way from the extreme east of the camp to the west, more than a league, and then stumbled back to his tent, still unable to sleep, but relieved at least to find the camp secure.

He lay on his camp bed and stared at the roof of his silken pavilion, which moved in the darkness as a cold wind blew across the camp. He couldn't get the smell out of his head, or the dead monsters' faces out of the gently moving shadows.

The day passed. The ditches deepened, as men dug them deeper, and the walls of dirt and the palisades were raised higher. De Ribeaumont stayed with the king, and Ablemont ordered Vasili to assemble the siege train—heavy catapults, onagers of ancient design, trebuchets of the very latest style, and ballistae that were like immense crossbows. The Etruscans sighted them carefully, but no one made any attempt to occupy the hill that rose behind the camp or the ancient hill fort atop it, and Ablemont, when at last he walked in that direction, thought the smell of death was spreading.

But it was a magnificent spring day, with the sun brilliant in a blue sky decorated with a few fleecy white wool clouds. It was hard for Ablemont to fully remember the terror of the night before.

About noon, the king emerged from his pavilion. "Well?" he asked.

De Ribeaumont stood by him in his magnificent dragon armour.

Ablemont could not hide a tick of frustration. "I'm sorry, Your Grace?"

"When does the *food* arrive?" the king asked. "So that we can resume our advance?"

De Ribeaumont nodded. "The essence of strategy is a strong offence," he said. "To attack is to seize the initiative. Whatever we are facing here, it fears us. These scorched-earth tactics—"

"Scorched earth?" Ablemont asked.

The king waved a hand in dismissal. "De Ribeaumont understands these things," he said. "Our opponent fears the might of our arms, so he drives off all the people and livestock to deny us food."

"We must push on and force battle," De Ribeaumont said. "Since clearly this is what our enemy most fears."

Ablemont felt ill at ease, which was rare for him. He could see that De Ribeaumont, usually his ally, was making a bid to become favourite. And somehow the terror of the night before had robbed the game of its savour. It was as if he didn't care.

In fact, he didn't give a damn. He was scared.

He shrugged. "Your Grace," he said, "we understand nothing of our foe. Last night, one of Your Grace's scouts discovered an old fort at the top of that hill. It is full of corpses."

"You see?" De Ribeaumont said.

"Corpses of creatures of the Wild," Ablemont said.

The king shrugged. "All the better," he said. "Your brother was not completely ineffectual in his defence of this realm of ours."

"And then he withdrew southward," De Ribeaumont said.

"Except that he came from the south, and so, as far as we know, did the Wild," Ablemont said.

The king shook his head. "I'm sorry you are so easily unmanned," the king said. "De Ribeaumont says that we should leave you here to command the camp and move south to attack the enemy."

Ser Tancred Guisarme was in full harness, as the law of war required, and he stood very straight despite his years. He had been silent thus far, but now he spoke. "Your Grace, it would be foolishness to move south without any kind of report on the enemy, his location, or his numbers."

The king merely glanced at his constable. "Old men are often cowards," he said.

Guisarme raised an eyebrow. "Your Grace, I will accept any insult from you, as you are my king. But I will insist that you acknowledge that I have lived to be an old man—an old man of war, who has seen a dozen great battles and a hundred skirmishes. My cowardice is such that many of my foes have regretted. I say, learn something of this foe before you strike."

De Ribeaumont nodded. "I say, ride now, and strike before the opportunity to do so is lost, while our horses and men have full bellies."

"There speaks a true knight of Galle," the king said.

"It is too late in the day to move today," Ablemont said. "Although perhaps the army would benefit by forming for battle on the plain in front of the camp. To better know their order on the day of battle. March tomorrow, Your Grace. By then, perhaps I'll have the first wagonloads of food from the north."

De Ribeaumont looked at Ablemont with a certain derision, as if to say *I know your game.*

But the king nodded to Ablemont. "Now you speak sense at last. Let's form for battle after the noon meal."

And in fact, as they all expected, the royal army took hours to form. Indeed, having started late, the last bannerette was placed in the line on the far left as the sun began to go down behind the hills to the west.

"Almost fifteen thousand men," Ablemont said. "A superb host. The main battle is more than a league long."

"No one is missing?" the king asked.

"A few dozen squires and light horsemen and hunters who are out scouting beyond the hills," Ablemont said.

The whole host made a magnificent show, and when they were formed, before the shadows of the tall pines across the valley began to fall on them, they waited in relative silence, and there was a moment when Albemarle thought that perhaps...just perhaps...something was watching them. Or perhaps some evil enemy army would suddenly appear on the plain in front of them.

No such thing occurred, and the army unfolded much more swiftly than it had formed, dribbled back inside the walls of earth, and cooked its meager dinner.

While Ablemont ate, he was served his scouting reports. His chief forester reported that he had seen rabbits and, to the west, squirrels in the trees.

"Nothing larger than a cat," the man said with a gap-toothed grin. "No deer, no bear, and this in the richest game country in all the southland. My lord."

"And no men," Ablemont said.

"Not a soul," the man said.

It was a day late, but Ablemont had to try everything at hand. "Do me a favour," he said. "Find the Etruscan, Di Bracchio. Ask him to show you where his men were when they deserted. See if you can follow them. Track them."

"Day-old tracks on dry ground, my lord?" The old forester shrugged. "Your faith in me is...probably a bit much, my lord. But I'll have a go before last light." He paused. "Deserted, my lord? That's foolery. No sane man would walk off right now. I been in the woods man an' boy, an' I don't like it out there alone."

The next man was a squire, a local boy who served in Ablemont's household. He was pale, and his eyes seemed odd. Saint Quentin. That was his name. Gaspard Saint Quentin.

"Well, Gaspard, *mon vieux*?" Ablemont asked.

The boy shook his head. "I have bad news, lord," he said. His voice was wooden.

"Out with it," Ablemont said.

"I found..." The young man drew himself up. "I found what must have been one of my lord's couriers. Here's his pouch."

Ablemont found that he was standing. "Damn," he said, far more mildly than he expected.

"He and his horse were..."

Ablemont sighed. "Take your time," he said quietly.

"Shredded," the young man blurted. "Oh sweet Jesus, I have never seen anything like it. Or the maggots and worms all over..." The boy bent suddenly and threw up. "Oh God, oh God," the young man managed, and retched again. "Something's wrong," he said in an odd, detached voice.

Servants saw to the squire, and towels were brought, rags, a bucket of water. The stench was foul, and it tickled Ablemont's throat. And his memory. Something of the smell of the hill fort.

Worms.

He dismissed his fears. He had a more immediate crisis, if his couriers had not gotten through. It had not, until then, occurred to him that he was surrounded.

Saint Quentin shook off the helping hands. He stood up. He seemed to have difficulty controlling himself.

Ablemont knew something was wrong, and got a hand on his sword.

Ah, there we are, said Saint Quentin's voice, except devoid of any nuance. The squire stood in an odd crouch, his weight mostly on one foot, as if he'd forgotten how to stand erect.

"Gaspard?" Ablemont asked.

You command these creatures? Saint Quentin asked.

"Messieur de Saint Quentin!" Ablemont insisted.

No. You command all these creatures?

Ablemont had a very able brain, but he could make no sense of the development. Except that his squire was possessed, and by some demon that could not fully control the young man's body. Even as he watched, it gave a convulsive step, a foot shot out and steadied him... like a bad marionette. Or a drunken man.

"Who are you?" Ablemont hissed. It was unseemly... and disgusting.

You command these creatures? Communicate. Now.

Saint Quentin took an ungainly step toward Ablemont.

"Guards!" the king's favourite shouted.

Another step. The boy swayed toward Ablemont.

A long, pencil-thin worm emerged from one eye.

In an eternity of fear and a need for action, Ablemont's arming sword exploded out of his scabbard. His draw was an upcut that severed the reaching hand and the worm as the blade rose, and the descending cut went deep into the boy's neck, a killing blow.

The squire was not-dead. A hand reached for Ablemont, and the mouth moved.

You command...

Disgust, terror, anger. Ablemont's sword arm had never been so strong.

Saint Quentin's head rolled away from his corpse.

"Stand back!" Ablemont shouted as guards began to pour into the tent. "Back!" he shrieked, his voice breaking.

"Sieur D'Ablemont is quite mad," De Ribeaumont reported to his king. "He has slain one of his squires for making a report. There is blood everywhere."

The king shrugged. "Ablemont has always been a very strange man," he said. "But he is my horse, and I will ride him as I please."

"He is demanding to approach Your Grace. I feel that this is unwise." De Ribeaumont was not quite gloating at the near destruction of his rival.

The king, however, was not quite so fickle. "I have certainly been tempted to kill squires," the king said. "And other bearers of bad tidings. Let him be."

The king went back to bed, and in the morning, he rose, and armed, and was pleased to see his orders obeyed, and the whole of the army forming in the meadow in front of the camp.

He didn't see Ablemont until his great charger was brought. A mounting block was being prepared, and then the man hurried up. He looked hag-ridden.

"You should be in full harness, sir," the king said.

"Your Grace, I beg your attention," Ablemont said. "This is not what it seems. This is not a straightforward war against a simple enemy."

The king reached out a hand and touched his friend on the cheek. "Ablemont," he said. "I am the king."

"Sire!" Ablemont said, and knelt. "Sire! There is something here that we do not understand. It tried . . . to communicate. Or . . ."

The king stepped up onto his mounting block, got a sabatoned foot in his great steel stirrup, and in one easy swing, he mounted. "Go and arm," he said.

Ablemont shook his head. "We have no food. Sire, it is possible none of our messengers have got through. We—"

"We will dine in Arles," the king said. "No more prevarication."

Ablemont drew himself up. "Your Grace," he said. "We have no idea what we face."

"We have the best knights in the world," the king said. "Fear nothing."

They moved across the plain in columns formed by battle: advance, main, rear. They crossed the stream to their front and climbed the next ridge, crested it, and scouts brought them reports of the enemy host waiting at the next ridge.

The army hurried forward. Even Ablemont, riding with his own knights, felt the thrill; to know that the waiting was over, and now they might come to grip with their foe, whether natural or infernal, was a relief.

A herald rode up, saluted, and requested Ablemont's presence with the king.

"Why?" he asked.

"The advance battle has taken prisoners," the herald said. "Or perhaps messengers. I do not know, my lord."

Ablemont and one of his squires rode forward. They went over the top of the ridge and for the first time Ablemont could see the size of the plain, which stretched for leagues, and the very top of the citadel of Arles gleamed in the distance.

Down on the plain, an army waited. Steel glittered in the sun.

The enemy had no flags. Ablemont had never seen an army without flags or banners before.

He pushed past a retinue of knights who were all counting their kills, bragging about how quickly they would break the enemy. A pair of priests were shriving foot soldiers. The king was sitting on his horse in the midst of a circle of courtiers and staff in a clearing in the pine woods just off the road.

Two men stood alone, surrounded by dismounted knights. The men were expressionless.

Ablemont frowned, noting the rags of their hose and shirts.

"Etruscans, surely?" he asked Ser Tancred.

The old knight made a face as if something smelled bad. "I should have known," he said. "The deserters. They demand to see the king."

Ablemont nodded, and the king took a pull from a flask and laughed.

"They do not look so dangerous, eh, Ablemont?" he asked. "Ribeaumont says we can scatter that host in one charge."

Ablemont saluted the king.

Before he could comment, the two Etruscan captives were summoned forward.

They walked badly, and Ablemont was immediately reminded of his young squire. His gorge rose.

"Sire, they may be possessed," he said.

The king turned. "Ablemont," he said, as if deeply disappointed, and the weight of royal disapproval silenced Ablemont.

The two prisoners were placed before the king.

"Are you the king?" asked the shorter one.

A knight tapped him, hard, in the back of the head.

The man's body moved, but he didn't even register the pain. *Are you the master of these creatures?* said the voice. It was almost the same voice that Ablemont had heard from his squire.

The king gave a twisted smile.

Ablemont said, "Yes, he is." His hand was on his sword hilt. His knuckles were white.

Good, said the unmoving face. *We have no need for your people. You may go.*

The king made a face. "I give the orders here," he said, mildly enough, for him.

No, said the voice. *We will direct now. For the good of all. All.*

The king was no fool, whatever his little predilections. He looked at the two prisoners, who spoke in perfect concert. "Something is channeling through them. I thought channeling was a myth. Ablemont?"

"Who are you?" Ablemont asked.

We are all, they said.

"You are not all," Ablemont said.

We are all. You can be All. All will be all.

The king laughed. "Well, you have certainly taken disrespect to the king to new heights," he said. "Kill them. Let's get on with this."

Go! said the two men.

"No, I'll destroy your army and your satanic monsters, and free Arles," the king said.

You are master of Arles? they asked. *Give us Arles and we will not molest you, or take you. For now.*

Ablemont smiled. "Your diplomacy is too honest," he said.

The king clenched his fist, and the heads of the two Etruscans fell from their shoulders almost together.

Even Ablemont, who expected the worms, was appalled at the size of the things that emerged from the necks of the dead men. They were like segmented snakes, long, grey and white, with tiny hairs and teeth in their mouths.

Neither worm made much headway against fully armoured men.

"Burn them," Ablemont said. "Sire, that was what inhabited my squire."

De Ribeaumont was having trouble breathing. He looked at Ablemont.

"I must apologize," he managed.

"Sire, we must show these...things...to the army." Ablemont caught the king's bridle.

The king made a face. "No," he said. "No, it would only unman them. Burn the dead. Come."

Old Ser Tancred still had his sword in his hand. "How long until they infest a man?" he asked. "And what's waiting for us down there? I don't see any monsters. I see men. Men who do not move, like these."

"Good, we'll slay them quicker. On me! Form for battle! Come, my lords!" The king swept past, and his household knights mounted and joined him.

Guisarme looked at Ablemont. "I mislike it," he said simply.

"Now we know a little," Ablemont said. "We should retreat and learn more."

"These things killed those irks," Guisarme said. "The Wild is no myth. So the priests are either ignorant or lying. But if the irks are the Wild, what in the name of the saints are these things?"

Ablemont shook his head. "After the battle. If we both tell the king…"

Guisarme shook his head. "See those men waiting for us?" he asked. "I'll wager you a gold ducat of Venike against a bowl of maggots that we're looking at the feudal host of Arles. Full of worms."

"Oh sweet Christ," Ablemont said.

"It's too late to stop the battle," Guisarme said. "Ride away and save something."

Ablemont smiled. "And leave my king at the edge of mortal battle? You must think me a bad knight, Ser Tancred. Not to mention the complete loss of prestige if the king should win."

Guisarme was looking at the valley. "Aye. I won't leave, either." He gave Ablemont a wry smile. "We'd best win, then."

It took them the better part of the morning to form the army on the plain. Ablemont was separated from the king and from Guisarme, who commanded the advance battle, and he had plenty of time to watch the unbannered line opposite, which waited in perfect array.

A little before the sun was high in the sky, the royal standard dipped, and the whole line started forward, a echelon of blocks of knights on horseback, with a second line of infantry at their backs.

The enemy host stood unmoving.

The royal standard gathered speed.

Ablemont let his mount go from a walk to a trot and kept his eye on the standard.

He looked to his front. By chance, he was almost perfectly aligned with the center of the enemy mass.

They were all on foot.

In one motion, all of them...thousands of them...lifted spears from the ground. The spears rose like a glitter of sun on rain.

And in the next heartbeat, the spears fell again, forming a dense thicket, points forward, breast high.

The enemy lines looked much denser than they had a few moments ago. Indeed, even through the slits of his visor, Ablemont could see line after line of men standing like puppets and joining the array.

The spearheads began to go back and forth, as each rank pushed, then withdrew their spears. The result looked like some steel-edged millipede, or a hermetical threshing machine.

The royal standard accelerated again, and Ablemont's horse flowed into a canter. He lowered his lance into the rest automatically.

The enemy spears ahead moved like waves of rain or snow.

Ablemont put his spurs into his mount, and the great horse exploded forward, unused to such abuse. The war cry of Galle burst from thousands of throats, and every lance came down...

The spear wall was unbelievably dense...Ablemont had an impression of an uncountable horde of glittering, empty-eyed men behind them.

And then he was lying on his back. He got to his feet, found his sword, and went forward. All around him were knights, down or rising, and ahead, the braver and more fortunate knights had penetrated the wall of spears and were killing.

Or being dragged from their horses.

Ablemont waded in, safe in his superb armour, and began to kill, aware that he needed to guard himself after successful attacks. It was not like fighting men; his adversaries made no attempt to guard themselves, and he hacked them down. He beheaded several and saw the writhe of their worms, guarded his visor, and kept forward.

But the press grew denser, not looser. He stepped back twice, risking glances to find his household knights, and he realized that he had gone too deep in the enemy host. He stepped back, and back again, and the adversaries around him ignored him, continuing to use their spears in near-perfect unison. He cut, and thrust, and his arms began to seem leaden, and there was still no shortage of foes, and none of them were fighting him.

Greatly daring, he paused to take breath.

He was ignored.

He didn't like what he saw, and he pushed straight back to his own knights, but they were now farther back than he'd imagined, and it was like a nightmare…they seemed to recede as he advanced.

He pushed faster. He was all but running through the ranks of the enemy, and no blow fell on him. He saw his own banner a few paces ahead and he cut, cut again, cleared a small space and burst out of the enemy and into open air.

There was dust in the air, and men were screaming. His own men.

But there were shouts of recognition, and he got clear of the battle line, backed again, and opened his visor.

It was difficult to see anything. The dust of the plain was rising as thousands of stamping feet, equine and human, pounded the moisture out. The sun glared down, but he was dismounted and he couldn't see over the men around him, and sweat was pouring down his arming cap over his eyes.

"Water," he said.

"What the hell is happening?" he asked. None of his captains were there.

A canteen was put in his hand, and only then did he see that they were already intermixed with the infantry line.

Losing, then.

The enemy remained perfectly silent. They simply pressed forward, in seemingly inexhaustible numbers.

Ablemont backed out of the new line and found the royal standard off to the right. Ser Geofroi had it up on a small, round hill. Ablemont looked back at the forward edge of the fight to see the threshing spears winnowing his infantry. Men were beginning to run.

Ablemont wondered where *any* of his household knights were, but he left his visor up. "Follow me!" he roared.

He ran to the royal standard. His legs were already very tired, and the deep earth of the ploughed field over which he was trying to run felt as if it were trying to suck him down.

Long before he reached the standard, he had to stop running. Had to breathe. But a dozen men, two knights he knew and some of his better armed foot, stuck with him, and they plodded across the open ground even as Ablemont saw the far right begin to collapse under some unseen impulse. The dust there…or was it smoke?

He began to climb the hill toward Ser Geofroi. He could see the man.

The center of the enemy began to come forward.

There were heaps of dead at the base of the hill.

Ablemont made it to the circle of waiting knights, and he saw Ser Tancred by the king, and he went to them.

"Ribeaumont is dead," the king said. His visor was open. "What is happening?"

"Get the king mounted." Ablemont heard his own voice begin to issue orders. "Sire, you must ride clear, immediately. This field is lost."

Guisarme nodded sharply.

Just behind Guisarme, the deep center of the enemy spearmen struck the Gallish knights.

Ser Geofroi didn't go back even a single step. His sword moved like a levin bolt, and he danced, pushed, and killed. He, at least, had worked out how to fight these things. His blows severed spines, and when his sword broke, he took an axe. Behind him, the standard flowed, silken and defiant.

A horse was brought, and then another, and Ablemont got the king mounted as if he were a page.

"Go with him," Guisarme said.

"But…" In fact, Ablemont wanted to go.

"I'm old, and have sons at home to avenge me." Guisarme nodded, a hand on his visor. He had a long, Alban-style poleaxe.

Ablemont's long years of service at court had not prepared him for this. "Thank you," he said weakly.

"Hah!" Guisarme said. "I'm delighted to find you are more a man and less an arse than I thought. Now go. Save the king."

He slapped his visor down and turned away into the maelstrom.

Ablemont mounted.

From here, on horseback, on a small hill, it was possible to see the extent of the battle. To the right, the marshal's advance battle was destroyed. But on the left, the rear battle had done terrible damage to the enemy at the onset and now struggled grimly with the horde that remained.

Except that beyond the far end of the rear battle came another army. Ablemont could see the spears. He could also see what appeared to be animals—horses and cattle.

All doomed.

He cursed.

The king looked at it, blank-eyed. "How can we be losing?" he asked.

Ablemont wanted to spit, *"How are we doing this well?"* Despite the odds and the nature of the foe, the line was still intact, and even as he watched, Ser Geofroi *cut* an open space into the front of the enemy. The wall of carrion in front of the king's standard-bearer was a testament of his *preux*—his prowess—and the monsters, or men, or whatever they were, had increasing trouble getting at the knight. But Ablemont wanted to scream at the king.

But the enemy was pressing along on both flanks of the hill, the wings moving straight ahead. The hill was going to be cut off.

"Time to go, Sire," Ablemont said.

The two of them started down the hill and headed north, straight away from the enemy. The army's left was beginning to break up and men were running. Nobles who had dismounted seized their horses, although sometimes their own men killed them and took the horses themselves.

The fabric of the army unraveled before his eyes.

But he took the king's bridle and rode, headed for the base of the ridge that they had descended to form for battle. As far as he could see, there was no pursuit.

It was as if the enemy had only one single will.

Ablemont thought that should have meant that any man who fled would be safe. He got them up the face of the ridge, hoarding the strength of the horses, because they had, by his estimation, two hundred leagues to cross before they reached a safe fortress.

Down on the hill, the royal standard still flew. They were too far to see individuals, but the line seemed steady, a ring that covered the hilltop, and the victorious wings of the enemy center had bypassed the little hill and moved on, almost to the base of the long ridge, and to the left, the stalemate had been broken, and the left was gone, shredded between two forces, and it was clear that the enemy possessed more than one will.

"Blessed Saviour," Ablemont said.

"I want out of here," the king said suddenly, his first words in many minutes. He turned his horse and rode over the ridge.

Ablemont was a courtier. He had betrayed his brother and his land to get the position he now held. He had stayed with the king through scandal and social peril and the near-ruin of his niece.

And now, for the first time, he *hated* the king. He didn't want to ride back and die with Ser Geofroi and Guisarme. But he knew he should, and he knew that were he the king, he could not have ridden away.

He spat.

He had hoped to gather fugitives into some sort of a rear guard, but the hilltop was curiously empty, and the moment they were over the ridge, the sound of battle vanished, and the world was mostly silent, although some screams penetrated the still air.

Ablemont opened his visor and rode down the ridge, his hands shaking while he held the reins. He rode carefully, unlike the king, who rode hard, and reached the distant plain well ahead of him.

Ablemont was beginning to consider rational things—like how the king would behave when he realized that Ablemont had seen him turn tail and flee; like what resources remained in their camp, and what orders he should give. Could they stop for provisions? What was behind them? *How soon would the enemy catch them up?*

Or would there be no pursuit?

Why Arles?

The king was headed for the camp, now visible as a long line of palisades.

Ablemont's battle shock was wearing off.

What do we do now? he wondered.

He was still pondering the future when the unmistakable form of a great black dragon rose from the camp. Ablemont's horse bolted, and his heart seemed to stop, and he was well to the west on the plain in front of the camp when he was finally thrown by the utterly panicked horse.

The dragon moved on rotting, silent wings. It was, perhaps, a mercy that in falling, Ablemont struck his head. He was unconscious when the dragon took him.

The king was not so lucky. He was still aware when the worms ate his eyes.

Part I
Alba

Across the north of the Nova Terra and the Antica Terra, summer came. It came in Etrusca, where every man's thoughts turned to war, and to Galle and Arles, where famine stalked, war prevailed, and the Wild washed like a rising sea around the settlements of men. In Iberia, peasants prepared for a fine harvest—and lived in fear of the news from over the mountains.

Summer came first to the grain fields of Occitan in the Nova Terra, where the wheat was already golden as a maiden's hair and the cornstalks were knee high, promising the richest harvest that any woman could remember. And on the hills, the olive trees promised another kind of riches, while bunches of grapes began to form in weights that had the farmers cutting stakes and propping vines across the whole of the south, even as they looked over their shoulders for bogglins and wights.

But even the promise of agricultural riches was not enough to keep men from fear of the Wild. Rumours came from the north—from Alba—of civil strife and victories—confusing rumours of Wild allies, of human perfidy, of a church divided, a king killed and a young king born. Out in the new country beyond the mountains, most families— those that had survived the spring—packed their poor belongings and fled to the oppression and relative safety of noble landowners and heavy taxation. A handful of people from Occitan and Jarsay—woods men and women, for the most part, who spoke with Outwallers and irks—felt a sea change. The Fox and the Sossag ceased to raid, and a few irks approached the westernmost human settlements to offer trade.

But the changes were most profound in Alba. In Harndon, Ser Gerald Random kept order—aye, and more—in a city that had seen fire and battle. Three thousand Galles prepared feverishly to sail for Galle, where the royal army had been shattered—destroyed, in fact—by a mysterious host from the Wild, and the King of Galle was feared to be dead. A year of bitter rivalry between the city and Galle was put aside, and ships from Genua, Galle, Venike, and Alba were put at the disposal of the Sieur Du Corse to launch his men to rescue Galle's desperate people.

And in Harndon, returning citizens, exiled by the now-discredited de Rohan's government, or merely having fled the fighting, spoke aloud of the queen and of her newborn babe, the king, in the tones people usually reserved for church. As workmen cleared the last timbers from the ruin of the great tournament grounds, and as those same beams, adzed clear of their charred portions, were turned into new dwellings for those burned out of the fighting, hope swelled in the people, increasing as fast as the heat and new summer sun.

And farther north still, at Albinkirk, the queen herself sat, the focal point of hope for her realm, on the warm green grass of Midsummer's Eve, her babe across her lap and her back to a great oak tree that towered above her with a magnificent, cool canopy that kept the new heat at bay. The tree was ancient, and grew at the head of a narrow, steep pass that ran from the country north of Albinkirk into the Wilds of the Adnacrags, and here, in long-ago times, so it was said, Men and the Wild had met in council. The king, in her lap, cooed, gurgled, and tried to use his newfound hands to grasp the spectacular golden fur of the queen's new friend Flint, who sat with her under the tree. Flint was a clan leader of the Golden Bears, and his presence, as a chieftain of the Wild, with the Queen of Alba, who might herself have been styled "Queen of Men" that summer, marked them as the very center of the change that rolled outward from them over the Nova Terra.

Before them, a young wyvern, head high, crest engorged with blood, spat his protests against the encroachment of the Abbey of Lissen Carak on the traditional hunting and breeding grounds of his clan. By the queen, the abbess, Miriam, representative of the abbey, sat with head bowed, quietly translating the wyvern's words. Throughout the meadow that surrounded them was a curious fair, where men sold every product of human hands from Venikan glass beads and Hoek bronze kettles to the best Etruscan steel crossbows and Albin-made knives and linen woven by women at the very foot of the valley. Merchants from the Antica Terra hawked their wares shamelessly alongside brass-lunged farm wives and local cutlers, cordwainers, and armourers. A tall, handsome man with a travelling forge fitted premade Etruscan breastplates to wardens (never call them adversaries, brother!) and

Outwallers who crowded his stall while a squire in the Red Duke's livery sat on a stool and sketched the scene rapidly, his lively charcoal capturing the beauty of the queen, the dignity of Flint, and the intense eagerness of one of Nita Qwan's young warriors to own a hardened steel breastplate, light as air, strong as magic. He negotiated quickly with his hands, offering so much Wild honey, so many pelts, and an agreement was reached for the Fair at Dorling, two weeks hence, without a word spoken. The smith measured the warrior with a tape of linen and made marks.

Adrian Goldsmith tossed his third sketch of the day aside and went on to his fourth, squandering a small fortune in paper because the captain had ordered him to do so. It was, in many ways, the richest scene of human and Wild interaction he had ever seen, or thought perhaps he ever would see, and he turned his back on the queen, who tended to draw every eye at the best of times, and then, against his will, turned back to her as Blanche, the captain's acknowledged mistress and the queen's handmaiden, leaned forward, her white-gold hair catching a ray of sun, her startlingly slender waist hard with muscle under her kirtle, to take the king from his mother's arms and change him into clean linen. The three of them formed something—it lasted only three heartbeats, and Adrian's charcoal fairly flew, capturing Blanche's attention, the queen's love, the king's fascination with Blanche's hair.

And then, freed of her son's weight, the queen rolled forward a little and bent her head, speaking quietly to Flint. The great bear raised his head, and nodded, slowly, and his muzzle opened and a series of short barks emerged—bear laughter.

The wyvern stood, poised as if for fight or flight, and perhaps, new to the ways of council and conciliation, that is how he saw the proceedings. Now the queen whispered to Miriam, and Miriam nodded. Then the Duchess Mogon—after the queen, perhaps the most important personage present—rose from her great chair of maple wood and joined in, her bronze and gold beak catching the same ray of sun that had penetrated the leaves to illuminate the light hair of Blanche Gold.

The queen bowed her head graciously to each, and then nodded to the wyvern, stretched her bare feet, and smiled.

"We find that the abbey is at fault in encroaching on your lands, Sythenhag. We will not attempt to examine the rights and wrongs—it is clear that these predate human occupation of the fortress. Nor is it the intention of this Tree of Judgment to force the Order from the fortress that they have protected so well most recently against our common enemy."

The wyvern bridled, its head shaking. Its great beak opened.

"But," said the queen, as if addressing a favoured suitor or a handsome squire, "It is clear to us all that the abbey need not resettle Abbington, which was destroyed in the late struggles. My justicar will assess the value—the human value—of the lost farms and make redress to the survivors in lands around Hawkshead and Kentmere, and the properties of the village of Abbington will be returned to the Wild."

Sythenhag—a very young wyvern to hold power in his clan—gave a screech. "But what of the other injustices we have suffered?" he spat at the Duchess Mogon. "What of the death of my father and mother at the hands of these—*garum*?"

The queen took a slow breath. It was the Red Knight who had, it appeared, killed Sythenhag's elders in the ambush on the Albin Gorge, and for that reason, he had been bidden to find other business while the council addressed the claims of the western wyverns. Which was as well. He was still recovering, and there were rumours…

But it was Mogon who answered. "My pardon, Your Grace," she said. "Sythenhag, you were informed—by me, in person—before appearing that the council had chosen to leave by any injury given or taken in open war. War kills. That war is over now. The abbey will return your easternmost lands. This is justice. Your elders chose to join Thorn, or were unjustly coerced, and fell afoul of men and their weapons, and are dead. Nothing can be done on this matter." She shrugged in callous indifference. "It is the way of the world… and a better justice than you would have in the Wild."

The silence that fell was broken only by the rapid sound of the armourer's hammer as Edmund Allen planished out his own raising strokes on an altered leg harness.

Sythenhag's crest remained perfectly erect. "Then I spit on your council, and when my people have grown in power and stature, we will avenge ourselves!"

The queen sighed.

Mogon snarled.

But now it was Flint—eldest of all the council—who rose. He

roared—an angry sound—and the force of his roar filled the whole clearing from wood line to stone wall, and every head turned.

"No," he said. The calm dignity of his voice was a superb contrast to the roar. "No, you will not have revenge, cub. If you attempt such a thing, every thinking creature's hand will be against you, and you will be outlaws in and out of the wall, and your clan will be destroyed, root, branch, and tree. What is done is done. That is all the justice we can offer you. Accept it, and be reconciled or go west—far west—and never return."

A terrible silence followed. And again, Adrian Goldsmith's charcoal flew.

But Sythenhag was not the only wyvern present. Mogon stared pointedly at an older female, and she spread her wings and hissed—and men flinched, and women hid their children behind their skirts. A handful of mountain bogglins, marked by their mottled green-and-brown skins, fell flat and pulled their wing cases over themselves, as if attempting to be invisible.

Crests began to rise among all the wardens present.

But Beltan—one of the few elder survivors from the war, who knew she owed her life to Amicia's intervention—was not to be dissuaded, and she pushed into the space Sythenag needed to fly—a breach of space, among wyverns. For a moment, scents and wave fronts of fear and dominance flew like arrows in a battle of men—so many scents that Blanche wrinkled her nose and the young king screwed up his whole face and burst into angry tears.

But as Mogon had expected—indeed, as she had calculated—Sythenhag lacked the years and the presence to face down an elder female, and Beltan cowed him, drove him to submission—and then bowed her neck and head to Mogon, a curiously human gesture.

"Lady Miriam; Good Queen, Lord Bear, and Duchess of the West, we agree that this is justice." She looked down at Sythenhag, who was almost prone on the ground. "War pushes the young males to positions that they lack the maturity to fill," she said.

"Not just among wyverns," the queen said.

Forty miles to the north and east, Ser Gavin Muriens, the Green Knight, Earl of Westwall and increasingly known as the Green Earl, sat in a clearing in the woods, his great green silk pavilion at his back and a hasty map drawn in charcoal on the surface of his camp table. Around him were gathered his own officers as well as many officers of the Queen of Alba and the empire—including the Count of the Borders, whose daughter he was soon to marry; Ser Ricar Orcsbane, commanding a squadron of the Knights of the Order, no longer attainted and now in the field in their more usual capacity as the kingdom's mailed fist against the Wild; and the Faery Knight, who reclined with inhuman ease, between a Wild bogglin wight on one side and a famous human outlaw Jack, Bill Redmede, on the other. To further confuse matters, Redmede's brother Harald had been appointed captain of the royal foresters during the recent fighting in the west, and now stood uneasily with the other royal officers—Ser Ricar Fitzroy, the queen's captain of the north, for example, who was commanding only a handful of knights of Jarsay and the southern Brogat, while Ser Gregario, Lord Wayland, the queen's new Warden of Albinkirk, just appointed and still recovering from severe burns, commanded more knights. It might have been a nightmare of divided command and conflicting jurisdiction, except that the recent, massive victory over the sorcerer Thorn had forced their alliance to thrive and cooperate.

But it was not either of the famous Redmede brothers who was describing the day's fighting—the fifteenth day since the great battle. It was in fact Ser Aneas, the Green Earl's youngest brother and acting Master of the Hunt.

Aneas bent his knees and prayed, then rose to silence and waved a short ivory baton over the carefully drawn charcoal lines on the table. By his side, Morgon Mortirmir crossed his hands like a priest saying mass and spoke three sharp syllables.

The charcoal marks on the table rose—and began to form lines in the air, and the lines filled in with colour and texture. Even as the two magisters powered their working, the flat charcoal sketch rippled, grew, and settled into a model of the Adnacrags—or that piece of the Adnacrags within ten miles.

Men coughed. Behind the Green Earl, Sauce coughed until her hands were flecked with spittle.

Morgon Mortirmir frowned, but the casting did its work, and the model *eventuated*.

Aneas bowed his head. "Gentles all," he said softly, but his voice carried. "The Army of Thorn and Ash has now, to all intents, ceased to exist."

The Faery Knight winced when Aneas said the name *Ash* aloud, but not for long.

The Green Earl rose from his stool. He had heavy dark circles under his eyes, and he looked as if he might be forty, or even forty-five. His eyes were bloodshot, and his hair had a thousand wisps that played about him in the breeze.

"I know that you have all wondered why we had to exhaust ourselves like this," he said. Even his voice was tired. "But it is essential to the next forty years of life here that Ash not have the raw materials to form another army of the Wild against the alliance. The only way to ensure victory was by ruthless pursuit—tempered where we could with mercy for those capable of surrender." His voice took on a quality of fatigue that was echoed in every face—Ser Thomas Lachlan looked as if he'd aged a decade, Ser George Brewes appeared dead on his feet, and Ser Michael looked old enough to be his own father—while his father, who had changed sides so many times in the last year that he had a little space around him, nonetheless looked old enough to be Ser Michael's grandfather. "Sadly, Ash chose to make sure they died. It is my opinion—and only an opinion, but shared, I promise you, by my brother—that Ash has moved this war into a new phase, wherein he will attempt to exhaust us and our will to fight through the endless attrition of his slaves."

They had all been fighting for weeks since the battle at Gilson's Hole, moving and camping in the deepest woods, sometimes without food or sleep for two or three days at a time, in clouds of insects, wading across desolate swamps and climbing pathless hills. This was everyday war for royal foresters and Jacks, but not for belted knights and heavy horse. Even the irks and bogglins showed signs of strain.

The pursuit had indeed been ruthless to pursued and pursuers alike, and now—deep in the Adnacrags, on the shores of the Great Forked Lake where few wardens or bogglins and even fewer men had ever been—they had trapped the last formed body of creatures enslaved not to Thorn but to Ash and destroyed them in a bitter, and very one-sided, fight. It was not a fight that men or monsters would remember around campfires for anything but one-sided brutality—a simple massacre of the last remnants of Thorn's great army, the creatures who would not—or could not—surrender. Hastenochs from the deepest swamps, bogglins raised in the north or far west, and men and even a few bears lost to all reason.

Repeatedly, Morgon Mortimir had used his powers—and the Faery Knight had used his own, Wilder yet—to try to break the chains by which Ash held them, but ever the distant dragon had contemptuously flicked their workings aside, dooming his creatures to a pointless death and mocking them all at the same time. But in the end, horrible, bloody, and exhausting, it was done, and nothing was left.

"We're done," Ser Gavin said. "Until Ash comes at us from the west. Even now, the queen is seeing to it that the Wild creatures in the rest of the Adnacrags are loyal to the alliance and not to Ash."

An old Outwaller hunter cleared his throat. He nudged Nita Qwan, the acknowledged war leader of the Huran and Sossag still in the field. Most of the Outwallers serving the alliance had gone home as soon as the great battle ended, but a hundred or so remained in the field.

Nita Qwan glared at his friend. But he knew his duty. "Where is Ota Qwan?" he asked. "We have not counted his corpse."

A collective sigh rose from the officers. It was followed by fits of coughing from a dozen men and women.

Aneas nodded to his brother and to his ally. "We have missed one of our principal objectives," he said, pointing to a red spot away to the north of the Forked Lake. "This is my best estimate of the location of forces still fighting under Kevin Orley. Ota Qwan. I would guess he has fewer than a thousand beings altogether—mostly men and daemons."

Ser Gavin looked at the glowing spot a moment.

Sukey, the company quartermaster, stood forth from the crowd of the company's officers. "Fuck," she said.

"That your professional assessment?" Tom Lachlan, Primus Pilus and the loudest voice in the army, except possibly Ser Danved, mocked his leman.

She looked at him and her eyes suggested that he could shrivel to ash and die. Even Bad Tom flinched at Sukey's anger. "We can't pursue any further," she said, her voice sharp. "There's no *road*!" she said. "We only have the food in our wagons, and then we start eating horses, and thanks to the horse plague, there's few enough o' them." She looked around. The Faery Knight looked at her in fascination, and Bad Tom growled at the silver-haired irk. The Faery Knight had proven himself to be...devoted to the pursuit of human women to a degree that some found delightful and others annoying or disturbing.

Sukey tossed her hair and rolled a bare shoulder at him, so that Bad Tom got halfway to his feet and Sukey laughed low in her throat. But she saw the look on Ser Gavin's face and straightened up. "And there's more men sick every hour," she reported.

Ser Gavin looked around—from Ser Christos and Ser Giorgos, who shared command of the imperial troops, to Bad Tom, who led the levies of the Green Hills and parts of the company, too. Both were allies—as much as the Faery Knight and his Wild Hunt and his bogglins and irks were allies.

"I propose we get out of here, at best military speed, with a good rear guard and appropriate caution," he said. "Anyone against?"

The Faery Knight stretched, more like a cat than a man, and rose to his feet. "I would like to have killed thisss Orley," he said. "Whatever he wasss born, he isss no longer man. Now, he isss sssomething rotten. I can tassste him from here." He nodded to Ser Gavin. "Where isss he going?"

The Green Earl nodded. "I, too, would like to finish him," he said. "But he's willing to starve his people to death, and I'm not."

"Perhapsss," the Faery Knight said. "Perhapsss we will hunt him from N'gara. He will crosss Mogon's landsss, or mine, if he stays on this course." His smile was pointy and predatory. "Let usss leave this fassstnesss of Wild beauty," he said.

Sauce coughed in her attempt to laugh. "Beauty, is it?" she asked. "Christ and Mary Magdalene and all the saints, I could do without Wild beauty. Give me an inn."

People laughed, and the mood was lightened.

Ser Gavin leaned forward. "Very well, then," he said. "Half the peasants of the Brogat are road building right now. We'll march east toward Ticondonaga, and link up with the main road crew." He looked around. "It is my intention to retake Ticondonaga—what is left of it, before we rest."

Sukey nodded. "Good. Better get some grain and some beeves waiting for us, Gavin."

Gossips noted Sukey's familiar use of his name.

Ser Ricar Fitzroy spoke up. "Surely we should make for the queen and Albinkirk?" he asked. Then, embarrassed, "I'm sorry, Your Grace. I had no intention of questioning…"

The Green Earl laughed—a tired laugh, but a genuine one. "Ser Ricar, as of now, you have no real reason to obey me. The emergency is over. But if you seek my rede—and if you will allow me to rule you a few more days—I would rather that the army dispersed from the Inn of Dorling than from Albinkirk. There are many reasons, and not least of them is that the inn is the most central place in the alliance. I'll add that after we've eaten and fed our horses and rested, it is my view that a force should be kept in the field—under you, Ser Ricar, or perhaps Lord Wayland—to cover the road builders. Finally, the Fair at Dorling…"

Almost everyone nodded.

"It isss the wrong way for me and mine," the Faery Knight said. But he smiled and shrugged. "But it isss long and long sssince I have ssseen the inn. And perhapsss I would like to dance and sssing. There hasss been too much war."

"My brother is thinking to hold a tournament," the Green Knight said.

Sauce coughed, and then whooped. "Now you're talking!" she said. She was not alone, and men drooping with fatigue suddenly began to perk up.

Bad Tom pumped his fist in the air.

Ser Michael laughed. "A real tournament, and not just His Nibs doing all the fighting?" he asked.

Gavin shrugged. "That's what I'm told. So. Fast as we can for the road head at Ticondonaga. Then rest, and make our way to the inn. I hope the queen and my brother will meet us there."

Ser Aneas spoke up. "My lord, some of our scouts have detected tracks moving *east* away from Orley's survivors."

"Oh, for some loyal wyverns," Gavin muttered.

The Faery Knight shrugged. "In time, if your queen isss fair, ssshe will have wyvernsss. They are loyal, when their loyalty isss fairly won."

The earl nodded. "I'd like to give chase—I wouldn't want any of Orley's monsters loose—"

Aneas bowed. "I would like to go, my lord. I have the needed powers. If I might have a few of the people who have worked with me since Gilson's Hole, I believe I could track the quarry and make a kill."

The Redmede brothers managed to meet each other's eyes.

"Suits me," said Bill Redmede.

Harald nodded. "Woods," he said. "It's what we do."

An hour later Aneas had his pick of the royal foresters and the Jacks. He was young, relatively untried, and he took his job very seriously.

Aneas was neither as tall nor as broad as his older brothers, a slim man of middle height. Unlike his dark-haired kin, he was blond, and had slightly slanted green eyes like his mother that gave him a very Irkish look. In point of fact, irks took to him easily; he already spoke many words of their ancient and complex tongue, and his mastery of the *ars magika* was odd and esoteric, covering only the aspects of the art that interested him. He had been his mother's favourite, and that marked him in other ways.

In the twilight of late afternoon, he wore a golden brown jupon in plain linen and deerskin hose in Outwaller moccasins. Instead of a long sword, he wore a heavy baselard and a pipe axe like those carried by Outwaller shamans. He carried a simple roll pack with one blanket, one cloak, and one clean shirt. He did not look like the brother of two of the most powerful men in the world.

He looked like an irk ranger, and despite his youth and their fatigue, when he chose a man or woman, that person grinned to be chosen. Whatever differences of height or power, he had the family trait.

People would follow him.

He chose three foresters, all northerners; Ricard Lantorn came from the company's rangers to continue his revenge. He chose three Jacks, and the first and most eager was Ricar Fitzalan. They were already fast friends. The other two were both women; careful, cautious, and deadly, the two had made a mark before the whole army in ambushing a rhuk in the swamps and finishing him—alone. They were Cynthia, a nobleman's daughter from the Brogat, tall and strong, with messy dark hair in a bad braid, and Cigne, a young woman who'd come north with the Prince of Occitan with no experience of the wilderness, and found herself in love with it.

And a pair of irks volunteered as well, Lewen and Tessen, as did the bogglin Krek. He was a mountain bogglin, an Adnacrag native, mottled and old enough to have moss at the base of his wing covers.

And Janos Turkos, who knew the north woods as well as any man, volunteered with Tall Pine and his warriors. The imperial riding officer was older than most of the others, a veteran and a captain in his own right.

Aneas hesitated. Turkos nodded. "I'm going that way anyway," he said. "I can follow as well as lead, Ser Aneas. And if we can't get along...well, the woods are large enough."

Looking over the resulting party as they pillaged Sukey's wagons for supplies, the Earl of Westwall shook his head. "I hope you catch your quarry," he said. "But by God, brother, if you come to civilization, you'll terrify every town you pass."

Aneas was quiet enough that his brother could sense his fear.

"You'll be fine!" he said, unhelpfully.

Aneas made a face. "You and bloody Gabriel make it look so *easy*."

Gavin nodded. No one was near them. "That's the trick of it, brother mine. Make it look easy. Never ever let them see you show anything but humour, and the rest is *easy*."

"Really?" Aneas looked more annoyed than pleased.

"No, I'm lying to make you feel better," Gavin said. "Really, you just make everything up as you go along."

Aneas sighed. But then he offered his brother a rare smile. "That sounds more like me," he said.

Long before the sun set, Aneas and his party were gone, headed north.

Dawn. A dawn without a proper breakfast—they were two days' march from the nearest supply, and out of grains and bread. With a lot of grumbling, the army rose, struck its tents, and formed to march east and south.

As men fell into their ranks on the impromptu wilderness parade ground, dodging young fir trees and raspberry prickers, one white wedge tent remained standing. A messenger brought word to the acting captain—the Green Earl—as his leg harnesses were buckled by his new squire, Isabeau. His stomach growled loudly enough that she laughed.

"Tell Sukey," Ser Gavin grumbled.

Sukey was high on the back of her wagon when the herald cried her name. He pointed out the lone tent still standing even as a pair of imperial soldiers ran up to tell her that something was wrong.

Annoyed, Sukey walked over, summoning two of her women to attend her, but the smell hit her before she was nigh the tent.

She shouted—the men inside were mountaineers from the south of Morea, and both had, it proved, been sick for days, but everyone was exhausted and most men had coughs and pains.

It was only when she looked in the tent that she paled.

She summoned Master Mortirmir by means of a working, to see the corpses. And in the same working, she informed the Green Earl that something was very wrong, and showed him the inside of the tent.

Ser Ricar Orcsbane was commanding the rear guard—he and his knights halted and watched.

Mortirmir rode up as the army vanished into the trees.

When the tent was pulled down, the corpses were fully revealed. Their faces were black.

Mortirmir entered his memory palace, cast a variety of workings, and then ordered everyone present to separate themselves from what remained of the camp. To their scandal and horror, he opened one of the bodies and revealed the lungs full of black ooze. He took samples—by then the grave diggers were flinching away—and sighed.

"Burn them," he told Sukey. "No—never mind. I'll do it."

He flicked two fingers, and the bodies immolated—burned so hot and so fiercely that nothing was left but marks on the matted ferns, which themselves were shriveled and smouldering, and a little black ash.

He gathered every witness and every person who had handled the corpses and began a great working that still occupied him as the sun climbed toward noon. Birds sang, and the sun beat down through the magnificent, tall trees, and Sukey had never been so afraid in all her life. She was coughing regularly by early afternoon, and the cough left little flecks of black on the backs of her hands. All of the Knights of the Order had dismounted—they were coughing too.

As the shadows began to lengthen, Mortirmir seemed to come alive. "Right," he said. "Gather round," he snapped.

Eager men and women pressed close to him—Sukey's two most reliable young women, a half-dozen junior archers who'd been told off to bury the bodies as punishment for some transgression including Wilful Murder, a dozen Knights of the Order and their squires.

Morgon raised an eyebrow at Sukey. "I need a canteen of water," he said. "Wine would be better, but I assume we're out."

"I'm not out," Sukey said.

She fetched him wine in an earthenware jug. He raised an enormous amount of *potentia* and turned it into *ops* so cleanly that it was almost contemptuous. Sukey had seen her mother handle as much, but not so casually. Practitioners seldom held *ops* for any length of time because of the effort of concentration required, yet Mortirmir held a vast globe of raw, barely fettered power over his head the way a strong man might hold a bar of iron—casually.

He took the wine and sniffed it. "Good wine," he said. "Morean?"

"Yes," Sukey managed. "Can you save us?" she asked.

Mortirmir narrowed his eyes. "Yes and no," he said.

Then he poured the globe of *ops* over his head into the ceramic wine jug as if volume had no meaning, as the jug was less than one hundredth the size of the glowing ball he'd had when he started. Throughout the process, he spoke, almost at random. He spoke single words, some in Archaic and some in a language none of them had heard.

Sukey coughed. It was a long, wrenching cough, and there were flecks of scarlet mixed with the black flakes on the back of her hand, and she began to shake. It was the oddest feeling—she felt hollow inside.

My mother died, she thought.

That hurt. She had been in the field almost without a pause since her mother died fighting the dragon Ash, and she had ruthlessly kept herself from thinking about it. She had drunk too much wine, mounted Tom Lachlan, and worked her people like slaves rather than think about her mother's death, but a little lung-blood on the back of her hand...

Mortirmir was very young—people said he was just seventeen. He was tall, and still capable of the kind of graceless, gawky movement that characterized adolescent boys without their full growth. He could also be very difficult, at least in part because he didn't always seem to understand what normal people did, or said.

He dressed like a knight and in fact was a passable jouster. At the moment, he wore black—black wool arming coat, black hose, black hood, with a gold knight's belt and an Umroth ivory-hilted dagger that went with his black hair and pointed black beard. A beard he was pulling at with his left hand even as his right hand made arcane gestures and left traces of a blue fire in the air.

The last of his refined *ops* vanished into the ceramic bottle. The displaced air made a small *pop* like the cork coming out of a bottle.

He raised one eyebrow at her and put the earthenware jug to his lips and drank.

"Mmm," he said. "Lovely—heavy. I wonder if heavier wines will hold more power? Wine holds more power than water. But why?" He stared off into space, his face almost frozen in concentration.

Sukey looked around at the knights and peasants, workers, archers, and wagoners gathered around. "Can you...help us?" she asked carefully.

He looked at her as if seeing her for the first time. "Possibly," he said. "Let's just see if there are side effects first, shall we?"

In fact, he began to glow a little, and he exhaled a short flame of blue fire and coughed.

"Hmm. Unlikely to set a new fashion among Nova Terra vintners, but it will do. Sukey?" He handed her the jug and then paused. "Do be careful. I'm not sure I could make another batch today."

"How much?" Sukey asked. Then she coughed. Mortirmir grabbed her hands as soon as she was done coughing and looked at the blood, phlegm, and black flakes through a lens, even while supporting the weight of the jug.

"Never mind," he said. "A full cup, then." He poured it out himself and gave it to her, and she drank it off. She looked at Mortirmir, winced at the taste, gave a sharp burp, and—

Mortirmir watched her fall and tried to catch her and succeeded in lowering her the rest of the way—on her back. Sukey's mouth opened and a bolt of blue flame as long as a man's arm emerged. Then she turned over and threw up onto the ground by her. Much of what she vomited was black. And stank.

Mortirmir shook his head. "Right, I'm a fool. Of course, I don't have the plague and she does. Well—it works. Next?"

They all hung back as Sukey's heels began to drum on the ground.

South and west of Gilson's Hole, Amicia's hospital continued to care for the sick. What disturbed her most was that two weeks and more after the great battle, the number of her patients was not decreasing, it was increasing.

Worst of all, people in whom she had invested power and healing were remaining abed, and not making the recoveries that medicine and hermetical practice should have allowed.

She stood over Ser Gelfred, who had been badly wounded—more than once—in battle. But he had survived the wounds and the first night after, and she had poured power into him, prayed by him, knit his bones and his arteries so that he had every chance of recovering the almost-severed right arm and the burnt leg.

Until the cough started.

Amicia had been awake for days, watching her people, and she could no longer remember when the cough went from an annoyance to a threat. But Gelfred started to cough after only a few days, and now he lay beside her, coughing and coughing. When he coughed into his pillow, black flakes emerged.

Amicia prayed. She had looked at the flakes, and she knew that they were the shriveled, necrotic remains of Gelfred's lungs. She had cast her most potent workings, and the disease had marched on, uninhibited, unslowed.

Gelfred's latest bout of coughing came to a merciful end and his eyes—clear and knowing—rested on hers. "I'm dying," he said. "I would like the last rites."

Amicia nodded. "I wish," she said. She stopped, because he might not have much time, and rose and went out of the tent into the sun-dappled day. She found Father François standing by the Mary shrine in the middle of the hospital camp.

"Father, Ser Gelfred..." She paused, afraid she was about to give way to tears. "Last rites."

She was unused to being defeated by mere disease.

Father François nodded. "Cough?" he said.

She nodded. "It was nothing...and now..." She took a deep breath.

Father François looked at her, put a hand to his mouth, and coughed.

"Are you sure this is a good idea?" Gabriel asked.

He was mounted on his griffon. It had reached a size somewhere between enormous and terrifying, and seemed, further, to have grown an immense amount in a single night after the great battle. The magnificent beast now sported an extravagant red leather saddle between its wings and long, shiny metal spurs attached to its already horrific-looking talons—each spur a long curving sword with complex attachments made by Master Pye's people in Albinkirk.

The griffon—Ariosto—was standing perfectly balanced on a

massive crosspole made from a single oak tree, set into the side of the highest tower in the citadel of Albinkirk, just outside the beast's sleeping chamber in the top turret.

Gabriel Muriens was sitting in the saddle, white as one of Blanche's new linen sheets. At each minute alteration in balance that the great monster made to deal with the various air currents that wafted over the city, Gabriel's look of alarm sharpened. It was more than a hundred feet to the ground below. The ground was the tiltyard—stone flags and brick.

"Look, I used all my courage just getting into the saddle," Gabriel complained.

Close by, on the same perch, stood a wyvern missing a wing. The wing had been replaced with a wing of pure *ops*, a massive thing of fire and cobwebs.

"You won't learn to fly a griffon by talking about it," said the wyvern. "Besides, he's made his first flights. He's confident. Can't you hear him?"

"All too well," Gabriel said.

"Then get over it. Time presses, my dear Gabriel. I need to be in my own realm. We are no closer to victory than we were before Gilson's Hole. Come!" With that, the wyvern leapt into the air—and sank like a stone in water. Gabriel watched, his heart in his throat, as the young wyvern with a wing of fire seemed to fall away beneath them—wings opening, then fully spread—

Halfway down the tower, the wyvern's plummet turned to flight. Just as Gabriel felt the griffon's weight go forward inalterably. He wrenched his eyes away from the wyvern to see the tower rushing past him—

The griffon had fallen off the perch. Or leapt.

The ground rushed at them faster than Gabriel Muriens, the Red Duke of Thrake, victor of Gilson's Hole, had ever moved before. The tower blurred past...

The great green and red and gold wings filled like the sails of a great ship in a changing wind, and under him, Gabriel could feel the change in tension in his mount's wings as the heavy muscles took up the strain—a crushing weight seemed to pull him back in his high-backed saddle, down into the leather, and a breath hissed out of his lips as his hips took the strain.

A wind of magical potency roared in his ears, and tears welled up in his eyes unbidden, and he could neither think nor work magic—

And then, in a twinkling of Ariosto's jolly, mad eyes, they were skimming over the town. If the griffon had to make any great effort to fly, it was transmitted only in the rhythmic pulse of his wings under his saddle and the sound of his breathing. Gabriel had the feeling of a huge, slow horse beneath him, the wings beating like the powerfully driving haunches of a charger, just slower.

Gabriel's throat was tight, and sore. The wind was cool, and he was chilled very quickly—he was wearing a light doublet and hose, and his understanding of flying was being changed with every wingbeat.

His great mount, who radiated love in the *aethereal*, was following the wyvern, and the wyvern was moving fast, far out over the plain between the distant Adnacrags and the great river. They were moving so fast that the ground was a blur, and Gabriel had to look around very carefully to figure out where he was. It was like looking at a map of undetermined scale. There was the city of Albinkirk—but could that really be the South Ford? Gabriel tried to calculate how fast they were going, but he could not be sure of anything—the distances, the height…

The wyvern began to descend.

Do you know where we're going, Ariosto?

No, lord. I follow the most noble one. Love you! Hungry!

Gabriel winced and flew on.

But it was not long before the wyvern descended again, turning, until they were all flying along at the height of the trees—the nearly endless trees. At this low altitude, it did rather seem as if the whole earth were covered in forests. The wyvern led the way down from the sky—banked suddenly over a stream that shone in the sunlight like glass, and followed it up stream and farther up, over beaver dams and through meadows where it wound, so that they cut across the snaking course in a few heartbeats and rejoined it—it turned in a long, lazy line, and there was a break in the endless trees that showed a flash of the great Albin River to the south, and then Gabriel, who was fighting both awe and terror, saw smoke from nearby chimneys and the wyvern turned more tightly.

Then there was a wheat field, the new grain waist-high and a lurid green, and the wyvern landed easily, running a few paces along the ground to lose the last of its velocity and momentum.

Gabriel's heart, already moving fast, threatened to burst out of his chest. The griffon flared its magnificent wings so that they seemed to catch fire in the sun, and he slowed, and slowed again, and then seemed to fall out of the sky...

And they were down. Paradoxically, as soon as Gabriel's senses told him that they were down and had stopped moving—as soon as the griffon's slightly mad eyes were on him, as the great head turned, as if to say *Wasn't that great?*—he wanted to do it again.

He reached out and patted his great bird-monster-thing, and clenched his arms around Ariosto's neck.

Love you, he said.

Love you! he was answered. *Hungry!*

He rolled onto his stomach and slid down from the saddle, savouring the warm sun on his cold skin.

The wyvern had just transformed into a dark-haired man with an elegant scar, a long nose, and no right arm. As Gabriel himself was a tall young man with dark hair and no left hand, they matched well.

"Where are we?" Gabriel asked Master Smythe.

"The Manor of Gracewittle Middlehill, Gabriel. Held of the Captain of Albinkirk in knight service by Lady Helewise."

"Oh," Gabriel said. "Yes. I needed to come here." His eyes went to the house. "Maybe not today."

"Reliable people tell me you are ready to return to your duties," Master Smythe said. "I thought we could kill two birds with but a single stone—your first flight—wasn't it easy?"

"My throat hurts. Otherwise, superb." Gabriel felt almost lightheaded. And he dreaded seeing Lady Helewise, lover of Ser John Crayford. The former captain of Albinkirk. Now, dead. "Why does my throat hurt?"

Master Smythe glanced at him. "If we had been higher in altitude, I'd suspect your sore throat was caused by the cold air," he said. "I told you to dress warmly. But as it is, I suspect you screamed your throat raw when Ariosto chose to launch."

"I did not," Gabriel said stiffly.

Master Smythe looked at him under his eyebrows. "As you like," he said softly. "All the way down," he said softly.

"You are enjoying this too much," Gabriel said.

Master Smythe shrugged.

Helewise watched her daughter, Phillippa, as the young woman stood on tiptoes, trying to see from the front door of their house what was happening in the fields closer to the stream. Helewise sighed, her only outward concession to the desolation that reigned in her heart.

The arrival of two monsters of the Wild had occasioned only the most temporary panic. Philippa held a heavy arbalest cradled in both arms, but it was not spanned.

"There's a man—two men. Oh, Mama! It's the Red Duke—not dressed in red. He has on a plain doublet, but I've seen him…"

Helewise did not allow herself another sigh. She got to her feet, steadied herself, and went to the great central fireplace and swung the copper over the fire. "Fetch bread," she said. "Hypocras, perhaps, if Mother Crabbe has any prepared. Look in the kitchen…"

"Oh, Mama, I can do all that!" Phillippa was perfectly capable of telling her mother that she was stupid, and that she had ruined Phillippa's life by dragging her from the glories of Lorica to this small manor house in the country bereft of fashion or eligible young men—not, strictly speaking, true, as the events of the spring had all but filled the manor with a series of attractive, muscular, brave, and dashing sprigs, but when the fit to yell at her mother took Phillippa, mere facts never stood in the way.

But Phillippa was no fool. She was her mother's daughter, and she knew that the death of Ser John Crayford in the great battle had been like a dagger into her mother's heart. In fact, for two weeks, she had managed to avoid telling her mother about her many failings.

She ran to the kitchen, told the women there about their august visitor, and then fetched Mother Crabbe's morning hypocras from its place by the kitchen fire, ordered a yule cake brought down and sliced, as the only sweet in the house, and washed her face.

When she returned to the hall, her mother was just making her curtsy. Phillippa joined her, watching the two men under lowered lashes.

The Red Duke, as everyone called him suddenly, was of medium height, with brown-black hair and a mustache and beard that suited him well enough. Phillippa had a little experience of kissing, and she loathed facial hair, but such was life, she thought with resignation. Beards, pointed or forked, were the fashion with men.

The man with the duke was as handsome as pictures of the old gods, with a magnificent mane of dark hair that curled, and pale skin, and red, red lips—he looked more like a painting of a man than a man, and the livid scar on his face only made him appear more handsome. He bowed to her mother and then caught her eye and smiled. His eyes twinkled.

The Red Duke came in, saying something polite about being in the area...fine house...clearing new fields....

He looked up, suddenly, and met her mother's eyes. He took both her hands. "I'm sorry," he said. "I'm so sorry."

Helewise was not quite twice his age. She did not burst into tears. "I'm sorry too," she said. "He was a good man, and he had good years left in him." She shook her head. "My mother said he was a bad 'un when we were young, and forbade me to marry him." She looked away, as if looking into the past. "So I didn't."

The duke nodded. "Without him, we would have lost," he said. "He saved the queen and the young king. He saved everyone."

"Everyone but himself," Helewise said. "Ah, my courtesy is lessened, my lord. Here is my daughter, mindful of your comfort. A cup of hypocras, perhaps?"

The duke made a face. "Not unless I must, my lady."

"It's very chivalrous of you to come all this way to comfort an old woman," Helewise said.

The duke bowed and looked at the handsomer man. "My tutor wanted me to see something," he said. "I was coming anyway. You are the most distant manor from Albinkirk, and I wanted to reassure you that we have a patrol system..."

Helewise nodded. "My lord, I appreciate your planning—but Sister Amicia comes here often, and I think her to be a better defence against the Wild than a legion of knights."

The duke nodded. "I suspect you are right. Is she here now?" he asked, his voice rising slightly.

Helewise looked at him with a frankness that he found a little hard. "She is in the fortress," Helewise said. She smiled—surprising herself, but there was something easy to speak to in the young duke. "My lord—how did you come here?"

"Please call me Gabriel. I came on the back of that griffon who is, even now, terrifying your field workers. They needn't be afraid. He is not only gentle but very friendly. Terrifyingly friendly, when he's hungry."

She laughed, and nodded again to the very handsome man. "I don't believe I caught your name," she said.

He smiled. His smile was wonderful—Phillippa sighed, a different sigh than her mother's. "I am called Master Smythe," he said.

Helewise put a hand to her throat and coloured, turning bright red for a moment. "You are the dragon!" she said.

Master Smythe laughed. "Well—I am *a* dragon, certainly," he allowed. "Although, to be fair, today I was a wyvern. And will be for many more days, while I . . . recover."

Lady Helewise curtsied again. "Well, my lords, you have caught us in our shifts, and in mourning. This is my daughter, Phillippa, who, despite her simpering, is a fine young woman. Most of the rest of us are working. If you won't have hypocras, may I offer a little barley soup? A nice green tea?"

Master Smythe turned his eyes on Phillippa. "Your daughter is very lovely," he said. "I would have some green thistle tea, if allowed."

Helewise didn't curtsy again. Her eyes narrowed.

The Red Duke put a hand on Master Smythe's arm. "I think the lady of the house would prefer fewer predatory comments and a little more action. She means that the household is busy, and we are in the way. So perhaps you can show me what we've come for." He smiled all the way through this little speech.

Helewise didn't turn her head. "Pippa? Fetch the gentlemen some cups. I've heated the water."

Then she followed them out the door and around the house. To the south, the griffon was so big that it seemed to loom over the field of wheat—a field that, thankfully, needed no work whatsoever so close to midsummer. Master Smythe led the way as if he'd walked over the springy turf of her dooryard and the sheep stubble of her near pasture all his life.

"You aren't going to the circle of stones?" she asked.

"I am, too," he answered in just her North Country accent.

"Oh, that thing." She looked at Ser Gabriel. "It's very kind of you to—well, I suppose even to know what John meant to me." Master Smythe kept walking briskly, avoiding sheep dip and goose turds as he went. "I met your mother," Helewise said. The words just slipped

46

out. She had been hoping to say something—she wasn't sure what—to indicate that she really did appreciate his coming out here to speak of John.

Gabriel stopped walking. "You did?" he asked.

"A month back, or perhaps a little more. She came to our little inn, with your brother and all his entourage. Your brother Aneas was the talk of our hall for a week." Helewise winced. "But your mother was—formidable."

Ser Gabriel laughed. "So she was," he said. He scratched his beard. "Did you like her?" he asked.

They had come to the hedgerow that some thoughtful soul had planted hundreds of years before to keep the ring of standing stones out of sight of the house.

Helewise wished she had a beard to scratch. "Yeeees," she said. "A little above my likes and dislikes, I think. She was grilling poor Amicia, and Amicia stood it well enough." She looked at the duke. "Do you love Amicia, young man?" she asked.

"And now," Master Smythe said, "we are on very dangerous ground indeed. Tell me, mistress, what do you see?"

Helewise had known the stones since she was a child. "Seventeen stones standing, and nine fallen. Maybe ten, too. And there—well off to the west—is another. We call him the Forlorn Lover."

"You've counted them, then?" Master Smythe asked. "How delightful! Count them now."

Helewise didn't need to count. She let out a small shriek, and for the first time in fourteen days, no thought of John and his death was in her head.

There were eighteen stones standing. One of them, the new one, stood a head taller than the other stones, and seemed dirty, stained with dark earth like rivulets of blood, as if it had risen straight up out of the ground.

Helewise stopped and put a hand to her throat. "Someone has raised one of the old stones," she said.

"Mmmm," said Master Smythe.

The new stone was different from the others. It had a curiously convoluted surface, that might have been carved, or might instead have been formed by the sudden fossilization of an infinity of snakes and worms. Helewise knew that some of the other stones had surfaces full of the stone worms, especially when the plough caught a little of the earth at the base. Most of the worms were eroded away by wind and water.

Helewise found herself almost frozen. It was as if the stone were attacking her will. She certainly did not want to get closer to it. She wondered, in fact, when she had last been here, in the enclosure.

"Well," Ser Gabriel said. "Well, well."

Master Smythe placed a surprisingly warm and heavy hand on Helewise's bare shoulder. "I think, my lady, that perhaps you should go back to the house," he said. "I forget how—fragile—people can be."

He looked into her eyes, and his own were odd—golden, and with pupils that seemed for a moment more like a cat's eyes than a person's.

"You are pregnant," he said quietly. "Protect your baby from this. Go back to the house. I'm sorry I brought you here."

Helewise jumped. His words were taking control of her, but the word *pregnant* carved through the fear and the subtle spell he cast. Especially as, in the moment he said it, she knew it must be true.

Ser Gabriel was doing something in the *aethereal*. She could feel it—she was no practitioner, but like most North Country people, she could feel a working and sometimes even see the threads that tied like to like, that sort of thing. She saw the red power pulse under his hand, and in a moment of sight also saw the lines of grey radiating like a wormy sun from the new menhir. Many lines, like thick spiderweb, but a majority of them reaching for her. For her *baby*.

She stepped back.

Ser Gabriel produced a blade of red light and cut with it.

The worms became smoke, and vanished, where they were cut.

"Worse than I thought," Master Smythe said, very calmly. His left hand opened, and a mass of what appeared to be hermetical bees flew out of his palm—each tiny animicule flew to a single writhing, worm-like strand and landed on its end.

Helewise turned, free of compulsions, and ran for her house.

Ser Gabriel continued to cut down any worm that tried to follow her, until Master Smythe's hermetical bees had done their work. Stung, all the worms drooped, and died.

The stone became, once again, a stone.

"Much worse than I thought," Master Smythe said.

"Is this an Odine?" Gabriel asked.

Master Smythe sighed. "Yes and no," he said. "But just now, more yes than no."

"I thought the Odine were all dead," Gabriel said.

Master Smythe began to walk around the tall stone. "Hmmm. Hard to explain, really. First off, I've never been sure that the Odine are alive—not in the way we are alive. Second, when we defeated them— and I mean we, the powers and our fine human slave soldiers—when we defeated them, we bound them. I'm not sure whether we killed them. I'm not sure they can be killed. I'm not sure, as I said, they've ever been alive."

"You are so helpful," Gabriel said. "This is a bound Odine?"

"Well, I wasn't here, and I didn't bind this one, so it is difficult to be sure. But I'll guess that yes, this is the site on which at least one of them was bound." Master Smythe suddenly stepped in, like a new lover wanting a kiss, and put his one hand on the stone.

Gabriel watched a titanic amount of *ops* flow from the dragon into the stone and vanish.

Master Smythe slumped and stood back. He pulled his spotless jupon down on his hips and straightened his hood where it lay over his collar. "I have reinforced the wards," he said. "What you just saw should not have been able to happen for eons. It wanted the new life in Helewise. It is very weak—probably only strong enough to take something unborn."

"Take?" Gabriel asked.

Master Smythe glanced at him like a disapproving schoolmaster. "What do they teach you?" he asked.

Gabriel looked at him, head cocked. "I never had a class on how to fight the Odine." He reached out his right hand to touch the stone, but Master Smythe caught it. "Don't," he said. "Don't let it know you. Something is happening."

"What, do you think?" Gabriel asked.

"I didn't fly all the way out here for the thistle tea or the pretty girl, although I rather fancy both," Master Smythe said.

"I think you'll have to confine yourself to the tea," Gabriel said.

"Hmmm," said the dragon. "I am reconsidering everything I think I know."

"That's not good," Gabriel said. "But I do it all the time."

They both looked at the unwrithing menhir.

"Do you know the sorcerer that men in Antica Terra call the Necromancer?" the dragon asked.

"Not personally," Gabriel said. "Yes, I know of whom you speak. In fact, Harmodius was just mentioning him. It."

Master Smythe looked at him. "Do you know what the Odine *did*?" he asked.

"This was what, ten thousand years ago?" Gabriel asked.

"About that," Master Smythe said.

Gabriel shook his head. "No," he said. "I have no idea what they did."

Master Smythe turned so fast that his fashionable cloak swirled out behind him. "I should go. I'm well enough to return to my own hold. It is important—that I return."

"What did the Odine do?" Gabriel asked. He was following the dragon-dressed-as-a-man out of the circle of stones. He looked back. "And why did you need *people*—humans—to fight them?"

Master Smythe led the way back through the hedge and across the field of goose turds and sheep dip. Safe in the kitchen garden, he turned with another dramatic swirl of his cloak.

"Let me explain. The Odine are not...alive. No, that is not where I should begin. The Odine seem to feed off that quality that, in most of us, makes us alive. I believe that to the Odine, you and I are close kin. No, that's foolish, you and I *are* close kin."

"We are? What?" Gabriel paused.

Master Smythe waved his left hand in dismissal. "Another story. The point is, the Odine leech life away, but they sometimes give it. They do not see the world as we do. One of us, who studied them, posited that they do not experience time as we do."

"But you fought them?" Gabriel asked. He wished he had Sauce, or Amicia, or Michael to hand. All three were adept at helping him listen to this sort of thing and sort it out. Especially Sauce.

He didn't, so he took a deep breath.

"Well, we fought them. Yes, for possession of the gates and this world and others. But..." Master Smythe looked away. Out across the fields, the griffon was surrounded by field workers and bathing in their admiration. He spread his wings—they all retreated—and for a moment, sunlit, he was the very archetype of a griffon, the heraldic beast come to life, silhouetted against the deep purple mountains in the distance.

Master Smythe shook his head. "The Odine can seize a living thing, take its essence, and then replace its will with their own."

Gabriel could smell bread baking, and he stood in the sunlight of a bright day, but he felt the chill.

"Even a dragon?" Gabriel asked.

"Perhaps...even a dragon," Master Smythe answered. "A horrible suggestion. They can project power from any body they possess. Any one. Well, there are limits...nothing much smaller than a wolf."

Gabriel twitched. Just for a moment, he felt a flare of pain in his missing left hand.

"But why did you need people?" he asked. But even as he asked, he saw it. "Oh sweet lord. Because they had armies of slaves. And you had to kill them."

"Every one," Master Smythe said.

Gabriel had grown better at talking to the dragon. "What is this to do with the Necromancer?" he asked.

"It is only a fear," Master Smythe said. "A fear that possessed me when I saw the stone manifest. I know little of the Necromancer, but I know he has the power to create the not-dead, and he made the Umroth, or brought them from outside." Master Smythe frowned. "I know that ages ago, Rhun...one of us...went to find out what was happening in Ifriqy'a. And he told another of us that all was well."

Gabriel nodded.

"But now I wonder if he lied," Master Smythe said. "I look at this and wonder if the Odine have in fact returned. There are other signs. Gabriel, this is what I was studying when you appeared at my door, so to speak."

"How long have you suspected?" Gabriel asked. "Crap, Smythe, you mean I'm a sideshow?"

Master Smythe closed both eyes, together, not a very human gesture. "I need tea, and perhaps a sight of the very attractive Pippa, to steady me. I have suspected, in a scholarly way, that something was amiss for half a thousand of your years. But today is different. Listen. I really do not want to tell you too much. I feel our friendship and our alliance is precarious enough. I know perfectly well that if it were not for you, I would be dead, if not at Ash's claws than at Harmodius's hands. Yes?"

Gabriel shrugged. "Perhaps."

Master Smythe met his eye, and for a moment, both of them were locked, like lovers, in a gaze.

"I do not want to tell you the details of my own race or even my part. Because, my dear friend, someday we may be foes." Master Smythe was looking away now, at the mountains.

Gabriel nodded. "I know," he said, without hesitation. "But I will do what I can to prevent that."

Master Smythe nodded. "I know." His face went through a range of patterns. In a human, they would have been emotions, but Master Smythe was like a classical actor trying on masks, unable to choose the appropriate one. The effect was unsettling. "There are not very many of us left," he said quietly, as if he feared being overheard. "We lost our home, and we almost lost this place."

Gabriel nodded. "So?" he asked. *We lost our home…*

"So I can envision a future in which I am allied with Ash," Master Smythe said. "Can you?"

Smythe meant to leave it that way with his excellent sense of drama. He turned toward the kitchen door, but Gabriel caught him by his good shoulder. "Against the Odine?" he asked.

"Gabriel," Master Smythe said. "It never ends. We hold a castle at a crossroads that others want. All the others. This is not a joust, where you can tell the marshal that you have done enough. This is not a child's game, where you can laugh and take your toy home. The races that live here… this is all we have. And those outside will keep coming. My people are forbidden to fight among ourselves…"

Gabriel looked significantly at Master Smythe's right shoulder.

"I told you that my… hmm. Side? Side… seeks to minimize negative outcomes. That's because we don't have resources to spare for internecine war. We must always be waiting for the next invasion." Smythe's face was calm now, and expressionless.

"And Ash has broken the agreement," Gabriel said.

"Yes," Master Smythe said. "But I'd like to know why." He shook his head. "I want to believe that he is merely greedy and unbalanced. But it is possible that he knows things my mother does not."

His strange golden eyes met Gabriel's, and like a viper biting, he was too fast for Gabriel.

He saw that Gabriel had caught "my mother." And that Gabriel knew. Or guessed… That his mother was Tar.

Gabriel chose to plough on. "So, in brief…the Odine may be waking up. The Necromancer may be one of them. The Odine. Do Odine have individuality? No—don't tell me. If the Odine are waking up—what does that mean? I'm still missing a piece. Or all the pieces. Damn, it's like playing cards with half a deck."

Master Smythe shook his head. "I agree. I have, no doubt, told you too much."

"Cobwebs and mirrors," Gabriel shot back.

"Welcome to my world," Master Smythe said. "Let me ask you some questions."

Gabriel bowed. "I doubt you will find me just as evasive and confusing, but I will do my best," he said.

Master Smythe shrugged. "It is not my intent to irritate you. Indeed, of all men, I find you easiest to understand, perhaps because…never mind. First, then. If you make the journey to Antica Terra, will you look into some things on my behalf?"

"Why on earth would I go to Antica Terra?" Gabriel asked. "The seas are swarming with newly woken monsters and there's still a war here, last I checked."

Master Smythe nodded. "Of course. Forget I asked. Only, if you do…will you look into the Necromancer?"

Gabriel's eyes narrowed. "Yes," he said, finally.

"Good," Master Smythe said. "If you go, come and see me before you sail. Or fly."

Both men nodded.

"Do you intend to pursue Ash into the west?" Master Smythe asked.

"That's an excellent question. I may," Gabriel answered.

"Hmm," Master Smythe said. "I would seek to dissuade you."

"I'll consider being dissuaded," Gabriel said.

"He's wounded. He's desperate." Master Smythe looked west.

"Good," Gabriel said.

"Hmm," Master Smythe said. "Time for tea."

Inside, Phillippa coughed.

Farewells said, Gabriel clambered back into his flying saddle.

Love you, said his mount. *Love these people. So kind. Love chicken and sheep, too. Love. Hungry.*

Gabriel thought that in another life, he might fancy being a griffon.

Taking off from a flat field was very different from taking off from the top of a tower, and although it involved a long and somewhat ungainly run by his beast, the griffon leapt into the air with an elegance belied by his size and then they were winging their way aloft in great, powerful downbeats of the vast wings. Gabriel watched behind as the long, lean lion's trunk stretched into a flat body, the enormous lion's paws stretched out behind into a more eagle-like tail, and they tucked in perfectly so as not to interfere with flight. Gabriel's mind was awhirl with Smythe's latest revelations, and somewhere in that whirlpool, Gabriel questioned the existence and design of the griffon—so spectacular, so clearly hermetical.

Ten thousand years.

How long did they fight? On how many...spheres? Who the hell were they? What did they fight over?

What dragon named Rhun?

Then Master Smythe led them through a series of turns and rolls and Gabriel almost lost his tea. And then they rolled in on the end of the great fair in the fields by the council tree and made three passes. A pair of genuine wyverns climbed up to meet them and led them in some wyvern sport, tossing a dead sheep around the sky. Gabriel was only a passenger, and a concerned one at that, but eventually, as the queen's train rode down from the hills to return to the castle for the night, the two wyverns shrieked something—disdain? approval?— and tore off into the gloom, and Smythe turned for home, swooping low over the mountain track where the queen rode with her ladies. Gabriel attempted to wave to Blanche and failed.

Then they winged away south over the Albin River and then south again over the Brogat. Gabriel noted that there was almost no traffic on the river or the roads, and no one was tilling the fields, which seemed odd, but high summer is the time that farmers take a rest. But it was eerie, and he began to watch the ground despite the ongoing terror of rapid turns and even flying upside down.

But none of the maneuvers practiced over the fields of the northern Brogat and the woods of the foothills of the Adnacrags terrified him as much as the landing.

They approached the citadel of Albinkirk from the north. Gabriel was able to pick out his tower against the sky from a great distance, and he settled himself in his heavy leather saddle, relaxing his muscles for the approach.

But nothing in his life had prepared him for the last ten heartbeats of the landing. Perhaps a hundred paces out from the tower, flying at a speed that left the rooftops below a blur of tiles and slates, Gabriel was sure they would slam into the tower, but then Ariosto pivoted on a wingtip, so that Gabriel's legs screamed at the effort of holding on to the barrel-shaped back and the restraining belt across the high back of the saddle cut deep into his gut.

They were fifty feet *below* the perch and still moving at an insane pace.

The great wings shot out, and up they went, a rising swoop, exactly like the rearing of a trained warhorse, except that it was a hundred-foot fall to a messy death below if Gabriel went over the back of the saddle. He was staring straight up into the sky one moment, and then the great wings on either side beat once and seemed to cup the air—their lightninglike progress was suddenly stilled, the rushing air in Gabriel's ears fell away to nothing, and they settled onto the perch. The griffon missed his grasp with one foot and they swayed a moment, and Gabriel's life passed slowly before his eyes...he thought of Blanche, and Amicia, and Gavin, and then Ariosto's head was turned, the great right eye was on him, and the griffon's thoughts beamed their affection and demanded praise.

It occurred to Gabriel that Ariosto had become his mother's enduring monument and her revenge.

Love you! Ariosto beamed. *Let's eat!*

Gabriel managed to hug his war beast before facing the horror of the dismount and the long, precarious shuffle along the perch, a hundred feet above the tiltyard.

Master Smythe watched him without doing anything helpful, head cocked slightly to one side like a large hawk.

"Problem?" he asked.

"I'm scared of heights," Gabriel commented as he took another shuffling step and the breeze nuzzled him.

"Ah," Master Smythe said. "Well, use makes master, or so they say. Come on, Ser Knight!" He laughed. "I have a gift for you, but not if you take all night."

"You could give me a hand," Gabriel allowed through gritted teeth.

"Oh, does that help?" Master Smythe asked. He held out his left hand, and Gabriel caught it and managed the last long step from perch to solid stonework. "Thank you."

"Think nothing of it," said Master Smythe. "Come."

They went down past the main hall and the kitchens, and out into the yard, and along the stables to the tiltyard. Gabriel looked up just as Ariosto looked down, and he was *loved* from a hundred feet above. It was curious that from the perch, the tiltyard looked miles away, but from the tiltyard, the griffon seemed quite close.

There was the sound of planishing coming from the armourer's shop, a permanent shop manned by whatever itinerant armourer could be persuaded to work on the castle's mountain of old and damaged harness.

Gabriel liked armourers. He liked them all, the old, bent ones and the young, intense ones. They were all mad, but all equally driven and passionate.

But the tall figure working carefully on polished metal was no man. He was obviously an irk. He had the high forehead and almost-pointed ears of his people, and far too many teeth, but the focused intensity of his stare at his piece of metal defined his breed more than his ears.

"Ah, my lord dragon," sang the irk. His voice had none of the sibilance of the Faery Knight. The armourer sounded more like a chorus of coyotes or wild wolves, his voice split into a strange polyphony. "And the famous Ser Gabriel. It is good to see you in person and not mere measurements."

Master Smythe nodded. "Gabriel, this is Cull Pett, the master artist of armour among all the people that you men call irks. He is just finishing my gift."

"You will have to finish it, lord dragon," Cull Pett said. "I do not play games with reality like some I could mention."

He took the plate he had been working when they came in, a small, roughly square plate with a decidedly curved surface and some form of articulation—something very fine. Gabriel thought that it might be part of a gauntlet.

He was pleased to find he was correct. A single left gauntlet lay on an old sack. Cull Pett took the gauntlet and snapped something, turned a threaded screw, and put the articulated plate across the back of the hand. He flexed it a few times.

Gabriel noted that the irk had done no measuring that he had seen. All by eye.

"Try it on," the armourer said. "I haven't had you to work with because my patron wanted not just the object but some form of surprise."

Gabriel realized it was not a gauntlet. It was a hand.

Even as he understood and reached for the thing, the armourer said, "It is foolishness, keeping the model from the artist. I should have had access to you and your stump a day ago at least. The vanity of the dragon is, of course, proverbial. Ah, there, it fits, but 'tis only luck. I should have made it better if I'd had you here. Perhaps it is too small..."

It was just like having a silver hand. It didn't work, of course. It was inert. But it was magnificent, and the size was perfect. It was as if he had a lifeless silver hand.

"Well?" said the armourer, somewhat pettishly, to the dragon. "You have to try it, Master. I can't close it up unless we both know it works."

Master Smythe created a working. It sometimes troubled Gabriel that the dragon didn't seem to have a memory palace or a working system. He did not hum, he did not sign, he did not manipulate beads. He merely cast. It was not a human thing, and to Gabriel it represented the single major difference between their kinds. Somehow, the dragons manipulated *ops* without ever converting it to *potentia* or working it.

The working crept across the worktable and then entered into the inert hand, which lay, attached to Gabriel's stump, in his lap. Tendrils of green-and-gold fire licked at the tips of the fingers.

Instantly, the tips of Gabriel's fingers prickled. Without a conscious thought, his fingers twitched... his *silver* fingers twitched.

"Oh my God," Gabriel breathed.

"Satisfactory?" the armourer asked.

Master Smythe beamed.

"Right, take it off," the armourer said.

Gabriel knew a prick of fear. He was trying to make the fingers close on one of the hammers left on the workbench. He was close.

Cull Pett came up close to him and lifted the hand. He stared at it a bit, moving the wrist articulation back and forth.

"I will do better if I am allowed to open your body and recut the wound," he said. "There will have to be wires... the cuff... you see? A small cutting." He pointed at the cuff, held on to another part by tiny screws. "This is only temporary."

Gabriel sighed as the hand was taken from him. "When will you finish it?" he asked.

"Oh, as to that, tonight under moonlight will be best," the armourer said. "And tonight, if you will bear it, I will attach the socket. It will hurt as much as any surgeon's work." He shrugged, as if Gabriel's pain were of no moment to him, which was probably the case.

"You are superb," Master Smythe said.

"It would have been better if I'd been allowed access to him earlier," the armourer said again. "Still, I suppose we were lucky."

They walked back across the tiltyard. Master Smythe paused, looking up at the perch. "I probably shouldn't tell you this," he said. "But before I even knew who you would be...when I first sensed you in the possible, before I became entangled in these threads...I saw this hand. I have no idea why. Actually, this is untrue, sloppy human emotional speech. I have a thousand ideas why. But I have made of that hand as potent an artifact as I know how to create. Before we part, I will teach you what it does. But the most important is, it will serve as a ready focus for power, the way Harmodius uses his staff. His new staff." Master Smythe smiled. "His old staff, you should know, is the stave of your weapon."

"I thought that was your notion of a wicked jest," Gabriel said.

"Hmm," Master Smythe said.

Full night. Gabriel ate with the queen, and there was formality, but not too much, and he sat with her ladies while they played with the king. Just as the sky passed from the last of twilight to full darkness, an imperial messenger came to the stables and a page brought him the messages, both from Gavin.

Gabriel read them through, first one and then the other. Then he read the first again.

"Madame, I need to speak to Master Smythe immediately, and then I fear I will have to advise you. You may wish to have all your council about you," he said.

"My lord, you scare me," she said.

"I scare myself. Ash has designed another plague. This one kills people. It is loose in the army, and the hospital, and I fear it is already loose in the northern Brogat." He thought of the empty roads and fields. He thought of Master Smythe, and Ash.

It was late when Gabriel made it to his apartments. He now had the whole of the turret top, with Ariosto in one open-roofed chamber, and he had the foyer as a receiving room and both bedrooms for his armoury and his newly appointed secretary. Master Julius was still writing—orders, the result of the meeting of the queen's inner council. Toby was directing a pair of maids and a new page, Anne Woodstock, in laying out clothes for morning. A pair of pourpointers, a furrier, and a leather worker were in the outer office, despite the hour, sewing a quilted leather flying doublet lined in fur.

It was the first night they had all been back in Albinkirk. Gabriel had only just been released from the sister's open-air hospital. The queen had stayed nearby, with the garrison at Gilson's Hole, for just as long, planning her summer progress and sparing Albinkirk. Money was short, and camping was cheap, even for monarchs.

Toby looked up, caught his chief's eye, and looked away. "Bad as that, sir?" he asked.

"Mortirmir has it under control for the moment but it is not beaten, and there's already people dead in camp and at the hospital. It may already be loose south of here, Toby, and even here in Albinkirk and there's a report from Harndon too. So have a care. If you start coughing…anyway, we'll be trying to get word out to people as soon as it is light. The church will play the lead." Gabriel put his hand in front of his eyes and yawned. "Damn it!" he said. "I can't be this tired."

Woodstock helped him with his boots. She didn't know him yet and he didn't know her, so she said nothing. He stretched his legs a little. "Thanks, Nell," he said.

Anne Woodstock glanced at Toby, who made a motion with his head.

Toby stepped forward. "Have you seen your leather pourpoint?" he asked. "Everyone will want a griffon, my lord."

Gabriel sat back and took the cup of wine that Toby pressed into his hand. "Everyone should want a griffon, Toby. He's quite wonderful, if just a trifle…overbearing." He rubbed his temples. "Where is Blanche?"

Toby smiled a slight smile. "Probably waiting on the stairs to be asked for, my lord." Toby's flat, matter-of-fact "squire's voice" expressed a great many opinions all at once...that this treatment was unfair to Blanche, and that Blanche deserved better.

Gabriel shot to his feet. "Damn it," he said. "Why didn't you just move her things here?"

He looked at Toby. Toby's closed face once again was its own signal. "Aha. Right. Apologies, Toby. Would you be so kind as to fetch her?"

"Might I be bold enough to suggest you might want to get her yourself, my lord?" Toby was laying out clothes for the next day. Light clothes. He had heard that the armourer was going to cut into his captain, and if he felt any apprehension, he hid it well.

"You are a very fountain of wisdom tonight," Gabriel said. He finished his wine. "Best pour me more. Stairwell?" he asked.

"Unless she's gone to bed in the queen's chamber, my lord." Toby hid his disapproval. His captain was tired, and when tired, the captain took people for granted. Squires, pages...lovers.

Gabriel ran down the first set of stairs to the floor below, where Galahad D'Acon and three other royal messengers shared one room, Harmodius and Payam shared a second, and the queen's ladies shared a third. He could hear voices—and laughter.

Pavalo Payam was as black as the irk armourer, but any resemblance ended there. Payam was tall but heavily built; his face was narrow and his limbs were long and graceful. He was dressed in court clothes, a pair of fine hose and a velvet doublet that some tailor had run up in a hurry, and he looked more elegant than Gabriel could have imagined. Lady Natalia and Lady Briar were sitting under a mage light working embroidery, while Lady Heloise wove a silken lace. Galahad D'Acon was providing the frame with his strong fingers, and Payam was playing an instrument that looked like a mandolin but had more strings and a complex, bent neck. The music he was playing sounded like nothing Gabriel had heard before.

Blanche was standing in the middle of the small hall, listening to the music. Her eyes were half closed, and her hips moved, suggesting how she might dance, and her elbows moved enough to show how her arms might move. It was quite unconscious, but Gabriel thought it unutterably lovely, and noted, too, that both of the older ladies' feet were moving, tapping, in time to the rich, complex notes.

Gabriel had a moment of what he had to confess to himself was jealousy as he saw her regard for the "infidel" knight, but Pavalo looked up from his music and grinned, and Blanche turned...

The impact she had on him remained the same. When she turned, and he saw her recognize him, and the instant smile that spread across her face, his heart seemed to explode. Irritation, fatigue, fear of the future and the plague—

Gone.

He took her hand and kissed her on the lips before he considered what he was doing, and where he was. Young Heloise turned her head away and blushed. Her mother smiled, and Lady Natalia smiled too.

I am a fool, Gabriel thought.

Part of him didn't care.

He sat by her, the two of them pushed against each other, sharing a stool, as Payam played another piece, this one very fast indeed, a thunderstorm of notes. And when the Ifiquy'an was done, they all applauded. He rose and gave a little bow with a broad grin.

"I found this in the hall," he said. "I saw it and I thought—that is something of my home. And lo, it is. It has taken me four days to teach it to play again, but it is a very fine instrument of its kind, and I like to think perhaps it was placed here so that I might please you all. There has been too much war and not enough dance."

Gabriel smiled and caught his eye. "You have the right of it," he said. Then, quietly, "Where is Harmodius?"

"He is *working*." The paynim knight shrugged eloquently. "He told me to go and make my mirth elsewhere, so I took him to mean this, and he is a good prophet."

"You have all but mastered Alban," Gabriel said.

"My master has always told me I was a quick study," Payam said with a sparkle. "But Master Harmodius has known me since I was a child, and he came into my head and began to teach me. Very rapidly." Payam's words were accurate but his diction was odd, very slow, almost too elegant.

Gabriel nodded again and ran his fingers through his beard, which was longer than usual. "He is exceptionally good at that," Gabriel said.

"It is the same with my own master," Payam said. "When something is important, always he can come into my head and teach me. If only the teachers at madrassa had been able to do this, perhaps I would be an imam and not a mere warrior."

Blanche beamed at him. "You are not a *mere* warrior. You have saved me twice, and the queen, and the young king—and you are as beautiful as a dancer when you fight."

Gabriel was aware of another stab wound near his heart. But Payam smiled.

"That is beautiful of you to say, Lady Blanche, and I will treasure this compliment like a necklace of jewels left me by my mother. But I have only done my duty." He nodded again. "And speaking of duty, I must go and see to whatever Master Harmodius may require."

Even as he spoke, Gabriel felt the accession of *ops* and its near-instantaneous remaking as *potentia*.

"Do not open his door," Gabriel said, rising.

Payam looked a question but obeyed.

Gabriel felt the release of the power, like the breaking of a dam, and it rolled away into the night, spreading seedpods or mayflies of power as it moved. One alit on Blanche's nose, and one on Gabriel's forehead, and one on Payam...in a single heartbeat, Gabriel saw that there was a point of fire on everyone in the room, and in his hermetical sight, he *could perceive the sparks alighting on everyone in the castle, even as a single bolt of constructed working sped east into the darkness.*

Gabriel did not lightly allow another's power to have access to him. He queried the tiny working, examined it, and even as it flickered, he opened himself and read it. Having learned it, he read the others, too.

"Master Harmodius has constructed a diagnostic. With help from Master Mortirmir, I sense. And now that he has completed it, he sends the finished working out even as he sends the blueprint of it to Master Mortirmir."

Harmodius was framed in the doorway, looking tired but extremely pleased with himself. "You read all that from my little hermetical bees?" he asked. "You are coming along very well, boy." He reached out, almost blind, and Blanche, ever thoughtful, pressed her own cup of wine into his hands. He drank the cup off, and Lady Natalia, unbidden, refreshed it.

Gabriel watched this and thought, *What a company we have become. How closely all these are bound.*

"I have always loved your oud, Payam, and I crave that you play again. Something old. And then I pray you all go to your beds and let me to mine," Harmodius said.

The older man—much older than he appeared, as he was presently in the body of a late-middle-aged man with a pointy black beard and pepper-and-salt hair—drank off a second cup of wine as Payam tuned his strings carefully.

"Can you tell me of the Brogat?" Gabriel asked quietly. Blanche had moved, and he was hip to hip with Harmodius.

The older man finished his wine. "It is bad," he said. "We do not have control of it, and people have been dying south of the river for two or three days."

Gabriel had expected very different news, and this was like a punch in the gut. "And the army?" Gabriel asked.

"Racing for supplies, and too deep in the Adnacrags," Harmodius said. "As I said to the queen, we must save the army first. I'm sorry for the callousness of this, but the loss of a hundred knights…anyway, I am drained now. But tomorrow, I will walk the Wyrm's way. And do what I can."

"I will fly," Gabriel said. "And see what I can carry in terms of food."

Harmodius nodded. "That is well thought," he said. "You see that this was all a trap," the older man went on, as the oud played.

Gabriel looked away. "Yes," he admitted.

"Ash didn't care a damn whether his forces won or lost. He left the plagues—and there are at least two—to kill the survivors. *All* the survivors. This thing is as lethal to bogglins as it is to men."

Gabriel found it difficult to breathe. "Sweet Christ…" he said. Religious imagery was creeping back into his conversation.

Harmodius nodded. "There is, in fact, an element of mercy. I have weighted the evidence. The army is so well protected—so many magisters, so much working, so many amulets—that in fact, the human plague has been held back, perhaps even lessened. Perhaps Mag's shields…I don't know. But Ash is not omnipotent, and he didn't predict that effect, or that Mortirmir had already solved the horse plague."

The old magister's eyes were closing. Gabriel had direct experience of casting until he was virtually empty, and he knew exactly how Harmodius felt.

Gabriel stood and, without too much effort, picked up the magister and carried him like a bride into his room.

"Bless you, boy," Harmodius murmured.

Gabriel put the older man on a bed and pulled two thick white blankets over him.

When he went back into the small hall, everyone was gone but Payam, who slipped past him into his room, and Blanche, who tossed her hair and looked uneasy.

Gabriel caught her hand. They walked up a few steps of the tightly wound tower stairs, and then she tugged at him until they were sitting.

He went to kiss her. She endured the kiss, but it was not very passionate. At least, at first. It grew with time into a much more rewarding kiss.

She broke away and laughed. "I have not been with you for two weeks," she said. "My whole body is yearning for you." She looked away. He felt her blush even in the three-quarters darkness, her cheek warm and close to his.

"I told Toby to have your things..."

"I told him to leave my things with the queen's," Blanche said. "I'll not be your whore, Gabriel. Or perhaps I will, but by the trinity, it will not be my *work*. I am the queen's lady, and I like it. If I'm to grace your bed, let it be my sport, by my will, and not...that other way."

Gabriel leaned back against the next step. "The queen is going south to Harndon, and I am going east," he said slowly.

Blanche kissed him a little, by way of communicating something. And then said, "You are going east, where mayhap they will crown you emperor. That is what Rebecca Almspend says."

Gabriel did not want to have this conversation just then. He had found the back of her neck, and his fingers were slipping to the neckline of her kirtle, and she was not making any effort at resistance.

There was more kissing.

"If you think you are going to make love to me with my spine pressed into a cold stone stair," she said, and she giggled, "you are mistaken."

Gabriel had, in fact, convinced himself that they were about to do just that, and he took a moment to master himself, and then he picked her up—and Blanche was not a small woman—and carried her up the rest of the steps.

Ho ho ho, said Ariosto inside his head. *And I love her. Oh, I remember her. So beautiful. Bring her!*

Gabriel shut the door on his griffon. There were some things he didn't intend to share.

Blanche put her arms around his neck.

Gabriel *entered his palace and winked at the image of Prudentia, and then examined the workings of his palace until he found the one he wanted, and then the wheels spun. It caused him a moment's unease in the* aethereal *to think that he had used this same working to get close to Amicia, not so very long ago.*

"Clementia, Pisces, Eustachios," he said in the palace of his memory, and the statue of Prudentia moved like a pantomime to point at one sign and then another.

And the room moved.

The windows rotated silently above the signs of the zodiac, and the statues below the band of bronze rotated in the opposite direction until his three chosen signs were aligned opposite to the ironbound door. And he winked again at Prudentia, walked across the tiles of the twelve-sided room, and unlatched the door.

He opened it on a verdant olive grove drenched in a dense golden light—the dream memory of the perfect summer day in Morea. It was not always thus, on the far side of the door. A richly scented breeze blew in. It was not always this strong, his golden power, and he deflected some with the power of his will, batting it into a ball and shoving it like a handful of summer leaves into a hempen bag he imagined into being and hung from Prudentia's outstretched arm. Against a rainy day when there was less gold. Despite the waves of lust—really, even love, as he could see clearly in his palace, or perhaps because of the love—he took a timeless moment to weave the dense gold into a shield, which he hung like a buckler from Prudentia's lifeless hand. Her lips twitched in a smile.

The insistent golden haze stirred through his hair and then reached the aligned signs on the opposite wall and—

Gabriel carried Blanche in through the door to his apartments. Toby was stretched out on a pallet of straw, and Anne Woodstock lay in her own blanket, wrapped tight, but just touching him. Gabriel managed to put a foot between them without either noticing, and Master Julius, who was writing out the last copy of a dense list of orders, raised his head at a scent of perfume but saw nothing.

Gabriel passed the two pourpointers, who were having a hushed discussion of whether to build a frame. He left them to it, and passed them into his bedchamber.

Toby had left a candle lit on one of his military chests. His bed had been hung—that is, his bed had been set up, and a sort of tent of linen hung over it by a hook in the ceiling. Gabriel almost pulled the whole thing down trying to lay Blanche on the bed.

She laughed. "Oh no," she said, and slipped out of his arms to the floor. She went to the casemented window and opened the shutters, and the full light of the moon fell in. It was a hot night—hotter outside than in the old stone.

Then she turned to him with a happy smile and began to unlace her kirtle.

He began to help her, and she to help him. The moonlight had its own magic. And he had not really seen her like this.

And then there was a soft knock at his door.

Blanche dove into the bed.

Gabriel cursed. His curse was sufficiently rich that a line of red fire began to move on the walls, and he had to recall it.

He managed to get to the door with his dirty shirt wrapped around his loins, and he opened it a crack.

Cull Pett stood in the sliver of moonlight, his light eyes sparkling in his dark skin.

"Excellent," he said in his rich voice. "There is moonlight, and you are already naked."

Of all the expectations Blanche might have had of the evening, becoming the nurse while a monster cut open her beloved was not one she'd ever imagined. But the irk knew she was there, and requested her most courteously, and Gabriel handed her kirtle in to the closed bed and she put it on with no linens underneath.

She wondered how the irk had come to the tower, but then, she wondered how Gabriel had passed all the people in his apartment, and she had a good idea as to the answer to both questions.

The irk unrolled a leather case full of tools and put a superb silver hand on one of the military trunks. She looked at it in wonder—she touched it with her hand and was shocked at its near-human warmth. It was not cold metal.

When the armourer was ready, Gabriel smiled at her.

"I have a notion," he said. "Sit just here, take my good hand, and look into my eyes."

She did as she was bid, aware that the irk had a keen-bladed knife that seemed to be made of stone; flint or jade, she thought. It had an alien, half-moon shape. His mouth had too many teeth; his skin was black, not the warm, rich brown-black of Payam but a colder, bluer black, and she felt a chill of fear.

She looked into Gabriel's eyes...

She had never been inside his memory palace before.

"I should have tried this weeks ago," he said. "In the hospital. Then we could have talked."

"Oh," she said, turning. She looked up at the cathedral ceiling, the stone moldings running like veins and arteries throughout the roof, the stained glass, the statues and the bronze and gold hermetical symbols.

"It is beautiful," she said.

And she could feel the warmth of his pleasure as a physical reaction.

He took her hand. "Have you ever worked ops?" *he asked. "You see everything here. I can feel your power—a steady flame. Fascinating."*

He turned to her, and she, without thinking, kissed him, as if they were in the real.

As her tongue reached to find his through open lips, she had the strangest feeling of falling, and for a moment—

She didn't know whether she was Gabriel or Blanche.

She broke the kiss in startlement and fell back into being herself.

Gabriel grinned. "My, my," he said. "The things Prudentia didn't teach me."

His smile was erased, and he flickered. And then grew solid.

"I'm going to guess that my armourer has begun work," he said.

Blanche pressed his hand, and kissed him again. But this time, as she kissed him, she felt a distant pain in her left hand and arm—a ringing pain, the aftershock of something worse.

"It is as if I am you," she said.

"I wonder how long this metaphor would last?" Gabriel said playfully. His aethereal fingers brushed her neck and shoulders suggestively, and she laughed.

"But I'm afraid I would awake and not know how to do the queen's laundry," Gabriel said. "And there you'd be, trying to fight bogglins with a clean shirt."

"Oh," she said in mock anger. "So you think my work is beneath you."

His face split in a grin, and she rolled her eyes. "Don't, for the love of God, play at being some hopeless castle boy with his double entendres," she snapped.

"I didn't say it!" he replied, all mock contrition, and then his face spasmed again and she held him tightly.

When he was calm and solid, he sat her down.

"I want to return to the conversation on the stairs," he said.

She smiled impishly. "Yes," she laughed. "If I had known what awaited in the bedchamber, I might have stayed on the stairs."

"Hush," he said. "Lady Almspend is right, and it is only fair, you know. I hope to be chosen as emperor."

"The queen is against it," Blanche said. "I'm sure you know."

Gabriel nodded. "I know. It will create a tangle of loyalties for all of us. You included. Me included." He shrugged. "It is hard to explain to you, my love—"

"Your love?" Blanche asked. "Tell me truly? I am your love?" She leaned close. "You do not need to say such a thing. I know you, Gabriel. I know you like me. But love?"

He paused.

She smiled.

"Are you always this blunt?" Gabriel asked.

Blanche shrugged. "This is new territory, Ser Knight. I'm sitting, next to naked, inside the head of a man enduring an operation, speaking of whether he'll be crowned emperor and how this may affect my life." She shrugged. "This hasn't happened to me before. I have to come up with new doctrines."

Gabriel leaned back. "I'm fairly certain that I love you," he said.

Her head snapped back as if she'd been struck. "Really?" she asked. "Why?"

She watched him a moment, enjoying his discomfiture. "My understanding," she said, "is that becoming emperor includes marrying Irene."

Gabriel nodded. "Leaving aside that she's tried to kill me at least once, yes, marrying her would ease the whole transaction. Good God, are we always going to be this honest?"

Blanche was surprised at herself. His ready admission didn't put ice in her belly. "Will you marry her?" she asked.

Gabriel stroked his aethereal beard. "I don't know," he said. "I don't think so.

"You will if you must," she said quietly.

"Yes," he agreed. "I have the sinking feeling that I should have made love to you before we started this conversation."

Then he froze. He gritted his teeth, looked elsewhere, and swore. She watched him a moment, then surrendered to impulse and kissed him.

Her left wrist was a ring of fire that burned and burned and . . .

The irk was rolling his tools in the moonlight, his fanged smile as terrifying as ever.

Blanche was herself, even as she looked at her own left hand and found it whole, and was surprised that she'd expected something else.

He was lying on the bed, peacefully asleep, and he had two hands, although one of them had a silvery sheen to it.

"But there is . . . no blood?" Blanche asked.

The irk smiled again and licked his lips. "I never leave a drop," he agreed. And slipped through the door.

Blanche put a hand on Gabriel's chest, but it rose and fell evenly, and his skin was warm—deliciously so.

He sighed.

Blanche leaned down, put her lips on his, and his eyes fluttered open.

"Ahh," he said, and pulled at her insistently. She had no interest in struggling. But she made him wait while she removed and folded her kirtle. And when he touched her . . .

"Your hand is warm!" she said.

He rose when Toby knocked, his bare feet on the little rug he always carried in his camp gear. He pulled the bed-hanging closed behind him, for Blanche's modesty and because she got cold.

Still half asleep, he yet had a moment to think that the real-life intimacy of Blanche was very different from his love-longing for Amicia. He wondered what that meant about him, as a person.

Toby looked wrecked. "My lord," he said. "There are messages. The queen is rising and has ordered the council." He leaned forward. "And begs the return of her lady."

Gabriel closed his eyes for a moment and his heart beat very fast. "Dress me in two minutes," he said. He shut the door.

Blanche was not a heavy sleeper. It was a piece with his earlier thought . . . the things he was learning about her, a whole realm of lovely and unlovely detail that went with constant intimacy. She was a delightful weight on him when she slept, curled against him . . . and she would suddenly talk in her sleep, which was less delightful.

She was awake, already off the bed. Her clothes, neatly stacked on a chest, went on.

"Lace me, please?" she said.

Gabriel still found her body fascinating, but this was not the time. He laced her up under her arm, resisted the temptation to either lechery or simple tickling, and helped her get her gown over her kirtle.

"Now the queen knows," she said. It wasn't bitter or accusatory. It was a flat statement.

"I think she already knew," Gabriel said. "Do you know that you have some hermetical talent?"

She looked at him for a moment by the light of the single night candle. "Is this a compliment?"

He shook his head. "No. Simple truth. Interesting, nonetheless."

"If you spend more time with Master Smythe, you'll end up sounding just like him," she said. She flashed a smile. "I'm afraid to face the queen," she said.

"I'll go with you," he said.

"No, you won't," she said. She put her hair up in three motions, put a veil over it, and nodded to herself. "Aren't you supposed to start buying me jewels and so on?" she asked.

"Only after you demand offices and money for all your relatives," he said.

She smiled. It was her real smile, and it was *beautiful*. "Sometimes, I'm still amazed I'm even talking to you. Or the queen. Or Becca." She shrugged. She leaned over and kissed him, catching his top lip between hers, softly, so that his whole body surged toward her, but she was out of his arms and out the door with all her long practice. He heard her exchange comments with Toby in the antechamber, and then Toby came in with his clothes. Anne Woodstock, in nothing but a shift, came behind with a flagon of something hot and a tart on a wooden board. She laid them on a chest.

Despite his near-panic at whatever kind of message got the queen out of her bed while it was still dark, despite the flush still on his body from Blanche's kiss, he had time to note that Anne Woodstock was not at all built like a boy. In livery, she merely seemed muscular. In a shift, she was heavily breasted, lithe and serious—and unconscious of her body as only a good dancer or a good swordsperson can be. She'd come to the company from one of the Brogat's noblest families. She was a hard worker, and Gabriel had some notion he'd called her Nell the night before. So he cut through all the piled lumber in his own head and nodded to her and smiled.

"Good morning Anne," he said.

She met his eye. "Good morning, my lord." She brightened up considerably. She was very young—perhaps sixteen or seventeen, dark haired, and she did look like Nell.

He took the steaming flagon from her hand, poured it into the silver cup she held, and smiled again. "Duke of Thrake as I may be, Anne, I like my morning cup to be horn, not silver. It saves on burnt fingers, and I've not always lived so well. Horn is fine."

She didn't simper or apologize. She merely slipped out the door, returned with a small horn cup, and poured the steaming hypocras into it before handing him the result. He raised it in a toast to her efficiency. Michael had chosen her in the days after the battle, and as usual, Michael knew what he was about.

While the little drama of cups played out, Toby was dressing him with efficiency. He kept lacing when Francis Atcourt, now an officer, bowed his way in. Gabriel had kept him as his aide while he recuperated. Atcourt's own wounds were all healed, almost scarlessly.

He nodded to Toby and received a nod from his captain.

"My lord," he said formally. Gabriel was now "Captain" or "my lord" the first time he met anyone. After that, he permitted more intimacy.

He blinked as he realized that he'd made this rule since Blanche came into his life, and he thought...

"Shall I read them?" Atcourt asked. "Sorry, copies of the messages." He waved a scroll.

"Go ahead," Gabriel said. Toby was lacing his inner doublet to his hose.

Atcourt sipped Gabriel's hypocras with the ease of long familiarity and began.

Riots in Liviapolis and plague. Demand immediate assistance. Irene.
Gabriel swore.

Venikan Duke has interviewed survivor of Battle of Gars. King of Galle dead. Lord D'Albemarle dead. Lord of Arles dead. Army shattered and nearly destroyed. Wild led by dragon. Citadel of Arles still in human hands as of last communication.

"What date?" Gabriel said. An icy fist clenched his heart.

"The report came in this hour, the date is yesterday." Atcourt whistled. "Someone got a messenger bird across the sea."

"Who is it?" Gabriel asked.

"E.23," Atcourt said, after staring at the parchment. "Christ, I need spectacles."

"Get them," Gabriel said. "I'm off my game. E.23 is in the Logothete's network?"

Atcourt made a face. "Must be. I'll summon Alcaeus."

"Immediately. He needs to know both messages. And probably get ready to ride. You have more?"

"Plague in Harndon," Atcourt said. "Random's doing what he can with confining families. Begs immediate sorcerous help."

Gabriel clenched and unclenched his fists. "Fuck," he spat. "I thought we were going to have a tournament."

Toby put his head in. "Master Smythe," he said, and then the dragon entered.

"Give me your hand," he said.

Gabriel felt the slow wits of early morning, and it took him several beats to realize that Master Smythe meant the silver hand. He held it out, limp but warm, and the dragon took it with a sharp click.

"A few hours," he said. He smiled and swept from the room.

"He frightens me," Atcourt said.

Gabriel smiled. "He's beginning to seem like family," he said.

Atcourt looked up in surprise.

Gabriel's smile was thin. "It's a Muriens joke," he said. "He frightens me, too."

Torches spat and gave off resinous smells. It was an hour until dawn.

"Well?" asked the queen.

She looked at Gabriel and Harmodius, who were sitting together. Gabriel was looking at Master Smythe.

Master Smythe was staring at the fire on the hearth and combing his beard with his fingers. As usual, his fingers were too flexible.

"We have underestimated Ash," he said.

Gabriel's heart sank.

Master Smythe rose, as if he and not the queen were the ranking person present. Mogon's crest rustled in annoyance, and Lord Kerak laughed aloud. Flint yawned.

The bear looked grey and old.

Smythe shrugged and looked at the queen. "But Ash has under-estimated you, too," he said. "Harmodius's diagnostic working is superb. Mortirmir's concoction can only buy time, but..." He looked back at Gabriel. "There should have been ten thousand dead already. Instead...you have a chance."

"Will you help?" the queen asked.

"Yes," Master Smythe said without hesitation. "Will you, in exchange, help me?"

"Is that not what allies do?" the queen asked. She didn't smile. She didn't look as if she had a smile in her.

He bowed. "Lady, I would ask that you, all your court, anyone infected or merely present on the battlefield in the last two weeks move immediately through the woods to the Inn of Dorling." He looked at Gabriel. "Within the limits of my power I can prevent the spread of the thing, and influence its effect. Here, I am not powerless, but I am much less powerful."

Harmodius stared at him, and then he, too, looked to Gabriel.

"What do you wish of us, dragon?" he asked. "I too would seek your aid, but we can defeat this by ourselves if your price is too high."

Master Smythe looked around the table. "There are too many here for me to discuss freely what I wish. But I will say simply that what I will request is well within your means."

"*You* don't trust *us*?" Harmodius asked.

Master Smythe looked at Gabriel with a little desperation.

Gabriel shrugged. "Can we discuss yesterday's adventure?" he asked. He thought he had it—the whole thread that led the master to look so desperate.

Master Smythe looked around the room pointedly.

Gabriel caught the queen's eye and she nodded, and he stood.

"Master Smythe, this is the queen's Small Council, with the addi-tions of some of the greatest lords of the Wild. We are allies, and we have chosen to be open with each other. If you wish to join our alli-ance, you will have to share with us."

Even the Golden Bear, Flint, nodded. Lord Kerak rose and bowed to indicate, in his fluid Irkish way, his complete agreement with the Red Duke.

The queen nodded. She had become less girlish and more regal, and her nod was that of the being in command.

Master Smythe went back to the fireplace and stared into it. Then he turned, very suddenly. And spoke.

"Very well, I agree," he said evenly. "Yesterday, on the moor only six leagues from this tower, an Odine attempted to seize the soul of an unborn babe." He put his hands behind his back. "I have known for some time that the Odine were stirring. But until yesterday I had no proof." He met Gabriel's eye. "And now..." He paused.

The pause lengthened.

"And now you know that the horde that crushed the Galles was led by a dragon," the Red Knight prompted.

Master Smythe's head shot round. But he made no denial. His nod was decisive. "Yes. Yes, Gabriel. You are very clever. That was it. The tipping point."

The queen leaned back. "I confess I have no idea what you are discussing."

Flint leaned back so that his heavy oak chair creaked in protest. "The Odine!" he said. He coughed the name, and Lord Kerak was seen to shade his eyes with his hand.

The rest of the council looked puzzled. The Grand Squire coughed into his hand. "Surely we need to concentrate on the plague," he said.

Gabriel frowned. "We must attack the plague with every resource to hand," he said. "But that is a matter of writs and scholars working until their fingers burn. We are going to take losses now." His voice was bitter. "I should have seen this coming," he admitted.

The Grand Squire nodded at him. "I am not sure that we could have done better than we did."

"And thanks to God," said Prior Wishart, "that we kept the army together and the hospital for the wounded down by Gilson's Hole." He looked around. "I have come from there. The cough is very bad...and many workers have already fled, carrying it south."

Gabriel nodded. "The camp was Amicia's inspiration, and may, in the last accounting, prove the most vital decision of the war. And we need her—as soon as possible."

Harmodius nodded sharply. "Except," he said quietly, and looked at Master Smythe, who nodded.

"Except that you will not have her much longer," he said quietly.

"Is this prophecy?" the queen asked. "She is one of my kingdom's most potent resources."

Harmodius and Gabriel and Kerak and Smythe all shook their heads in unison. "Not prophecy," Harmodius said.

"Apotheosis," Master Smythe said.

Becca Almspend, who was acting chancellor, sighed. "Your Grace, I am not usually the slowest or least-informed person in any room, but I do not understand half of what I'm hearing. May we suspend general discussion and force the interested parties to *tell us what they're talking about.*" She favoured them all with a thin smile. Ser Ranald grinned.

Master Smythe nodded. "First, in the matter of the Odine. The Odine are an ancient race here. Perhaps even the first. Eons ago, they fought...us. We, whom you call dragons. For possession of this world."

"Men were the slave soldiers of the dragons," Gabriel put in, helpfully.

"Irks were the same for the Kraal," Kerak said. "Until our masters found another way. And fled to the oceans."

Mogon rumbled. "I know too much about this," she said.

"These are dark waters," Kerak said. "And best left untroubled. The Odine were...not like us. Even dragons," he said. "Yet you defeated them."

Master Smythe played with his beard. "Yes," he said. "We did. As they defeated the Kraal, and drove them into the sea. But did not destroy them." He shrugged. "I have two theories, equally viable, and I will share them. One is that Ash has awakened the Odine to use them against the rest of us. I can tell you that at some point, his sole objective became, and remains, the complete destruction of humans. I suspect he may be adding the irks and wardens to this by now." He looked around. "My second theory is that Ash has taken the actions he has taken *in response to discovering that the Odine are awakening.*" He shrugged. "If this is the case, he has elected perhaps to act against men before they become pawns and slaves of the Odine, rendering the Odine more powerful than they have ever been."

He looked at Becca Almspend. "Madame," he said, "I am surprised that a person of your knowledge does not know that the use of power has an effect on any creature. It is not quantifiable, and it is different from individual to individual, but the eventual end is the same. The person fades. Or...becomes..."

"Becomes what?" Almspend asked.

The dragon shook his head. "No one knows. Some of them seem to linger and exert great power, and some simply vanish." He laughed. "It doesn't seem to happen to dragons."

"The saints," said Prior Wishart.

"Perhaps," the dragon said, in a voice that suggested the opposite.

The queen looked around. "That was fascinating, and perhaps terrifying. Now let us get down to the business of the realm. I cannot affect the Odine. But by God, gentles, I can fight the plague. Are we in favour of Master Smythe's offer?"

Gabriel looked around. "Yes," he said. "I confess it falls in with my other plans, but yes. We must preserve this council and our court against the plague so that we can continue to rule and direct the war." He shrugged. "I know how that sounded. But if we advertise the fair and the tournament, we'll bring many, many people into the circle."

The queen nodded. "Draconian," she said. She even smiled.

There was no dissent, and Lord Shawn, who had just coughed black flecks onto his hand, was distracted. But his courage was of a different order. Calmly enough, he said, "I want to hear the cost, first."

Harmodius nodded to Lord Shawn and escorted him out of the room and placed him in isolation. When he returned, as soon as he entered, he recast his working of the night before.

"No one else," he said. "Yet. What have we decided?"

Almspend held up a stack of parchments. "Six acts for isolation and comfort of the inflicted," she said.

Gabriel was writing on a wax tablet. "We're off to Dorling as soon as we can arrange it. I'm not—I have another errand, but I'll meet up with you and the queen. You and Master Smythe and Amicia and Mortirmir will try to crack the plague there…then we act." He paused. "You realize that we will lose many of our soldiers and knights, and that this will impact the harvest and the urban economy. There may be no taxes this autumn, Your Grace."

The queen nodded. "Better no taxes than no people," she said.

But Prior Wishart looked at the queen. "No taxes, and no army," he said. "That is when Ash will attack. In the fall."

As the councilors hurried out to pack and move, and as Ser Ranald began discussing the evacuation in detail with Lady Almspend, Gabriel knelt by the queen's chair. Master Smythe came up behind him.

"What of the Etruscans and the Galles?" the queen asked.

"What of them?" Gabriel replied.

She met his eye. "Will you be emperor?" she asked. "If you are, it is very much your problem." She raised an eyebrow. "And where is Ser Alcaeus?"

"Already acting," the Red Knight said. "I have given orders and taken steps. Yes, Your Grace. I will probably be emperor."

"Liviapolis?" she asked.

"I must see the west secure before I can act. I will need my company." Gabriel met her eyes.

"You swore to uphold me and my son," the queen said.

"I will," Gabriel said. "I will be the best ally any Queen of Alba ever had."

"Would you decline the title if I so ordered you?" she asked.

Gabriel was still kneeling at her side. He took a breath. People were looking at them. Master Smythe was close behind him. But it seemed a day for truth.

"I would not take this thing, if I thought there was another way," he said. "Indeed, I have already refused it once," he went on, with an attempt at humour. Seeing nothing but fear in the queen's eyes, he shrugged. "Yes, Your Grace. I am your man. If you tell me to decline, I will decline, and do my best to support Irene in making the decisions she must make. But..."

"But you do not trust her," the queen said.

"I do not think she has the training to actually be empress," Gabriel said. "None of them have had to...bah. Never mind. I may be full of hubris. My greatest lesson in the last year has been that I am not the center of this, any more than you or Amicia or the babe."

The queen leaned down. "And Blanche? What becomes of her, if you marry Irene?"

Gabriel smiled. "I will not marry Irene." He made a face. "Your Grace...this is not the place. But I have learned things in the last few days about myself...about Blanche." He shrugged. "I am not sure I could now marry Irene just to be emperor. What if she snores?"

"I snore!" the queen said, and for some reason, Master Smythe laughed very hard.

Gabriel raised an eyebrow.

Master Smythe waved a hand, rather weakly.

Gabriel turned back to the queen. "And she has tried to murder me at least once. Possibly as many as three times."

The queen sat back, eyes steady, large, and deep. Some men found her eyes difficult to meet. Some men made the mistake of confusing the frankness of her gaze with interest, or romance.

"Will she attempt to murder Blanche?" the queen asked. "That would not please me at all."

"Nor me, Your Grace." He accepted her nod as a dismissal.

"Towbray's son married a laundress, did he not?" she asked. "The two of you might start quite a fashion."

"Think of the poor laundresses, Your Grace," Gabriel said.

The queen smiled. "You will consider marrying Blanche?" she asked.

Gabriel knew that many paths branched from this point. He could imagine being angry at this intrusion into his private life . . . except that really, Blanche had probably done more to save the queen at Eastertide than any other person except he himself. And the queen had every right—feudal, human, even, by the rood, hermetical—to view Blanche as *within her circles*. He could imagine lying smoothly, except that, after a spring of war, childbirth, and camping, they all knew each other very well. Too well.

He frowned. "Your Grace, the lady in question and I have not discussed this. At all." He bowed his head. "I am not ready . . ."

"But you are not against it," she shot back.

"I do not regard Your Grace's lady as a trull sufficient only to serve my needs and to be discarded at will," Gabriel said, discovering that he was, after all, angry at this intrusion into his private life.

The queen leaned back and breathed in. Her face was brightly flushed, her eyes sparkled, and she, too, was angry.

The two of them looked at each other, eyes crossed like blades, for too long, and then both of them cracked. Gabriel had to work to quell a snort, but he managed.

The queen nodded. "Very well," she said. She rose, and the people left in the hall all froze, turned, and bowed. "I suppose that *is* what I wanted to hear, and I will equally suppose that I deserved the arch tone for my impudence, but at least today, Ser Knight, you are still one of my gentlemen, and she is one of my ladies, and all the rules and lessons of my court of love apply to you and she, the more so as both of you conduct yourselves on the public stage." She leaned down. In his ear, she said, "Many a maid, and many a matron, would think you the prize of all prizes just now, Ser Gabriel. So pity Blanche, who must see every woman about her with better blood, more land, and more dowry as her rival or her superior."

She stood back from him. "Do you by any chance know when your brother intends to wed my Mary?"

Gabriel bowed his best bow. "Madame, it has been mentioned in my hearing, but not, if you take my meaning, discussed. The press of the war."

The queen looked down the hall, where Becca Almspend was motioning insistently. She came forward. "Your Grace, we must move. Ser Ranald is loading wagons even now…"

"And when will you wed your paramour, Becca?" the queen asked.

Becca curtsied. "When I have a minute to breathe, Your Grace. Now—"

"No, Becca. This is as important as the conduct of the war and the new exchequer and the harvest and the fur trade. Pax. Ser Gabriel, what would you say if I endowed Blanche with…a new creation, perhaps a barony in the west, on the wall?"

Gabriel didn't like being badgered, and he was feeling the spark of animosity that could make him say things he might later regret. He bowed. "Your Grace," he said coldly, "do you imagine that I will bargain with you for titles when I have just declined to be Earl of Westwall?"

"You may go," she said. "You may come back when you remember how to speak to me."

The Red Knight did not, quite, spit at her feet. He bowed, a little distantly, nodded civilly enough to Lady Almspend but without any form of eye contact, and walked from the hall.

At the foot of the steps, he found a long line of people, mostly squires and pages, each with what appeared to be a sack of flour.

"Duchess Mogon requests a moment," Toby muttered behind him. Gabriel turned, glared at Toby, and walked back down half a flight to where the great duchess stood in the yard, watching the sky.

She wasted no time on ceremony. "You go to fly to the army," she said.

"Yes," he said.

"I have four wyverns willing to accompany you," she said. "They will carry flour too. And fight, if need be. They owe the alliance and they are ready to begin to prove it."

Despite the extremity of Gabriel's annoyance, he grinned. "I accept," he said.

Mogon motioned to a wyvern who waited in the midst of the courtyard. People flowed around the monster on both sides. A few glanced at the great winged beast, but most concentrated on their errands as if there were not, in fact, a giant, beaked terror sitting in the middle of the courtyard.

"Ser Gabriel, this is Beltan," Mogon said. "Beltan will take a full wing of the Wolfshead Mountain wyverns to follow you."

Beltan nodded slowly.

The Red Knight stepped forward into the aura of fear that Beltan cast by her nature and placed a hand on the breast of the wyvern. She regarded him with some surprise, like a cat who had not expected to be patted.

"It won't be fun carrying all that baggage," he said.

She raised her wings slightly.

He tried again in Low Archaic, which he had heard wardens use. This time she nodded again.

"Let the handlers be attentive," she said. "I will do thy bidding."

Gabriel bowed to her, then ran for the stairs, calling for Toby.

The tailors had his entire flying ensemble ready to wear, and he changed from a light doublet to the leather one with padding, like an arming coat, and over it, a breastplate and his arm harnesses. Over that went a white wool gown lined in squirrel fur, which was long enough to reach his ankles. A saddler had just finished making adjustments to the harness, and even as he changed, Master Smythe came in and placed a burlap bag on one of Gabriel's chests. The bed was already gone, and so was his harness.

"Cull Pett has gone, but he was kind enough to make you another gift. From me." Master Smythe reached out. "Show me your arm, then."

The silver-and-steel cuff with a decorative brass band ended with a short silver spike where the bone would have been. The cut that Cull Pett had made the night before had already healed, and the cuff looked as if it were part of him in an organic way. If he had been made of metal.

Master Smythe looked at it. "Mine is already growing back," he said. "But this may be *better*." He took the silver hand from the burlap sack and slid it down the spike, where something engaged with a sharp click.

There was no warning. A spike of pain struck Gabriel, and he flinched and cried aloud, and then it was gone, and in its place...

...the hand. He flexed it and it *worked*. He had trouble making the fingers match up exactly.

"Touch your nose with your index finger," Master Smythe directed him. He came close several times.

"Practice. Really a foolish thing to say...you'll use it constantly. It will improve." The dragon smiled. "I'm coming with you," he said.

"You are?" Gabriel asked, delighted. Master Smythe might be annoying, godlike, endlessly patronizing, but he was, at some odd level, a good comrade. *Like family.* Like Gavin. Like his mother...

"I may even carry a sack of flour," Master Smythe said. "I will see you in the courtyard." He smiled. "No, I'll see you in the air," he said, and stepped out.

It was Toby who opened the burlap bag. Ser Gabriel was armed with his own long sword and his magnificent dagger. He was ready to go, and avoiding the walk out on the beam.

"It's a helmet," Toby said. "Damn!" he said, pulling it clear of the bag.

The helmet was blue-white steel, edged in gold. It was beautiful, but it wasn't like any helmet Toby or Gabriel or Anne Woodstock had ever seen.

It was composed of a simple skullcap—deceptively simple, as it had complex planes and curves for glancing blows, and two hinged cheek pieces that conformed to the shape of the head and the upper neck, locking under the chin. The protection offered was superb, as was the visibility. There was a visor that locked both up and down.

It was fully padded inside, and it was as light as air.

It took the squire and page a little while to understand the helmet. In fact, to Gabriel's delight, they put it on Anne Woodstock to learn how all the catches fastened. But when they had it on Gabriel, he grinned.

"I love presents," he said.

It took him five long minutes to get into his saddle. Even the lightest helmet ever made, atop a heavy garment and with some armour added, made the climb along the perch more perilous, and the heat inside the new leather doublet was stifling. To add to his discomfort, he almost missed his foot entering into the stirrup. He couldn't bend his neck in the new helmet.

He took a long moment to breathe, steadied himself as best he could, and tried not to think about the roughly hundred or more people watching him, to say nothing of wyverns.

Love you, said his mount. *I won't let you fall.*

Gabriel smiled inside his helmet. He got a foot into the stirrup, gathered the shreds of his courage, and swung his left leg, and then, with a bit of a bump, he was in the saddle.

You weigh more, Ariosto said. *And I am laden with all this milled wheat. Is this to see how strong I am?*

Gabriel felt a new bolt of fear. *Is it too much?* he asked.

I don't know . . . Ariosto said, and leapt off the perch.

They went a long way down. Gabriel's heart went into his throat, and so did his stomach and a good part of his intestines, but the long drop to the ground was nothing compared to the moment at which the griffon altered the geometry of his wings and the plummeting rush became . . .

. . . a stooping glide. The deceleration was worse than the acceleration, and Gabriel was forced back into his saddle, his lower back muscles relieved only by the steel back plate. It was exactly like being hit hard in a joust, and Gabriel thought fleetingly of fighting de Vrailly and being stretched over the crupper, and then the griffon's powerful wings were beating, and they were skimming over the rooftops of Albinkirk.

A wyvern with a wing of green fire rolled in ahead of him, and the sinuous neck reached back and there was a long screech, to which Ariosto responded. Gabriel hadn't known him to be capable of such a terrifying sound . . . it rendered the great monster's childhood screams from the tower nothing by comparison.

My bones hurt, his mount said.

You are having a growth spurt, Gabriel said, a phrase he'd learned from Blanche. Blanche . . .

They were beating slowly up and up. Already, despite the bright sunlight, his fur-lined gown was no longer oppressive. Suddenly he was in shadow and he looked up, and there was Beltan, her head mere inches from his.

She screamed something, and despite a steel helmet and padding, she deafened him.

Ariosto sounded rueful inside his head. *She says, if you will fly, you must learn to look around all the time. That the sky, by its emptiness, is very dangerous, and that the rush of wind deafens all.*

Gabriel rolled his head left and right. He spent a little time learning to look beneath them, by rolling Ariosto slightly left and then right. He practiced looking behind and so learned why all the flying creatures of the wild had long necks.

The other wyverns fell into formation, a long wedge with Master Smythe at the apex. After a few leagues, he slipped off to the right and Beltan took the lead with a single, sharp *raaack*.

She immediately banked, hard, to her own right, cutting across their line of flight at a ninety-degree angle. Gabriel was alert and ready, deep in his saddle, and he took the turn in his hips, already leaning into it, and Ariosto kept his place in the formation well enough, although he had to power forward with his wings to close the gap he briefly created. Behind them, a younger wyvern gave a sharp cry and rolled up, so that its head was level with Gabriel's, its wings vertical.

Gabriel guessed it was merely showing off, and managed a grin. Then he reached up and closed his visor, and instantly discovered what was magical about his new helmet.

Even at this high, bitterly cold altitude, and at this speed, no wind penetrated the visor. Gabriel probed it lightly in the *aethereal* and there was a barrier where the eye slit was.

And then he nearly lost his seat. A moment's inattention and he was turning hard to the left, and falling.

It became obvious over the next hour that the wyverns were playing with him. But Gabriel guessed that Master Smythe had arranged this, and it was certainly excellent training. The griffon's superior wingspan and size was placed against their vastly superior experience of the air, and the wyverns were decisively better at everything. But Ariosto, deprived of parental training, seemed to inhale the lessons as they went, so that as fast as the wyverns pulled a trick on him, he would learn it—rolls, deceptions, wing-folded dives, use of the sun and clouds . . .

A childhood in the air, compacted into an hour.

They are much better than we are, Ariosto said.

You are trying to do all the flying for us both, Gabriel said. He, too, was learning. There were ways that he could help or harm his mount's performance. Luckily, they were very like the tricks of riding, and he had the muscles and the experience to experiment immediately with postures and leans. For his own comfort, he found that leaning forward, balanced on the balls of his feet in his stirrups, legs like springs, helped him tolerate the rapid decelerations at the end of dives.

But when the wyverns began—playfully, he hoped—to spar in the air, he almost lost his seat in the first exchange. A wyvern changed direction as fast as a flock of starlings in autumn, and Ariosto did the same, pivoting on one wingtip, his great body contorting in a sudden and exuberant left bank, and Gabriel was for a moment unable to think or act, and only the force of the turn pinning him to the monster's back saved him from a seven-thousand-foot fall to the Adnacrags below.

Love you, Ariosto said, chagrined.

Love you too, Gabriel managed with his teeth gritted.

Over the high peaks there was cloud cover, and the whole wing cavorted, flying along canyons of cloud, brushing the insubstantial stuff with their wingtips. And suddenly, as before, Beltan turned. This time she went into the cloud and vanished.

Ariosto followed her, and Gabriel clung to his saddle and reins and suddenly his head was everywhere, and they were lost, blind, and in danger of collision. A wyvern screamed near at hand and then another, and like a curtain lifting they were back in sunlight. The formation was a shambles, and a wave of wyvern recriminations passed over them, but Beltan beat her powerful wings and turned along a tendril of cloud, and there was Wolfshead Mountain, one of the tallest of the Adnacrags, so close that its stony immensity was its own terror.

Gabriel learned that lesson, too. In cloud, mountains can kill you. But he had also experienced something else...the sheer, unbelievable wonder of flying. Of being free of the constraints of mere earth.

Don't forget, comrade, Gabriel said, *that if we fight, I won't be useless weight.*

Ah! Ariosto said. *What can you do?*

Gabriel had prepared a number of options. *I need to practice*, he said. Certainly the difficulties of preparing a hermetical working, summoning *potentia* and creating *ops* and casting in an aerial skirmish looked dire. Much less the dimension difficulties of aiming and hitting a target.

He experimented a little while they were in level flight at high altitude. With a steady seat and no interference, it was no harder than working on horseback...difficult enough, for all love. He summoned power and tested various workings until he found two that might serve, but by then they were descending.

Gabriel made his now-routine check, looking all around, and found the allied army under his left heel, moving slowly with their wagons along the high beech woods of a ridgeline.

All along the ridge, steel was flashing, men were pointing, archers were dismounting, and...

A heavy arrow rose from the center of the army.

Gabriel felt like a fool.

Tell the wyverns to back off! he shouted.

Ariosto let loose a trumpet blast, and Beltan understood immediately and her dive became a stoop, her wings filled, and she rose. The heavy arrow completed its climb and seemed to hang in the air under Ariosto's talons and then fell away.

"Damn," Gabriel said aloud.

And then something happened. And he had already summoned power...

Sauce cursed God and Satan equally as she dismounted. It was their second day of retreat, the plague was taking its toll, Mortirmir was running low on *ops*, and now...

They had chosen to move along the ridgetops because the ground was clearer. It had been a good decision, and they were within a day, perhaps two days' march of the new road. It hadn't occurred to any of them that their adversaries had wyverns left, and now they were exhausted, at the edge of starvation, and totally exposed to aerial foes on the high ridge, and the soldiers who did not have the cough didn't want to stand in formation with those who did.

Cully, a few horses from her, launched a ranging arrow. Sauce knew he'd loosed it short. He was capable of more and wanted to lure the beasts lower. The archers were leaping from their equally tired mounts, and searching quivers for the right arrows while eyeing their mates for signs of disease.

Something caught her eye. One of the wyverns seemed to breathe fire...or the light caught it oddly. It was...

It had a wing that seemed to burn.

She got her leg over her mount. "Save the horses," she said. The last attacks they had experienced from the air had been from wyverns and barghasts delivering the horse plague. But even as she watched, the lead wyvern rose suddenly, and the rest of the formation rose away with the leader, leaving one monster, almost twice the size of the others, glowing red and green and gold in the midday sun, to roll away in a showy display of wingspan.

"Wait for it," roared Wilful Murder. But then he began to cough.

"What the hell?" Gavin said.

The Faery Knight began to chuckle.

In letters twenty paces high appeared the word *Friends*. It seemed to be written in red smoke.

"I'll be damned," Sauce said.

Tom Lachlan's roar sounded through the woods as the griffon turned and began to dive.

The wyverns chose to land on a bare outcropping at the east end of the ridge. It was early afternoon, and the exhausted army tottered to a stop and the people not yet afflicted with the plague began to set up tents in the stony soil. The flying creatures left five hundredweight of flour and turned for Albinkirk, where, after a meal of their own, they took up a second load, and then, passing low over the dwindling herds that Gabriel had purchased for supply and that were already being driven back toward Dorling by Donald Dhu and his clansmen, each great creature snapped up a protesting animal and, with mighty wingbeats, carried it up the ridges and deposited it gently by the sacks of flour.

Gabriel dismounted and saw that Ariosto was unsaddled and his back feathers carefully cleared of sweat. The saddle hurt him, that much was obvious, and he seemed to expand with joy when it was removed. But the moment he'd been lightly curried and scratched, he grunted and leapt from the cliff to find his own supper with the wyverns.

Gabriel found himself surrounded by his army. They had not seen him since the formation the day after the battle.

He walked through camp and had to fight to avoid despair.

They had been used too hard, and they were in terrible shape. Much was purely superficial, although still bad enough. Their shoes were ruined by just two weeks in the deep woods, and many men were barefoot or wore scraps of hide bound to their feet with rags. Hose were ragged or worse, and the smart doublets with puffed sleeves so beloved by his archers were fit only for polishing armour. And the armour was brown and scrofulous with rust. This was as true of his brother's magnificent harness as of Cully's breast-and-back.

That was the superficial, but under it was tension, fatigue, and the makings of despair and panic. The wagons were full of men and women with plague, and the rest of the army knew that their turn must be close. Morgon Mortirmir was fed like a child, the trance of utter exhaustion on him, and he had black thumbprints under his eyes and his skin looked transparent. The Brogat levies were dead on their feet, and the Albinkirk-area lords looked like a pack of mongrel brigands.

Gabriel felt fat and overrested and pampered. But he walked up and down as people were fed, doing his best to shore up Mortirmir's workings against the plague, to see that everyone was fed, to compliment the officers on making it this far.

And food was like a tonic. They had gone too long without a full meal, and without good sleep, and the results had taken them very close to the edge. But they were on a high ridge, out of the midges and the heat of the marshes and deep valleys, and they had food.

In late afternoon, as the army collapsed into a desperate sleep that could not be put off, Gabriel put the saddle back on Ariosto's back with a long apology and set off, alone, for Lissen Carak.

Ariosto created the same consternation among the nuns and novices as the wyverns had created for the army. They arrived at the very edge of darkness, and the layered workings of the ancient fortress closed against them like a great shield of fire.

This time, against the edge of darkness, Gabriel wrote on the sky in white lightning, and Miriam came to the walls and ordered the workings lowered.

There was a huge crane of heavy wood against the stub of the north tower, and the griffon settled at its base. The courtyard of the fortress abbey was filled with new-cut stone.

Miriam hurried along the wall, with Amicia at her back.

"Stop!" called Gabriel.

Both women, and the novices behind them, froze.

"Pardon me, ladies. It is Gabriel Muriens, and I have need of instant succour. But... I would not come any closer to you. I almost certainly bear the plague." He tried to bow, but his head hurt and the twilight seemed to undermine his balance.

Miriam nodded. "We are preparing a great working. And I have teams already in the countryside..."

"I'm sorry, Lady Abbess, but it is the army. It is running unchecked... Mortirmir has done his best to contain it, but they... they are carrying their sick in the wagons."

Amicia nodded. Even in his fevered state, even at twilight, fifty feet away, the merest shake of her head made his throat tight. "I had a message from the queen," Amicia said. "I'm to go to Dorling."

"If you can be spared," Gabriel managed.

Amicia nodded. "I can come now," she said.

Gabriel nodded, and began to cough.

The first day was hard, but then, the woods were never easy. All of Aneas's party were loaded with food, and Tall Pine's warriors had both food and loot from two great battles, although they carried their loads without complaint.

Aneas felt the weight of responsibility constantly, and wondered how his brothers carried it so well. Practice, he thought.

He wanted to show them all how skilled he was at the Wild magik and the woods, but he guessed that they were watching to see if he would fail. All of them seemed so *experienced*.

As he crouched over a muddy hole with tracks all around it on the main trail going north from Forked Lake, he debated asking for advice, or letting the decision rest on his own skills. He cast his working twice, his slim ivory wand moving over the tracks, and received two very different answers; the first time, tracks glittered off to the west, the second, to the east.

Behind him, two of Tall Pine's warriors used flint and steel to light their pipes as most of the party shed their heavy loads. Fitzalan smiled at him and slipped past without a word to go on watch while others rested, and Krek, the old bogglin, made a sign with one of his legs that he would watch the rear. Tall Pine and Janos Turkos watched the old bogglin, but more with interest than suspicion.

Turkos turned his head, as if the Morean warrior felt his regard. The older man winked.

The wink settled it. Aneas waved to him, and the Morean officer came over after begging a pull on a young warrior's pipe. He crouched by the mud and swatted a mosquito.

Aneas motioned east and west. "My workings are…" He paused. "Inconclusive," he said, using a word his mother had used often. Usually with contempt.

Turkos walked cautiously along the edges of the mud hole. In the strange way of the Adnacrags, the mud hole went uphill for some distance, and stopped abruptly downhill, which seemed contrary to nature.

Tall Pine came over, picking his teeth with a piece of liquorice root he'd bought from a trader.

Turkos pointed at the tracks. "Captain here says he's baffled."

Tall Pine nodded. His face was impassive. He looked at the tracks and walked around just as Turkos had, and then cast farther west, off the trail, and farther east.

"Their party split, I think," Aneas said. He spoke in Archaic, in hope that the tall Outwaller understood it.

Tall Pine nodded.

"Something here I don't like," Tall Pine said.

Aneas thought it remarkable that, through the haze of green workings and the scent of hastenoch and behemoth and bogglin, Tall Pine could find something not to like.

The tall Outwaller muttered to himself as he cast a little more west, and then started north, right on the edge of sight.

Aneas went to follow him.

Turkos smiled. "Stand here and be the captain," he said. "He's very good at this."

Aneas took this as criticism. "I am too," he said.

Turkos nodded. "But you asked advice," he said.

Aneas caught himself when he was about to deny having asked advice. "I—" he began, and looked away.

Turkos nodded. "When an Outwaller offers help, it is a free gift," he said. "Accept with grace."

Aneas took a deep, steadying breath. "Thanks," he managed.

Turkos laughed. "Not laughing at you," he said. "No, I am. Hah!"

Tall Pine came back and beckoned to them, and the two men went forward. Fitzalan was just visible at the next stream, bow strung, leaning against a tree.

Tall Pine led them unerringly to a clear space with a cut sapling in the center. Feathers had been tied, and blood spilled.

Aneas looked at Tall Pine and bowed. "I missed it," he said.

Tall Pine allowed himself a very thin smile. "You were meant to," he said. "Can you unmake it?"

Aneas looked at it with his wand, making a hermetical lens. He was careful and tried to forget twenty people waiting for him in a haze of heat and bugs back on the trail.

But this was exactly the sort of thing for which his mother had prepared him...a curse and a making and an illusion, all nested, expertly worked. And a trap for the hand that pulled the cut sapling from the ground, an ugly thing. In the *aethereal* it was black, not green. He was aware, in an academic way, that black existed: the colour associated with death. A particular set of necromantic workings that his mother spurned as amateurish and desperate.

This didn't look amateurish.

Any working could be unmade, with time, and patience. *It was like unpicking a garment. Some opened as if unbuttoned. This one looked as if it had been embroidered, the work was so dense.*

He liked the image, and he applied it in the aethereal, *seeing the working as a piece of embroidery, knotwork and chain stitch. With his allegorical view in place, he turned the working over and exposed its less-perfect underside, and began to cut threads and pull at bits. He bent his will upon it and worked slowly, aware that the insects were feasting on his exposed face. He found one particularly long thread in the black projection, paused in pure fear, and then, setting his* aethereal *will, pulled, and the curse unraveled.*

Aneas got to his feet from the crouch he'd had. He had been in the crouch a long time...his young knees were stiff.

But with a smile and a small flourish and a frisson of terror, he reached down and pulled the sapling from the ground.

There was a small pop.

He was not turned to black jelly.

He turned to smile at Tall Pine, but he was alone.

Turkos hurried up a few minutes later, crossbow loaded.

"I disarmed it," Aneas said with what he hoped was his brother's cheerful voice.

Turkos looked around, all but sniffing, and Tall Pine came up behind him.

"When you started messing with that, we…" Turkos grinned. "We thought we'd let you do it without us. Christos, he got it. He broke the working."

Tall Pine nodded courteously. "This is well done," he said. "Now see."

A third set of tracks now went off almost straight north. There were men's prints, and many other things.

Aneas was suddenly aware that in breaking the curse and unworking the illusion, he'd told the enemy practitioner who he was and where he was. And they outnumbered his party.

"I want to follow this group," he said. "But I want to follow them to the west, well off their line. We'll have to cross their trail from time to time…" He was thinking aloud.

Tall Pine raised an eyebrow. "You fear ambush?"

Aneas sighed. "I have just told them that I found their trap," he admitted.

Tall Pine nodded again. "Then we must be cautious, brother," he said.

In minutes, they were moving again, this time downhill into the edge of beaver country in the valley. Tall Pine led them, choosing a path between huge trunks blown down in some titanic storm and the dense alder thickets that ran along the valley edge. They caught tantalizing glimpses of open, grassy meadows that every ranger knew were crisscrossed with sharp stakes and deep troughs of muddy water maintained by the beaver.

Aneas stayed on the enemy trail. He moved as quickly as he dared, but either his adversaries had assumed that the working would cover them, and made no effort to hide, or the whole thing was a trap. Aneas kept his eyes on the ground in front of him, guided by prints and scuff marks. The trail itself was an artifact of Outwaller hunting in the deep woods in autumn; it was the main route that the Huran and Sossag used to hunt the interior of the Adnacrags, but now it was deep in old leaf mold.

He kept watch in the *aethereal* too, stopping from time to time to look ahead, to the sides, watching Tall Pine and the rest of the party.

He was terrified. But exhilarated at the same time, because he was doing it. He was leading a war party.

Kevin Orley, count your days.

A little after noon, he cut back over the lip of the ridge and waited by a downed log for the party to reach him, which they did quickly enough. They put out a pair of sentries: Ricard Lantorn from the green banda of the company, and one of the royal foresters, Alan Beresford.

The Outwallers ate like mad. In Archaic, Tall Pine said, "Easier to carry inside," and many laughed.

Turkos squatted by Aneas. "I mislike you out there by yourself," he said. "I have no skill in the *ars magika*, but... it seems to me that if you found one trap, there'll be another."

Aneas nodded. "I'm careful," he said. *I'm scared every second, and this lunch with sentries is me at the end of my tether for fear.*

"I'd rather you took a pair of rangers," Turkos said. "Or... Tall Pine has a young dream walker. The... woman. She's called Looks-at-Clouds." The Morean's brief pause between "the" and "woman" was odd.

Aneas shrugged. "I'm fine," he said. Even he could hear the lie in his voice.

Turkos smiled and put a hand on his shoulder. "No, you are not," he said quietly. "I wouldn't walk that trail alone, and I've been a few dark places, eh?"

Turkos went and sat with Tall Pine. They both laughed a few times, and then one of the Outwallers came to them, sat on his haunches while a story was told, and nodded. The warrior came toward Aneas and he saw that the man might be a tall woman with small breasts, wearing a red daubed shirt and deerskin leggings. She— or he—had silver ball-and-cone earrings, but then, so did most of the men; the face was painted a flat ochre red, which hid any femininity s/he might possess.

The Outwaller touched his/her forehead in greeting, face impassive.

Aneas bent his own. "Are you Looks-at-Clouds?" he asked, in Archaic. He used the feminine form.

S/he looked at him for a long time, his/her eyes travelling over him slowly, as if he was being reckoned. Finally s/he grunted.

Only when s/he moved did s/he display any femininity, and under the paint, he could not discern his/her age. S/he might have been fifteen or fifty, except her hands—the only part of her flesh that was visible and unpainted—which were heavily scarred but appeared young and smooth where not scarified or tattooed.

Had he not been told s/he was a woman, he'd never have assumed it.

"You work with *ops*?" he asked.

The warrior's eyes narrowed at the word.

Again, Aneas was answered with a grunt. It seemed affirmative.

"Looks-at-Clouds is *bacsa*," Tall Pine said. He had come up so silently as to be unnoticed. Aneas tried not to leap to his feet.

"What is *bacsa*?" Aneas asked.

Tall Pine shrugged, just like an Etruscan. "Walk a few days," he said. "You will see."

Turkos nodded. "Take Looks-at-Clouds," the Morean said. "We'll all be easier in our heads."

Aneas, fascinated, agreed with a nod.

The Outwaller moved well in the woods; not as silently as Tall Pine, but no twigs broke. Aneas could walk silently as well, and they moved back to the old trail together, and spoke no word. Aneas struggled not to resent that the older captains felt he needed help. He knew he was being foolish, but there it was, and the strange man-woman creature looked at him as if he were a child, or so he felt.

Looks-at-Clouds insisted on examining the trail. Aneas watched as the lithe figure crumbled dried leaves, and was fascinated when there was a burst of *ops*, expertly shielded.

He smiled without meaning to.

The *bacsa* looked back at him, caught his smile, and replied in kind.

They still exchanged no words, but moved, one to the left of the old trail and one to the right, pausing from time to time to look at tracks or other things, otherwise almost running. Aneas's pack straps bit into his shoulders cruelly, but he was enough of a veteran woodsman to know that it was the first day, and he'd eat the weight in two days and miss it by the fourth.

An hour passed, and another.

Looks-at-Clouds made a clicking noise and he froze, and then walked toward the *bacsa* on the trail.

He saw what s/he saw, three very clear prints at the edge of another small mud hole in the center of the trail.

One print overlay another. The third was fully clear, a bogglin, and a large one, perhaps even a wight.

The *bacsa* raised an eyebrow.

Aneas went *into his palace and began to move things. His palace was his mother's casting room at Ticondonaga, preserved in his memory, although he'd added long columns of writing to the whitewashed walls. He had a mirror there, and some other potent interior workings his mother had gifted him.*

He walked along the walls, touching the words that interested him, and the letters glowed.

He'd spent a good deal of his youth hiding things from his brothers and his mother. He'd never realized what a wonderful talent this might be in war. But now he conducted his working, which in his mental imagery consisted of a tree leaning over a fire and hiding the rising smoke.

Only when his system of deception was in place did he cast his main working, and beams of coherent light crisscrossed his chamber until he'd made a little multipointed star in many dimensions, and he released it, and it burst like a slow-motion flower.

In the real, a full-sized wight in stained ivory-coloured chiton appeared over its track, frozen in the act of raising its head to survey the trail.

The *bacsa* laughed, eye sparkling. One of the *bacsa's* hands slapped his back lightly.

He grinned at him/her ... it was an unusually successful working. He was quite pleased with himself, and as usual he allowed that to warm his opinion of others. "More than two days ago," he added in Archaic.

The Outwaller shook her head—his head. Aneas could not be sure. The warrior's arm muscles were outstanding, and yet the tattooed arms were smooth.

Aneas held up two fingers and pointed at the sun, and then the tracks.

The *bacsa* brightened in understanding. "*Geer-lon-sen,*" s/he said, as if this explained everything, and loped off.

That night, Aneas lay next to Ricar Fitzalan. He was looking up at the stars.

"I'm tired," he admitted.

Fitzalan laughed. "You spent the day looking for traps at a run," he said. "I didn't. All I did was carry my pack and climb over a thousand blown-down logs, and I'm tired. Sweet Christ, this is my everyday life. How do the Outwallers move so fast?"

Aneas shook his head.

"What of the witch?" Fitzalan asked. "Man or woman?"

Aneas shrugged. "Sometime I think the one, and other times the other," he said. "But I like him. Or her."

Fitzalan laughed, but his laugh was uneasy and his jealousy obvious. "Don't like him or her too much," he said.

Aneas squeezed his friend's hand. "You have a sweet friend at N'gara," he said.

Fitzalan shrugged. "She's at N'gara and you are here," he said, with all the sincerity of the young.

Aneas lay and looked at the stars too long, and Ricar went to sleep and snored.

After a while, he rose from his blankets and drank from his canteen, relieved himself, and sat under a tree on the pine needles, exerting himself, *reaching into the darkness in the* aethereal. *And there they were. It was sheer luck, or great fortune, or a trap.*

He caught the enemy in the very act of casting. The casting was shielded but the shielding was hasty. He watched carefully for colour and application, and he watched long into the night.

He awoke under the tree, and it was dawn, with Fitzalan standing over him and glaring at him. "Something I said?" the handsome young Jack muttered. He was fully dressed, his bow strung in his hand.

Aneas shook his head. "I felt something in the night," he said. "Orley, casting something."

Fitzalan sneered. "Of course, *my lord.*"

Aneas was not at his best when he awoke. "Grow up, Ricar," he said snappishly. "I *am* a lord."

Fitzalan shook his head. "I'll just cast about and see if the enemy have left us any little surprises," he said. "Before I say something we'll both regret."

He walked off. Aneas admired him in that moment. The Jack was very self-possessed. He didn't threaten to walk off. He did it. And he didn't say anything he had to regret.

Aneas saw a lot in that to admire. "Be careful," he said.

He helped with breakfast. He had a packet of Etruscan kahve, and he made a little in his copper pot and shared it with Captain Turkos, who enjoyed it a great deal. Most of the Outwallers chewed dried meat, and a few smoked, and then they were packed. Once again, Looks-at-Clouds joined him on the old trail. When the warrior saw him eyeing the shaman, s/he grunted.

Aneas felt rude. He flushed, and then started down the left side of the trail. He moved along too fast, and made too much noise, his attention already reaching for the place that his enemy had cast the night before.

As they moved, it occurred to him that he hadn't shared his information with the others, and that seemed foolish. As he moved, his feeling of foolishness spread, and he slowed, took more account of his surroundings, and froze.

Then he reached into the breast of his cote and pulled out a horn whistle, which he blew, short and shrill. Looks-at-Clouds turned. S/he moved, and Aneas held up his hand: "Stop!"

A horse-length away was a split sapling with two dead black moths and a messy spiderweb of feathers and moss and excrement.

Shit, Aneas thought. *He cast last night to draw me. This was the real trap—a mile from my camp. . . .*

. . . they could be right here.

. . . they must be. This isn't just a curse. It's the trip wire of an ambush. I'm a fool.

Looks-at-Clouds was moving along the ground, crawling to him. He went down immediately, feeling foolish all over again.

He got the *bacsa*'s attention and pointed at the curse.

He saw the warrior's nostrils widen. Then the *bacsa*'s eyes closed.

Aneas reached out a very tentative curl of the *aethereal* toward the curse.

The *bacsa*'s eyes opened. S/he shook his/her head and began to crawl again.

A few inches away, the *bacsa* whispered, "Tall Pine knows."

Aneas had not been aware that the shaman and the chief could communicate. "Tell him to stop moving and lie down," he whispered. And then, "You speak Alban!"

The *bacsa*'s eyes twinkled. "A little," s/he said.

"Tell Tall Pine that there is almost certainly an ambush," he said. "Within half a mile."

Eyes closed.

And opened. "He says 'yes.'" The warrior looked very slowly to their left, from whence s/he'd come, and then right. A hand reached out, and Aneas followed it.

Another curse tree.

Very, very carefully, he reached out in the *aethereal*.

It was brutally hot, and a mosquito landed on the very tip of his nose, and began to drink his blood, and he didn't move. He felt the insect's proboscis go into his flesh like a little knife driven into his flesh, and he was *deep in contemplation*.

Last night's casting—the one he'd been meant to see—rang out like a tocsin, and he felt even more foolish.

But the line of small curses was dark and palpable. It was subtle, but not subtle enough, hence the casting behind, to lead him on.

Damn. The line was half a mile long, but curiously, only from the huge beaver meadow on their western flank to the ridgetop.

He described this in a whisper to his companion.

"Turkos says, 'Come.'"

The two began to crawl backward. It was painstaking and uncomfortable, hot, humid, difficult, and nerve-racking.

In fact, the two of them took almost an hour, the sun rising high to the right, to recross the main trail and move down the ridge to the beaver meadow.

In among the alders waited Turkos and Tall Pine. All the rest were gone.

"We'll flank them," Turkos said tersely. "Squirrel Who Hunts says the beaver meadow is clear. He would know. Now we are bait."

Tall Pine smiled. "Bait," he said, relishing the word.

"I can set off one of the traps," Aneas said. He was considering being annoyed that the two veteran war leaders had just usurped his authority and ordered the battle, but that seemed foolish, give the situation.

Tall Pine said something in Huran to Looks-at-Clouds. The *bacsa* spread his/her hands and smiled.

Turkos understood. "Do it," he said.

Aneas *entered his palace. He reached out, felt a tree he'd marked, and set it up to drop on the trap nearest the trail. For good measure, he worked a long scream in illusion and prepared a working that would move twenty paces through the woods, thrashing. Illusion was easy.*

"Now?" he asked.

Turkos had a finger in the air.

Something sparkled far out across the beaver meadow.

"Wait," Tall Pine said.

The four of them lay in the mud under the alders, and hordes of deer flies, horse flies, mosquitoes, and even a few late-season black flies fell on them.

Looks-at-Clouds suddenly tensed. S/he put a hand on Aneas's arm. "*Gots onah!*" s/he said. "Now."

Aneas took the time to shield his working.

Then he loosed it. It was a very, very small working…

The aethereal *exploded.*

Trees burst into flame, or fell. Explosions crackled along the line of curse markers as tree splinters swept the woods at head and ankle height.

Safe in the alders, Aneas watched as the heavy, dark *ops* ripped at reality over an enormous and very wasteful stretch of woods. It was a remarkable display of power. Because he was safe and unthreatened, and had no other role, Aneas watched and measured, tasting the colours and smelling the nuances.

Aneas's little deceptions began to take effect.

Just a few hundred paces away, shapes *moved*. Aneas couldn't make out what they were. In his memory palace he began to gather *potentia* and make weapons.

The shapes were dark, and they screamed as they came.

There were several hundred of them.

"Shit," Turkos said.

It was difficult to follow a combat in the woods. This Aneas understood; he'd been fighting in deep woods since he was old enough to follow his father's battle cry. He had to listen to the music, as his father had used to say; the bellows, the shrieks, the song of bowstrings, the rattle and clank of blades and harness.

The strange dark shapes flitted like shadows, and cried like wild wolves or coyotes in chorus.

They had about a hundred heartbeats until the line of shadows hit them. More, if they had to spend time looking. Aneas's ears were still ringing from the explosions resulting from his release of the curse trees, but he had learned a great many things in that small hermetical encounter, and now, he thought through the possibilities, examined them like a determined student with a difficult math problem, and guessed—he couldn't do better than a guess—that his idea would work.

"I'm going forward," he said to Turkos. "I'll be right back."

In front of them was a new downed tree: an old maple with wilted leaves still clinging to its upper branches. The last storm had dropped the old fellow. Aneas noted that the dead tree had fallen in parallel to all the other blow-downs, some of which had been massive giants and now, mostly rotted, were like small ridges on the forest floor. Indeed, the five of them had been crouched behind the westernmost blow-down, just at the edge of the alder swamp.

Aneas leapt over the huge rotting log and ran lightly over the loam, directly at the onrushing shades.

One of the shapes crossed a patch of sunlight, perhaps eighty paces away, and paused for some reason of its own, sniffing the air, and what Aneas thought he saw made his hair prickle on his neck—a human build, but massive, with muscles like a caricature of a man's muscles, a heavy lower jaw with backswept fangs, burning eyes, and a mighty rack of antlers like a stag, all jet black, and bearing a heavy spear.

Aneas thought he saw arrows fly to his left, but he got to the old dead maple and crouched amid the branches, his whole attention focused on the *rough bark under his fingers*.

Deep in the old tree was a stirring of life.

Aneas paused. In the aethereal, *he cried out, "Oh, old man! My need is great. Forgive me, I will take your life."*

The tree said nothing.

Aneas had no time for a misplaced mercy. His hand on the tree, Aneas aligned the symbols of his mother's favourite working. He altered it, greatly daring, intruding on her elegant simplicity. Her working drained all the water from a living thing, leaving a dried husk to fall to ash and dust.

His alteration took the moisture and concentrated it all in one place, in the very midst of the tree, a long, thin thread of water forcing itself between the innermost rings of the old man of the woods.

In the aethereal *he heard the ripping sound as the water cracked the trunk, but it held; the trunk remained intact.*

Aneas jerked himself out of his light trance to find Looks-at-Clouds crouched next to him, loosing arrows.

The antlered ones were just a few bounds away, and even as he glanced, one of the Outwaller's arrows went into the heavily muscled gut and the thing continued forward, two long strides, and fell with a coyote scream.

Aneas let go one of his carefully built weapons, and green lightning played over the next three antlered giants.

They shrugged off his potent magery, even as he turned to run.

"Run!" he screamed.

Looks-at-Clouds swung a hand, a casual gesture, and one of the shades went down as if struck with a huge rod of iron, heavily muscled shoulder and rib cage crushed. But the warrior turned, even as a dozen arrows hissed into the antlered giants from the west.

Aneas didn't dare look back. He ran—one, two, three paces, long, panicked strides, the working still balanced in his mind the way a child balances an egg on a spoon while running.

Turkos rose from his hiding place and shot a crossbow bolt. Aneas had a moment to think it was loosed at him, and then he made another stride and another.

"Down!" he roared.

He realized the *bacsa* could not possibly imagine what he intended.

Turkos dropped as Aneas hit his eighth stride. No other heads showed above the rotting trunk of the fallen forest giant.

Aneas slowed his stride...

...the *bacsa* came abreast...

The horned ones were crossing the dead tree behind them, twenty or more, baying—

"Down," Aneas screamed.

His arm was around the shaman's waist and they leapt, and he carried the lighter warrior to the ground, crushing the breath out of his/ her *and he superheated all the water he'd gathered along the core of the dead tree, a small working, easy, not requiring touch like the difficult desiccation.*

The utterly dry maple exploded, a ninety-foot-long cylinder of flechettes that flayed the wilderness for forty paces.

Hermetical protections were worthless.

When Aneas raised his head, his ears were ringing, nothing sounded right, and branches were still falling. There was not a leaf on a tree as far as the eye could see, and one of the horned ones was pinned to the rotten log that had sheltered them, his ruined body spiked to the mossy wood by long splinters of dried maple. Splinters decorated every surface—and red, red blood.

The *bacsa* squirmed under him, and he rolled off, drawing his dagger because his arming sword was gone, lost somewhere in the run or the fall. He didn't imagine that he'd got them all.

Turkos said something—at least, his mouth moved. He leaned out over the ruins of the rotten tree and loosed his small crossbow.

Tall Pine stood. He put a horn to his lips and winded it, and Aneas heard a little.

The blast of the old maple, and the earlier, larger explosion from the curse trees had cleared the foliage, and now bright sunlight flooded the wreckage of the forest floor.

Aneas felt *awareness*. Something was looking for him—at him.

He was *revealed*.

He shielded himself. And then, aware of the pressure, he raised shield after shield in concentric circles.

Another shield crossed his as the bacsa, *a glowing golden figure at his side, raised defences too.*

The attack came. It was green and black, and it struck his outer shield like a hammer and cracked it, but the golden shield carried the weight.

Aneas fought as his mother taught. He launched a subtle, quiet attack straight back along his adversary's strike before he was even sure his shields would hold. His adversary had to raise a shield and was thus, in turn, revealed, and Aneas, ever a faithful pupil, went over to the attack. Seizing the initiative, he threw his entire arsenal without stint, three illusions of attacks, one massive electrical discharge, and one tiny act of creation, difficult, puissant, carefully practiced.

He made a deerfly.

His enemy parried the electrical discharge, poured power into defeating the illusions—launched a counterstrike, black lightning.

A curtain of golden fire fell into the black lightning like rain on a forest fire. The bacsa *was potent—no doubt of that. Curious that the shaman used gold and not green.*

In the real, the deerfly flew through the violet-black nimbus of a shield, and through the heavy, semen-scented green of another.

It was Kevin Orley.

At least, the man at the center of the shields was a sort of flesh-parody of Kevin Orley in antlers, a hulking brute in black and pale flesh, his antlers lush with engorged blood and velvety blue-black, and eldritch runes were tattooed to his face and hands, and he wore black armour. But the face remained Kevin Orley's face, in a rictus of rage.

Aneas wished his deerfly were more potent. But it landed and stung, even as the sorcerer's hand moved to crush the simulacrum of life.

The horned sorcerer staggered as the poison struck him.

Drops of the bacsa's *golden fire burned through the sorcerer's outer shields, and struck home, and he...*

...vanished.

"Fuck!" Aneas barked.

A horned man vaulted the huge tree trunk in front of him, ignoring the dozen shards of wood stuck in his massive body. He landed, striking Turkos to the ground with the butt of his heavy black spear.

Looks-at-Clouds swayed like a branch under the backswing of the spear, an almost inhuman movement, and kicked even as the knife in his/her left hand went into the horned man's bicep, and s/he turned him, his weight leading him off balance, and s/he kicked again with incredible speed, her bare foot, hermetically *enforced*, shattering his giant knee. His/her knife slipped free of the bicep and cut, severed the giant's sex and cutting deeply into his inner thigh, proving that his arteries were the same as a man's as blood fountained and the thing died in four obvious beats of its great heart, the spurting arterial blood flying ten paces in the clear air.

Aneas might have paused to admire the work—the hermeticist in him wondered why he, a slim man, had never thought to use the hermetical to put force in his blows—but he and Tall Pine had their own problems as the horned men closed. There were more than Aneas, in the heat of the fight, could count, and they stood more than seven feet tall, and every one bore a hideous wound; transfixed by arrows, punctured by splinters, burnt or cut.

Their eyes were insane.

Aneas's immediate opponent lunged with his spear from the other side of the downed, rotten tree, and Aneas flowed with the attack. His opponent had attacked a little out of distance, and the point flickered too long in front of him. Aneas got his dagger blade, held point down in his right hand, on the spear point, and then his left hand on the haft—

—the antlered thing pulled at his spear haft—

Aneas wrapped the spear with his left arm and rode the pull, levering his legs up the surface of the rotten log and getting a heavy splinter in the back of his thigh, his own work turned against him. But he was taller than the antlered man for as long as he held his balance, and very close, and he buried his dagger in the muscle between jaw and shoulder and leapt, wrapping his legs around the big torso, pinning them even as the eyes lost their mad will and the big body crumpled.

Tall Pine's adversaries were both messily dead—one with a fine Etruscan axe protruding from its head, a superb throw at five paces, and the other was sitting with its entrails across its hands, its eyes already glazing as Tall Pine beheaded it.

Aneas rode his dead foe to the ground, and rolled, forgetting he had a bow still on his back. The roll ended badly and Aneas tried to rise and felt the pulled muscles in his back and would have felt a fool except that he lacked the time. And his best bow was broken.

He got his feet under him anyway. Looks-at-Clouds threw another one of his/her *aethereal* punches at the last horned man close to them, and Turkos shot him from a few feet away with his powerful small crossbow and drew his sword.

Aneas had loosed every aggressive working he had.

The horned ones were running.

"At them!" Aneas called, and winded his horn. Fitzalan's horn sounded in answer, and two others, and then, blood flowing from his thigh and ignoring the pain in his back, Aneas ran forward, plucking his lost arming sword from the ground. The explosion of the maple tree had removed the scabbard and it lay waiting for him, naked, and came to his hand like a falcon, and he ran on.

Looks-at-Clouds bounded along beside him like a deer given human form, and then passed him. With his/her came the two irks, Lewen and Tessen, and Aneas, eyes opened, saw how like an irk Looks-at-Clouds was.

Tessen paused—just a glance, and Aneas put his head down and ran harder.

Whatever virtues the horned men had, they were slow. In fact, now that a little of the terror of combat drained from Aneas, he thought that they had been slow in all their movements.

They caught two immediately, wounded creatures, and Looks-at-Clouds knocked them down from behind with his/her *aethereal* fists and Lewen killed them before Aneas could catch up. But even the *bacsa*'s ferocious energy dimmed in half a mile of pursuit, and Lewen was resting against a tree, panting like a dog, when Aneas caught the fastest runners just as the young shaman attacked a wight, its chiton glowing a malevolent ivory, facing Ricar Fitzalan and Bertran de la Mothe, one of their royal foresters. There was crashing off to the west, and a heavy company bow twanged where Ricard Lantorn, his stance easy, had just put a heavy shaft in the back of a fleeing horned one.

The wight was as unnaturally fast as the horned men were slow. His two long swords scissored, catching Fitzalan's sword and disarming him, covering against de la Motte's desperate arming sword and casting a pulse of raw *ops* at the *bacsa*.

Its other arms had daggers, and its dirty-white wing cases were like razor-edged shields.

The thing was tired, its four mandibles parted and its purple maw showing. It, too, could run no farther, but it was determined to sell its life hard.

Aneas had his dagger in his left hand and sword in his right, and he cut from far behind his right shoulder, the "long tail" of his master-at-arms, a heavy blow even with a light sword, and when the wight committed two arms to cover his blow, Aneas's dagger went in and skidded off carapace—he let go the dagger and seized a lower arm, his arming sword covering the resultant countercut to his head. He was infighting against a creature that was stronger than he and had more arms.

He had no choice now.

A dagger blow struck him in the chest. Only the natural armour of his all-too-human ribs saved him, as the dagger penetrated his mail and cracked a rib—but went no further. He didn't even notice the pain.

He wrapped the arm he had further in his own left arm, locking it and breaking it without any more conscious thought than the wight exercised as its backhand long sword cut, beheading Ricar Fitzalan as he, game to the last, drew his dagger and died.

Aneas saw his friend die.

In his surge of hate and grief, he ripped the wight's arm off its carapace and unbalanced the thing—it spared two arms for balance, and de la Motte's desperate cut caught it in the armoured head so hard it was stunned, and Looks-at-Clouds struck, crushing its side so that ichor flowed. The irks flowed in, their slim swords probing, their faces transformed from unnatural beauty to fanged horror.

Ricard Lantorn, sword bloody to the hilt, came out of the trees and joined them, his company long sword rising and falling like a peasant axe, each blow driving the dying wight's guard down and down and down, and Aneas put his sword into the thing's eye.

The rest of the company came out of the woods from the east and west, calling to each other in high-pitched voices, high on fear and victory.

Aneas went and knelt by Fitzalan.

Looks-at-Clouds brought his head.

Aneas was not aware he was crying. He was only aware later, when he found his face wet.

Ricard Lantorn, of all people, came and put a hand on his shoulder. "Lost Garth and Beresford, too," he said. "We beat 'em. Like a fuckin' drum. They left corpses all the way back t' ta trail. Look at yon, Ser Knight."

Aneas mastered himself. He was used to hiding his feelings from his mother and father, and this was no different, really, except that apparently they all knew what he felt for Fitzalan.

He'd reached some sort of dull equilibrium when de la Motte muttered, "Look at that."

The smallest Outwaller, Squirrel, was cutting the antlers off one of their fallen foes, twenty paces away in the open woods, while another warrior held the dead thing's skull and grinned.

Lantorn laughed his nasty laugh.

"I want a set too," he said, and loped off. Then he called out, and Aneas rose like a man who'd taken too much drink and moved away from his friend. One of the irks had a small shovel. He'd have to borrow it.

The horned one lay full length, almost eight feet of him. He stank of warm death, and flies were already gathering. Lantorn had taken his antlers, and he looked—pitiful.

"Thinkin' o' takin' 'is balls for a 'bacca pouch," Lantorn said, with a grin.

It was difficult to believe, sometimes, that the beautiful Kaitlin was this Lantorn's sister.

But Lantorn raised a heavy dead arm to show him the tattoos. Aneas was sure enough, but he called for Turkos and Tall Pine with his horn, and after a long pause they came.

"Naming calls, and so do horns," Turkos said. He made an avert sign with his hand. "The woods is full of things today."

Aneas nodded. "I thought you'd want to see this," he said.

Tall Pine spent a long time on the corpse, examining the tattoos.

"Not my people," he said. "Sossag, maybe. Northern Huran, maybe not."

Aneas rubbed his beard, finding it filthy. "But they are men. Were...men."

Tall Pine shook his head and ran his hand over the absurd muscle structure. "Yes," he said sadly. "Men." He got up and dusted his hands. Then he took tobacco from a pouch around his neck and threw some to the cardinal points: north, south, east, and west.

Aneas had very little prepared *ops* but he did what he could, using his little bit of astrology with his simplest, cheapest investigation working.

The answer was the obvious one. "Ash made them," he said warily.

Aneas sat heavily on the rich loam of the forest floor. His hose were damp with his own blood and his friend's and the red, human blood of the dead horned one. Flies began to settle on him.

He couldn't get his mind to work. Nothing came to him. He just sat and breathed, like a tired dog.

No one was moving much, and Aneas knew that they were waiting.

Looks-at-Clouds came and squatted with almost inhuman posture. S/he was too close.

S/he put her hands on either side of his face. They were warm, and sticky with blood.

The shaman's eyes bored into his, and he felt *that s/he was pulling him into her palace, and let go, although he had never been offered such intimacy.*

In the aethereal, *s/he was no more female than in the real. But something...*

Aneas had always been...wary...of women. His mother in particular. S/he had nothing of his mother.

S/he stood in a clearing in eldritch woods, alone. And naked. His/her arms were clothed only in power. Aneas wondered if he should be afraid.

S/he seemed to encircle him with her arms, except that they grew longer and longer, as if s/he could attenuate his/her view of herself at will, even in the aethereal, *and suddenly she might have been he; he seemed more male, his muscles more pronounced. But this flicker of masculinity was only one of many manifestations of change—change and change, as if Looks-at-Clouds was not one settled thing.*

Aneas felt his mind unglue, wondering if perhaps his/her attitude to gender was reflected in his/her powers. It must be so. Looks-at-Clouds was a changeling.

Aneas was seated on a log, and the wound in his chest was already healed, and the pain in his lower back and thigh were mere pulses of the earlier agony, and his grief for Fitzalan was sharp, but not debilitating.

S/he was seated by him, working the edge of his/her knife with a sharpening stone. Other men were mending clothes, and Cynthia Durford, the woman from the Brogat, helped Krek the bogglin hammer a rivet.

"I do not know all your words," the *bacsa* said. "But you threw too much. And your lover died. This is a bad way, for our kind."

Aneas nodded. "I need to walk around," he said.

"Good," the *bacsa* said. "You are strong. Go."

Aneas hesitated. "You are...part irk?"

The *bacsa* shrugged. "I am what I am," the Outwaller said. "Part irk and part human. Male and female." A broad smile followed. "I am myself. Changeling."

Aneas clamped down on his temptation to kiss the Outwaller. It hurt him...he felt disloyal to Fitzalan, who had been jealous of the shaman just a few hours before.

Fickle, fickle.

And he's dead.

And I am alive.

And so is Kevin Orley.

*

He came back to them with his kit packed and on his back.

"We're not done," he said.

Tall Pine got to his feet. "*Gots onah*," he said, which meant "Let's go." Aneas had heard often enough to guess the meaning of it. All the rest of his war party were on their feet in ten beats of a calm man's heart, and Turkos grinned and put his blanket roll over his shoulder.

The two irks looked at each other and shrugged.

"Even we are tired, young man," Tessen said.

"We are not done yet," Aneas said. "We need a good campsite tonight, and we have some dead to bury."

The battle had moved over almost a mile of ground. The enemy they left to become one with the forest. Garth had fallen first, a spear in his heart at the edge of the beaver swamp, and Wart, the only surviving Jack, joined the two irks in digging the rich loam at the edge of the swamp. Looks-at-Clouds started a fire with his/her powers, and they drew the doubtful swamp water in two brass kettles and boiled it for a long time and made tea.

When Garth was in the ground, his sword and bow with him in the Outwaller way, they drank the tea, and the *bacsa* poured the leavings over the new grave and said words in Huran, and all the others bowed their heads.

Then they walked north along the ridge. There were already wolves moving off to the east, sniffing at the dead of the maple tree explosion, and they gave that charnel area a wide berth and then, woodsmen all, found the other graves by dead reckoning. Nothing had disturbed the dead, and they buried Fitzalan and Beresford together with their swords.

Wart threw a coin in Fitzalan's grave. "He were a good one," he said. "He kilt the great wight, when we was fightin' out west. Wi'out him, I'd be dead."

Aneas threw a gold leopard into the open maw of the grave. *He made war into fun. Can I say that? He saved me. I loved him. I think. Sweet Christ.* "He saved me too," Aneas said.

Hands reached out and touched Aneas.

He was so unused to the mere comfort of other people that their concern cut through him like knives. He could all but hear his mother say, *People are cattle.*

Maybe you were wrong, Mother, Aneas thought.

But he held on to his hate for Kevin Orley. Orley killed his mother and father. Orley killed Fitzalan.

Orley.

He was still weeping when he led the way along the old trail, headed north.

He—

Part II
Etrusca

"Y ou said we'd need a ship," Lucca chortled.

Indeed, the ship was the same Venikan merchant that had brought Pavalo Payam to the Nova Terra, which was the sort of information that was flesh and blood to Jules Kronmir. She was a small round ship with the new, sharper bow that several nations were trying, faster in light winds and a little more of a risk in heavy weather. Kronmir had some experience at sea, and he liked the ship, and he liked the captain more, a Venikan adventurer with a sharp eye for a cargo and plenty of grey in his beard to indicate storms survived and tempests conquered or endured.

"Capitano Parmenio, at your service," he said with a bow, and Kronmir returned the bow with interest.

"Your man said you had a special request," Parmenio said. He was mild, for such an old salt, and although his eyes remained on the lading of his ship—just past him, teams of labourers were moving bales of furs and raw wool into his open holds—he beckoned with open hand to demonstrate that even while working, he could concentrate on the needs of a passenger.

"I need to reach Etrusca at the earliest possible moment," he said.

Parmenio turned and met his eye with the smile captains reserve for potentially annoying customers. "Of course," he said, his tone unchanged, and yet Kronmir's minute attention revealed his assumption that Kronmir was the usual run of busy or greedy fool who thought that a ship could go faster than the wind if one paid enough.

Kronmir was an intensely private man, but there were times when a level of crisis was reached that forced him to share a confidence. He drew from his bosom a folded sheet of translucent imperial messenger paper.

He noted that Captain Parmenio truly was a man of the world. His expression changed at the sight of the paper alone, and when he saw the imperial seal, he straightened.

The emperors of Liviapolis had not exercised anything like control, government, or even taxation over the free cities of Etrusca and Arles for many hundreds of years, but they remained, at least nominally, imperial subjects, more so in some cities than others. Venike had never ceased to use the imperial eagle with her own lion as a badge, and a gentleman of Venike was naturally inclined to some small feeling for the needs of the Imperium.

Parmenio bowed.

"You know of the defeat of the King of Galle?" Kronmir asked.

"By my faith, sir, the docks are alive with it, and yon Galles have offered me a fortune to carry part of their company to West Galle, but I'm bound for the Inner Sea. It took me too long to reach here. I must away, or my fortune is broken." Captain Parmenio glanced back, twirled his mustache, and shouted at his mate, Sim Atkins, who had a small fortune in Wild honey suspended from a slender rope and couldn't find a man to belay. Parmenio ran to help, and there was a long lacuna in the conversation while the two officers sorted their sailors.

"Half my crew has deserted, and I have Albans and Galles and every other nation on the face of the earth. And the plague is panicking everyone," Parmenio said. "I beg your pardon. I would do anything in my power to aid a servant of the empire."

Kronmir bowed again. "I need to land in Etrusca at the first possible instant," he said.

Parmenio nodded. "I can weigh in five hours, on the tide," he said. "If the weather holds, we could sight Iberia in five days. Then it is in God's hands how long it takes us to weather the Gates and raise Gelon and Charybdis." He shrugged. "Ten days at best. Fifty days is not impossible."

Kronmir looked at the sailors, the dock, and the captain. "In fifty days, the world may have ended," he said.

Parmenio frowned. "Bad as that?" he asked.

Kronmir shrugged. "An unfortunate turn of phrase, Captain."

Parmenio straightened his mustache and looked at his cargo. "I will do my best," he said.

Kronmir nodded. "We'll be aboard in two hours. There will be three of us."

Parmenio nodded.

Kronmir came aboard with Lucca and one other man, a nondescript servant who was not introduced to anyone and went directly below. Each man brought two small leather trunks and no other gear besides signed parchments from the port captain that they were free of the plague. Already, the Alban authorities were acting on the queen's orders. Kronmir was astounded and a little pleased that Alba was not as barbaric as he had feared.

As the sun began to set in the west, the tide changed and, without any fuss, the round ship dropped her lines and slipped out under sweeps into the offing, dropped her sails in a neat way that spoke of a good crew despite Parmenio's pronouncements, and heeled slightly in the fine breeze. Water began to gurgle along her tubby sides almost immediately. Kronmir went below, as he was sharing the captain's cabin, and there he browsed the captain's truly stunning collection of books, from the latest romances of history to books of mathematics. He chose a historical romance about the times of Empress Livia and her legions and opened it.

It was the lookout who spotted the strange bird and hailed the deck. Kronmir was summoned and came on deck, and a heavy black-and-white messenger bird circled the ship twice and came to his fist.

The sailors watched with a sort of awe. Imperial messengers were the very epitome of information transfer, and, in a way that knowledge is power, the possession of one indicated power more clearly than fancy clothes or magnificent armour.

Kronmir took the tubes from the great bird's legs. He gave the bird to Lucca to feed and slipped below. He'd been offered the prize accommodation, the second cot in the captain's gallery, and he had accepted, and it was there, by the light of a swaying lamp of beaten gold with eight Saffish seraphim beating their six wings in hermetical majesty, that he read the message appointing him Logothete of the Drum and granting him the master code.

But there was more, a whole second sheet, and he decoded as quickly as he could, his work interrupted by incipient seasickness as the ship hit the chops of the open ocean and the ship's motion changed accordingly. It was difficult to concentrate. But Jules Kronmir did many difficult things, and he bore down. He had the presence of mind to take his work with him when he went topside to vomit over the side, and then he went back to the captain's cabin and continued. He had reason to believe that the Red Duke had penned the message himself, and in some detail. Kronmir, who had killed more men than most, found his hands shaking as he read. *Kraal... Odine... dragons... nexus... pillars... Necromancer...*

The stern windows showed stars before he came to the end of the second sheet. When he was finished, he folded the results into his jupon and went on deck. There, he bowed to the captain, who stood on the high quarterdeck and invited him up the ladder.

"Captain, I request a word," Kronmir said formally.

"At your service," Parmenio said. "You are, if I may say, very pale. Seasick?"

"What do you know of the Kraal?" Kronmir asked. He was, he thought, *information sick.*

Parmenio fingered his beard. "I know we do not generally name them, at sea," he answered.

"I am to warn you that... forces of the sea may attempt to intercept us." Kronmir felt odd saying this. He was relatively unversed in the ways of the Wild. His life had been lived in the world of men.

Parmenio looked at the star-filled heavens for a moment. Kronmir had had suspicions that the man had deep intelligence. Most of the Venikan sea lords were thinkers. He walked up his deck and back with the ease of many repetitions, never glancing at the bulkhead or the binnacle and moving past them with a rolling gait and a finger's width to spare, and then he returned by the same route.

"This is related to the business in Arles?" he asked.

Kronmir bit his lip because he hated to share intelligence, but the captain had his life in his hand and seemed an ally. And Kronmir was not travelling as a spy. He was travelling, in a way, as an official person. Almost an ambassador. "So it appears," he said.

"Christ and Saint Mark," the Venike captain spat. "Very well. My wife was speaking of this three months ago, when we first had word of your sorcerer. I will see what can be done. We wanted speed anyway. Atkins! All hands on deck."

In minutes, half a hundred irritated, sleep-deprived sailors were expertly spreading canvas. The bow bit deep and the captain grunted in dissatisfaction over the lading of his ship.

"The bow is too high and the stern too deep," he said. "I'll move the cargo tomorrow, perhaps put something heavy in the bow." He shrugged.

"You can outrun them?" Kronmir asked.

Parmenio shook his head slightly. "No," he said. "Or rather, yes, but only over time. For a short sprint, a sea monster can take any ship. But for a day, no. And unless they're waiting off the harbour mouth"—he rubbed his mustache—"it becomes a problem of geometry, Master."

He laid it out for Kronmir with a straightedge and a lead pencil, and the spy understood even as the numbers were laid down.

"The faster you go, the less chance they have to make an intercept," Kronmir said, impressed despite himself.

Parmenio shrugged. "So the theory runs. The last year has seen more monsters attacking ships than in all my life ere this. Are they in league?"

Kronmir looked at the distant stars. "It is not for me to say," he said.

Parmenio bowed. "Or you cannot, and I can respect that, Master." He exchanged quiet words with Atkins, the Alban mate, and left the Alban at the helm. "My watch below. I recommend sleep. If the monsters want us, tomorrow will be the day of highest danger, and then four days hence, when we raise Iberia. If God loves us and this magnificent breeze holds, I think I can promise you a fast run and relative safety."

Kronmir put his head down and had the best sleep he'd experienced in fifty days, free from seasickness and worry. Someone else was in charge. It was the greatest relaxation a spy could have.

The sun rose on an empty ocean all round the compass, and the little round ship raced east into the rising red orb.

The sky was just moving from salmon pink toward a golden yellow when the lookout hailed the deck that he could see movement on the sea's surface to starboard.

Kronmir awoke to the rattle of a drum over his head and a hundred voices shouting. He'd undressed to sleep and he lost valuable time lacing his doublet to his hose; then he got out the cabin's main door and, at a nod from the captain, raced up the starboard-side ladder to the high quarterdeck castle.

"Three of them," Parmenio called. He pointed, and Kronmir's sense of scale did a flip inside his gut.

"Watch 'er spout," grumbled an old salt at Kronmir's elbow.

Kronmir watched under his hand. Parmenio told Atkins to summon the weather mage on deck.

Kronmir's experience of the sea had been limited to a youth spent in fishing boats. He leaned well out, shading his eyes. "How do you know they are not whales?" he asked.

Parmenio smiled, but the smile didn't reach his eyes. "I do not know," he said. "But there are three, and they are fetching our wake and accelerating, so it seems likely to me that they are sea monsters."

"Weather mate, sir!" Atkins reported.

The weather mate was young—absurdly young for such an important post. He was Alban, like most of the hermetical practitioners, who all seemed to come from Alba or Ifriquy'a. He had sandy red hair and thin arms and looked too small to be taken seriously.

"Can you make a working to see clearly across distances?" Parmenio asked.

The boy—it was absurd to call him a man—looked under his hand; paled, if a person as white as ivory could be said to turn pale; and then flushed, his freckles seeming to burn with inner fire.

He raised his right hand and sang a few notes, and the air before his hand seemed to shimmer and take on shape.

Parmenio grunted and bent to look, but the boy waved him away and cast a second time, and then a third, spectacularly, casting a rod of pure light that seemed to hold the two air shimmers together. And a fourth casting, something very small indeed, and the whole hermetical artifact began to move slightly as if it had a life of its own.

Parmenio was looking through it. He raised his head. "Have a look," he said. "By God, young man, you have just earned your full pay."

The boy flushed again, this time with pleasure. "That's how they teach it at the academy," he said. "I've never been, but I read all the books."

Kronmir bent his head, and there, in vivid detail and suffering only from a slight heat shimmer, were three innocent whales basking in the sun.

"How long will this thing last?" Parmenio asked his weather mate. He turned, not waiting for the answer. "Watch below can go back to their hammocks. Whales and no Eeeague."

"As long as I concentrate on it, and perhaps a little more." The boy shrugged. "I'm more of a scholar, so far, Lord Captain."

Kronmir looked again. "This is better than any distance device I have ever seen. You say this is from the academy? In Liviapolis?"

The boy smiled. "Just this spring, they sent a whole manuscript of these things, each better'n the last. My maître got us two whole days to read it, before the Galles killed him in the riots."

"How old are you?" Kronmir asked. At a remove, he wondered when children had begun to slip through his armour of indifference and cynicism. He also wondered if the government in Morea knew that the academy was sharing hermetical secrets with ... the world.

That would be a revolution, of sorts.

"Fourteen, and it please you, my lord," the boy said.

"I'm no lord," Kronmir said.

The boy bobbed.

"How much wind can you make?" Parmenio asked the boy.

The redhead shrugged. "Never tried," he admitted. "I mean, I know how."

"How much *ops* can you master?" Kronmir asked. "What's your name, anyway?"

"Kieron Hautboy," the young man answered. "I can master a fair amount. But ..." He looked at Parmenio as if fearing rebuke.

Parmenio shrugged in a very Venikan gesture. "My old weather mate was lost in the last storm." He shrugged. "Mage craft is common as dirt in Alba compared to Venike, but just try to hire a master!"

"Let me try, gentles," the boy said. He went to the foot of the towering mainmast and began to chant. It had a religious sound, and he went twice through his piece before anything manifested, and then the effect was gradual. The breeze stiffened and the only exact evidence was from the tell-tales, hanks of yarn that hang at the end of the booms to show wind strength.

"Perfect, lad," the Venikan captain shouted. The boy turned his head to listen, and the new breeze died away.

"What?" he asked. "What, sir?"

Parmenio's face flushed, and anger turned down the corners of his mouth ... but he mastered himself in an instant, and Kronmir, who prided himself on his imperturbability, felt a kindred spirit.

The captain put his arm on the boy's shoulder. "You have to be able to hold your working and listen for my orders, or Master Atkins's. You're no use to us if you can only do one thing at a time. But that was a fine breeze. How long can you hold that?"

The boy rubbed his chin. "An hour?" he said. "It would be quite painful," he admitted. And then he waggled his head, a curiously feminine gesture. "But on the other hand, excellent practice. An exercise in concentration. Lord Captain, please allow me to raise the wind again, and then you give me an order."

This time Kieron was swifter at raising his breeze, and the captain nodded to Atkins at the tiller.

Atkins looked fore and aft. "Ready," he called.

"Turn us four points to starboard," Parmenio said in a conversational voice.

"Four points to starboard it is, Cap'n," Atkins said.

"If this boy is as good as he seems, he and Atkins will alone have made my crossing worth my while. My former mate was a drunk," Parmenio said.

Atkins moved the tiller. Half a dozen men immediately began to trim the sails, as the round ship did not like to point off the wind at all.

"Can you bring the wind around four points?" the captain said to the redheaded boy.

The boy listened. This time, he hummed throughout the captain's explanation.

"Right behind us, then?" the boy asked.

Parmenio shook his head. "That is not the ideal," he said.

"Just point where you want the wind," the boy said tersely.

It was quite possible that Captain Parmenio was not used to being told what to do on his ship, but he merely glanced at Kronmir and winked. Then he walked to the rail and pointed his right arm directly at the boy from ten paces away, a little to the side and well behind.

Almost immediately, the breeze came round, alarming the sailors and forcing a new rush of sail trimming on the mainsail and the headsails.

The captain ran up his quarterdeck ladder and leaned out over the side. He took the tiller from Atkins and stood there for several long minutes while Kronmir watched the distant horizon.

"Perfect!" the Venikan said. He relinquished the tiller and came back down his ladder to the half deck. "Let it go, young man. I do not wish to use you up. Master Atkins, four points to port."

"Four points to port, aye," Atkins called.

An older sailor with gold earrings and a deeply tanned, deeply lined face and a superb baselard at his belt, laughed and said something to his *capitano* in the liquid Venikan dialect. Parmenio grinned and shrugged, and both men laughed.

"Antonio, who has been with me since I was a newly entered noble archer on my uncle's ship," he said. "Antonio says that if I hire more Albans, he will have to learn to grunt as you do. He means no offence."

He put his arm around young Kieron. "I think that you will have to learn how a ship works," he said. "But your skills are excellent."

Kieron flushed again. He seemed to go from red to white to red very easily. "I thought they would be," he said. "But then, I was afraid they wouldn't. That probably doesn't make any sense."

Kronmir nodded. "It makes perfect sense. An experience I have almost every day." When the captain began describing his ship as a box pivoting on a single point, and the different aspects of wind, Kronmir withdrew to the romance in his cabin. The author was very capable and his fancy suited Kronmir.

Later, he came on deck to find young Kieron aloft in the crow's nest with a sailor, and the sun setting rapidly off to the west over Alba. Lucca came on deck with a pair of practice swords, and the two of them fenced up and down the deck. Lucca was better than merely competent, but Kronmir was better yet, and he would stop to teach his apprentice the finer points of timing and, in most cases, the judgment of distance.

When Kronmir went to see if he could keep a cup of wine down, Lucca began to practice his cuts against the foremast until Antonio came and moved him along. He mimed sanding and painting the mast, and Lucca, appalled at the damage he'd done, went and confessed to the captain.

Kronmir returned to the deck to find a hardened killer patiently sanding away with a bucket of fine sand and a big piece of flax tow. Parmenio was standing at the foot of the mainmast, exchanging hails with a countryman in the tops.

Kronmir offered a greeting. "What's the trouble?" he asked.

"Our young weather worker has rigged his far-seer in the crow's nest, and now we find that our three whales have stayed with us all day." Parmenio shrugged. "Whales are probably smarter than men. I cannot guess what drives them."

"But none of the deadly Eeeague," Kronmir said.

"Very difficult to tell at this distance," Parmenio said. "At darkness, I will try a little trickery that I usually save for the Iberians."

As soon as it was full dark, the mate set a barrel adrift with a lit lantern in it. The ship then turned north, almost eight points of course change, and the boy powered them for almost an hour before the captain ordered a return to their original course.

In the morning, the horizon was empty in every direction. Parmenio was particularly satisfied with himself, and after he took his noon sightings, he had young Kieron drive the ship with a mage wind for a little more than an hour, which caused the boy to look like an Etruscan ascetic saint but made the captain very happy indeed.

Atkins, newly risen from his midday nap, went forward and threw a small floating log attached to a line. He let line off until the captain ordered him to stop from the stern.

Kronmir, for whom any form of science of mathematics was fascinating, came aft. "You are measuring speed?" he asked.

Parmenio smiled with pleasure. "You are just right."

Kronmir bowed. "My childhood on fishing smacks did not include all this scientific seamanship."

Parmenio nodded. "The log is simple enough. I have a set distance—the length of my ship. I have a minute glass. But I don't need it—I am no longer green behind my ears, and I can count the time in my head, like any musician. Eh? And I can check my work against Master Atkins, as he has knots on the line by which to measure speed."

"Eight knots and a touch," Atkins reported.

"I make it more like eight and a half," Parmenio agreed. "It is not an exact science, but it is better than no measurement at all." He nodded aft. "If the boy can move us at eight knots, I suspect we can outdistance most pursuit."

"And the whales?" Kronmir asked.

Parmenio smiled and ran a thumb along his mustache, of which he seemed rather proud. "No idea," he said. "I have fought the Iberians my whole life, the Genuans a dozen times, and the ships of Dar as

Salaam once, but I have never faced a sea monster. Before my voyage here, from Dar, I had never even seen one."

Kronmir sighed. "My apologies."

"None needed. If there are pirates to be exterminated, I'm your man. But for this, I am working with myth and rumour and gossip, and my friend, I tell you, the gossip of sailors is something to make a soldier blush."

They shared a glass of wine and played chess, and then the captain went on deck to take his watch. Kronmir shot at targets with a marine's crossbow, and then with his balestrino, a tiny steel crossbow. Lucca used an easterner bow with either hand and could loose arrows in a steady stream even while running or leaping. The sailors enjoyed their antics, and the watch below came up to do laundry and some of the more daring souls took turns with the practice swords. Kronmir exchanged a dozen blows with Captain Parmenio, who was both strong and clever.

"Fighting pirates has given you a strong wrist," Kronmir said.

Parmenio wiped the sweat from his mustache. "I'm damn glad there are not many pirates like you, sir."

The lookouts declared the horizon clear at sunset, but Parmenio did the lantern trick again.

"It is every night in pirate waters," he said. "I feel that our adversaries should be treated with the same respect."

Another night passed without incident, and the ship ran on. The third day dawned cold and wet, and there was patchy fog, but despite the perfect weather for some dread event, the ship ran east and east without let or hindrance. Toward evening the wind backed and moved from their starboard quarter to the port quarter, and became fitful, and there was much fiddling with the sails, but before dark, the wind steadied and grew stronger. Parmenio tossed the log himself and came aft twirling his mustache in satisfaction.

"Almost nine," he said. "Were I a praying man, I would say it was God's will. I have seldom made a passage so good." But he touched wood when he said it, and behind him, Antonio scratched a backstay with a callused finger.

The fourth day dawned fine, with clouds few and white and billowy. Before noon, they had seen land birds, and Parmenio was unavailable, as he was standing at the tiller with Atkins, alternating between log casts and using a lead weight on a line with tallow to test the bottom. Kronmir fenced and ate, feeling well enough at last, and in midafternoon he was finishing his second meal of salt cod when Parmenio joined him in the coach, the long bench with a velvet cushion along the magnificent stern windows.

"I wonder if you will be good enough to sign my log," he said. "No one will ever believe that I passed from Harndon to the Eagle's Gate in four days. But we had white sand in forty fathoms at daybreak, and now the Eagle's head is in sight from the masthead. We might *just* weather the entrance to the Inner Sea before nightfall. I wouldn't do it in the dark, I can tell you."

The captain had a glass of a fine sweet red wine, a true *riccoto* of Berona, in celebration, and he shared it with Kronmir, who went on deck, saw the huge white rock called the Eagle's Head from the deck, and signed the log.

The sun was sinking in the west, and still they ran east.

"I am taking a risk," Parmenio said conversationally. He'd invited Kronmir to the quarterdeck, a rare honour. "I probably ought to anchor and ride out the night, but..."

He had Antonio up in the crow's nest, and the Etruscan mate was waving. He shouted, and there followed a long exchange.

"Pass the word for Master Hautboy," Atkins called down into the waist of the ship, but Kieron was already on deck, and he swayed himself outboard on the shrouds and began to climb toward the mainmast crow's nest.

"Antonio does not like something ahead," Parmenio said. And..." He paused.

"And there is also something like a pod of whales behind us," Kronmir said. "I beg your pardon, Capitano, but I speak Etruscan, even the kind you and Antonio speak."

Parmenio raised an eyebrow, but his head was too engaged with the problem of the moment to consider Kronmir's facility with Etruscan.

There passed a general alarm as a young boy appeared with a drum at the head of the companionway and beat it, if not well or rhythmically, at least very loudly. Aloft, young Kieron had his far-seer up.

"Never seen anything like yon," he shouted. He was looking astern of them.

Parmenio never hesitated. "Man the sides, serve out the crossbows, and rig the boarding nets," he called. He turned to Kronmir. "You and your companion seem to me to be good men of arms. Please join me here to defend the quarterdeck," he said. "You have armour?"

"Just a mail shirt," Kronmir said.

"You might want to fetch it," Parmenio said with a ghost of a smile.

"I never part with it," Kronmir admitted. "I have it on this minute."

Parmenio started in surprise, but he passed it over and demanded something called the siphon to be rigged forward.

Kronmir fetched Lucca and their bows. From his own case he fetched a black stone jar. Wearing gloves, he carefully dipped each of ten crossbow bolts and all of his tiny steel spikes in the tarry stuff in the jar, and then when the job was done, he put oiled silk over the top of the stone jar and tied it back on tightly, placed the whole inside a copper container with a lid, stripped off the fine chamois gloves...and threw them over the side.

To Lucca he said, "Do not scratch yourself with the heads of the bolts."

Lucca raised an eyebrow. "Fatal?" he asked.

"Unpleasantly so," Kronmir said.

The ship ran on. Now the White Eagle was towering over them to port, and in the distance, the lights of Southern Iberia began to twinkle. Kronmir had time to imagine the slim hands of some Iberian woman lighting the candles in her seaside home, and to wish...

"Sternward pod is coming up hand over fist," Kieron called. "They ain't no whales, Cap'n. Tentacles and beaks."

"Jesu Christe," Parmenio swore. He knelt, crossed himself, and leapt back to his feet. He had his mail on, and Atkins, already armoured, closed a fine browned breast-and-back on him and two sailors began to fuss with the buckles.

Kronmir's servant came on deck. He was difficult even to notice, a nondescript man in nondescript clothes, but where the eye lighted on him, men noticed he had a long copper or bronze tube and that it appeared very heavy and it had something like a hook or an axe blade.

"Whale! Port side aft!" Hautboy yelled.

A great head—terrifying, needle pointed, many-toothed, black and yet patchy with sea growths—broke the surface of the sea, and the whole great beast broached, three-quarters of its vast, ship-sized bulk coming free of the water before it slammed back, half turned. Just for a moment, Kronmir saw one of its great eyes—indeed, horrified or not, he had the impression that he had truly been eye to eye with the thing, and it had seen him, and then it crashed into the sea and through half the ocean aboard them. The ship heeled, the sails were wet, and the thing gave a flick of its tail and was gone. It seemed to run alongside them for a few ship's lengths, a pale green smudge under the clear water, and then it rolled and went for the depths.

Parmenio crossed himself. "Jesu Christe," he said again. "It almost had us."

Kronmir frowned and looked over the side. "I do not think so. I think that was a warning, and well meant." He shrugged. "I cannot tell you why, but I live and die on my opinion of men's souls."

Parmenio looked at him a moment.

"That animal had a soul," the assassin said.

"What else do you see?" Parmenio called to the top.

"The things with tentacles are gaining!" Hautboy called.

"Two leviathans off the starboard bow, between us and the straits," Antonio called in Venikan.

"Leviathans?" Kronmir asked.

"Sea serpents. Larger than whales, and more malevolent. We have seen them lately in the Inner Sea." Parmenio shrugged.

Kronmir looked aft. "Could the whales and the leviathans be enemies?" he asked.

Parmenio looked at the compass. "I wish I knew. It's is a beautiful theory, and in less than a minute, when I have my last chance to commit to the straits or turn south, I will have to decide whether I will risk my ship, my cargo, and our lives on this insane but delightful theory." He smiled. "Are you a betting man, Master?"

Kronmir could not hide his snarl of disdain. "No," he said.

Parmenio shrugged. "Alas! I am."

"Serpent!" screamed the lookout.

A triangular head, the size of the forecastle, surfaced alongside. The head moved, striking the ship a glancing blow.

A volley of crossbow bolts tore at the head, and the beast went under.

"'Ware the tail!" Parmenio roared. He had the tiller, and he laid it hard over to port.

The round ship jibed, the wind filling her mainsail as she turned hard across it. She heeled heavily as the whole mainsail took the wind broadside on, but the coils of the sea serpent struck only empty water.

"Weather mate!" Parmenio roared. "Wind! For the love of God and Mary the Virgin!"

Kieron stood by the mainmast, one hand around the stained wood, and began his song.

Kronmir, gazing over the size, saw an opaline flash and then another, as if there were oil on the water. It took him a moment to register what he was seeing...

"Eeeague!" he called. He had a light crossbow in his hands, the head covered in sticky black tar. He snapped the bolt at the nearest jellylike beast coming sluglike up the side.

The bolt struck home, and a dozen of the Eeeague screamed together, a terrible choir of agony and sea-stink. The one he'd struck turned jet black in the blink of an eye and fell away into the sea. The others climbing the ship's side seemed to lose animation. Their oily, reflective skin grew dull, like worms drying in the sun after a rain shower.

Kronmir leaned well out and shot straight down with his little balestrino. The Eeeague he struck turned black. The others gave a mewl of sadness, and all fell away. The ship, released from their grasp, began to gather speed.

Away forward, another half dozen of the Eeeague—or perhaps each one had six arms? Six bodies? Kronmir couldn't think. He had never seen anything so alien, and even as he rewound his balestrino he had a hard time grasping what he had just seen...

Away forward, his anonymous servant spun along the side as six more attacked. The Eeeague had trouble with the forecastle's high sides, and the ordinary little man used a ship's pike and then a sword so fluidly that he appeared to be dancing, and when he stopped moving, the forecastle was clear.

The ship's contingent of crossbowmen and several sailors loosed bolts into the waves until Parmenio ordered them to cease, and the ship raced away into the east again, having returned to her original course and slowly gathering way as the weather worker's magery added to the wind.

Captain Parmenio was examining the three-quarters of his great sword of war that was left to him. He had struck repeatedly at something gelatinous that had come into the waist of the ship, and its flesh had eaten the point of his sword.

"I gather that we have met the Eeeague," he said, but his voice was high and a little wild. Atkins, who had a heavy axe in both hands, came up behind his captain and two sailors poured seawater on his back plate without warning. Parmenio sputtered and was then shown the hole a hand span wide in his back plate.

"Christ and all the saints," the captain swore.

The coast of Iberia raced at them. The Eagle's Head was tall and white crowned on the port side, and to starboard, Ifriqu'a loomed in an evening haze of purple-pink mountains, but there were lights on that coast, too.

"Faster," Parmenio called to the weather mage.

Atkins shook his head. "Topsail and foremast can't take too much wind, Cap'n. We took an almighty jolt when the serpent hit us. Foremast stay parted."

Parmenio ran aft. Kronmir thought that they might as well be speaking another language, and went back to watching the sides.

Just aft of the stern and the wake, the sea grew suddenly dark.

"'Ware!" Kronmir called.

The enormous triangular head rose swiftly from the wake and lunged on the sinuous serpent's neck. Kronmir's hand came up and he shot into the great eye, a single malevolent wheel of liquid ebony in the heavy, crystalline brow.

His heart seemed to stop.

The head fell toward him, and then, almost under its jaws, so close that the whole of the ship shuddered, a mighty whale broached, its tapered head striking the serpent under the head where the snout full of needlelike teeth met the diamond-riveted coat of the long body. The sound of the impact was like a thunderclap and the two monsters fell away, sliding into the sea like sinking ships even as a wall of spray and solid water fell into the ship, drenching the sails, knocking a sailor over the side and slamming Kronmir into the after mast so hard that lightning streaks of red crisscrossed his vision.

Another rush of Eeeague came up the sides. These screamed as they came and emitted torrents of their acid.

Lucca stood over Kronmir. His heavy arbalest blew one into black fragments, and then another as he shot again with Kronmir's spare weapon.

Kronmir gained control of his trembling hand and loosed the tiny bolt from his balestrino.

Then Lucca and Parmenio and a dozen sailors were fighting with staves and pole arms, at least until the heads of the weapons melted or rusted away, but even as the Eeeague took a sailor and dismembered him, the Eeeague themselves were suffering the effects of Kronmir's poison, which seemed to dry them, rot them, and weaken them—and drive the survivors to a frenzy.

Revenge? Kronmir's mind asked, lazily. *Do they feel? Do they think?* The poison was an Outwaller concoction he'd become aware of in Liviapolis. It was cruel to men and horses. He was unsurprised that it was hellish for the Eeeague as well. He began to span his balestrino, painfully aware that his hands were not interested in obedience, aware too that the circle of armoured men defending him was shrinking.

White lighting played against the nearest glistening mass. It froze as if galvanized and then exploded, showering everyone on the quarterdeck with acid. Lucca fell, a mass of burning sludge on his face, and Kronmir forced his head and body to cooperate, got himself to his feet by rolling to the left and got his hands on one of the pails of seawater that the sailors had used on Parmenio. It was half full and he hurled it straight at his partner, who inhaled half of it and went down sputtering, but the acid was washed away, and he was left screeching in pain from the salt.

Lucca whimpered, got a hand under himself, and his good eye met Kronmir's. And then he passed out and his head hit the deck with a thump.

Parmenio's arming coat was full of holes under his shredded metal armour, but he was delivering a stream of orders, and the mainsail, with fifty holes burned right through, was being stripped off by eager sailors as another was brought on deck. The weather mate was leaning over the side, working. Kronmir saw the whale slam into the serpent again, and the disturbance of their two bodies in the water was so great that the ship turned on its beam ends, and men were thrown into the scuppers and worse.

Parmenio was looking back, past the two monsters. He had an odd smile on his face, and not a particularly pleasant one.

"Ready about!" he called.

The sailors were hauling the new mainmast taut. Less than two minutes had gone by since the first contact. The ship, despite the loss of her mainsail, had never stopped her long turn to port that had taken her from a northeasterly course with the wind on her starboard quarter through a southeasterly course with the wind perfectly on her port quarter and past that again to a broad reach with the wind coming right over her gunwales, pushing her far down in the water as she ran due south, but now, all standing sails trembling, she was turning back west, having already passed through half of the compass rose. The wind was against her now, and all her sails were flapping or even fighting the wind, but she still had way on her, and the two fighting sea creatures were now a hundred paces off the starboard side, the weather-worker quite competently keeping the wind steady in the foresails, reenforcing the shredded main until it was down, and casting offensive workings at the serpent each time it broke the surface.

Atkins, the mate, was in the ship's waist. "At the serpent, lads!" he called. "The whale's a friend!"

A dozen heavy bolts vanished into the green scales of the serpent as a coil rose from the water. Bubbles burbled to the surface everywhere. Kieron leaned out from a shroud and a bolt of red lightning leapt from his hand and struck the triangular green head. The ebony eye moved, and like lightning the great head shot around, the mouth opened—

Flayed and bleeding, the whale rose from the sea like a vast, injured wrestler who has not yet surrendered, and came down across the serpent's midbody, dragging the thing down even as Kieron landed another bolt of red lightning.

Kronmir was not focusing well, but he was on his feet, a tridentine spear in his hands. There were men gathering in the waist.

The ship was now running almost north, broad reaching with the wind on the port quarter, having passed through almost two hundred seventy degrees. The breeze had crossed her bow while she still ran on from the rapidity of her jibe, and her odd round hull and sharp bow seemed in perfect harmony in the rising sea. Kieron's bursts of mage wind had helped, and now the ship was completing her turn, still at speed.

She passed the rising bubbles that were the only evidence of the fight between serpent and whale. The party in the waist were putting their crossbows, loaded, on the deck.

Kronmir turned to Parmenio, who was watching the water, his head well out over the starboard side as he steered very carefully.

"One chance," he called.

Atkins waved.

At some point, Kronmir understood what he was seeing... the mad Venikan captain had gone back for the man who'd gone over the side.

It was mad, but it was, in its own way, magnificent. The lone man, swimming strongly, waved. Almost under him, the monsters turned, their bodies creating a treacherous current, an undertow. The man swam desperately for the ship, Parmenio nudged the tiller, and Atkins leaned far out with a poleaxe. The serpent's head ploughed a wake just a horse length from Atkins's outstretched hand, but the man didn't flinch. He reached with the poleaxe...

...one desperate hand caught the weapon's head. Two men pulled on the haft with Atkins, and the sailor all but *shot* out of the water. Behind, a fourth sailor raised the crossbow he'd had trained... on the man in the water.

"If we hadn't got him"—Parmenio nodded—"Alberto would have killed him. It is far kinder, I promise you, than leaving a man in these seas."

But Alberto shot anyway—at the rising head of the serpent, coming up now on the starboard quarter.

A great section of bloody, mangled whale came to the surface, ribs exposed, entrails trailing, quite dead.

Kronmir plucked his black stoneware pot from its copper container. He opened it.

The serpent was not undamaged. It seemed to list, to swim slightly on its own left side, and the shape of the triangular head was changed. Many of the hundreds of vicious teeth were broken. But it came on, and fell on the ship, the jaws yawning wide.

Kronmir reared back and threw the black container as hard as he could. It rose—and by his side, young Kieron reached out with a web of fire and placed it, almost gently, on the sea serpent's great purple tongue. A single bolt of red lightning forced the monstrous jaws to snap shut.

Parmenio had all the wind he needed, and a fresh mainsail newly bent. He threw himself on the tiller, and Kronmir joined him, and the round ship turned again, still to port, completing her journey around the compass and returning to her original course, one point north of due east with the wind on her port quarter. The ship crested the rising waves, and Kieron threw wind into the mainsail, low, at deck level, so that sailors went flat even as the deck surged beneath them.

The triangular head shuddered. The black eyes blinked, and the head fell away to the left, crashing into the sea and throwing spray high in the air. Before the head went down, it vomited black.

"Christ and all his saints!" crowed the captain.

Fifteen minutes of terror later, they were in the straits, running before the wind, and without a sight of monsters—natural, Wild, or otherwise. The only sign of their trials was a cloud of gulls descending on the floating whale's carcass far astern, and a slick of black that was just discernible as a discolouration, like a matte stain on the ink-black nighttime sea.

Within it, hundreds of dead fish bobbed like the corpses of a defeated army.

The Venikan ship ran east.

At first light the next morning, Kronmir sent his bird. He debated it as soon as his head was clear enough to think, and decided, in the end, that he was unlikely to submit a more important report than one about the sea fight.

The imperial messenger launched from the deck and, with powerful strokes, vanished heading north and west. Kronmir watched it fly until it was out of sight, annoyed to find that he felt more alone and more afraid once it was gone, as if it were a palpable link to the world of Alba and Morea. Then he sat down by his own cot, now holding Lucca, who had lost an eye and was in terrible pain, lashed by storms of agony. The anonymous little man came, mixed a potion and then another, then left in irritation and returned having fetched young Kieron, who made two workings that brought Lucca some relief. The ship had lost a dozen men dead and two more so badly injured that they had little chance for life.

Parmenio, entering the cabin for a cup of wine, glanced at Lucca. The younger man was finally asleep.

"Terrible losses," he said. "Blessed Mary, we wouldn't have lost as many in a long sea fight. With men, I mean, even vicious brutes." He frowned. "The transparent things...they are the Eeeague?"

"I believe so," Kronmir said. "And are the serpents the Kraal?"

Both men shrugged.

Kronmir shook his head. "I confess I may never be able to face the sea again," he said. "That thing...the scale of it...the jaws, reaching for the stern..."

"Kieron says you killed it," Parmenio said.

Kronmir's eyes narrowed. "Perhaps," he said. "But I will not be in any hurry to see one again."

That evening, they passed the Wine Islands and ran due east and a little south. "It would not be so funny," Parmenio said, "to be killed by the Genuans after escaping the monsters. I will make Venike's Lido on the morning of the third day from now."

And on the third morning, Lucca awoke from his fever, cried a little for the loss of his eye, and then sat up. Kronmir led him on deck as they passed the fortified sea-gate of the Lido, with the great lion of Venike flying over the double fortresses that covered the great chain, and beyond, a series of three fortified islands, the third of which raised a flag. Parmenio responded with a coded signal, and they landed on the third island by midafternoon, with the magnificent city of Venike, dazzling in the brilliant midsummer sunlight, sparkling just a few hundred paces of seawater away.

The round ship kissed the quay and the sailors swarmed down the decks to the pier, put hawsers to the iron bollards, and then knelt on the stone and gave thanks to God, to the saints, to a hundred dubious devils and a dozen curious amulets. A pair of inspectors came aboard and began to review the cargo, and with them was a magister who cast repeated detection workings, on the ship and on the sailors. Then every man aboard had to walk under a curious bronze arch set in the stone of the pier. Parmenio paid a fee, a document was sealed with a very official-looking seal, and they were free to travel on to the city.

"It is the best-run port in the world," Parmenio said proudly. "They already know of the plague in Harndon." He nodded at the bronze arch. "The work of Hermes Trigeneris himself, or so it is said." He crossed himself.

Years had fallen away from his face, and Captain Parmenio appeared a much younger man.

The city, beautiful at a distance, became even more magnificent closer up. Kronmir was unimpressed by the muddy barbarism of Harndon, with her unpaved streets and fortress-palace, but Venike might have been built by the same master sculptors who built Liviapolis, except that her streets were not manure-covered marble, with sections of cobble, dirt, and mud. Instead, the streets of Venike were paved in water, and small boats ran in every direction, hauling cargo or passengers.

When they found their moorings and came to rest in one of the city's two great S-shaped canals, Parmenio insisted on taking Kronmir and his two companions to his home. "It is a very expensive city," he said.

"I will need to go to work immediately," Kronmir warned the captain.

Parmenio shrugged. "I have made the run from Harndon to Venike in eight days," he said. "Surely this was fast enough for you?"

Kronmir raised an eyebrow. "Is that roast eel?" he asked, breathing in.

"Squid in squid's ink," Parmenio said. "A dish of my city, which perhaps we will share tonight. You will meet my wife, who will, I hope, not be too amazed that I have returned." He nodded. "And, to be honest, I suspect that you will be required to meet with officials of the city."

"I would expect as much," Kronmir said. He noted that Parmenio was hiding something.

"You have been to Venike before?" Parmenio asked.

Kronmir shook his head. "Never this far north. Listen. I need..." The habit of privacy and stealth bound Kronmir like a vow of silence, but he needed to move very quickly. "I need to speak to someone who will know...the news."

Parmenio smiled. "My wife," he said.

Kronmir's brow furrowed. "No, I mean someone in government. I understand that they will want our news. I am content to *exchange*. With someone with access to the news from Arles and even Nordika."

Parmenio led the group, which included the sailor Antonio and two others, along a broad street. Their ship was not even the largest, and hundreds of ships lined the canals and a forest of masts seemed to hang over every building.

"This way," Parmenio said. "I think you will find my wife meets your criterion. Perhaps you are unused to women holding positions of power. I find Alba terribly backward in this regard." He led them along a walkway scarcely wide enough for a man to walk safely, with a wall on the right and a four-foot drop to the water on the left. They walked fifty paces and came to an ornate door set in a high wall with an iron grating.

Paremnio slapped the grate with one hand and said some gibberish. The gate opened without a sound.

"Your wife is in government, Captain?" Kronmir asked.

Parmenio was at the foot of a stone external staircase that wound up three flights. At the top, a heavy woman in a shawl was cleaning clams. She looked over the stone balustrade and shrieked with evident delight.

"Il Capitano!" she roared. She turned and vanished through the doorway behind her.

Parmenio grinned and began to run up the stone steps. Kronmir had to follow suit to keep his attention.

The ornate door on the second landing opened, and two liveried servants stepped out, one adjusting his jupon. Behind them was a middle-aged woman with a magnificent mane of red hair and a severe but possibly beautiful face. When she caught sight of the captain, her face lit with joy and her beauty was evident. She threw her arms around him.

Parmenio looked over her shoulder at Kronmir. "My wife," he said, unnecessarily.

Kronmir looked away. When he looked back, she was holding him at arm's length as if to see if he was real. In very precise Etruscan, she said, "You are alive! We hear of nothing from Alba but war and pestilence."

"It has both," Parmenio said. "But I am alive, and with a beautiful cargo and some new friends."

"Come and tell me all your news, husband," she said. "Tell me quickly and I will report to the Thirty. There is much..." She looked at Kronmir.

Parmenio nodded. "He saved my life and my ship. He is an officer of the empire."

Kronmir bowed, unused to having his status as an officer announced. But under the circumstances, a little openness did seem the fastest solution. "Am I to understand," he asked, "that your wife is..."

"An officer of the Thirty," Parmenio said. "Theresa."

Kronmir bowed; Theresa curtsied.

"Is...are you..." Theresa struggled to control herself. "Is the emperor coming?" she asked.

Kronmir sighed for his lost secrecy. "Much has yet to be decided," he said. "I am here to gather information."

"For the emperor?" she asked. "Who is emperor? Is it true that the emperor was killed in battle? With...the Wild?" She drew a breath. "Ah, messire, my apologies. I would never interrogate my husband's guest on our very doorstep, but by the graces, messire, the Thirty are desperate for information."

Kronmir bowed. "I will do the best that I can," he said. Behind him, Atkins and Antonio carried Lucca's stretcher in.

Servants bustled about. Parmenio paused. "Wasn't there another man?" he asked.

Kronmir looked interested. "Another man?" he asked.

"A servant?" Parmenio asked, and then shrugged. "Perhaps not."

Donna Theresa sent a runner. Before the *norcini* was set in steaming bowls on the sideboard, before wine was poured, a knock interrupted the clamour of the servants, and Kronmir, sitting in the shifting light of an upstairs balcony that overhung the canal and enjoying a sweet and bitter drink that seemed to smooth away eight days of sea monsters, saw boats pulling up to the small dock at the front of the house—first one small black boat, and then two larger boats, and then a magnificent barge that seemed to be plated in solid gold.

"Your wife is quite important here, I gather?" Kronmir said to Parmenio.

The ship's captain smiled. "More important than I am," he said. "This might hurt some men. But she is..." He made a little sign in the air. "It is a miracle to me that she married me."

Kronmir made no comment. People's marriages mystified him. But he put on a genial smile. "You know, sometimes I almost believe in God," he murmured.

Parmenio finished his drink and stood. "I dreamt of this," he said. "A glass of wine on my own balcony, looking out over my city. When the serpent's coils went past us, I told myself that we would, with a little luck, be here." His smile grew broader. "I see we are to have company for dinner, my dear!"

She leaned over and kissed him. "My darling, the duke has come, with the duchess, and all of the Seven."

Parmenio leapt to his feet. "Sweet Christ!" he said. "I need to bathe, change, buy clothes!"

His wife smiled. "I know it is not what you want, but your guest and your news are of the utmost importance." She shrugged in a very Etruscan manner. "More important than clothes."

Parmenio shrugged. "We survived the sea monster. The duke should not be so bad."

And then, very suddenly, the great, well-lit rooms of the second floor were full of people, men and women in the most beautiful clothes, and Kronmir felt terribly out of place. He was introduced to so many people, so fast, in a language that was not his best language, that even his remarkable memory was stretched to its capacity, and he found himself finally bowing over the fingers of the duchess and unable to remember what to say in Etruscan or any other language. But despite the age of her spouse, who looked to be a somnolent centenarian with a death's skull for a face, the duchess was very young, blond, and had a charming manner. She rang all sorts of alarm bells in Kronmir's head. Her face was tanned, and her pretty, tapering fingers in his were hard with muscle and had ridges of callus that told him that her right hand was her sword hand. Her smile to him was direct, eye to eye, and held no nonsense and no flirtation.

Kronmir noted that she gave Donna Theresa a particular look and there was a small motion of her hand, and Donna Theresa opened her fan. All conversation ended.

"Gentles all," Donna Theresa said. "This gentleman is come as a sort of unofficial ambassador from the emperor."

Kronmir was not used to being the center of attention.

He bowed again to the elderly duke and presented his papers, such as they were—the letter from the Duke of Thrake with the imperial seal. The other letter, with the codes, he had destroyed.

Donna Giselle—the duchess—took the letter and read it, and then leaned over to the duke and spoke quietly.

The death's head turned and he was fixed with a basilisk stare. "The Duke of Thrake is to be emperor?" he asked in a firm voice, only a little weakened by age. His eyes glittered with intelligence, and Kronmir controlled a shudder. He knew a dangerous man when he saw one. The two of them...they spoke to him, their bodies close. They were not a political match of an old man and a young woman. They were, however it had come about, partners.

"If he chooses to accept the iron sceptre, he will be emperor," Kronmir answered.

"On what grounds?" the Duke of Venike asked.

"Acclimation by the army," Kronmir said. "He has won a great victory over the Wild. Two great victories."

The duke seemed to sag. "And the king? And Rohan?" He glanced at his wife, whose face was impassive.

"The Sieur de Rohan is dead. The King of Alba is also dead. Queen Desiderata is now regent for her son, who will be christened..." Kronmir stopped. He blinked. "Perhaps was christened yesterday. My apologies, my lords, I have lost track of the days."

The duke snapped his fingers and silence fell again. "And the emperor?" he asked.

"Was killed in battle against the Wild," Kronmir said, and bowed his head. "At the first battle, at Dorling."

"And then your Red Duke, having sacrificed the emperor, came up and defeated the Wild?" the duke snapped. "And assassinated all his rivals?" he said, as if asking for jam. Suddenly he did not seem old or weak, but Kronmir had met such men before.

Kronmir bowed his head. "The emperor insisted on engaging an enemy too strong for his forces."

"But you confirm that he is dead," Donna Theresa said. "And Irene, his daughter? Is she not empress?"

"Has she not tried to make herself empress before?" the duchess asked.

The duke snapped his fingers for silence. "The King of Alba and the emperor are *both* dead. The Sieur De Rohan is dead, and his party is fallen. Do I have the facts correct?"

The lords of Venike were all speaking at once. Kronmir followed their babble easily enough because it was his duty and pleasure— amazement that Rohan had fallen, pointless speculation as to the manner of his fall.

The duchess leaned back—a graceful movement—and Donna Theresa leaned forward. They spoke together.

The duke frowned. "He has defeated the Wild?" he asked, or rather, barked. "This upstart Duke of Thrake? Is he some marauder? Some sell-sword?"

Donna Theresa nodded. "He was a sell-sword, Your Grace." She made a sign in the air. "But he was, I believe, the commander of the imperial armies." Her lips moved, but Kronmir could read lips. *The yellow folder.*

Kronmir let them talk. This was a game as old as thrones, and they would do more for the Red Knight's myth by making things up for themselves than he could add by telling them the facts, bare or embroidered.

"This is the same who defeated our fleet at Liviapolis?" the duke asked.

All heads turned to Kronmir. He took a deep breath and smiled.

"The same, my lords," he said.

"The same of whom young Baldeske reported so favourably?" he asked. He looked at Donna Theresa, as if to say, *I read your damned report.* Kronmir hid a smile.

"And now his army will make him emperor?" The duke all but spat it. "How long will he last? A week? These soldier emperors are all fools and brutes."

But his wife shook her head. "My dear," she said, "if he has defeated the Wild, perhaps he is the man for the hour."

The duke's skeletal face turned back to Kronmir. "You are not precisely an ambassador," he said.

Kronmir was pleased when a servant put a glass—a beautiful, elaborate piece of Venikan glass—into his hand. It was brimful of wine, and Donna Theresa caught his eye and her expressive eyebrows made a small movement that said, as clearly as speech, *Endure this, and we will be friends.*

He had a sip of the wine. It was delicious.

"Your Grace, I am here to gather information for the empire. I am an officer of the empire, from which you, in person and ex officio, have requested assistance." He bowed. "Unless I am mistaken?"

The duke pursed his thin lips and nodded. "Yes," he said. "We are close to desperation."

Parmenio's head came up.

The duke looked at his wife, and then at two young men who stood together. There must have been nonverbal clues passed, as he looked satisfied. It was interesting that in a room with a dozen men and women, the duke only looked at a few.

"Can you promise assistance?" the duke asked.

Kronmir shrugged. "I am an officer, not the empire."

"I'm sorry," the duchess said. She was like a gem—a beautiful round face, small hands, sparkling eyes. And yet, instead of the vulnerability of a small, pretty woman, she looked...hard. "What office do you hold?"

Kronmir bowed silently. He did not want to state his office. It was not done.

Donna Theresa seemed to understand, because she smiled and stepped forward. "Dinner is being served," she said. "My husband and Master Kronmir have endured perils beyond anything you can imagine, Your Grace. Let's allow them a dinner before the interrogation continues?" she said, and the two young men in the matching hose laughed. One came forward, as pretty and blond as the duchess and revealed at close range as her brother. He bowed. "Corner," he said.

His friend had jet-black hair, which he wore like a Galle, shoulder length, and he bowed as well. "Dolcini," he said. "We are both named Lorenzo, so waste no time calling out to us. Surnames are the fashion here."

Kronmir smiled to both. They were obviously intelligent men, used to governing others, but what interested him was that Donna Theresa used the pause to whisper to the duchess and she turned a mild shade of pink and looked at Kronmir—and was embarrassed to be caught at it.

They all went into dinner, the two Lorenzos chatting away as if their sole duty in the state were to entertain visiting imperial officers. The duke was placed in a chair very like a throne and carried to the head of a long table. Kronmir sat where he was told, by the duchess and across from Parmenio, who told the tale of the eight-day voyage and told it well, with only a little embellishment, two timely quotes from the ancients, and a bit of poetry.

Kronmir's role was, if anything, elaborated, and at one point Parmenio paused.

"But there was another man—a fighting man. I would swear it. Yet I cannot remember what he looks like." He glanced at Kronmir, who looked at his hands and said nothing.

The story drew to its end, and the audience was appreciative even as they ate their pasta course and went on to fish—the clams Kronmir had seen earlier, and another dish, a risotto with squid's ink that was among the most delicious things he had ever tasted.

"And what office did you say you held?" asked the duke.

His wife leaned over him attentively. "Ah, perhaps you'd like a little more wine?" she asked. "I would rather hear about this battle, wouldn't you?"

Kronmir, who had been plotting the death of the Archbishop of Lorica at the time, did his best to describe the demise of Thorn and the defeat of his army.

The duchess put a dramatic hand to her throat. "The Red Duke is allied to the Wild, as well as fighting it?" she asked.

"Yes," Kronmir said, after a moment's thought. *It was true, and it was pointless to hide. Lying needed to be saved for special occasions.*

His affirmation did not create consternation, but something like it, and there was a buzz for several minutes in Etruscan and Low Archaic, as if they might imagine he didn't speak the latter. He stared into space and tried not to let his eyes rest too fondly on the graceful form of the duchess.

I am getting old and simple, he thought.

But he gathered from their informed babble that they had already faced and defeated a wave of the Wild; irks and the eastern clans of the *adversariae*, who had struck over the mountains to the east, the mighty Sellasia range that ran from Arles in the west all the way east almost to the ancient borders of Dakia. They had come in waves and been defeated only recently at the edge of the mountains. He gathered that the duke and duchess had faced them in person. He gathered that the Patriarch of Rhum continued to refuse to believe that there were such Wild creatures and had contributed no forces, and neither had the Duke of Mitla to the west.

It was clear from their conversation that Venike believed that the Wild was real. But that they had no idea of sides, or the existence of Ash. And they were afraid.

"It is not enough that we have defeated a few irks," the duke muttered as beautiful ricotta gnocchi with truffles were served. He looked around. "You know that the King of Galle is dead?" he asked.

Kronmir was careful. "I have heard a rumour."

"Well, young man, I haven't seen his corpse, but I suspect he is dead. His army destroyed, and the army of western Arles. Eastern Arles is already overrun. And three of the northern states of Etrusca sent contingents. Mitla, Genua, Voluna." He steepled his fingers.

A hush fell.

"None returned. My own theory, or rather, Giselle's, is that what we faced here, in the plains north of our lagoon, was merely a harbinger. Or even possibly a defeated rival, driven before the massed horde that now fights in Arles." He looked around. "Let me be a little more precise, Imperial Officer. Our reports tell us that one man...just one man survived the rout. Somewhere north of the city of Arles, there is a deep dark hole into which has fallen all the truth and all the lies. Out of that hole comes...*nothing*." He shook his head.

The hush became silence. The almost-whispered word *nothing* seemed to hiss around the edges of the room like rats in the wainscoting.

Kronmir leaned forward. "Nothing?" he asked. His professional interest was piqued.

Donna Theresa nodded. "We have had no news at all since before the battle," she said. "Couriers go and do not return."

"Indeed," one of the Lorenzos said. "We begin to see a spread of this darkness. Now *nothing* comes to us from all of western Arles. Except one man of the militia of Mitla, who saw nothing of the battle, and who is quite mad."

"Nothing from Galle, either," whispered the other Lorenzo.

"You have sent trusted men?" Kronmir asked.

The duke looked at his hands. "I sent my son," he said. "He has not returned."

They sat in silence. The old duke looked up. His eyes were a vivid green, a surprising colour for so old a man. "It is like the end of the world," he said. "Listen, young man. I am old, and I have seen many crises. Many moments when other men and other women cried that this incident or that war was the downfall of our state, but I weathered them all, and so did Venike." He drew a deep breath. "This is different. Nothing natural destroys an entire army and leaves one survivor. Nothing natural eliminates...everything. My son was a careful man, and a deadly blade, and he has not returned."

"Nor the fifty lances he took with him," one of the Lorenzos said.

"You must have a theory," Kronmir said.

Theresa looked at the duchess, and the duchess glanced at the duke, and he made an impatient gesture.

"Let us not dance while the city burns," he said. "I believe that we face the Necromancer of Ifriquy'a. Or some lieutenant of his."

He waved. "The only survivor is in the care of Magister Petrarcha of Berona." He looked at his wife.

She looked at Kronmir. "You cannot be expected to understand the mare's nest that is our politics," she said. "But this one man, he did not return to his home city. Instead, he went to...Berona. As if drawn to Magister Petrarcha. Berona is our closest ally. And no friend to the Patriarch in Rhum."

Kronmir could see that something was not being said. But he nodded. "The possibility that the Necromancer was involved is contained in my instructions," he said carefully, "as a possibility. Indeed, Your Grace, there has been some...contact, at the highest level...from my master to the powers in Dar as Salaam."

The duke sat back. His uncanny eyes went to his young wife, who was drawing in wine on the tabletop.

"We also think that we are betrayed from within," she said, her face etched in a misery that could not, Kronmir thought, be manufactured.

Ah, Kronmir thought. He had wondered at the barges, the visit, the relative informality.

The presence of only three servants for one of the most powerful men in the world.

"Will you help us?" the duchess asked.

Kronmir knew he should temporize and carefully avoid committing himself or his principal, who was, for all he knew, planning an autumn campaign in the west country against the dragon Ash.

But Kronmir loved the game, and the game called to him, not just in the handsome person of the duchess, but in the seductive evil of a dark hole from which no information escaped. The challenge was magnificent.

The threat, vast.

Kronmir bowed. "Let me see what can be done, Your Grace," he said. "The Duke of Thrake sent me to see what could be done."

"You are his military John the Baptist?" the old duke asked with bitter humour. "Remember how he ended, young man."

Kronmir found that he *liked* the skull-faced old man. Here was a professional, a man skilled at the art of government. "If I cry his name, in the wilderness, he will come," Kronmir said.

Their faces brightened, and Kronmir wondered if what he had just said was true.

Kronmir reviewed the single paragraph that the Red Duke had written him on the Odine and the Necromancer. He read it many times, and tried to imagine...

Then he tried to imagine what kind of person would sell himself to such an enemy.

Eventually, he slept.

In the morning, he woke to light and beauty, the ripple of light on his ceiling reflected from the canal outside his window, and the smell of the sea. He stripped to braes and padded down to the loggia, where he found a dozen men already swimming. The water in the canal was seawater, changed with the tide, clean and wholesome. He leapt in and swam for some time. He noted that the local service was very efficient. He was watched throughout his swim, and indeed he was able to spot several watchers because of the early-morning hour and their habit of standing in the middle of the great bridges to watch him.

He swam slowly, almost lazily, along the many palaces that fronted the canal. The water was clean, but he swam past the corpse of a donkey and what might have once been a man, and took more care. Venike was as grand a city as Liviapolis, or perhaps grander, and the there was so much wealth concentrated there, and some terrible poverty. He had never imagined the Nova Terra as a backwater before, but Harndon, which he had just left, seemed antiquated, even barbaric, by comparison.

Toward the end of his swim, he went up the small canal that ran by Parmenio's small palazzo and under the bridge and there, as he hoped, was a mark: two chalk marks in white, and a third in pale blue.

He climbed out of the water by the small jetty, and two servants wrapped him in a towel softer and more luxurious than he had ever known before. He went to his room, dressed, and had a hasty breakfast of bread and cheese. Parmenio was still asleep, and Kronmir had no intention of waking his hosts. He bowed to the majordomo and went out into the sunshine to walk the city.

He was followed from the moment he left the iron gate. He was careful, as he went, to keep his watchers satisfied. He made no attempt to lose them. Indeed, he calmed them with many small stops. He paused in a coffee house, and drank the beverage for which Venike was famous. It was available in Liviapolis, but even better here. He had two small cups, and then, filled with energy, walked across the great central square and came at last to Parmenio's ship. He felt he had given a creditable performance as a man of average intellect who could not quite remember the city grid or where the bridges were, and then he went aboard. A dozen workmen were unloading, carrying barrels of Wild honey and boards of furs ashore. He slipped past them up the gangway and went into the captain's cabin, where he fetched his shaving kit, left the night before in the hurry of leaving, and flourished a little too dramatically for the benefit of his watchers as he left the cabin.

He wandered a little, investigating the smelly wonders of the fish market, and made his way back to Parmenio's palazzo in time to find a disheveled Theresa and a rather smug Parmenio sharing a cup of hypocras and some sweet cakes, waited on by their servants who seemed more like family.

"You *walked* all the way to the ship?" Parmenio laughed. "One of my *riggazi* could have rowed you there in five minutes."

"I like to see a city. This one is magnificent."

"You have never been here before?" Donna Theresa asked.

"Never," Kronmir admitted.

"Yet your Etruscan is bold and fluid," she said.

He smiled at her compliment. "I thought of being a priest," he said, "and studied for a while in Rhum."

Her smile flickered for a moment. "But you are of Morea," she said.

"I was a contrary youth," Kronmir said.

"You would have to be very contrary indeed to want to leave the benevolence of the Primate of Liviapolis for the rigours of the Primate of Rhum," Parmenio said. "I for one bless the day that Venike chose the imperial primate."

His wife looked at him. Kronmir noted that look, adding it to the very slight hesitation that had come to her when he said "Rhum."

He went up to his room and lay on his bed, opened his shaving kit, and withdrew the folded piece of paper that had been tucked neatly inside.

Kronmir went out a second time with Captain Parmenio in the early afternoon. Both men had appointments at the ducal palace: Parmenio with the naval board, to report on the methods used to combat the sea monsters, and Kronmir to meet with representatives of the Seven.

They shared an *ombre*, a small glass of wine, in a quiet square shaded by a magnificent old tree, and the world did not seem under so much threat, but there was a hush to the city that seemed odd even to Kronmir, who didn't know its rhythms, and odder yet to Parmenio.

"Most of our shipping is here," he said. "Four-fifths of our ships must be in the docks, and no one is under repair."

Kronmir thought, *The old man is thinking of packing his citizens into the ships and running.*

That's how bad he thinks it is.

The two men parted in the great square before the ducal palace and the magnificent basilica. Kronmir went into the church and, after whispering a question, was directed to the priest hearing confessions by the altar of Saint George.

He knelt. The priest was old, with a strong face and a very old-fashioned tonsure.

"What do you call yourself, my son?" the priest asked.

"Dragon," Kronmir said, giving the code of the day.

The priest's breath caught for a moment, and then he knelt beside Kronmir. "I have waited a long time," he murmured.

As it turned out, Kronmir made no confession. In fact, he listened a great deal more than he spoke. An onlooker might have thought it was the priest confessing to Kronmir.

Eventually, he bowed his head, received a blessing, and departed.

When he entered the ducal palace, it was more magnificent than any public building he'd ever known except the throne hall of the emperor in the palace of Liviapolis. The stairs were all marble, and even small stairwells had coffered ceilings, recessed niches of statues—Saint Aeteas repeated endlessly, a superb tapestry of the Battle of Chaluns that filled one huge wall of the waiting room, where more than a hundred gentlemen and women, nobles, and merchants cooled their heels and waited, some with visible anxiety. Kronmir passed his name to the functionary and was almost immediately greeted by a liveried servant in curious white face paint who led him silently to a small door.

"God bless you, brother," said a total stranger. The man made the sign of the cross.

Kronmir understood that the men in the waiting room feared the door he was about to enter. He bowed to the man and ducked through the door.

The stairway climbed away at a steep angle, the stair treads narrow and wooden, but the walls of the stairwell were figured walnut in carved panels that flickered by him in the dim light. He understood few of the scenes, and wondered if he was meant to understand at all. Men were tortured in one, their entrails being pulled out and wound on a spit over a roasting fire painted in lurid colours. In another, two women flayed a man whose face of agony was so lifelike that Kronmir thought perhaps he could hear the scream, and in another a headman's axe descended.

The message was tolerably clear.

Kronmir was alone, as far as he knew, on the stairs, and he wondered what would happen if he simply turned and walked back down, and walked out of the palace and into the great square where men and women walked free and sold fish. He told himself that he had nothing to fear, but despite his life of action, he feared torture. He had many secrets to disclose, and he would attempt to preserve them, and this would cost him much pain and humiliation.

Kronmir knew all this, because he had been taken and tortured before.

His legs continued to take him up the steep steps until he reached the dim light of a single small window, and then he came to a door that was closed. There was nowhere else to go, so he tapped once.

A voice said, "Enter."

Kronmir pushed and the door gave easily. The room beyond was dim but not dark. Four robed figures sat at a bench. All wore red robes and white masks with white wigs.

Kronmir bowed.

All four heads nodded.

Kronmir noted that the bench was sized for more, and he guessed it was intended for seven people. He also noted that the two figures on the left sat very close, so that their hips touched, and the one on the farthest left had a lock of pale golden hair escaping from the wig.

They examined him in inhuman voices for more than an hour, mostly on details of the battles fought with Thorn and the role of the Sieur de Rohan and the Archbishop of Lorica. The questioning on the archbishop became more and more sharply focused.

"And you are absolutely sure," said the woman that Kronmir guessed was the duchess. "You are absolutely sure that this archbishop is dead?"

Kronmir frowned. "Yes," he said.

"Why?" she asked.

"I killed him myself," Kronmir said. He leaned back and folded his arms.

The silence was profound.

"May we speak of your office?" asked a fourth voice, hitherto silent.

Kronmir sighed. "Gentles," he said, "I assume that the custom of ancient times preserves the necessity that you, members of the Seven, should preserve your identities. And that if I should be able to name you...well, it would be rude and even impolitic to do so. And in the same way, I would prefer that my office not be named."

The four conferred a moment.

"I would like to go a step further, gentles. I would like to suggest that I know the source of your discontent. To the outward enemy you add an inward one. You fear that the Patriarch of Rhum, who works actively to eradicate the use of hermetical powers, who claims that there is no power of the Wild and who preaches directly against Alba, and, I understand today, is threatening to preach a crusade— you fear that this voice, the voice of the church, is itself controlled by an enemy."

If his dry assertion that he had personally killed the archbishop had brought silence, this second assertion seemed to quell all comment. The four sat still as plaster images in a church.

Finally, the duchess raised a hand. "We will be in touch," she said.

Kronmir stood. "I am not against you," he said. "But I have my own resources and my own plans. And I must say that there is someone in this city working directly against you. Unless you had me followed here when I was walking with Captain Parmenio, which seems to me a waste of manpower."

"What do you intend?" asked the one he thought to be the duchess.

He bowed. "I will go to Berona and search out Magister Petrarcha. Beyond that, I cannot guess."

She leaned forward. "Will you go to the Darkness?" she asked.

Kronmir smiled. "If the Darkness can be said to have an edge," he said, "and if I learn the appropriate information from the magister, I will go to that edge, and see what can be seen."

She spoke in an inhuman, multitone voice. "We approve," she said. "We will support this."

All four heads bowed, and Kronmir went back down the stairs. His emergence was greeted with a heavy silence, and Kronmir had to assume that more footsteps went up than came down.

Parmenio was nowhere to be found, but Kronmir bowed to Master Atkins, who was waiting for his own interview in the naval department. Kronmir was not used to reassuring people, but he spent a moment to tell Atkins, in his smooth Alban, that he had nothing to fear from the Venikan naval department, and he repeated his words to young Kieron.

The weather mage was dressed in a very long gown, almost a fashion of another age, and wore his hood up despite the warm weather outside. Kronmir had much to do, but he was almost certain he'd be dead if not for Kieron, so he made the time.

"A walk with you, Magister," he said.

Kieron looked at the number of people waiting ahead of him and bowed. "I'm not a magister," he said. "A mere student."

The two of them passed outside unchallenged, and into the square. Kronmir immediately detected one of his surveillants from the morning, and he made no attempt to make the woman's life difficult. Instead, he walked with Kieron to near the center of the square, under the marvelous clock tower.

"Listen. I think you saved all of our lives. I wish to do you a favour." Kronmir wished he had the time to be more careful. Or less blunt.

Kieron bowed, face mostly hidden.

"It appears to me that you are a woman," Kronmir said.

Silence. Around them, hawkers sold curious toys and pilgrims badges and two prostitutes called their skills to the crowd. They seemed to be bidding against each other in levels of obscenity.

"My understanding is that you will be welcome here for your skills. But these people are deeply suspicious of anything hidden, and with reason. I recommend you appear as a woman, apologize to Captain Parmenio for the deception, and move on. Women are more nearly equal here than at home."

Kieron bowed. "I am what I am," he said.

Kronmir had the sticky feeling that he had interfered in something, and his interference was not wanted.

"I will leave you to it, then, with my thanks," he said. He bowed, and left the mage standing amid children playing with new baubles.

He himself joined one of the throngs of religious pilgrims. He looked at them, and thought about religion, which didn't usually interest him much. He thought about the Archbishop of Lorica and his actions. It had never occurred to him before that the archbishop's program in Alba was one of deliberate obstruction and sabotage.

He saw a doublet that he'd registered earlier, and something clicked in his busy mind, and he bowed to a pretty woman and slipped down a flight of steps to water level and boarded a water taxi just pushing out from a jetty. Two men on the bridge above him leaned out, both dressed as pilgrims, and Kronmir saw the twinkle of sun on metal and he rolled and shot before he considered his actions.

The man leaning out from the bridge crumpled, arms outstretched toward the water, and then, very slowly, slumped forward and fell off the low bridge into the canal just aft of the water taxi.

The other man ran.

The waterman in the stern had eyes as wide as dinner plates. But he kept poling.

A large steel spike was inches deep in the floorboards of the taxi, and a little water seemed to be coming in.

The waterman's eyes went from the spike to Kronmir.

Kronmir leaned down and placed a gold coin on the steel spike, and looked up at the waterman. He nodded, pursed his lips as if he'd just smelled something bad, and looked elsewhere.

Kronmir's sense of urgency peaked. He had intended to wait for Lucca's recovery but now had little choice. At the palazzo, he checked on his apprentice and exchanged a few quiet comments and two codes. He packed a small script, like any pilgrim on the road.

He met Parmenio in the hall.

"You are leaving?" Parmenio said with a bow. "You are good company and you're welcome here..."

Kronmir smiled. "As are you, and your selection of books is a delight. I must meet all your authors! But listen. I must be away, and your wife knows why. I need transportation to the mainland. And perhaps a horse." He shrugged. "A guide would not be amiss, either," he admitted.

Donna Theresa emerged from the hall. Her severe face was tense, but she granted him a deep curtsy. "Master Kronmir," she said.

They know my name.

"All is arranged, including the guide," she said. "Go. With God. And all our hopes."

Kronmir nodded. He was not particularly good at having allies, but he tried to be gracious. "I will certainly need local help," he said. "And horses. Someone just tried to kill me."

Parmenio's face grew red. Theresa shrugged.

"It is pilgrimage season, and our city is full of visitors. We screen them for disease and for weapons, but we cannot be perfect. We will apprehend those responsible. All day, as you moved, our people were following those who followed you."

Kronmir bowed, deeply impressed. "I look forward to working with you, *ma donna*, and I see that you are as good at your business as your husband is at his."

She curtsied. Kronmir and Parmenio exchanged an embrace, and Kronmir set out.

Before the sun set, he was landing at a small town in the middle of a vast marsh. In the last light, he saw a causeway running away to the west into the marshes with a good road atop it. There was a storm to the west, the lightning and the thunder rolling at him like a harbinger.

He was met at the pier by a young fisherman who escorted him to a sailor's inn where he had a clean bed, on which he sat while he sharpened his sword and poisoned the darts for his balestrino. Before it was time to sleep, a nondescript man in plain clerical brown appeared, fluffed his pillow, and settled into the armchair without a word exchanged.

When Kronmir awoke Brown was gone, but the man was only as far as the main room, where he was eating a breakfast of fish stew, slightly cold, as the maid had forgotten him, as people usually did. Kronmir sat separately, relished his fish stew and his small beer, and failed to hide his startlement when the duchess ducked her head and entered the low door. She was dressed like a man, in doublet of green wool and plain black boots. The maid curtsied and they spoke. Then she came to his table.

"May I sit with you, Master Kronmir?" she asked.

He nodded.

Her eyes flicked to Brown. "He is wonderful," she said.

Kronmir scratched under his beard.

"I am your guide," she said.

"Is this some misplaced chivalry?" he asked.

"No," she said. "I am down to about forty people I trust, and the one that can be spared just now is me."

Kronmir noted that with her nails trimmed close and all the rings stripped away, her hands looked very competent.

"We can be in Berona this evening if we ride hard. I have two changes of horses arranged, and the Tyrant will receive me, where he might ignore you."

"You have nothing to prove to me, Donna. I have worked with women all my life." He rose.

She smiled. "Well," she said. "That will make a refreshing change. Usually, I have to train each man to my hand, like a falcon."

Kronmir looked away. "I sense we could be uneasy allies," he said.

She shook her head. "No. We are, truly, at your service, and despite my husband's distaste for warrior emperors, you are virtually our only hope of salvation. But...I must see this Darkness for myself."

The quarter hour rang from the church, and they were ahorse, the three of them, with three more horses behind them. They rode quietly until they were clear of the town, and then the duchess leaned forward on her horse's neck and broke straight into a gallop. The two men followed, and the three of them pounded across the long causeway and onto the road through the marshes, and the duchess led them, never glancing back, until the horses were lathered in sweat and the long-awaited rain began to come down. Then she reined in, opened her saddlebag, and pulled out a cloak.

"You'll find the same in each," she said.

Brown quietly transferred the saddles to fresh horses, and they ate slices of bread spread thickly with goose liver ground fine with pepper, and drank a little wine. The rain went from a scatter of drops to a downpour.

They rode across the rainy morning, and as the noon bells rang they rode into a fine town with a magnificent cathedral and more churches than Liviapolis. Brown, whose indescribable face seldom changed expression, registered satisfaction.

The duchess raised an eyebrow.

Kronmir shrugged. "What should I call you?" he asked.

"Call me Giselle," the duchess responded. "Also, please allow me to save you time and insist that I'm quite as fond of my husband as any man I've met, and that a day's riding never raises the least amorous thought in me."

Kronmir couldn't think of what to say in response to this flat delivery, but he decided to smile. "I do not think I deserved that yet," he said.

"Exactly," she said. "That's the time to say such things. In my experience."

"Do we expect to be attacked?" Kronmir asked as they remounted on fresh horses. Vadova, as the city was called, seemed to abound in good food and beautiful horses.

She shrugged. "Why?"

"I was attacked yesterday. In Venike." He shrugged.

"I know," she admitted. "We caught the man you didn't kill. That's when I decided to come myself."

Kronmir paused. "Am I allowed to know why?" he asked. It was like flirting, conducted with pieces of information.

"Because he was one of the Corners' most trusted people," she said. She glanced at Brown. "You trust him?" she asked.

"As much as I trust anyone," he said.

All three of them were soaked to the skin by the time they entered Berona—soaked, and stiff as boards. Kronmir could just manage to walk, and his memory of the crossing of a high pass was so hazy that he wasn't sure he hadn't dreamt part of his day away.

They were ushered into a fortress—another magnificent building in the local style, a great castle of red brick. The guards were alert despite the weather, and Kronmir noted, favourably impressed, that every man-at-arms on duty had full harness and polished silver despite the rain, and that the captain of the guard was polite but very careful with them.

For example, he took all of Kronmir's weapons. He remained courteous as the arsenal was disclosed. Giselle smiled and handed over a sword and dagger, prettily handled in Umroth ivory, and they were escorted into a superb hall, illuminated with tall windows all along the south side, and with frescoes from floor to ceiling.

The Tyrant, as he was sometimes known—Il Conte to his own circle—was a dark-haired, handsome man of middle height. He had a pointed black beard and heavy brows, but his intelligent face and elegant dress relieved him from a look of brutality, and he moved with dignity. Furthermore, he rose as soon as Giselle entered his hall, and came down from his dais to bow to her, as did the men and women of his court.

"*Mi fate honore*," he said. *You honour me.*

The introductions were brief and the formality light. A group of young women began dancing with a dozen of the count's knights. Giselle was taken away, to wash and change.

"You are an officer of *Il cavaliere rosso*," the count asked.

"I am," Kronmir said with a bow.

"Tell me," Il Conte Simone asked. "Is he the very paragon of chivalry that has been described to me?" He leaned forward. "Is it true that he killed the Galle de Vrailly in single combat?"

Kronmir bowed. "So I understand."

"How I wish to have seen this!" the count murmured. "The woman currently calling herself Giselle says that perhaps he will come here."

Kronmir bowed again. "It is possible."

Count Simone smiled. "That would give us some hope," he admitted. "I used to brag that I had the best knights in Etrusca," he said. "And perhaps I do, yet. But my gut tells me that knighthood is no match for the Darkness."

Kronmir spread his hands.

"This is our magister, Master Petrarcha," the count said. "This is one of my staunchest knights, Ser Tomaso Lupi."

Kronmir bowed to each. "Master Petrarcha?" he asked, to be sure.

"Yes," the old man answered.

Kronmir reached into the breast of his doublet and withdrew a scroll tube. He handed it to the old man with a bow. "From Magister Harmodius," he said.

Ser Tomaso smiled as the old man cracked the seal on the scroll tube. "I gather you intend to try to scout the edge of the Darkness," he said.

Kronmir cursed inwardly. "How many people know this?" he asked.

Tomaso made a face. "Perhaps three. Watch the dancers. Comment on how beautiful that woman is. My wife, by the way." He grinned. "The duchess is being very careful. There will be an entertainment and no public gathering. You will leave in the morning, with me as your guide to the hills. When you go to relieve yourself, you will be met."

Kronmir felt naked. "How bad is it?" he asked.

Lupi shrugged. "I trust everyone in this city," he said. "We take these precautions because the duchess asked us. Berona is not Venike, and the Patriarch of Rhum has no friends here."

Kronmir did not protest to this nice young man that almost anyone could be bought, something in which he had some experience.

An hour later, when the dancing—brilliant—and the music—dazzling—was over, and Kronmir had been introduced to the Beronese chivalry; Ser Alessio, Ser Maurizio, Ser Achille, Ser Lucca and a dozen more knights and their ladies. Ser Tomaso introduced him to Sophia di Castlebarco, a famed beauty, and Kronmir allowed himself to be dazzled. But even while playing the courtier, Kronmir noted that Master Petrarcha returned briefly to the hall, met Lupi's eye, and vanished into a dark doorway. Kronmir rose and begged to be excused every eye was on Ser Maurizio and Donna Sophia and he made his exit unnoticed.

He was taken to a bedchamber hung in embroidered linen. The old hermetical master was sitting behind his bedcurtains.

"Really, I'm too old for these games," he said, but he smiled. "I have already prepared your workings. I will offer you another one. My own theory."

Kronmir bowed.

"If this is indeed our enemy from Ifriqu'a," the old man went on, offering a selection of phials of glass, "then I suspect that this will act as a specific against his intentions. I have no idea how long it will last or what side effects it will have." He shrugged. "It is a matter as simple as like to like, however." He nodded. "Or in this case, unlike to unlike."

Kronmir had endured more than a year of Askepiles, and he was used to the torturous reasoning of hermeticists. "What is it, Magister?" he asked.

"Umroth ivory, powdered," Petrarcha said. "The very bones of the not-dead."

Kronmir twitched.

Petrarcha shrugged. "I take it as a sign of hope for us that Harmodius, Al Rashidi, and I all have a common theory," he said. "Let this be my contribution. It should work, but I have no means to test it unless I walk into the clutches of the Darkness myself."

"But you have ingested this?"

"Of course. And so does every ivory worker! It is harmless." He wrinkled his nose. "It stinks, I confess. And the smell lingers," he spat. "As does the taste."

"Why?" Kronmir asked.

"The man who lived," Petrarcha said. "One man. He never even reached the fighting, if I understand him. But nor was he seized in what seemed to have been some hermetical panic, some blind terror that seized the whole host and destroyed it. He alone...ran. While the others...he says they began to fight among themselves, or became demons. Or," he said, "simply fell dead. Or stopped moving, and stood perfectly still."

Kronmir nodded. "But?"

The magister shook his head. "No *but*. I tested him, I pricked him and drew his blood. I have had a month, messire. I have run every test my arts could imagine, and nothing would explain why this simple, mad craftsman in the militia survived where men—men I knew, wearing amulets I crafted myself—died instantly or perhaps turned against their brothers, their fathers, their allies and friends. This Darkness is only perhaps three days' ride away. And we have one survivor."

Kronmir nodded, examining the mage's slight emphasis on the word *craftsman*.

"He was an ivory worker," Kronmir said.

Petrarcha nodded. "Very good."

"Something about the bones of the not-dead confers some immunity," Kronmir said.

"Now that I have this missive from Harmodius," Petrarcha said, "I am even more confident."

Kronmir felt his heart rate accelerate, even though he was safe in a palace surrounded by men-at-arms. "Master, if the enemy is this powerful, why have they not taken all Etrusca?" He looked at the rough map that the magister had appended to his written notes. "If your estimate is correct, the Darkness hovers a few miles from the richest, most populated portion of...of the world. Or at least, of the world we know."

Petrarcha sighed. "I had no idea," he said. "But Ser Tomaso is a widely read young man with a masterful grasp on the story we all call history, and he has a theory that, I am sad to say, stands every test so far."

Kronmir nodded. "Yes?" He waited. "Why is the enemy not coming?"

"Because they do not want Etrusca," Petrarcha said. "Or they do not need it *yet*."

Kronmir winced.

The next morning, they took the road a little after dawn and moved north and east, into low hills and long ridges. They rode around a magnificent lake set in wooded hills, and then took the broad road east to Mitla.

"Mitla is not an ally," Giselle said. "Let me be clear, friends. If the Duke of Mitla knew who I was, he would make me prisoner. At least."

Kronmir thought for a moment, striving to be politic. "But perhaps you then put us all at risk?" he asked.

They rode along for a hundred paces, their horses and the tinker's cart ahead the only noise.

"Master Kronmir, I am no more eager to show you my loaded dice than you are to show me yours," Giselle said. "But I know the ground north and east of Mitla well, and so does Ser Tomaso here."

Kronmir looked at them both.

Tomaso Lupi looked away, into the distant mountains of Sellasia.

"Because you have planned to make war on Mitla?" Kronmir asked.

"If you are so very intelligent," the duchess said, "perhaps you could simply keep your brilliance to yourself?"

Mitla was as quiet as a city of the dead. They came to the great gates—magnificent gates, fifty feet high, set in walls that appeared to Kronmir to be virtually impregnable. The traffic was very light; only a scatter of farmers' carts headed in. Ser Tomaso rode ahead and spoke to a tinker. Kronmir watched him with a critical eye. The knight was good; he bought a small item and paid the top price, a sort of easy bribe. He shook the man's hand as if they were equals, and rode back.

Kronmir disliked the lack of bustle intensely. It made the hair stand up on his neck. The tinker hadn't liked it either, and stopped his cart well short of the gates to set up his little shop.

Kronmir shook his head, fifty paces out from the gates, which were open like mouths set to swallow them, three gates all together.

"I say we go around," he said.

Ser Tomaso and the duchess exchanged a glance.

"It will look odd," the duchess said.

But the Beronese knight nodded. "Not so odd. That fellow says there's an Ifriquy'an horse trader working the north wall." He raised an expressive eyebrow. "Perhaps we can buy a couple of remounts at the horse market on the north walls."

Giselle smiled at Kronmir for the first time. "It cannot be happenstance that there is an Ifriquy'an selling horses at Mitla," she said.

They turned their horses and followed the circuit walls, and the city remained quiet on the other side. There did not appear to be anyone looking over the walls, which itself was odd.

The horse market was virtually empty. There were only two sellers; an Ifriquy'an in a burnoose with the superb horses of his country, and a local seller with warhorses from the plains. The two men were standing together, complaining about the lack of customers, when the duchess approached them. Kronmir studied the horse sellers and remained silent. Giselle negotiated rapidly for four Ifriquy'an geldings and a mare, a large purchase, and M'bub Ali, the horse seller, praised Allah and gave her many deep bows. When she had made her purchases, she went to talk to the local breeder, and Kronmir bowed to the Ifriquy'an.

"It must be a difficult journey with horses, across the sea from Dar?" he asked.

The dark-skinned man bowed. But his smile was genuine and seemed to lighten the creases in his face. "Bah," he said. "I have made it sixty times. I know more about crossing water with horses than any man alive." He grinned more widely. "And I am modest," he added.

Kronmir smiled. The trader snapped his fingers at a boy, and the boy ran off.

"I would have bought the lady coffee, but she was in too great a hurry to have a little *conversatione*," the horse trader said.

"Hmmm," Kronmir said. The horse trader was trying to draw him. "Was the most recent trip any harder than the others?" he asked.

The man's eyes seemed to double their intensity. "That is a very interesting question," he said.

Kronmir shrugged. "I have just come on a voyage myself," he said.

"Ah, I did not think you were from this place," M'bub Ali said. "Although your tongue is very easy."

"I am from the empire across the sea," Kronmir said with perfect honesty.

The boy came back with a brass tray, a pot, and tiny brass cups. Ser Tomaso stopped ogling the warhorses like an adolescent boy in his first brothel and joined them.

Kronmir leaned back against an offered cushion and drank his coffee. "I saw two sea monsters fight," he said. "It made me think that shipping horses..." He let his words go, hoping they would hook the man.

M'bub Ali frowned, shrugged, and drank coffee. "It is a strange time," he agreed.

Jules Kronmir was almost certain that he was dealing with another of his own kind. "Strange how?" he asked. "Strange enough that the Kalif can lose money on fine horses just to gather a little information?"

M'bub Ali paused, his coffee cup on the way to his mouth. His eyes narrowed.

Kronmir closed both eyes and opened them. "We are not from here," he said carefully.

Giselle came back, her business done, and knelt on the horse trader's carpet and took a cup of coffee. She raised it. "My thanks. I love coffee."

M'bub Ali scratched his beard. "Hmm," he said. "Let me just allow you to imagine that this might be true, this thing that you suppose." He shrugged. "Whatever you suppose, it cannot harm me, I think."

Kronmir nodded.

He smiled at Giselle and tried to pass with his eyes that he was engaged in delicate negotiations.

She looked down, he thought in amusement.

"I think we might exchange more than money for horses," Kronmir said. It was too bald. But he was in a hurry, and something about Mitla made him want to leave as quickly as he could.

The horse dealer's eyes didn't flicker.

"Do you know a man named Pavalo Payam?" Kronmir tried. It was a little like a drowning man grasping after a straw.

But in this case, the right straw.

The man's face changed. "That is a very interesting name," he said. "A...friend. A compatriot." He paused. Sipped coffee. And sighed. "And one of my master's most powerful servants. The veritable drawn sword of the faith. The terror of the not-dead."

"I met him in Harndon," Kronmir said.

"In far-off, mythical Alba?" the horse dealer asked with a flash of his teeth. "I begin to think that either you are a snare set for me, in which case I must tell you that my horse boys are very well armed, or that Allah has ordained this meeting."

Giselle leaned forward. "It is the latter, M'bub Ali. We are going to look at what we call the Darkness. Your people face the not-dead. Are they the same?"

M'bub Ali set himself on one elbow and drank more coffee. "I think," he said, "that we should travel a ways together."

They left before dawn, riding east into the red stain of the rising sun. The rain had stopped, and the mountains to the north stood like a stark barrier, capped in white. They rode along the richest agricultural plain that Kronmir had ever seen, past field after field of ripening wheat.

The fields were empty. There were people in the villages, but their doors were locked. There was a steady stream of people passing away south: some dressed as pilgrims, but some obviously fleeing with their animals and their possessions.

The four of them rode into a village with a small inn at noon. The bell rang, and they saw a small market in progress in the square...a dozen peddlers with their packs open, and women buying vegetables from farmers. M'bub Ali and his two horseboys dismounted.

"We are not always well liked," he said.

Giselle nodded. "I understand, but I am quite sure that I can arrange a good reception for you at the inn."

The Ifriqu'an bowed gracefully. "I will await your word, demoiselle," he said.

They dismounted by the inn and took tables under one of the spreading trees.

"I don't believe he's a horse trader," Giselle muttered.

Kronmir nodded. "His hands are strong, but very clean," he said. "He has worn more rings than he does now. And the hilt of his sword..."

Ser Tomaso nodded. "I may lack all your assassin's skills," he said, "but I saw the sword. That's a rich man's sword."

"A rich *swordsman's* sword," Giselle corrected him.

"Amen," Ser Tomaso said, as the wine arrived. Giselle turned to the servant and spoke in rapid patois. The young man nodded twice.

"Of course we will serve your infidels," he said in good Etruscan.

Kronmir sent Brown to fetch M'bub Ali and his men. As he watched, Brown approached a child and gave the little thing a sweet. The child smiled and Brown slipped away. Kronmir took his hand off his sword hilt.

"I am too much on edge," he admitted.

Giselle nodded. "As am I," she said. "Everything seems wrong. I have no benchmark for this sort of thing."

"I found Mitla...very *difficult*." Kronmir rubbed his beard.

Giselle tasted her wine. "Why are they not clearing these villages?" she asked.

Tomaso shook his head. "If Mitla won't, perhaps we should," he said. It was clear that the "we" he intended was Berona, not the four of them.

Kronmir was looking at a man who had to be the landlord, headed for them across the tables in the square. "I'm going to ask. It will save time."

Giselle gave a small nod.

Innkeepers specialize in gathering and dispensing information, and Kronmir was in a hurry and prepared to pay.

The man came up and bowed low. "My son says you have infidels travelling with you. I have never served such before, and it is possible the priest will make trouble." He was apologetic.

He spoke to Kronmir as if the other two did not exist. Kronmir decided to play the situation as he found it. "May I convince you?" he asked, laying a gold coin on the table. It was a round rose noble of Alba, one of the largest gold coins in the world. It was worth twenty-five Venikan ducats; probably a week of profit for the inn.

The man took a deep breath. "You should speak to my wife," he said finally. "She is the last word."

Kronmir nodded at his companions and went to the serving counter inside, where a heavy woman was pouring wine into pitchers.

"Donna?" he asked.

"Who wants to know?" she said. She looked up. "Ah, messire."

"Your husband," he began.

161

"A useless drunk," she spat. "He sleeps all day and eats and drinks free. What lies has he told you?"

"We are travelling with infidels from Ifriquy'a. I wish you would serve them." He laid the yellow gold coin on the counter.

She took it and bit it. "Of course we will serve messire's friends," she said. "The priests tell nothing but lies anyway." She looked over her shoulder. "And more lies of late," she said, looking east.

"Can you tell me what is east of here?" he asked her. Even as he asked, Giselle came into the big room behind him. He tracked her by her footsteps.

The woman frowned. "Vilano is the next town, and then there are hills," she said. "Travellers from Arles come over the pass in good years," she said. "This year, no one since the…" She swallowed. "The battle."

"Has anyone come from Vilano?" he asked. "Today?"

She looked at him, and her eyes were frightened. "I know about the Darkness," she said.

Giselle's breath went in sharply.

The woman's eyes darted around the room. "The priest says we should stay," she said.

Kronmir's eyes met Giselle's.

Giselle put a hand on the woman's shoulder. "The priest…never mind him. Lock your inn and go to Berona. Do not go to Mitla."

"Who are you?" the woman asked.

Giselle smiled. "No one you ever want to meet," she said.

The woman crossed herself. "I will serve your infidels, take my money, and go. Shall I leave the husband?" she asked.

Giselle laughed. It was a brutal, callous laugh, that seemed too old for her, too evil for her golden hair. "Only if you truly hate him," she said.

Outside, the infidels sat at their own table and drank a local grape juice with relish. They also ate six whole chickens.

Giselle nodded and ordered more meat. "I am going to guess this is our last meal for many days." She asked the serving boy to bring them whole sausages.

Kronmir sat with the horse trader. "Will you come with us?" he said.

The man shook his head. "More is not better, in this," he said. "I will ride north from here, as I had planned, and see what I can see. But food is good. Not everyone will sell to a black man. I am lucky I met you." He bowed to Giselle, who had a dozen beef sausages done in a bundle and handed them over.

"You know our ways," he said.

She shrugged. "I serve Venike. We trade with all."

He nodded. Then he glanced at Kronmir.

Kronmir had nothing to lose. "My principal believes that the Necromancer has crossed from Ifriqy'a to take Arles," he said. He raised an eyebrow. "Bah. Precision counts, here. My principal suspects that this is a possibility."

M'bub Ali had a fine red beard, somewhat overdyed with henna. He ran his fingers through it thoughtfully. "This is what I think I see as well," he said. He shrugged. "My master believes it too. We have fought four campaigns this year against the not-dead, but Al Rashidi says this is merely a diversion." He shrugged. "Who *is* your principal?" he asked.

Kronmir smiled. "The Duke of Thrake. Soon, I think, to be emperor."

M'bub Ali smiled. "This is good. A year ago, I confess that news that the lords of the west might come here would have filled me with fear, and perhaps a desire for jihad." He flashed both eyebrows up and down. "Now, it is good to have any ally at all. It is a strange time."

Kronmir nodded. He took a glass phial from his pouch.

The Ifriqy'an took it, shook it, and smiled.

He took an ivory tube from his own sash. "Each of us carries three or more. Have your reasoned this for yourself, or did Payam tell you?"

"Umroth ivory?" Kronmir asked.

"Mmm. I only use the stuff. I don't make it."

Tomaso shook his head. "This Al Rashidi is a famous philosopher," he said. "Magister Petrarcha knows of him. Perhaps they correspond?"

Giselle raised an eyebrow too. "If they didn't before, we must see to it they do now. Anyone have letters? The donna is closing. She will go to Berona."

All of them except Brown wrote notes—even the horse trader.

The infidels were ready first. They packed two heavy skins of current juice and a stack of loaves and beef sausage on two handsome mules, and with a salute of riding whips, rode off north.

East of the town, the fields were empty. Brown met them as they rode past the small manor house of the town's lord, which was empty.

Vilano was less than two miles farther east, across a narrow stream that seemed still full of rage and snow from the mountains.

They rode across the stone bridge and their hooves clattered, far too loud in the still air. No bells rang from the village, and nothing stirred. No chickens called, no birds sang, and no dogs barked. The only animal Kronmir saw moving was a cat, with a dead mouse in her mouth. He watched her until she disappeared with her prey.

Sole survivor?

There were no people.

Kronmir handed his companions each a glass phial of pale dust, and all of them took it with wine. Almost immediately, all four began to cough. The stuff was disgusting, like eating powdered dog shit.

The cough passed, but the tickle at the back of Kronmir's throat was like the harbinger of a winter cold.

Giselle spat. "That was disgusting enough to be truly powerful," she said. She loosened her sword in its scabbard.

Brown raised an eyebrow. He made a sign, Kronmir nodded, and the smaller man turned and rode away south along the stream bank. Tomaso Lupi checked his weapons and stood in his stirrups.

"You think we are close to the Darkness?" he asked. "Blessed Saviour, that tasted like crap."

Kronmir looked around. "I think we are *in* the Darkness," he said.

Ser Tomaso crossed himself. "It is not dark," he said.

"It is a name," Kronmir said.

"A metaphor," Giselle said.

Tomaso spat.

They rode forward for two hours, moving no faster than a walk, raising no dust. Giselle proved a skilled scout; she never broke a ridgeline, and she seemed instinctively to know when to lean low on the neck of her horse. Kronmir watched her carefully.

She had been trained to do these things. Carefully trained.

Toward evening, they were all of them exhausted from a full day of moving from cover to cover. They rode well out of their intended path to climb a long ridge, one of the outliers of the great mountains to the north, a barrier that Etruscans were used to thinking impregnable against their foes. But as they made camp, Lupi regaled them with tales from the time of Saint Aeteas, when the Wild boiled over the mountains and the sorcerer Il Khan penetrated Etrusca as far as Rhum. Giselle watched the woods below them, and Kronmir watched her.

Lupi was easy to read. He moved well, even in armour; he was well-read and probably an excellent dancer. A knight. Kronmir found him unexceptional beyond his obvious intellect and devotion to reading, rare in warriors anywhere.

But the duchess was another matter entirely. It was not that Kronmir disliked or mistrusted her particularly. It was merely that she was an anomaly many times over; a young wife of an old and powerful man, who nonetheless claimed to love her husband; one of the richest women in the world, who nonetheless seemed to possess similar skills to Kronmir himself; a woman of vast political power, risking herself on what had to be a mixture of whim and desperation.

She knew how to build and start a small fire and how to place it among the roots of a great oak tree so that the smoke rose invisibly into the branches. The smell would carry, but neither flame nor smoke would show in the deep valley at their feet.

Nightfall was perhaps more eerie in the Darkness than daytime. Insect noises rose, and Kronmir noted with something akin to relief the rustling of squirrels in the trees.

Lupi sat with his back to the oak. Away to the east, there were lights. West, there was only darkness. "Squirrels," he said.

"And cats," Giselle put in. "And crickets and grasshoppers."

When the sky was a delicate charcoal pink and the first stars were out, there was a rushing noise overhead, and a long cry—a piercing cry like a soul being wrenched down to hell.

Lupi flinched and leapt to his feet. Giselle produced a long knife that Kronmir hadn't seen.

But he knew the sound, and his heart reached to meet it as he imagined other people reached for loved ones.

He rolled to his feet, snatching his armoured gauntlets from the ground and running for the center of their small clearing.

The enormous black-and-white bird emerged from the west, its wings beating hard as it reached, reached for his wrist, straining with its talons, and settled.

Kronmir had handled imperial messengers for years, and never before had one leaned and rubbed its feathered, bicoloured head against his cheek.

Kronmir's lack of empathy was a byword with his colleagues and victims but did not extend to animals. He held its weight by bracing his arm on his saddle, kneeling, and talked to the heavy bird.

"You are very beautiful," he said, "and I am very happy to see you. And oh, my love, you crossed the Darkness, did you not? You crossed. So brave. So *talented*." He turned to the two people at the fire. "Sausage, please," he asked.

Giselle knelt next to him. "I have seen them only in books," she said.

"This one is a she. She has no name, only a number." Kronmir slipped the golden tag on her right leg so he could read it. "Number Thirty-Four," he said.

Giselle patted the bird, smoothing her feathers and offering bits of sausage, which the clever beak took delicately and made to vanish with little tosses of the great, owl-like head.

Kronmir sat again when the bird was fed and opened the sheet that Thirty-Four had brought him. He read it several times.

"News?" Giselle asked.

"Yes," Kronmir said. "The plague is ravaging Alba and Occitan." There was a dense paragraph on the working of gates. No need to share that. "My...employer expects to be crowned emperor in Liviapolis. Very soon. Perhaps this week." He met Giselle's eyes. "I believe he will come here," he said. "He needs to know if the citadel of Arles has fallen."

Giselle made a noise of annoyance. "Of course it has," she said. "The battles were lost almost two months ago. Two of them, or even three." She looked east. "Or four," she said.

"I would appreciate understanding your four battles," Kronmir said carefully.

She shrugged. "We *know* there was a great battle between the Count of Arles and the Wild. By the wild, I do not mean the Darkness. I mean irks, and perhaps these new bogglins."

"Yes?" Kronmir said helpfully.

"Then many Etruscans went north to fight, as many as we could spare from our own defences. I'm going to posit that they fought the Darkness, and lost. And I have to guess, and it is no more than that, that the initial army of the Wild that I faced east of here and that the Count of Arles faced in the north also fought the Darkness, and was defeated by it."

Kronmir pursed his lips. "Why...you think there are more than two sides?"

"Since when does war only have two sides, Master Spy?" Giselle shook her head.

Kronmir shrugged. "You said four," he pointed out.

"Well, at some point the King of Galle went to raise the siege of Arles and died trying," she said. "But I do not know in what order these things happened, and I do not know for sure that the Darkness and the Wild are adversaries. But when we fought in the woods of Istria, I can tell you that the Wild creatures were not on a raid. I saw one of their camps. They were...fleeing. Or moving. Or invading."

"Fascinating," Kronmir said. "Why do you think Arles has fallen?"

"It's been under siege for at least two months," Giselle said.

"It is reputed one of the greatest citadels in the world," Kronmir said. "How far is it?" Kronmir asked.

"Sheer suicide," she said. "Too damned far."

"We haven't been attacked yet," Kronmir said. He'd just been given a two-paragraph outline of the powers of the Odine. The cat, the mouse, and the squirrels made sense to him. In fact, they, and the insects, were evidence of a sort. But the bone powder was clearly unknown at the other end, and that suggested that other things might not be known.

Kronmir opened an oiled leather wallet and extracted writing materials. He had a report, written in code; it covered every aspect of his trip, of Venike and what he'd found there, and even his thoughts about Giselle. He took a fine gold nib, fit it to a steel stylus, and began to write. He disliked writing in front of her; he disliked it more when she helped him by bringing light. He disliked having anyone who even knew he wrote in code.

But he disliked the Darkness more. He wrote swiftly, pen dipping... the day, the insects, the cat. And the performance of Thirty-Four, flying over the Darkness from west to east, as she must have come.

"She cannot fly again for at least twelve hours, and given...the situation..." Kronmir stared out to the lightless west. "Giselle, who are you?"

She smiled, her even, perfect teeth showing neatly. "The wife of the Duke of Venike," she said evenly. "I thought you'd never ask."

Kronmir looked at her. "I think I can take both of you," he said.

Giselle rolled on her haunches. Lupi, who had been cooking, froze.

Kronmir remained still, and his hands didn't twitch. "I am a careful man, and my understanding of this situation is flawed." He looked at her. "But if you do not explain to me how you and your golden hair and flawless skin display so many of the talents of an assassin, I will have to assume the worst."

"Looks are a curse," she said. Her right hand showed the glint of polished metal in the firelight. "I am not an assassin. But I have been a ranger."

"Ranger?" Kronmir asked.

"From Venike, into the mountains. All about us, there are trees. Ancient trees. We keep the borders." She nodded. "We protect the trees." She shuffled. "We fight the things that people think do not exist."

Kronmir thought about that. "Really?" he asked.

She smiled. "Think, Master Kronmir. What is the one thing on which a fleet of warships depends?"

Kronmir understood. "Trees. Old, straight, tall trees."

"It is none of your business how I came to be married to the duke. Only *perhaps* it is your business that I saved him. And we met." She shrugged. "This campsite is one of ours, though we seldom venture into these settled lands. But in the mountains north of Fruli, there are irks and other creatures that the church denies. And here...our ill-feeling for Mitla is not new."

Kronmir nodded, and his hands relaxed. "I find it...unlikely... that a woman of your status would come on such a mission."

She smiled thinly. "You know what is sad, assassin? The world is in danger; may be about to end, for me and mine. My family lives in the plains north of the city. I could lose them very easily. And yet..." She shrugged.

"And yet, you are *happy* to be here." Kronmir nodded.

By the campfire, Tomaso Lupi snorted.

"I am," she admitted. "Out under the trees, on the edge of battle?" She looked at Kronmir. "May we all live?"

Kronmir nodded.

"May I make bold and ask *you* some questions?" she asked.

Kronmir shrugged.

"Where is the small man whose face is so very easy to forget?" she asked.

"Somewhere close," Kronmir said. "He is covering us."

"Doesn't he eat?" she asked.

Kronmir smiled and looked away.

"Let's eat," the knight said. Like any competent huntsman, he could cook in the field, and he'd made them a fine camp dish, cutlets of beef rolled with slices of beef fat and slices of bone marrow, skewered and done on the fire. He'd made eight, and each of them took two. He also produced a bottle of good red wine and a loaf of bread, a little stale, which they toasted on sticks and ate with beef fat.

Kronmir nodded and wiped grease from his beard. "You can come with me any time, Ser Tomaso."

Lupi laughed. "I lived by myself a whole year," he said. "I learned a great deal."

With their cups in their hands, they went to the edge of the bluff beyond the fire. It was fully dark at last, and to the west, the shapes of hills were just visible in the moonlight, but there were no torches, no candles, not a fire burned.

"Am I in command?" Kronmir asked.

The duchess was unreadable in the Darkness. "We are allies," she said. "Not subordinates."

Kronmir considered how little he enjoyed working with amateurs, and contrasted this with the excellence of their camp. "I would like to withdraw from the Darkness the way we came," he said. "I want to move south and release my bird where she will *not* cross the Darkness going home. Then I want to ride west, and see if my guess that the Darkness is roughly circular is correct."

Giselle sighed. So did Tomaso.

"I won't pretend. I'd be delighted to leave this blight and never return," Lupi said.

Giselle nodded. "I feel it like sickness. Those who are chosen to be rangers . . . we are attuned. To the Wild. We do not hate it."

Kronmir nodded. "Of course. To hate the Wild is to fail in understanding."

She grunted, a very un-duchess-like sound. "I need to see what is happening to these people."

"I'm sure we will see," Kronmir said.

Kronmir lay awake, aware that the duchess was also awake. Lupi was on guard. It might have amused him, that all three of them were awake in mutual distrust, but instead it seemed wasteful.

And yet he had a hard time trusting her.

He lay, thinking about her hard hands and soft face, and he felt his irritability and his fear rising. He listened to his heart beat too fast.

What is happening here? he wondered, and for a long moment, he lay wondering if he'd been poisoned.

Thirty-Four was sitting on her makeshift perch, a dead branch laid across two small logs. She continually raised her wings and baited. But she did so in silence, having been trained to be silent. Her rustling disturbed him, and only gradually did he realize that the great bird was as disturbed as he was himself.

He rose, throwing off his blanket and his cloak, and moved to the bird's perch.

"What is it?" Giselle asked.

Kronmir put a hand on the bird and calmed it. As the bird's wings quieted, Kronmir could hear clearly, and he heard wings again.

A vast, slow beating of wings at the very edge of his hearing.

Kronmir listened until he was sure he was not creating the noise out of fear and panic and his own fertile imagination, and then he knelt. "Giselle," he said. "Something is above us. Hunting us."

She came out of her own cloak in a motion largely hidden by the darkness. There was no firelight and no smoke.

"Tomaso!" she called.

The Beronese knight came out of the trees.

"Something above us," Kronmir whispered.

He kept stroking Thirty-Four. Now he was looking up, his attention focused by the bird's agitation.

"See to the horses," Giselle said. "No, I'll go myself," she muttered, and slipped away.

Kronmir stayed, kneeling by the perch. Tomaso slowly cocked his heavy crossbow, a windlass that could put a bolt through an armoured knight and his horse, too. "What is it?" he asked very quietly.

Kronmir shook his head. He heard the long whoosh again, very far away, more the suggestion of sound than a sound.

And then he saw it. Or rather, he saw its absence; the stars went out to the north.

Unbidden, Kronmir's heart began to race as a tenth of the sky was blotted out altogether. He gathered Thirty-Four to his chest and made himself as small as he could.

"Saint Maurizio and all the saints of war!" he whispered. "What is that?"

Then they could hear nothing but their breathing. It was so quiet that they could hear Thirty-Four breathe, and then Giselle was back.

"Brown had the horses. What is it? I feel afraid. I don't even know why!"

"It's big, and it flies," Kronmir said. "I feel...better." He looked at the sky, and it was clean. "I think it's gone."

"I think you are premature," Giselle said. "But I hope you are right."

An hour later they agreed it must be gone, but no one slept.

They retreated from the Darkness with less care than they had entered, and still endured two hours of riding across an empty landscape devoid of life, almost noiseless besides the sounds of insects and the wind on the ripening wheat.

They left the Darkness at the same bridge where they'd entered, and Brown was waiting there, and followed them across. Lupi became cheerful, almost ebullient. Giselle kept looking back.

Thirty-Four rode on Kronmir's saddlebow, her head turning back and forth. She ate every time she was offered food, and when they left the Darkness, she spread her wings and gave a great cry, as if in triumph.

Giselle wanted to return to the small town from which they had started into the Darkness, and they did. To everyone's relief, the inn was unlocked, although the town was virtually deserted. They took food for travelling and left coins on the counter.

Lupi spoke to two old people who sat alone on the steps of the church. "One of my comrades came yesterday and led the people away," he said. "Il Conte has sent knights into the land of Mitla to move the people east if they will go. He has declared a state of siege, although there is no obvious enemy. People are obeying. The priest is a fool, but"—Lupi flourished a heavy bottle—"we'll be the better for it. I told him to go. I told him the Wild was on his doorstep." He looked at Giselle, who frowned.

"Well, my lady, I had to tell him something," he remarked pettishly.

Giselle shrugged. "Rumour will be as much our enemy as the Darkness," she said. "Let's ride."

They rode south for two hours, and Thirty-Four rose from Kronmir's fist to take a bird in the air, which she ate greedily, and then later climbed away to take a small goat, which Kronmir suggested was going to start its own rumour somewhere. She ate the goat more fastidiously, and appeared restored.

In midafternoon, they entered a small village that was empty, but tracks and dung in the streets and on the road south of the village showed that the populace had moved away in a natural way, and they found two old people sitting in the town square, drunk. Most of the livestock had left with the people, but there were pigs out under the trees and someone had left a forlorn dog. Giselle fed the dog, and it followed them.

They rode south, with Kronmir using a staff to take sightings on the mountain peaks of the north. "We are now four miles farther west than last night's camp," he said, in late afternoon.

Giselle nodded. "You do not need to use an instrument to know that," she said.

"I do," Kronmir said. "I need to be *sure*."

"I *am* sure," Giselle said.

Lupi tried, and failed, to hide a smile. He dismounted, and the dog was there again. He went into the woods, came back, and started scratching the dog's jaw.

No expression crossed Brown's face, as usual.

A little later, taking advantage of the long evening, they turned north, and climbed another ridge, lower than last night's but still prominent. There was, at the top, an old fortification of the ancients. It was square, covered in trees, but at the north end of the ridge there was a collapsed tower, an old gate, and a single room preserved by chance.

Closer to, it was clear that it had not been preserved by chance. The old tower's north wall had been carefully repointed, and the single intact room had a working fireplace and a roof. Giselle led the way unerringly.

"Another of your secret places?" Kronmir asked.

"Yes," Giselle said. "I see that you must make an effort to trust us. Let me say that I, in turn, break an ancient rule in leading you to these places."

Lupi looked out over the valley. "I do not think that you two need a guide so much as a referee. Perhaps I might go home to my wife?"

Kronmir smiled at the young knight.

Giselle laughed. "Who would cook?" she asked.

Just for a moment, it seemed that Brown might have smiled.

Thirty-Four hunted again at nightfall and brought back a large piece of a deer, which she laid beside Kronmir with touching grace. He ruffled her feathers and helped her clean the blood off her talons, and Lupi took the meat and turned it into a stew with herbs. Thirty-Four shared the scraps with the dog.

Kronmir penned his thoughts and observations from the day at the base of his report, rolled it fine, and tucked it in the tube for the bird's right leg.

In the morning, after taking a sausage, she launched away from the rising sun, and they saw her powerful wings taking her higher and higher as she bore away west, travelling in almost a straight line.

Two hours later, they crossed back into the Darkness. None of them wanted to, and the dog sat and howled. But in the end it followed them.

Now they were attuned to it, and they all felt it as soon as they entered, even without the dog's howls, the horse's pricked ears, and their own immediate depression of spirit. Once again they swallowed doses of the horrible powder, and then they rode north and a little east, going deeper and deeper in. Before noon, they reached a village that was utterly silent.

Just west of the village, Giselle, casting wide, found tracks.

The tracks went straight. They were as unnatural as the silence, because the whole trail ran almost as straight as a tailor's ruler, and every person walking had a stride of exactly the same length. The trail didn't go around a pigsty or a low stone wall. It went straight over both, so that all those who made the trail crossed the same rambling stone wall four times in twenty paces.

Giselle walked around and back, and Kronmir followed the trail up to the edge of the deep woods. There was birdsong in the woods.

"This morning," Giselle said, her eyes everywhere. "Last night at the earliest."

"I think I should go on alone," Kronmir said.

"I don't think you'd make it," Giselle said. "I'd like to send Tomaso home."

Their eyes met.

But Tomaso shook his head. "Do not disgrace me," he said. "I am a knight."

Giselle put a hand on his. "Ser Tomaso," she said. "It is very likely we will all die."

"Or worse," said Brown, the first words he'd said in days.

Ser Tomaso made a brave face. "Perhaps," he said. "But we will eat well."

They went up the ridge into the woods following the straight trail, which went over the top of a low ridge, through the woods, and down the other side. At a ten-foot drop, there were two bodies. One was dead, and one had broken both legs and a number of other bones and lay, perfectly silent, eyes open.

Alive.

Or not.

"Stay back," Kronmir said. His balestrino was in his hand.

"Hello," he called.

Not a blink.

"Hello?" he said again, edging closer.

Giselle coughed. "That's why they're called *not-dead*," she said. "Because they're not. Dead."

Kronmir had, of course, heard. But he had never seen. "Christ," he swore.

The dog began to bark.

The not-dead face was smooth and devoid of thought. The eyes—the body was that of a young, active, handsome man—were open wide.

The other body's eyes were closed.

Giselle was looking at the tracks.

"They all came this way," she said. "The first one fell and died. Or whatever happens to them when their spinal cord snaps. The second fell atop, and the third went around, leading the others. Here." She pointed to a new path, a few paces off the line of the original, that descended sharply away downhill.

Kronmir began to understand. Or thought he might.

The dog's barks rose to a crescendo.

"There is but a single will," he said. "They have a little volition, but not much."

Her head turned sharply, and just at that moment, the eyes of the body at his feet focused.

The body seemed to exhale a mist—tendrils of pale grey that moved almost as fast as thought: a dozen reaching for Kronmir and the rest reaching for Giselle.

Kronmir rolled to his right and put his bolt into the thing's head. The eyes closed immediately—the black poison was the deadliest hermetical toxin known to the empire.

The wormlike tendrils thrashed, a few inches from Kronmir's face, and then crumpled to dust and blew away on the summer breeze.

The dog was growling, the hair on its neck and back standing up like a garment it was wearing, making the dog look alien, feral, and dangerous.

Kronmir spat. He breathed out, very carefully, as he backed away, the same technique he would have used if he'd been under threat of a poison gas or a venom. He spat again and looked at Giselle, who was frozen in place.

He watched her carefully as he reloaded his weapon and ignored the dog.

"Look at me," he said softly.

Her eyes moved. "One of them touched me," she said. The fear in her voice was controlled. But very close to the surface. "Blessed Mother of the Forests. I saw it close. It had a tiny mouth. Oh Virgin Goddess..."

She fell to her knees.

"What's happening down there?" Lupi called.

"Do *not* come down," Kronmir called. "Giselle. Look at me."

She did.

He drew a glass phial from his belt pouch. "I'm not willing to come in range of your arms," he said. "I'm sorry. Can you catch?"

"I think so," she said tightly.

He tossed the phial, and it flashed in the air. But her arms only spasmed and didn't move.

"It is trying to take me," she said.

"Try to defeat it," Kronmir said.

"Kill me if I lose," she said.

"Of course," he said. "Now make your body bend and take the phial."

"It is toying with me because it wants *you*," she said.

"How would you lure me to come to you?" Kronmir asked.

She coughed a little. And fell to her knees.

She'd fallen the wrong way, too far from the phial.

"Brown," Kronmir said.

"Right here," the man replied.

"I'm going to try to save her. You see how it works."

"Yes, boss."

"If I fail, kill us both and go. Report to Petrarcha all you have seen. That is the whole of your duty." Kronmir placed his unloaded balestrino gently on the ground.

"Yes, boss. How will I know if you are alright?" Brown asked reasonably.

She was losing.

"If you can't trust us, kill us," Kronmir said. He took out yet another phial and, turning his back on her, consumed the contents. He coughed.

"This ain't like you, boss," Brown said.

Kronmir agreed, but he moved forward anyway, unarmed. Unarmed, so that if he fell to the thing, Brown could kill him the more easily.

She was on the ground. But of course, the *will* rolled her over now, even as he knelt swiftly beside her.

She gagged.

The dog's growls deepened. It was almost like a low song of hate.

"Look at me," he said.

It wanted him closer. He moved close enough... almost... to kiss her. His left arm went to hers, and in the time between one heartbeat and another, he had her in a joint lock.

The *will* struggled.

It made no difference to Kronmir's lock.

The tendrils of pale grey smoke began to gather around her mouth, and her eyes reflected the horror of her inner struggle.

His left hand went deep behind her, like a cruel lover's, and took her hair and snapped her head back, and his right hand, armed with the phial from the ground, dumped its contents between her lips even as the grey tendrils batted about his eyes, wormlike segments pulsing, tiny, tooth-filled mouths ravenous and like a minute vision of hell. Then he put a thumb to her throat and forced the swallow reflex just as he would in making a man take poison, and rolled over her, scissoring his legs in the air and thrusting free of her with his arms.

He landed on one knee and raised his hands.

She was on her hands and knees, vomiting.

"Say something, boss," said Brown.

"Calpurnia," Kronmir said. An operation performed long ago, in flawless secrecy.

"True for you, boss. Although a damned odd choice." Brown was still looking along his weapon. "As we failed."

"No, everyone who hired us died. We didn't fail." Kronmir moved a little farther from the duchess. "The Darkness can't get us easily, thanks to Master Petrarcha, but it can get us."

"Her?" Brown asked, his voice perfectly steady.

Kronmir had a rare desire to go somewhere and shake. "Give her time."

"You sound like you," Brown said. "Except for the whole saving-other-people part."

"I try never to lose an agent," Kronmir said.

"Eh," Brown said. "True for you, boss."

An hour later, Giselle was sitting at a small fire. Her colour was returning.

Kronmir sat with her, and Brown sat well away, with three loaded crossbows.

"Tell me what you remember," he said gently.

She took a deep breath. "It was fucking *inside me*." She breathed. "It was eating me. Inside. I could feel it. My—spirit. I still feel the wounds." She looked out across the valley. "But it was slow. I could feel that too. I saw it . . . in images. Oh, this is foolish, but it was as if—have you ever come across a corpse, and when you touch it . . . it is not the dead thing, but only its shape? And the hole of the thing's substance is maggots?"

Kronmir looked away. "I can't say I have had this experience," he said.

"I have. In the woods. And that is what it wants to do to me. And when it does this, it feeds. And keeps me a slave. A bag of maggots."

"Is it still in you, Giselle?" Kronmir asked gently.

"How will I ever be sure?" she asked.

Kronmir left her by the fire and went to the two men across the clearing.

Ser Tomaso was cooking, as much to fill time as because anyone was hungry.

"I should kill her," Kronmir said.

"You what?" Ser Tomaso asked. He had been crouched by the fire, but now he stood.

"I should kill her," Kronmir repeated.

Brown nodded.

Lupi shook his head. "She's the Duchess of Venike! You cannot just kill her. I'll take her back…"

"If the Darkness has her," Kronmir said, as gently as he could, "her position as duchess would probably guarantee the complete collapse of northern Etrusca. She could be the center point for…" Kronmir searched his mind for the word he wanted. "For the infection. She could subvert and sabotage. Frankly, I cannot even guess what she could do. Is your soft heart worth the deaths of everyone you love, Ser Tomaso?"

"You saved her, boss," Brown said. "Odd call."

"I propose that you, Master Brown, take Ser Tomaso back to Berona and report to Magister Petrarcha everything you have seen here. Everything. And then await orders."

Brown shrugged. "I obey. You know that."

"I think we may need to do something about the Patriarch of Rhum," Kronmir said.

"I'll look into it," Brown said.

"I hope to be back in five days," Kronmir said. "I'll take Giselle. By the end of the mission, she will or will not be fit to…trust."

"That thing got into her mind," Brown said.

Lupi shuddered.

"If it gets you—" Brown raised an eyebrow.

"Best be sure that doesn't happen," Kronmir said. "It can't be you."

"It won't be me. There isn't enough gold in all the world to pay me to go to Arles," Brown said. "I'll tell you this for free. I think you should walk away. After you waste the duchess." He shrugged at Tomaso. "Sorry."

Kronmir nodded slowly.

"I'm sorry you have to hear all this," Kronmir said to the knight.

Lupi shook his head. "I do not want to know more," he said. "But I will guess that if you kill the duchess, you will kill me as well. In fact, I will insist upon it, because I could not stand such dishonour." His voice shook.

Kronmir looked at the stars rising above them, and at the silent, darkened plain at their feet.

"No," he said. "I will kill neither of you." He pursed his lips.

Brown made a little motion with his head, and shrugged. "I will see about the Patriarch," he said. "Listen, boss, I can do the woman for you, if it's a personal thing."

Lupi put his hands over his ears.

Kronmir shook his head.

"This ain't like you," Brown said.

Kronmir pursed his lips. "I know what I'm doing," he said.

Brown shrugged. "Sure, boss," he said. "I expect you want me to take the dog?"

Kronmir looked at him.

Brown nodded. "You didn't want me to save the dog?"

"I didn't give it any thought," Kronmir said.

Brown nodded. "Good to know it's you, in there. But I'll take the dog."

In the morning, the two men rode away south, moving quickly. The dog followed Lupi very willingly.

Kronmir and a very quiet Giselle rode north, down the ridge and then through a silent town and across the great plain. The sun rose, hot and yellow, and their shadows seemed like black pools at their feet as they rode, and their horses began to flag just after noon.

Giselle had not spoken all day. Kronmir was still tracking the people of the village, and they had joined another trail and another and another, until they had all reached one of the main roads. He guessed they were now thirty or forty hours behind the tracks.

"They know we are here, now," Giselle said.

Kronmir looked at her.

"Even as we ride toward them, they are sending agents to us," she said.

"You know this?" he asked carefully. He'd had a weapon covering her all day.

"No," she said. "But I am guessing that's how they work."

"They?" he asked.

She shrugged. Her shrug made him relax. It was the same half-angry, half-amused shrug, the shrug of a woman used to men taking her for granted or assuming her ignorance on matter of which she was truly expert. It was a complex muscle movement, a subtle social cue.

And thus, not something easily pretended by the not-dead.

"I read them as them," she said. "I'm not really ready to discuss it," she went on. And a little later, "You have me with you in case you have to put me down," she said.

"Yes," he said.

"I understand," she said. "You saved me yesterday," she said.

"Yes," he admitted. "I still don't know what came over me." He tried a laugh.

She smiled.

He nodded. "Humour," he said. "Interesting." He paused. "How many are they?"

She shrugged. "I think they are legion," she said. "But they are like a chorus. Or several choirs." She closed her eyes.

Kronmir watched her. "Interesting," he said.

Late afternoon, and they saw dust on the road. Kronmir got them off the road into a patch of woods and laid the gem that contained Magister Petrarcha's small working in the road, and he smashed it with the hilt of his dagger, crushing the stone to powder.

Almost immediately, he was facing an image of himself. "Declare yourself!" it said.

He smiled and replied, "A fool." He stepped back and left the image of himself standing with a horse in the middle of the road. The simulacrum was excellent, delicately coloured, and so realistic that every time it spoke, Kronmir was tempted to turn his head.

He slipped into the trees, and just for a moment he knew fear. Giselle was not where he had left her. She had, instead, moved into better cover to the right and had further begun to weave a screen of branches.

He joined her, and they raised the screen before a dozen men, all walking swiftly, came over the next low hill and marched, in step, along toward Kronmir's double, who, as if trained, drew his sword, waved it, and demanded that they identify themselves.

They, for their part, halted. It was not like watching a man stop walking. They all simply *stopped*, together, better than the best soldiers ever trained.

"Oh Virgin Goddess, I feel it," she said.

Kronmir wasn't really so interested in the manifestation of the Darkness taking place in broad daylight on the road. He was more interested in her reactions, and he used his peripheral vision.

Out on the road, a grey mist rolled forward, over the simulacrum, which was not, however, affected.

Kronmir smiled a nasty smile. "It is a terrible thing when you depend entirely on one sense," he said. "Score two to our magister."

She shook her head.

"The things operate on sight alone. Or so I guess." Kronmir nodded. "Let's be on our way."

"Let's end them first," she said.

"I can't let you inside their reach," Kronmir said. "And our horses are not protected. I think that the loss of the horses would be the start of the end."

"You have a plan?" she asked.

He nodded. "I do," he said. "And if you are still recovering by this time tomorrow, I'll assume it is safe to tell it to you."

She managed half a smile. "You are too kind," she said.

They made no real camp. No fire, no beds. Each took turns lying quietly. Kronmir didn't trust the duchess enough to sleep, and he suspected from her breathing that she didn't sleep either. Yet nonetheless he was rested in the morning and ate his garlic sausage ravenously.

Giselle ate too. "I want coffee," she said suddenly.

He smiled, and then frowned as tears came to her eyes and she turned away.

She turned back, rubbing her face with a grubby hand. "I want something," she said. "I have not wanted anything since...they... tried for me."

Kronmir was fascinated. "You keep calling the thing *they*."

She shrugged. "I felt them. They are...a mare's nest of thought. Of *will*. Worse than a single will." She shook herself. "I have no experience with which to compare...it is not enough to say I was violated. I was...*taken*."

Kronmir had both their horses tacked. He'd prepared hers to keep her talking. He didn't like the way his spare riding horse was acting. The gelding was tossing his head and rolling his eyes and there was something he didn't like, and Kronmir listened to horses. He looked carefully, and listened, and calmed the gelding.

Then he walked back to Giselle, and sat with his back against a great old tree, facing her.

"You were not taken," he said.

She looked at him with a spark of anger in her eyes.

"It will grow more important to you as the days pass," he said mildly. "What story you tell yourself about yourself. I think that thing almost defeated you, and it left you with doubts, but this is what I saw. I saw you fight it. I saw you take action to save yourself, to the best of your abilities, and I saw you hold some ancient evil back long enough for me to get the medicine into you."

She was gazing into his eyes like a lover.

"This thing has undermined your image of yourself. It has told you a story that you are starting to believe. It is still in you, still working. You can defeat it with will. Your will." He stood up.

She looked away, hiding her eyes. "I dislike being taught by men," she said.

He shrugged, and took no offence. "Imagine me a woman, then," he said. "Let's ride."

He led them up the next ridge. The ridges were beginning to come more frequently, like wrinkles in a blanket, and he had a notion that the not-dead would stay in the valleys. The not-dead, as far as he could observe, did very little, and only when they were touched by the *will*. Climbing took effort. They seemed to exert as little effort as possible. Or perhaps, their masters were the ones saving effort.

And, he thought, they depended on sight very heavily. And didn't seem to be able to see in the dark.

Kronmir turned to his companion. "Do you have access to power?" he asked.

She shook her head. "None," she said. "You do know how rare it is here? Magister Petrarcha represents a level of power we haven't seen in five generations. It is much more common in Ifriqu'a and Nova Terra."

He nodded. She spoke naturally, in complete thoughts.

"There are better ways of travelling these ridges," she said suddenly. "If that's your plan."

He smiled. "Lead me, then."

She took him at his word and cut her horse in front of his, and took a much steeper route for almost an hour. It wasn't brutal; it merely killed conversation and took them up a deep gorge littered in rocks tossed down both slopes like a child's playthings. Most of the rocks were bigger than the big gelding; smaller rocks rolled under their feet, making the footing treacherous for human or horse.

But two-thirds of the way up the little valley, a path appeared at the base, winding between boulders, fitful at first and then bolder and wider.

"Really just a cattle path," she said, and examining a round cowpat. She dug in it with a stick, exposing the fly eggs, her reins across her left shoulder. "Four days old," she said. "Maybe five days old."

They went along the ridge for several miles, and the mountains rose ahead of them and to the north.

"You plan on going all the way to Arles?" she asked.

"I don't know yet," he said. "I'm not sure what I'm doing or what I'm looking for."

She nodded. "That's the everyday life of being a ranger," she said. "We have to cross the valley at some point. There's a stream—quite a deep stream. There's a stone bridge. The next ridge is higher, as you can see, and ten leagues long. After that—" She shrugged. "After that, it's mountains and mountain forests." She met his eye, and hers were clear. "It's more than a hundred miles to Arles and we only have food for two days." She frowned. "And at some point, we have to go over the big mountains, and that means one of the passes."

He was watching the valley floor. "We can steal food," he said. "What do the not-dead eat? They aren't dead. They are still alive."

She shook her head. "No idea."

"I need to catch one and kill it," Kronmir said. "Perhaps more than one."

She took a breath. "It doesn't trouble you that these are people, who have had their minds taken over?"

He thought for as long as it took his horse to reach down, pluck a tender shoot from an old stone wall, and chew it. "I suspect it would be better to tell you that it doesn't trouble me," he said. He watched her carefully now. "But the truth is that I cannot cure them, and I do not know them as people, and this is my mission, and it must be done."

"What if there is a way to save them all?" she asked.

Kronmir shrugged. "Perhaps. If there is, Harmodius or Petrarcha will find it. I won't. But I can help them by learning the parameters of the threat. By gathering intelligence. This is what I do. We need to know what kills them."

"Whatever kills the living," she said.

"No," he said. "Give me your hand," he said.

She extended her hand willingly enough.

He took the pricker, four inches long, a needle of steel, from his knife scabbard, and stabbed the palm of her hand.

"Ow!" she spat. "Damn you!"

He withdrew the pricker, which had gone right through her palm like a stigma. "Ow?" he asked.

"Fuck," she said. She sat staring at her hand. As she stared, it began to heal. Before her eyes.

"Oh Huntress!" she said.

"You are afraid?" he asked.

"Yes, damn you to seven hells!" she spat.

He nodded. "You are recovering."

She turned. "You think so?" she asked.

"Yes," he said simply. *Simple lies were better.*

They rode down the steep slope, both of them skilled riders who could manage the ground. They emerged from cover carefully, about three hundred paces from the bridge. Almost immediately they came to the corpses.

Kronmir rode along, looking down.

Mostly they had been dogs. A few had been goats, and two had been children, although the desiccated corpses were like unwrapped mummies, something of which Kronmir had a little experience.

"This is how they end," he said.

She dismounted, and he readied his weapon. Just in case.

She rolled the girl child over. She had had long, chestnut hair, and it was still bright, and had a ribbon in it, an incongruous horror over the skull-face and shriveled lips drawn back from her healthy teeth.

He moved among the corpses.

"All about the same weight," he said.

She was already working to bury the two dead children.

He joined her.

The graves were shallow, but then, there wouldn't be any scavengers for some time. They both washed in the stream, and he looked down into the water and saw trout in the mountain stream.

"You think this is about will?" she asked suddenly.

"Yes," he said. "That is, no, I don't perceive that you or I have the will to resist these things. But in the state in which you are now, yes. And you are winning."

"And you are an expert," she said.

He shrugged. The both remounted, watched the valley carefully, and rode for the next ridge. There was a road on the far side of the bridge, and it was deeply trodden. She looked at the tracks, and he turned his head away.

"So many," she said.

"Mitla?" he asked.

"No. If it were Mitla, there'd be a river of not-dead," she answered. "This is a thousand people and as many animals. I don't know... I've never had to track a horde. But not fifty thousand. Saint Michael protect me."

"Fifty thousand people," Kronmir said. He considered. "This thing has to be stopped before it gets to the cities," he said.

She raised an eyebrow. "You have a plan to stop it?"

He shook his head. "No," he admitted. "Not yet."

They made it to the end of the next ridge before daylight failed them, and the ridge ended in a cliff with a view over a dozen miles to the mountains rising like a wall, a great slope rising, grass covered above the tree line, to a high pass far above them that contained the road to Arles.

A steady stream of beings, smaller at this distance than ants, toiled up the immense slope toward the pass. From his vantage point, Kronmir could only see them as a thin black thread, but given the distance, it was a matter for awe.

And at their feet was the tail of the immense snake of not-dead. A column that covered a mile or more, fifteen or twenty wide; animals and men and women and children all intermixed. They walked in step, all together, so that the entire column seemed to bob in unison.

"Ten thousand people," he said.

"Your math is very good," she said with some asperity.

They picketed their horses and sat with their backs against two different trees.

"Trust me yet?" she asked.

"Almost," he said. He got up, fetched a shovel, and walked around their clearing, looking at trees. Finally he chose one. He began to dig.

Later, they shared cheese and bread. The bread was stale and delicious. The cheese was marvelous.

"I don't want to die," she said.

He made no reply beyond a smile.

"Do you mean that if I were to surrender to it, I would become one of them?" she asked quietly.

He shrugged. "I really have no idea. I suspect it has…allies. I have no notion of what bargain you can strike with it. I believe it is still…aware…of you."

Her eyes widened in the last light. "Do you? Won't it send some of its people for me?"

He nodded. "I hope so."

She let her eyes meet his. "I am your bait?" she asked.

Kronmir thought a moment. "Yes," he said.

An hour later he heard the whooshing sound again, louder and closer than the first time, and he rolled out of his blankets and moved to his tree, but the sound diminished.

"What is it?" she asked.

"I don't know," he said. "But it appears that it hunts by sight, even at night. We are being hunted. It knows where we are. It wants you."

Her eyes shone in the darkness. "Fuck," she said.

Kronmir smiled, and went to check his trap and man his station. He watched a long time, and saw nothing more.

They came when the sky was just beginning to whisper of a coming day. They were not very quiet, and three of them went into his net trap immediately.

The rest went straight for him, not her. He was lying with his head on his saddle, and the first not-dead, a big man-at-arms in armour that still appeared shiny and well kept, swung a heavy poleaxe at his head.

The weapon passed through his head and struck the saddle.

The simulacrum vanished.

Kronmir leaned out from the branch of his tree and put a dart behind the man's ear, and the man fell, skin blackening, eyes already blank.

There were almost a dozen of them coming into the clearing.

Giselle had a little bow, no longer than one of her legs and bent in an almost ridiculous curve. She'd strung it when he'd explained the situation, and now she began to put arrows into the not-dead.

She hit. It was superb shooting; six arrows loosed, six shambling warriors struck. One, shot in the throat, crumpled and went down.

The others kept moving.

So did Kronmir. He racked his crossbow and loosed it into the least-armoured foe, who froze, began to turn black, and fell.

The only sound was his breathing and her grunts as she pulled and loosed. Her bow was very powerful; some of her shafts blew right through her targets' chest cavities to emerge in red-brown ruin from their backs.

Another fell.

They surrounded his tree.

But their attempts to climb would have been humourous if the situation had not been so dire.

One fell into the pit he'd dug.

Giselle began to improve at downing them. She was forty feet away, on a platform she'd built herself in the crotch of a huge tree, well off the ground.

Eventually, they were all accounted for. They were eerie in their silence, and their teamwork was perfect; four of them would cooperate perfectly to thrust the fifth one up into the tree where Kronmir sat. But they were not good at simple muscular coordination. And they had no distance weapons.

Except the writhing grey worms. And those seemed to reach about two feet from the eyes and mouth of the host.

Kronmir took his time, experimenting. When the attack was over and the last active one down, he examined those who were left. He had four in various states of injury, and he expected it to take his foe a little while to process its little defeat.

He cut the throat of one. It continued to struggle until all the blood had pumped out of it, and then a little while after, and then its eyes rolled back and it collapsed and began to desiccate—a year's drying in a hundred heartbeats.

He made notes on his wax tablets.

He tried three poisons on a second. He had darts prepared, and he stood by his net trap and shot into it—shot a dart, waited, made notes. Shot another dart. Made more notes. Used the third dart.

He took the dead thing's poleaxe and pulped the head of the fourth one.

It came for him. He was surprised, and it was fast, and almost had him.

Giselle's sword severed the thing's hand on the forestroke and cut the tendons behind the leg in a wrap blow, and then her pommel caught the thing's chest and knocked it flat. Hamstrung, it could not rise, although it tried.

He bowed to her. "You didn't say you were such a blade," he said.

She smiled. "You didn't ask," she said. "Trust me now?"

"Since they attacked," he said. "Our enemy didn't attack until it could no longer hope for your conversion. It is very subtle." He looked at the squirming thing at his feet, which had once been a strong man, a farmer, perhaps a father and a husband and a son.

"The spine," she said. "Why?"

"No idea," Kronmir said. "Stay back," he said, as a grey worm erupted from the thing's severed neck. It was thicker, and as it emerged it hydra'd. But it had no more reach than the other worms, and he pulled her back as she stared, fascinated.

"That is disgusting," she said.

Aiming carefully as the half-*aethereal* thing thrashed, he shot with his crossbow and missed. It took him three bolts to sever the worm at its apparent base in the creature's spine.

Severed, it vanished.

It was growing toward full light, and Giselle was looking out over the far valley.

"We need to go," she called. "Now."

He backed away from the corpse and ran to her side.

Out in the valley, a phalanx of not-dead was raising dust on the road. They were marching in lockstep, headed their way.

Kronmir had the horses saddled. He shot the last not-dead in the net, a simple dart with the black poison. It unmade rapidly.

"I was going to take one back," he said, as he mounted.

"Huntress," she said. "You are a cruel bastard."

"I almost forgot that they could track us by just one. And that its worm, if I understand, could take the horse." He looked back. "But they take time to *inhabit* a new host. Time for the worm to grow? I'm inclined to believe that the new worm can't hydra until it has matured in the host." He shrugged.

She spat.

"So much to learn," he said.

They rode along the ridge, down into one valley and then another, backtracking the way they had come as the sun rose higher. Always, a little cloud of dust betrayed pursuit.

"They are moving fast," Kronmir said.

"They are angry," Giselle said.

Kronmir watched another moment. There was a raven or a crow far off, but rising. "I don't think it is anger. Curiosity, perhaps?"

They rode on, moving as fast as they could without exhausting their horses, riding on the main road to Mitla. They rode into early afternoon, over one of the great ridges through the woods, but then they cut down the ridge to the open road. The sun was descending but still hot, and nothing seemed to move or breathe except the rising dust cloud to the north.

They'd lost time in the woods. The dust was close—less than a mile.

Giselle changed horses, and so did Kronmir. He took a moment to feed his mare from a nose bag.

"I am waiting," he said to her. "I want to see them more closely."

She took a deep breath. "Very well," she said.

The horses ate. One defecated on the road in a typical horse display of normalcy, and then the dust rose, and the silent not-dead were running at them, five hundred paces away.

Kronmir nodded. He looked at Giselle, his almost blank eyes betraying satisfaction.

"Let's go," he said.

"Was that bravura?" she asked. "What was the point?"

Kronmir straightened his back. "You were right. We hurt them, and this reaction is anger," he said.

They turned and rode another league, and then Kronmir slowed his horse and looked back.

The phalanx of not-dead had stopped. But over the distant mountains circled a great black bird of ill omen, rising against the northwestern sky that was already tinged with the salmon-orange of summer sunset. Even as he watched, the black smudge turned and began coming toward them, a speck against the brilliant western sky.

"I don't like that," Kronmir said.

Giselle stopped, looked under her hand, and spat.

"What?" Kronmir asked.

"It's enormous," she said. "I can't get a sense of … it must be huge. Look at it."

"I agree. Let's ride," Kronmir said.

"It is fast, too," Giselle said. She sounded more tired than scared. "Damn."

They turned their horses and rode, flat-out; a dead gallop along the river. Twice Kronmir looked back. Both times, the enormous carrion bird, or whatever it was, was closer. Night was coming. They first star appeared, and the long twilight of a summer night began.

When they came to the bridge, and the flowing water, and the grave of the little girl, Kronmir called out.

"Your way," he said.

"It is slower," she said. "In fifteen minutes it will be difficult to see under the trees."

"Good," he said.

She raised an eyebrow. "You think it has to see us?"

Kronmir wasn't able to conjure a confident smile. "I'd like to think so," he said. He withdrew the third of Master Petrarcha's workings from his belt purse, invoked a prayer that was entirely voluntary, and dashed the jewel against the stone of the bridge.

As if he had sown the proverbial dragon's teeth, the simulacrum sprang to life; this time it was three of them, and they took up a little too much space for the roadbed of the old bridge.

He didn't have time to adjust the working. He turned, and they went up the ridge as the great wings beat behind them, and they were under the oak tree canopy before the dark thing entered the valley behind them. Kronmir looked back in time to see a shape from nightmare cresting the last ridge; he'd never seen anything like it, and he had an impression of titanic size, of a wingtip of fantastic dimension. Strips of flesh hung from it, and there were gaps in the fabric of its wings.

He had difficulty breathing. The thing was out of all proportion to his idea of the world.

The thing's sinuous, impossible neck moved, and the head turned to the bridge, and it stooped.

"Go!" Kronmir said, and they bolted over the ridge even as they heard the bridge crack as the thing's weight crashed into it.

They made the crest of the ridge, and the monster was still savaging the bridge. It was breathing something that smelled of rot and acid and roared like a furnace casting bronze.

Twilight deepened, and night was close.

"I think it can also see hermetical power," Kronmir said, looking back. "So if you have any items on you, I suggest you leave them here."

He reached into his saddlebag and produced a small bronze pot, which he threw into the trees.

"What was that?" she asked. "I have an amulet."

"Throw it away," he said.

She hesitated.

"It didn't save you from the worms," he said ruthlessly.

She ripped open her shirt and pulled a chain over her head.

And then they rode along the ridge. They didn't gallop, and they were cautious when they came to open ground, but they moved deeper into the trees when they could.

Evening made its subtle change toward night, shadows deepened and the stars lit the east, and they could hear the beat of the great wings, somewhere to the north.

"And you wanted to go to Arles," she said, at one point.

"What the hell is that thing?" he asked.

"I assume it is a dragon," she said. "It is as long as a war galley." She sounded cheerful.

Kronmir made a face. "I have never seen a dragon," he said. "But this is not what I have been led to expect." He wrinkled his nose. "And it smells."

They rode on.

When the moon rose, they halted and changed horses again. Both of them fed their horses and watered them at a tiny rivulet, and both of them filled their canteens.

"I begin to be cautiously optimistic," Kronmir said.

Giselle looked up in time to see the stars go out to the west.

"It is hunting us," she said very quietly. "Damn it. I want a weapon that will harm it. I hate feeling this helpless. Like prey."

"The Duke of Thrake has a weapon that will harm it, and allies," Kronmir said, watching the Darkness. "He needs to know about this."

"I'm in favour of our surviving to tell him," she said.

"We should split up. One of us will make it. I don't think it will leave the Darkness."

Giselle laughed in the dark. "Why?" she asked. "Why should it stop at the edge of the Darkness?"

He cursed. Then, more mildly, he said, "Well, I don't care to split, anyway. Only you know the terrain."

"I know a ranger post..." She sighed. "I do not like to go to a bolt-hole and wait for death. That's not my way. But if we can wait it out..."

"How far?" he asked.

"Come on," she said.

They rode along another ridge, trusting the horses to pick their way through deep woods. The woods were open, with little undergrowth, and some moonlight penetrated the canopy, and so did the sound of great wings beating.

Twice they halted, with the shards of moonlight leaving bright patterns on each other's faces; the first time for water, the second time when Giselle admitted she had lost her way.

"It is all so different in the dark," she said.

She tethered her horse and walked up and down while Kronmir's heart beat too fast and he watched.

There was a cry. It wasn't far, and it was long, terrifyingly loud, inhuman, a rising scream with a breathy quality...

EEARRGGGGGGGAAAA

And the sound of the wings, everywhere, and Kronmir's spare horse spooked, ripped the reins from his hand, and ran.

Kronmir hung on to his remaining horse grimly, and when Giselle's reins showed signs of strain he stopped calming his own horse and went to her two, murmuring, muttering...

There was a scream, abruptly cut off. Not far.

The horse. The monster had taken the horse.

Kronmir readied his tiny crossbow with shaking hands. He had to kneel, breathe deeply, think of nothing...nothing...nothing...

He stilled his hands, and very, very carefully he put the small steel bolt tipped in black into the weapon. His last poison bolt. The last tin of the nightmare stuff was somewhere else in the woods; its dark hermetical aura was probably enough to attract the monster.

He'd rather hoped the dragon might try to eat it. But it was not a fortunate day, that way.

He didn't really think that his tiny balestrino bolt would injure a not-dead creature the size of a war galley. But he felt better having it prepared.

After some time, he allowed himself to admit that Giselle had been gone too long.

He whispered to the remaining horses, watered them again, as quietly as possible, and thought terrible thoughts. Temptations arose in legions; to walk off and find her, which was a foolish notion; to ride for Berona, and abandon her, which was cowardly but at least practical.

He had to admit that he didn't want to leave her.

He examined that for a while. And then realized that more time had passed, and he had not heard wings, and she was still not back.

He cursed. He hadn't slept well in days, and the woods seemed full of ghosts.

Of course, if the thing got her . . . it would leave. It didn't know about him. The worms, whatever they were, only *knew* her.

He didn't think that had been her, screaming. He certainly hadn't thought so at the time, but his confidence in everything was eroding.

Kronmir took a deep breath. He began to breathe as he'd been taught, shutting out panic, monsters, Darkness, and Giselle.

A black mirror.

. . . be the mirror . . .

He opened his eyes. It was lighter; just barely, perceptibly, but he was focused and he knew that dawn was less than an hour away.

It was his duty to take the horses and ride. Stark, obvious. He'd waited three hours. She was dead or lost, and his duty was clear.

He didn't move.

The horses began to shuffle, to be restless, and when he feared they might make noise, he put a corner of his cloak over the geldings' eyes.

Then he heard the movement. He glanced without moving his head, and in the morning half light, fifty paces away, he knew her shape.

He smiled.

"You waited," she said, when she was close. She smiled.

He shrugged. The crossbow wasn't pointing at her, but she'd been away in the Darkness a long time and he was careful.

"I lost a horse," he said.

She nodded. Her reactions were natural, smooth, controlled.

"I found my bolt-hole," she said.

"I haven't heard the thing in two hours," Kronmir said. "We should ride."

"Food. Sleep. Ride at twilight," she said.

He nodded. "What's the Beronese knight's name?" he asked.

She looked at him. "Why?"

"Please tell me," he said.

She turned. "You think..." she said, her voice rising.

Kronmir was very quiet. "Giselle. I waited for you. Longer than anyone with my training should have. Doesn't that make you cautious? I could have a worm in my spine right now. *Tell me the Beronese knight's name.*"

"Tomaso Lupi. I take your point." She frowned.

He let his breath go and carefully uncocked his crossbow. "I am sorry," he said.

"Now I really think you are possessed by daemons," she said. "An apology?"

"You can ask me," he said.

She shook her head. "When I first spoke to you, you shrugged. Not-dead don't shrug, or anything else. It's extraneous to the needs of their masters." She took her horses. "Come on. Let's eat. And sleep."

They had to cross a creek in early-morning daylight, and Kronmir's sense felt leaden, and his eyes felt as if they'd been rubbed with sand. But he was good at working with fatigue, and so was she.

Her bolt-hole was a cave that had been improved by a wooden door carefully camouflaged. The cave was deep, and they coaxed all three horses undercover.

The hay was musty, but the oats seemed to make the horses happy enough, and there was some old green bacon that, when cooked over a tiny fire, proved delicious.

They lay down on the fern and alder bed and pulled their cloaks over them, and she was asleep and snoring softly before he had his cloak over his legs. Her hair smelled of bacon.

Jules Kronmir lay down and allowed himself to be happy for a few minutes, then went to sleep.

They awoke at sunset, and Kronmir felt as if sleep had robbed him of his vitality.

He saw her open the door, and go out, and he considered going back to sleep, except that fear outweighed even fatigue.

"Unless the cursed thing is watching from a mountaintop, we're free," she said, coming back.

They tacked up the horses, ate some burnt rice, and drank water. Before full darkness, they were moving east.

Around midnight, they struck a major road, and before the next dawn, they had crossed the river. Kronmir knew immediately when they were free of the Darkness.

They embraced. They were on horseback, and he had his arms around her, and hers were around him. It went on too long.

And then she disentangled herself. "Well, well," she said. "I think we're going to live."

He shook his head, his thoughts a whirl of emotions and questions. "I need to send a report."

"You are a strange animal," she said affectionately. "I need a bath. Thanks for not trying to kiss me."

He laughed. But indeed, he had been very close to kissing her.

"Come on," she said. "Berona in three hours."

"My horse is done," Kronmir said. "And I'm not sure we're . . . free. Let's take our time and lift a nag from one of the abandoned farms."

"Noted," she said in her duchess voice.

But there was no horse to be had. He looked for a donkey, a mule, but they were gone. They ambled into daylight, and birdsong.

But a few leagues farther east they met a dozen Beronese knights led by three that Kronmir remembered; Ser Alessio and Ser Luca and Ser Achille, who were shepherding refugees up the road.

One of the knights exchanged horses with Kronmir.

"You survived the Darkness!" he said, and then all of them were kissing the duchess's hands.

Alessio smiled at Kronmir. "The count has been beside himself since Ser Tomaso returned; worried about the duchess. And you, too, messire. Let me escort you to Berona."

The duchess bowed.

Kronmir was already separated from her by a great distance. The thought made him sad. *Last night I smelled the bacon in her hair and slept with my arms around her*, he thought. But his mission was a success, and the world turned.

"Nothing would give me greater pleasure, Ser Alessio," Kronmir said.

Part III
The Empire

T he Red Knight awoke in comfortable linen sheets and for a moment, a year was gone from his life.

There stood Amicia. She was smiling. He was at Lissen Carak, in the all-too-familiar hospital. He took a deep breath.

"You are awake," she said.

He found that she had changed. He still could not take his eyes from her face, but it was not the cheerful, slightly tanned face he'd known during the siege. It was different, subtly, as if she had grown to great maturity in a short time. But mostly, she shone.

"You emit light," he said.

"You always say the nicest things," she said. She sat in a chair and put her hands in her lap and smiled at him.

"You cured me?" he asked.

She made her frustrated face. "Yes and no," she said. "We are still linked. All that... all that drama, and the link is still there."

He reached out in the *aethereal. And then inside his palace, in Harmodius's mirror. And there it was. A golden thread.*

She met him in his parlor, and she smiled at Prudentia, who smiled back.

"This is a much brighter place than it was when I first visited you here," she said.

He grinned. "It's my life of ease and all my clean living," he said.

"You still have the plague. I am... controlling it." She smiled. "I owe you several lives. This one's on me."

They laughed together.

"I love your hand," she said. "So clever."

In the aethereal, *its hermetical working glowed with a special light.*

Very much the way she glowed. All the time.

"You emit light," he said again.

"Yes," she said. She looked at her hands.

"Master Smythe thinks you are about to perform an apotheosis," he said lightly.

He saw a shadow pass across her face.

"What?" he asked.

She looked at him. "I am afraid," she said. "I would not be afraid of death. But what is this?" She reached out a hand so they could both see it. It gave off a golden light. "My faith has no room for this."

He could not face her like this. It made him think...things. He surfaced. "How long have I been down?" he asked. "The army is dying."

She put a hand on his. "Two hours. It is dark, and Harmodius and I have channeled what we could to young Morgon. You may sleep. We will go in the morning." She squeezed his hand and rose. "I do not want to go to the army. I want to be in the Brogat. People are dying there."

"People are dying everywhere, and you don't know how to cure it yet," he said. "And every time you work *potentia*, you are closer to... whatever you are closer to."

"Yes," she said. "I knew you'd understand."

He put his arms around her and tried not to move his head so that kissing her would be a natural option. She put her head on his shoulder.

"I never wanted this," she said.

He laughed. "Which?"

"Not that," she said, sitting up with an unsaintly giggle.

He touched her face. "You are still the woman who only wants everyone to be happy," he said.

She smiled and put her hand on his.

"Someday, I'll be able to say I comforted a saint," he said.

She flinched. "I am no saint," she said. "I do what good I can, as much in expiation of what I've done as because I'm *good*. And just today, I feel useless and incapable. I watched two farmers cough their lungs out, and all I can do is slow the horror and ease the pain. Both of them will die." She paused. Their eyes were very close. "And what if you die?" she asked him.

He looked at her. "I will die," he said. "And you will die, golden brown and brave to the last. All of us will die, and so will all of them." He smiled. "Despite which, I will not die today, because of you. And perhaps because of both of us, many will live longer and better."

"Who made you so wise?" she asked.

"Increasingly, I think it was my mother, for all my bitterness on the subject," he said. "Maybe eventually I too will be a saint."

"Only if arrogance is a secret holy virtue," she snapped back.

"I'd like that," he said. "I think I'd look rather splendid in stained glass."

Her hand went to her mouth. She made a splorting noise.

He shrugged. "I have very little faith, but it amuses me to think of how they were...really. All the saints. Bickering, puking, farting people. Who snored and did tomfool things. And yet became saints."

"Stop!" she said. "I'll go to hell!" But she was laughing.

"I think you'll be a splendid saint," he said.

She got off the bed in one sudden movement, like the strike of a swordsman, and she shook her head. "I think I remember what you are like, until you are there." She smiled, but she was wary. "Very unsaintly."

He nodded. "Same, here," he said.

He rose in the morning and left the hospital under his own power. He coughed, and there were tiny black flakes, and that gave him a frisson of fear. So he stood in a corridor and breathed for a little, and he didn't cough again.

He went down the familiar main steps to the chapel, and then across the great courtyard. A dozen nuns and novices were already hanging washing. Some watched him as if he were the devil incarnate, but others—a pair of older nuns—called out to him, and he stood in the new sun and helped them hang washing for a few minutes. Sister Anne put a hand in the small of her back.

"It's good to have someone tall," she said.

"I'll send you Bad Tom," he said.

She laughed. "I liked him," she said. "How does he?"

"Hale, when last I saw him." *God send he's not got the plague*, Gabriel thought.

"Still breaking heads?" she asked. "Tell him I'll pray for him, just for fun." She laughed her jolly laugh and picked up an empty basket. "Come on, girls. I can't find you a handsome knight every day. Don't be shy."

Gabriel went on his way whistling, thinking about very little. He went up the steps to the abbess's audience chamber. It was empty, although the two hermetical spell books still sat in their niches, and he went and leafed through one and then the other, recalling workings he had not practiced since Pru was alive.

He looked up, and there was her chair... the old abbess's chair.

He thought of meeting Amicia.

He thought about the plague, and Ash, and Harmodius's enmity for the dragons; of the Wild, of his alliance with the Wild, of Master Smythe, and by a process of nonlogical connection, he thought about the Odine. And dragons. *Rhun. Who is Rhun? One of us studied them...*

"Amicia is almost ready to go," the abbess said behind him.

He turned. Just for a moment... but it was not the king's former mistress, but Miriam, now dressed in a long grey gown with a high collar. He bowed deeply.

"Looking for something?" the abbess asked.

"Yes," he admitted. "May I have a look at the gate?" he asked.

She met his eyes. "You don't mean the fortress gate," she said.

"No," he admitted. "The true gate. I've been through it," he said. "I knew something was... different. But I was busy."

"I know," she said. "Come, then."

He stopped to check on Ariosto and then followed Miriam into the tunnels below the fortress, where their glistening sides looked as if they'd been polished, and they wound as if they'd been eaten by snakes. But the wardens and their successors, men, had left marks to prevent people from wandering lost.

"Do you know what's happening to her?" Gabriel asked at some point, deep in the bowels of the mountain.

Miriam stopped. "No," she said. "It is terrifying. We have never needed her more than now." She frowned. "Spiritually terrifying, too."

Gabriel laughed. "I've always found her spiritually terrifying."

Miriam smiled, but it was an automatic reaction. She had never found Gabriel's blasphemies funny.

They followed the winding tunnels along, down man-made stairs built in the wormlike tunnels. Several times, Gabriel stopped and raised his lantern to look at the alien paintings on the walls, but eventually they emerged from the winding way and into a hall. The hall had been carved by the wardens or their slaves, and was built to their titanic scale. Only the center of the great steps had been recarved to human scale. The stairs on either flank of the great doors were almost three feet high each tread.

Gabriel was surprised to find how little he had remembered. The doors were higher and wider, and the steps more majestic.

He cast a simple working of mage light and raised it to the ceiling. There were, as he had remembered, constellations painted on the ceiling between supporting flutes that divided the artificial sky into seven panels.

He spent several minutes looking at them. "Would you do me a favour, Abbess?"

She shrugged. "It's just past sunrise and I'm deep in some ancient horror with you. I'm probably good for another favour."

"Can you get someone to copy this? In detail?" He tried to look apologetic. "Today?"

She surprised him by smiling. "Is that all?"

He shrugged. "You have the key?" he asked her.

She produced it from around her neck.

He reached for it.

"There is something on the other side that wants in," she said. "I don't have to be Amicia to know that."

"I won't open it," he said. "I need to understand . . . something."

He took the key and *instantly went into his memory palace, where he duplicated its shape.*

Prudentia reached out. "Two workings," she said. "Very clever."

He touched it to her marble hand. "How old?" he said.

She frowned. "Two or three hundred years."

"Damn," he said. "Wrong again."

"Why?" she asked.

"I thought it would be thousands of years old. That it is relatively new means that this is a copy. It means that someone out there has the older key. I bet Ash has it." He shook his head. "Damn. And damn."

Nonetheless he worked on copying it, and Prudentia coached him on the way the workings had been conducted.

He stepped back into the world with the key in his hand, and he put it into the ornate box by the door. It was a golden star with nine sprays of golden light.

Instead of turning the key all the way, he turned it one stop, from one ray of gold to the next.

The door grew cold.

He looked at the ceiling. "I didn't spend enough time on this the last time," he said.

Miriam was silent.

"Have you always known about the gate?" he asked.

Miriam sighed. "I still don't know, the way I know God's love or that it will rain tomorrow or that the thing you came on is hungry."

Gabriel unclicked the key, back to its starting position. The door warmed almost instantly. He withdrew it carefully, and turned.

He *went straight back into his palace and looked at the key again in the* aethereal, *but nothing new was revealed. He shrugged, and Prudentia's stone shoulders shrugged in reply.*

He hung the key around Prudentia's neck and took the copy back to the real.

It wasn't a bad copy, and he handed it to Miriam.

The look she gave him suggested that she was no more fooled by his hermetical sleight of hand than by any small boy's protestations of innocence, but then, she made no protest. They made their way back, almost twenty minutes of walking, and then climbed the stairs where the bogglins had broken in and Sim had died.

Gabriel stopped and thought of Sim.

And then, after bowing to the abbess, he took Amicia to Ariosto. And the great griffon bowed low, and said, *I love this one! You love her too!*

Amicia looked startled.

"I can hear him!" she said. "Is this... the bird your mother..."

"No bird," Gabriel said. "Ariosto, can you carry two?"

She weighs less than a sack of grain. Ah! Do you mate with her like Blanche?

Amicia made a face. "I think that's a compliment," she said.

"Just a measure of his reality," Gabriel said, rattled and talking to cover his embarrassment. "Come on. I've wasted enough time this morning. Let's go save the army. Please."

"What were you doing? With Miriam? In the old tunnels?" she asked. He'd insisted she bundle up.

"Trying, for once, to be a crisis ahead rather than a crisis behind," he said. "This time, I don't want to ride to the rescue. I want to kill the monster in its sleep."

Two hours later they descended onto the high ridge and found, not the army, but only the army's sickest and some of the older archers burying the dead. Amicia was off the griffon with a sigh of relief that suggested that budding immortality did not cure fear, and she followed an exhausted Morgon Mortirmir into the tents that were pitched haphazardly in the stony ground.

Gabriel found at least a dozen imperial magisters and students from the academy working in the impromptu hospital. He understood that they were recently arrived, and that they had all set to work immediately, and his Archaic was good enough to understand that they had set out as soon as they heard of the disaster at Dorling, determined to do their utmost to avenge their fallen comrades.

Thorn had destroyed thirty of them in a wave of his hand. Thirty practitioners, of all levels. A third of the most promising crop of magisters and philosophers of hermetical principle that the imperial academy had ever trained.

That they had arrived to find a plague before them and rumours of a plague behind them might have sapped their wills, except that one of the leading instructors of the academy, the elderly master grammarian, Master Nikos, insisted that they apply themselves immediately to the work at hand.

Which was why the very pretty and almost comically stern Despoinetta Tancreda appeared in front of the Duke of Thrake. "Your Grace," she said, her jet-black, almost straight eyebrows raised. "I understand that you, too, are a practitioner."

"I am," he said.

"Would you please come with me?" she asked, and walked away into the camp, stepping over tent lines as if she had every one memorized. The Red Knight tripped several times.

Eventually he found himself entering Gavin's tent, a flame of magnificent green silk, lit from inside by lanterns. There was the master grammarian, and there was an exhausted Morgon Mortirmir. Amicia was nowhere to be seen.

"You can work *ops*?" the older man asked. He taught young people every day, and he was used to being obeyed.

Gabriel hid his smile. "Yes, sir," he said.

"Why didn't you volunteer this morning?" the grammarian asked.

"I wasn't here," Gabriel answered.

The grammarian sneered. "That sounds unlikely. Very well, please open to me, and I will take what I can from you."

Gabriel shrugged and allowed *the grammarian into his memory palace. As soon as the older man in magnificent red and gold walked onto his parquetry floor, he froze.*

"Jesus wept!" he said. He looked around. "How is it that I do not l know you?" he said, and he had power rising in his own right hand.

Gabriel shook his head. "I know you, Master Nikos. I am Gabriel Muriens, the Duke of Thrake."

The grammarian had the good grace to bend his knee; a full reverence. "My lord. I understand you are likely to be emperor. I had no idea that your powers were so . . . developed."

"High praise indeed. I may be emperor, but I believe that some discussion is yet required. I already have the plague, and so I need to keep this power; and these powers are my reserves for combat. The rest is yours." He swept his hands, gathering ops *inside his own palace, a trick that had taken him time to master but greatly sped his casting.*

The master grammarian accepted the power and subsumed it.

"How are we doing?" Gabriel asked.

The grammarian raised an eyebrow. "Well enough. We've only lost a dozen, and I think we've stabilized all those who can be saved. Tomorrow, at first light, we'll move to Dorling. Mortirmir must sleep. I cannot allow him to work any longer. This wild user, this so-called nun . . ."

Gabriel bowed. "More powerful than you or I," he said.

The master bridled. "Really?" he said. "I doubt that."

Gabriel shrugged. "Raw ops *runs through her palace," he said. "I've never seen anyone with her access to power."*

"I must witness this prodigy," the master said, with some sarcasm.

"Master Smythe believes that he can help us once we enter the circle of his power." Gabriel pushed more power at the master.

"The Wyrm of Ercch?" the master said. "This is the world of myth walking abroad in daylight, to be sure." He frowned. "But at this point I will accept any help. This plague is nefarious. It employs forbidden techniques as well as necromantic working and a natural host."

Gabriel, drained of ops, *was suddenly very tired. "You must excuse me," he said, yawning.*

"Ah. I will go work." The master was gone as swiftly as he had come.

Gabriel found his way to an unoccupied camp bed and went to sleep fully dressed. Twice in the night, he awoke, coughing.

In the morning, he woke late enough to find the healers loading the most serious cases onto carts. He only learned that Wilful Murder was dead by seeing the man's corpse being prepared for burial, and his death struck him hard, so that he had to turn aside. He leaned on a tree briefly, and then he went and touched the grey hand.

"May you go well, old friend," he said.

There were eight company archers there to bury him, and Gabriel went with them, and helped them dig in the stony earth of the Adnacrags, and then lower in the body. The new Archbishop of Lorica came and said the words.

"They say he was the last to die," Smoke said.

Tippit spat. "Fucking plague," he said.

"He saved my life a dozen times," Gabriel said.

"He always tried to take my fucking wine ration," Tippit said. "He was sometimes an awkward bastard, an' he had *theories* about yon; dragons and bogglins, as could make your head spin." He paused. "But he were a fuckin' wonderous archer."

"Bastard always said he wanted to die in bed," Smoke said. "An' look ye, he did."

"Who gets his bow?" Cully asked. "He pulled a heavy bow."

They all looked at Long Paw, who, despite his new rank as a knight, was still thought of as a master archer.

"Ricard Lantorn could draw that bow," Long Paw said.

"So he could," said No Head.

"Like fuck," Snot whined. "I can."

"No, you can't," Smoke said, with finality. "The Lantorn boy's good."

"As good as Dan Favour?" Cully asked.

"Favour's got his own bow," Smoke said. "Anyway, he's going to be a knight. Ask the captain. He's right there."

Gabriel realized that he had not given any thought to his company, and he didn't like the light in which that cast him.

"Who else did we lose, Smoke?" he asked, dreading the answer.

"Ser Gelfred," Long Paw said. "We buried him yesterday."

"Ser Bescanon, Ser Gonzago, Gawin Hazart from the men at arms," Smoke said. "An' Hetty and One Lug and poor Gezlin."

"Casualties like a battle," Long Paw said.

Cully nodded. "You know what Wilful would have said. Half us got it. There'll be more in the ground presently."

"*Mark my words,*" came a chorus of voices. Some laughed.

"Oak Pew's got it bad," Long Paw said. "You might want to go see her."

"I'll see everyone at Dorling," Gabriel said. But when he slipped away—some of them were pouring wine on Wilful's grave—he made the time to find Oak Pew. She was just being hoisted into one of Sukey's wagons.

She was far gone. Her skin had the silver sheen of the worst cases, many of whom had complex webs of magery in them, trying to hold their lungs together for a little while more while the magisters and the masters sought a cure.

"Cap'n, she said in her low voice, with a sad excuse for a smile. "I ain't drunk. Not this time."

He took one of her hands and she snatched it away. "I got it bad, Cap'n," she said.

"I already have it, Sally," he said. There were very few in the company still left who knew her real name was Sally. And even that was the rags of a fancier name. A Gallish name.

"Oh," she said. "Well. I think I'm going soon." She shrugged. "I can't say I'm altogether sad." She smiled a little. She was having trouble breathing.

Gabriel thought he'd never heard her so sober. Never heard her use a word as long as *altogether*. "I'm going to wager you pull through," he said.

She nodded. "You do that," she said. "Tell that pretty nun to fix me up." A smile crossed her face. "I rather fancy her," she said.

He squeezed her hand and she squeezed back.

Ariosto covered the distance to the Inn of Dorling in minutes; it would take the supply wagons, toiling through the last of the thick woods, many hours. But Gabriel was heartened to see the road-building crew, more than a thousand men and women, working toward the wagons, and he brought Ariosto in a tight circle.

The road moved forward even as he watched. It was stunning—perhaps almost frightening—how fast a thousand people could work. Trees fell and were dragged to the sides, trimmed, hewed, the wood stacked for travellers or for accordion road repairs in damp ground.

He dove low, skimming the treetops, Ariosto grumbling between his legs, his great wings sweeping up and down. The workers already knew him; men waved their hats, and women veiled against the mosquitoes waved their tools.

He was heartened again to see how close the wagons were to the spur of the road, and how close again was the next camp, at the road junction, where six wyverns rose from a clearing and headed south to bring more beeves. And now at the great fork in the road, Ticondonaga was already close besieged; he turned once over the outworks, where Gavin's advance guard had occupied Ser Hartmut's siege lines. The Orley garrison was doomed and knew it. There were huge gaps in the ancient walls, and the sack had ruined most of the defences. And thanks to Aneas, Orley was close pursued in the great north woods and not in a position to relieve his garrison. Aneas was his least favourite brother, but the slim boy was pulling his weight and more. Orley's attempt to turn east had been stopped by Aneas and his rangers. Ticondonaga had perhaps a day or resistance left in her.

Gabriel flew the last fifteen imperial miles contemplating the possibilities of moving human soldiers with even a little support from the air. The difference in scouting, the incredibly enhanced power of a magister, the communications...

He considered visiting Aneas, who would need a resupply in a day or so.

Below him, six miles out from the inn at the edge of the rolling downs that marked the Green Hills, the veteran armies of Morea and Alba marched. Again he dove.

Every time you go down to wave, I have to climb back up! the griffon said.

Love you, Gabriel said. He was thinking that yesterday, he had flown with Amicia's arms around his waist, and today, if he was lucky, he would find Blanche...

Thinking of Blanche immediately led him to consider that Irene would naturally expect him to marry her to be emperor. And she had tried to kill him. And she could not be trusted.

Marry them all! Ariosto said, helpfully.

Gabriel coughed.

Then he passed through the invisible boundary that marked the edge of the Wyrm's demesne and felt an immediate lightening in the work his body and his mind had to do the fight the sorcerous plague within him.

So many questions.

The byres around the inn were half full of beasts—an odd sight as the *lorilindel* was in bloom on the hillsides, and the eastern edge of the Green Hills was already more purple-pink than green, something never seen during the annual drove. But Donald Dhu and his men had brought half the drove back to feed the armies. This made Gabriel consider that he'd mortgaged his own riches to pay for the animals, and that the Brogat, at least, was unlikely to pay any taxes for a year or even two. He wondered about Thrake, which had known two years of war.

He wondered how long the merchants of Harndon could fund the war. Even if he and the queen pledged their credit, it was ultimately the merchants who handed over their money, and it was the merchants who took the greatest risks.

In among his other pastimes, he needed to find a great deal of money.

He skimmed over the full byres, looking for a landing spot. He was ahead of the army here; he could see Count Zac toiling up the switchbacks on Heartbreak Pass to the west, and thus he knew that he would have no harbinger but the Wyrm himself, but he expected that some arrangement would have been made for flying creatures.

But even as his eyes scanned the ground, his thoughts were on logistics.

There will be no taxes from the Brogat, and Jarsay is not much better, thanks to bloody de Vrailly. Harndon had a major fire; a third of the waterfront warehouses were burnt. Albinkirk is still half a ruin, and half of the fields around Albinkirk are abandoned. Occitan, by reports, is better, but not much better. Morea is stable because of our fighting a year ago, but Thrake was burdened with taxation for two years before that to support the usurper, and Lanika is too poor to tax.

We're winning the battles. But we're losing the war.

If the Outwallers have enough people to collect furs, we'll have cargoes for Galle and Hoek, but if the rumours are accurate, there's no one there with the gold to buy them.

The Etruscan cities ask for imperial aid. The Imperium has little enough aid to give... but if I am going to fight Ash this year, or next, I will need to be able to borrow money in Venike and Genua.

It will be ten years before the revenues of Alba and Morea are fully restored. In those ten years, we will have won or lost, and we will still be paying. If we win.

If we lose...

If Galle is truly being destroyed...

He saw a tall man—no, an irk—standing in an empty pen, fifty paces on a side, waving two scarlet flags. When he leaned out and looked carefully, he saw that each flag had his six-pointed spur rondel painted in gold.

Heraldry. So useful.

One of the unique qualities of the helmet that the irk armourer had made him was that, when closed, it was silent inside. It did not cut off all sound; it was clearly hermetical. It simply eliminated the sound of the rushing air over his head, so that he could hear other sounds, like the wingbeats of approaching wyverns.

But sometimes, it was pleasant to flip the visor open and let the wind touch his face, and he did this as Ariosto, screaming his pleasure at the two fat sheep penned for his pleasure in a corner of the fold, descended from the heavens like the raptor he truly was, at least from the waist up.

He was crushed into his saddle as the great beast decelerated, wings cupping air, the magnificent pinions of his wing edges rippling and sparkling, red, gold, green, white, black in the sunlight. He screamed a hundred feet above the sheepfold, freezing both petrified animals in their tracks, and then, as delicately as a dancer placing her foot, the griffon's talons shot out and took a sheep and swept along a few inches from the ground. He flew another thirty paces and landed nimbly on his leonine back legs, dropping the newly dead sheep at the feet of the irk, who bowed.

Want some, friend? Ariosto asked.

You know I like mine cooked, Gabriel said. *Don't you think you could kill your sheep after we land?*

What's the fun in that? Ariosto complained. Then he was eating, the welter of griffon impressions replaced with a simple, almost transcendent pleasure.

Gabriel was lucky to get free of the meal before the blood spurted. The lion was clearly very much present in the hybrid, especially at meal times.

The irk nodded. "Ser Gabriel? Master Smythe is at the inn and requests your presence."

Gabriel nodded and followed the tall figure as it walked down from the high fells along a stone wall so ancient that Gabriel couldn't even reckon whether men had built it, and then along a running stream to the vale within a vale that was the ground immediately around the inn.

The inn itself was more like a small town than a simple inn. At its heart sat the oldest building, a tall pile of stone with a central tower and two long wings that faced the inner stables, two more long low buildings, across the central yard. But outside the central yard was another ring of buildings: workshops and lodgings, a complete outer inn with its own kitchens and common rooms and snugs, and yet another tall stone tower both for defence and to lodge more travellers. The walls of the original inn rose sheer from the rock, and at the corner of the tower, the besiegers had set their ladders and climbed, attempting to take the inn by surprise, just a month before.

The inn had already been stripped and emptied, and Gabriel expected to find things out of place, things missing or forgotten. Or perhaps he expected to see some sign of the assault, or of fire. He had heard that the frustrated attackers had used fire on the roof beams.

If they had, there was no sign whatsoever of damage. The outer buildings looked as they always looked, at some comfortable midway point between newness and shabby decay. And the Old Inn was untouched. Inside the great main doors, the ancient, somewhat grimy settee, a huge bench with a leather cushion shining and black from years of dirt, made of some unknown and incredibly tough hide, sat in its accustomed place.

"This way," the irk said.

Gabriel saw the Keeper standing at the bar in his enormous common room, and the two men bowed low. The Keeper of Dorling was every bit as much a personage as the Duke of Thrake.

"Your son is with the army," Gabriel called out. The Master of Dorling had served throughout the campaign with Tom Lachlan, and had won himself some renown. And lived to bask in it.

But the irk was already vanishing up the well-remembered corridor to the paneled room.

And there, smoking, sat the dragon. Master Smythe.

He rose, and nodded. "Pipe?" he asked. "There's a nice Etruscan red wine on the sideboard."

"How much wine do I need?" Gabriel asked.

Master Smythe smiled. "I have acted in your name. Time is very… difficult. Is that the right phrase?"

"Time is tight," Gabriel said. He poured himself some wine and smelled it. It was a delicious smell, like autumn and smoke turned into liquid.

The irk handed him a cup of clear water. "Flying can dry you out," Gabriel said. He looked—really looked—at the irk. "You are also a dragon," he said.

The irk frowned.

"I told you," Smythe said to the irk.

The irk was clearly annoyed. "How did you know?"

Gabriel shrugged. "Just to start, it's extremely unlikely that there'd be an irk here before the Faery Knight rides in."

The irk's face shifted, and suddenly Gabriel was looking at himself.

He shook his head. "No," he said. "Most of the people I know have already decided that one of me is quite enough."

"He's young and still learning." Master Smythe winked at the irk. "Sit quietly and learn." Master Smythe gestured and the Gabriel changed back into an irk.

The real Gabriel pinched the bridge of his nose, tried not to laugh or cry, and sat with his wine. "You acted in my name?" he asked.

"I have invited all of our major allies to dinner. And your eternal displays of mock violence." Master Smythe shrugged.

"Tournaments matter," Gabriel said.

"Of course. They are barbaric and a colossal waste of money and energy, people die, bad feelings are born…" Master Smythe sat back. "Shall I go on?"

Gabriel shrugged. "All that may happen, but a tournament is…the best way to cover our meeting. And I am about to begin a great *empris*."

"Yes, yes. Princess Irene was already at Middleburg with some of her people. I have invited her. In fact, I used her fear of the plague to lure her. She must be dealt with. Also, the queen is on her way, and the Prince of Occitan. The Faery Knight, Kerak, Harmodius, your brother, the pretty nun, Tom Lachlan, the Keeper himself, the Duchess Mogon, the leading Outwaller sachems and war leaders." He shrugged. "And me. It will be quite a feast. I have called it the Tournament of the Dragon." He smiled, and blew smoke. "I can't think why."

Gabriel lit his own pipe. The tobacco was from the Outwallers, and was light and easy. He tried to blow a smoke ring and began to cough.

"And the plague?" he asked.

"As soon as all the leading hermetical workers are present, we will begin work. But already we have several areas that show promise. It is clear that the plague is not as natural as we first believed. It has both a sorcerous component and a necromantic component. It is, in fact, a blend of three kingdoms of magery, and..." Master Smythe smiled nastily. "And from it, I am learning...we are learning. Learning things I do not think our adversaries wished us to know."

"Here we go," Gabriel said. "Off into a world of mystery."

"No. But I do agree that the single most important thing we can all do, now, is to join together for dinner. And then talk. And then, after that, act."

"And the plague?" Gabriel asked again.

"I know you fear it. You do well to fear it. To all intents, you are already dead, and only Mortirmir's brilliant sleight of hand is keeping any of you alive. But you see, now that you are here, that sleight of hand can be maintained almost without effort. And..." He shrugged and blew smoke. "I think we have understood it now. Hermetically."

Gabriel nodded. "Then..."

"Get some rest. The army will come in tonight."

"Except for the siege of Ticondonaga."

"Hartmut left some Gallish sailors as a garrison. They have already offered to surrender, in exchange for being allowed to go north to their friends on the Great River. Your brother will accept. Ticondonaga will be rebuilt." The dragon blew a smoke ring.

"Gavin will be pleased," Gabriel said.

"You will have almost five days to prepare. The tournament will begin on Monday, and I have it in hand with the Keeper. We will have the tournament that the king failed to hold. Every knight in all three realms who is not incapacitated or destitute will attempt to appear."

"From Occitan?" Gabriel asked.

The dragon shrugged. "Ask me no questions..." he said.

Gabriel nodded, drew in some smoke, and then tried, again, to blow a smoke ring, and failed.

"I went to Lissen Carak," he said.

Master Smythe's head turned.

"I went and looked at the gate," he said.

The dragon allowed a little smoke to trickle from his human nostrils.

"I have questions," Gabriel said. "How many gates are there? Is it seven?"

"There may be as many as fifteen," Master Smythe said.

"So why the number seven?" Gabriel asked.

Master Smythe sat back and looked at the young irk and then back at Gabriel. "The gates can go to seven places," he said. "Some gates only go one," he went on. "The master gates, at Arles, and Lissen Carak, and Such Zen, at least, go to all seven. The rest go to one, or two, or three.

"Where is Such Zen?" Gabriel asked.

"It lies as far beyond Etrusca as Etrusca is beyond the seas, and then that distance again. Or so I am told. I have never been, and neither has any other of my race in fifty lifetimes of men." Master Smythe shrugged again. "Such Zen is beyond our ability to cover. Arles is either fallen or under siege. Ash has made one or two attempts on Lissen Carak..."

Gabriel shook his head. "Ash's allies *had* Lissen Carak until it fell to the knights of the order after the Battle of Albinkirk." He met the dragon's sharp eyes. "Just two hundred fifty years ago. And he tried to get it back in the old king's lifetime, didn't he? In the events that led to the battle that my father and all the old men thought had settled the Wild for good. At Chevin. Except that Ash is working to a schedule, is he not?"

Master Smythe smoked in silence. Outside, they could hear Count Zac swearing, and the sounds of men dismounting and calling for wine or ale.

"Mogon's people," Gabriel said.

Master Smythe nodded. "I see," he said.

Gabriel shook his head, his anger sudden and uncontrollable. "Why do I have to work this out for myself? Why won't you just *tell me*?" he asked. "My world is teetering on the edge of extinction and I'm being made to work on puzzles! I just buried a man—a strange, bitter man whom I, God help me, loved in my own strange, bitter way. I wasn't there when he died, because I'm running about solving puzzles, and by God, Wyrm, if I didn't have Ariosto, this would take me weeks. Is that what it was supposed to do? Take me weeks? Are we on the same side, or not?"

Master Smythe didn't flinch. "I believe we are on the same side. More strongly, since I reentered my own realm and got to examine the plague in detail. I told you I learned from it. The necromantic marker tells me a great deal. It tells me that we are not on the wrong side. It tells me that it is Ash who has brought in these awful things from the past." He released a puff of smoke. "As to the puzzles," he said. "I am bound. Surely you, of all people, understand a binding. And honestly, Gabriel, I am making this as easy as I can for you. I promise."

Gabriel looked down at his wine cup. "Apologies," he said. "People are dying. I feel impotent. I don't even want to face Irene, much less... much less." He looked up. "We have to save Arles?"

"If it has already fallen, we have already lost," Master Smythe said. "No, now we are in a grey area. If it has already fallen, we *may* have already lost."

"The gates only open at certain times," Gabriel said.

"Yes," the dragon answered, obviously pleased.

"Only some gates open at those times, which are conjunctions of the spheres." Gabriel leaned forward.

"Probably. I really don't know. I'm too young. I wasn't... around... last time." Smythe toyed with his pipe.

"Ash wants to let something *in*," Gabriel said.

"Perhaps," Smythe said.

"The Odine want to get *out*," Gabriel said.

Master Smythe smiled. "There you have it," he said. "Well deduced."

"Why don't we let them go and slam the door behind them?" Gabriel asked.

"Because that would unleash them again, to move unchecked, and breed. Even if I didn't think they would come back here eventually, when they had made a wasteland of everything," he shrugged.

"You are still not telling me the whole story," Gabriel said with some of his earlier anger.

Master Smythe turned away. "Why do you think that? Of course it is fiendish and complicated..."

"No, damn you," Gabriel said. "If the Odine are so terrible—which I fully believe! And you and yours came here to bind them, then you are so clearly the better people that you had only to tell us and we'd have supported you."

Master Smyth raised an eyebrow. "Really?" he asked. "Askepiles? The former Duke of Thrake and his son? And, pardon me, your mother? Let me push the dagger in deeper, Gabriel. Irene! Irene would have allied with Ash. Still might. She is the very archetype of human very eager for power. Many will trade almost anything for power." He sighed. "Some of my kind too, and Mogon's and the Faery Knight's. All of us share this."

Gabriel narrowed his eyes. "Simple fear?" he said. "No more deep dark secrets?"

Master Smythe shook his head. "I have a dark forest of secrets," he said. "But I promise you that simple fear, and a passion for secrecy, is at the root of most errors. Never ascribe to some conspiracy of evil what can be explained as easily by ignorance and fear."

Gabriel nodded. "I'll drink to that," he said. Gabriel looked at the young irk and raised an eyebrow. "You have new allies?"

Master Smythe's blank eyes gave nothing away. "Circumstances are changing," he said.

"What does that mean?" Gabriel asked.

"It means that evidence—hard evidence—of the nature of Ash's fall, or perhaps merely of his allies...either way, the evidence suggests that events since at least Chevin have been manipulated. My isolation is ending. But..."

"But?"

Master Smythe stood up. "You know, Gabriel, the truth is that I find you a very easy man with whom to speak. Too easy. I have been alone too long, and what Ash says of me is true. I love men, perhaps too much. I have already told you far more than I should."

"But still less than I need to know! Damn it! Harmodius and his circle believe that you are all in this together...you, and Ash, and Tar." At the last name, the irk raised his head suddenly.

Master Smythe nodded. "I suppose we should have planned for a moment when humans began to cooperate instead of endlessly playing the factions," he said. "But like you and all the other sentient species, in general, we do what works until it explodes." Master Smythe looked at Gabriel. Both men were standing.

"Do you believe in...a higher being?" Smythe asked.

Gabriel choked on the smoke from his pipe. He coughed. "No. Or yes. No, until I met Amicia, and now..." he shrugged. "Now, I confess to fearing to ask any more questions. Not of you. Of the world."

Master Smythe looked out the window. The strong light made his too-perfect features look as if he were in fact a manuscript illumination. The sun placed his face in bright light and his back in too-heavy shadow. "I don't know why I have this urge to confide in you," he said. "But it has begun to occur to me that there is a string of coincidence too strong to be likely. That four of the great human mages should ally just at the time when the gates were preparing to open. Just in time for the fates to provide a human whose actions were nearly invisible to Ash. Because of your parents you are almost ideally suited to the moment. As is Amicia. And dozens of others—perhaps even me. And you came to me just as I began to see the probabilities. Thorn allowed Harmodius to take him. *Why?* The faeries who helped Tom Lachlan wound Ash...*why?*" He shrugged.

Gabriel joined him at the window. Only as he approached it did he understand the light. It was not the light of day.

It was *aethereal* light. The window was, at least at that moment, looking out at everything, and nothing.

"Are you saying it is all predestined? I'd hate that," Gabriel said.

"You know something, Gabriel?" the dragon asked. "Just this once, I don't know what I'm saying. No one could follow all the arcs from here. Or at least, none of my kind. And yet I have a feeling that there's a hand on the balance."

"Helping the side that minimizes negative outcomes?" Gabriel joked.

The dragon turned from the window slowly. "I do believe that's the most profound thing you're ever said to me," he said.

"What?" Gabriel asked. "What? I was teasing you."

The dragon made no gesture, but the quality of light changed, and they heard voices outside...voices of men-at-arms and pages and archers.

"What did I say?" Gabriel demanded.

"Let me think on it. In the meantime, please understand that many, many refugees are coming here simply for protection from the plague, and I am content that it be so." Smythe went and sat, his limbs only a little inhuman in their motions.

"Any advice on how to deal with Irene?" Gabriel asked.

"Please. I understand the appeal of humans and sex—better than you might think. But your endless rituals of mating? Not my business. I will say, however, that she's coming here as much for protection from the plague, which she fears, as because she actually intends to ally with anyone. She shares her father's belief about the importance of the empire. She will almost certainly demand an oath of fealty from the queen." The dragon made a face. "She thinks you will marry her and give her the future of power and stability that she wants."

Gabriel groaned. "A moment ago you were conjuring a higher power. This is the sublime to the ridiculous. From stopping a sorcerous plague to the petty politics of one dangerous young woman."

Master Smythe blinked. "Gabriel. This is the great game. Everything matters. You *know* that. We watch even the sparrows fall, because we know that everything is everything."

Gabriel felt a little like a small boy being lectured by his tutor, and his resentment rose. "Some problems seem a little more heroic than others," he said. "I have another question. You said there was one of you...a dragon? Who had learned about the Odine. And that one of you...I can't remember...had reported? Had lied?" Gabriel paused. "I'm not sure what I'm asking, but it's a damn sight more interesting than Irene's love life."

Smythe released a long stream of smoke. "That is the failing of many beings," he said finally. "They solve the most attractive problems. If we are going to win, we must solve *all* the problems."

"I don't think I can kill her," Gabriel said, a little wildly.

"Perhaps you should just mate with her," Smythe said. "Need you make it so complicated?"

"That would needlessly entangle my personal life," Gabriel said.

Master Smythe blew a smoke ring. "Surely this kind of thing is normal to your kind?" he asked.

Gabriel stared at him. "What? Having multiple wives?" he laughed.

Master Smythe let out a little smoke. "It seems to me that most of the males have multiple partners while pretending to have just one, and most of the females have single partners only when these limitations are imposed by males. It all seems inefficient and...traumatic. Much time could be saved if only—"

Gabriel rose and bowed. "I think I'd rather hear you discuss the endless hermetical complications of the negative outcomes," he said. "Probably less terrifying. I do not wish to marry Irene, and she would not settle for any lesser status. I am not interested in forcing Blanche to accept a lesser status to suit my political career; indeed, that's exactly the advice my mother would have given."

Master Smythe sat back. "Wise woman, your mother," he said. "Marry your empress and have your sons with your laundress."

"Fuck yourself," the Red Knight spat. He left the paneled room and slammed the door.

Only later did he realize that Smythe had not answered his questions about the dragon and the Odine.

Gabriel changed into riding clothes instead of resting, his head roiling with new information that fell like grain from a field cart after harvest whenever he confronted Master Smythe. He borrowed a pair of ronceys from the inn and headed out down the road to the west. His own household was already in the courtyard, under Francis Atcourt, and he took the time to embrace men, to lament the loss of Wilful Murder, and then he was away. He found Gavin and the main body just three miles from the inn. Unaccompanied and out of harness, many men didn't recognize him, but Gavin did, and his brother crushed the breath out of him before Bad Tom came up on horseback to do the same.

"Just in time to take all the credit," Gavin said, but his grin said it was raillery, not malice. "Christ crucified, we're going to make it. Two days ago, I thought we were going to lose to the wilderness."

Gabriel watched the column going past. Men's heads were up. Their equipment was wrecked, and their clothes shredded, but what they had was clean and neat, and they had some fire in their eyes.

"Well done," Gabriel said.

Gavin nodded. He was scratching under his pauldron, trying to reach his shoulder under the mail.

"You are free of the plague?" Gabriel asked.

"Oh yes," Gavin said. "I have a new problem; my scales are spreading. Again!"

Gabriel frowned. "Let me have a look tonight."

Gavin grinned. "Just the reason to have a sorcerer brother. To cure your scales." He laughed.

Bad Tom slapped Gabriel's back. "Dull wi'out you. Your brother's no slouch, but he's careful."

Gavin narrowed his eyes. "Ticondonaga is surrendering, damn it," he said. "We didn't *need* to fight."

Gabriel put a hand on his brother's shoulder. "Tom, I think you've managed to offend us both."

Tom laughed, as was his wont. "Well," he said, "where next?"

Gabriel looked at the distant inn on its ridge. "We'll discuss it there," he said.

Sauce came up, coughed, and shook her head. "Not in harness, riding about alone. And when did you last practice? Eh?"

Gabriel looked around. "Why do I miss you people?" he asked.

"No idea why anyone would miss Tom," Sauce said. "Me? You need someone to tell you all the things no one tells you."

"I do?" Gabriel asked. "Never mind. Where's Michael?"

"Rear guard," they all said in a ragged chorus.

He rode farther west, and found Michael and George Brewes riding nags at the head of a mixed force. He had never before seen a version of George Brewes that seemed happy to see him, and both men had to exclaim over his silver hand.

"We have a horse crisis," Ser Michael said. "If we're going to fight, we need horses."

"We have a plague crisis," Gabriel said. "That's first."

"Oh aye," Michael said. "How's my da?"

"Right now, he's not my favourite," Gabriel said. "Does he ever stop scheming?"

Michael laughed. "No," he said simply. "Why?"

Gabriel shrugged. "We can talk over dinner. I want to get the sick wagons in. Would you allay my fears and send me half the rear guard to cover?"

Michael nodded. "I'll do better. I'll come myself. Ser George had only this moment proposed the same; that the sick were too naked, even with most of the archers. And Ticondonaga safely behind us."

The rear guard, most of the white banda and some of the green, turned about without a murmur. Every man and woman of the green banda wore a black armband. Ser Gelfred had been one of the best-loved men in the company.

The horses were in terrible shape. They were the survivors of the horse plague, and the company had stretched itself very thin to remount the white banda. The normal losses of a battle and three weeks fighting in dense country had done the rest.

Michael saw where his eyes were going. "Some will be restored by rest and food. But the rest..." He shook his head.

Gabriel's fears swelled to a ridiculous height as they rode back, and he rode faster and faster, regardless of the state of the rear guard's horses.

But Sukey's wagons were all together, the company's archers riding along either margin of the road, and they were moving smartly when Gabriel found them, seven miles from the inn.

Sukey looked bad, but Gabriel knew he wore the same look; too much magery, and not enough appetite. The same working that froze the disease seemed to lower other functions. He kissed her without fear—he already had the disease.

The knights of the rear guard split into two bodies to cover the front and rear of the wagons.

"We can't spare one man or woman," Gabriel said. "There's a thousand years of military experience lying in these wagons, and I need them all." He rode along the wagons, leaning in through the canvas covers, and when he found the master grammarian in a wagon, he passed him as much stored *ops* as he felt he could spare.

The grammarian took the power. He came and sat on the wagon box, and nodded. "As soon as we passed the Wyrm's boundary," he said, "we passed out of the immediate crisis. The issue is no longer power. It is now technique." He sounded as if he were lecturing students.

Gabriel put his head in every wagon and told them that they were in the Wyrm's circle, that they were safe from the plague, and that they'd have a week or more of rest.

Michael nodded when they reached the end. "At least a week," he said. "Better two. The heart of the company has been fighting far too long. We almost lost it in the woods."

Gabriel nodded. "But you didn't," he said. "Where's Aneas?"

"He took some of our best and went off to hunt Kevin Orley," Michael said.

"I know," Gabriel said patiently. "He defeated Orley yesterday, or so Alcaeus tells me. Do you have his location fixed? Hermetically?"

Michael looked abashed. "Damn."

Gabriel knew it was because Mortirmir was fighting plague and Alcaeus was already on another mission.

"Never mind, I'll find him with a messenger," Gabriel said. "We're spread too thin."

"Damn, it's good to see you again, and to see the Inn of Dorling between my horse's ears. Gabriel, I'm not afraid to say…I need a rest, myself. I'll bet Tom and Sauce need a rest."

"A nice restful tournament?" Gabriel asked.

Michael laughed. "I hope the queen brings Kaitlin!" he said. "And my son!"

"Since you're in a rush to see them," Gabriel said, "you could take the red banda out at first light and meet them on the road."

Michael smiled. "I walked into that."

Dinner—their first dinner together in three weeks. The whole of the officers of the company, gathered at one immense table in the courtyard of the Old Inn. There were faces missing; Bescanon and Gelfred were the highest ranking, but Chris Foliak was not there either and a half-dozen other corporals who had eaten their meat with their captain in early spring, just three short months before, in the same yard.

But Sauce sat by Count Zac, now an honourary officer; Bad Tom had an arm around Sukey while he propounded his latest theory of how to conduct the expected autumn campaign against Ash, and Sukey leaned against him as if she needed his warmth and his solidity. Michael sat by Gabriel, with Gavin on his other side, and Ser Milus Dunholme sat by Gavin with Ser Francis Atcourt.

They ate beef—excellent beef, cut thin and served with little cellars of flavoured salts and a great bowl of pepper that was itself worth a small fortune. Wine and ale flowed, and all around the central tables, archers and men-at-arms and pages and company servants from highest to lowest were waited on and served as if they were all nobles. At other tables sat the survivors of the Nordikaans, and Zac's handful of Vardariotes. The Scholae and the rest of the Vardariotes had already gone east to meet Princess Irene, cursing their ill luck and vowing to make up on their drinking time as soon as they returned. The leaders of the royal army had their own tables, and the infantry had their own feast, but several officers of the royal foresters sat at the central table, and so did Lord Wayland and Ser Ricar Fitzroy. The forces of the Wild—the Faery Knight, Lord Kerak, and their people—had all been invited by the Wyrm to a separate feast.

When the first edge of their three-week appetites had been taken off, and before anyone became too drunk, Gabriel mounted a barrel and they all fell silent, or mostly silent.

"Friends," he said.

Some cheered. People laughed, there was a snatch of song—

"Listen up," he snapped. They fell silent.

"I think that Ser Michael and Sukey have already spread the word. But let me confirm it. A week of rest. The inn will provide you. Sleep. Eat. Do anything else you like, as long as you drill and sew. Expect that we will be marching away in ten days. Sukey will serve out wool and linen. But that's for later. For now—well done."

"When do we get paid?" called someone. Almost certainly Cat Evil.

"Pay parade on Saint Catherine's Eve," the captain said.

"Where next?" another voice called. It sounded like Wilful Murder to Gabriel. He knew that couldn't be.

"Ask me in a week," he said.

"Who's paying for all the wrecked kit?" called another man.

"The awkward sods who wrecked it!" roared Tom.

Gabriel shook his head. "We have a dozen armourers coming with the queen. We'll do our best to restore our kit." He looked around. "You aren't paying."

That got a cheer.

"On Saint Catherine's Day, we'll have a tournament," he said. "Archery, swords, jousting, a melee on foot and on horseback. We'll post all this in a day or two. The prizes will be splendid. Contests will last three days, and we'll end with a great feast."

"And then we march away," groaned a lugubrious voice.

"And then I'll give you a day to sleep it off," Gabriel said. "And *then* we'll march away."

They cheered and cheered. Most of them hadn't had ten days of rest—archery tournaments and foot melees were restful—since the Winter War began.

Harald Derkensun got to his feet. Men fell silent.

"Are you the emperor, or not?" he roared.

Men and women began to thump the tables with their fists.

"Imperator! Imperator! Imperator!" they called.

Gabriel had the strangest feeling, of love and of invasion. He wanted the adulation and he was afraid of it. He wanted to be emperor because he knew what he could do with it. But he was afraid of it, and what it would do to him.

But inside him was a boy who'd craved the good opinion of others and seldom had it. So he drank in their cheers.

Derkensun was still standing. "Don't make me hoist you on a shield again!" he called.

Gabriel smiled, and realized that this was getting out of hand. He also knew that he couldn't tell the Nordikaans that he wanted to negotiate with Irene before he accepted.

"I am too tired to be emperor tonight," he called.

Derkensun frowned, drank some ale, and sat. He glared at Gabriel.

"Eat and drink and sleep," he said. "Red banda knights must turn out to escort the queen at first light."

Archers jeered their social superiors in a way that only the broad-minded could have understood as good-natured.

"Next formation, under Bad Tom, in three days."

A hearty cheer. This meant they could get especially drunk.

"Carry on, then," he said, and jumped off his barrel.

Michael nodded. Atcourt knelt by his captain.

"All the knights will go," he said. "We discussed it. Even Ser Christos and the Moreans."

Gabriel nodded. "Well, if you can manage it," he said, "I guess I'll have to lead you."

He walked over to where Derkensun sat. "I need you to give me a day or two," he said.

Derkensun looked at him. His look held something—bitterness? Disillusion? "Acclimation is supposed to be spontaneous," he said. "You do not *tell the guard* when we may acclaim you."

Gabriel took a proffered mug of dark ale, drank some, and sat back. "I need a few more days," he said. "I'm not discussing the politics of Morea. I'm asking on behalf of all the people who will die if we fuck this up."

Derkensun drank. He looked at his own corporals; Bregil White-hair, the oldest survivor of the Nordikaans, who had a scar that crossed his face and divided his beard in a way that always made Gabriel wonder why he was alive; Thorvin Lakbone, who was as big as a house and wasn't actually a Nordikaan at all; Erik Snoder, with his glorious mane of red-gold hair and his brilliant accumulation of gold arm rings, all of which he wore, so that some called him Erik Goldarm. They were all big men, and all tended to be silent until they were drunk.

"Fuck," Goldarm said. "Whatever he says, he'll be emperor. So who cares? Just obey and drink your ale, Harald."

"*Ja!*" muttered Whitehair, who was already working on getting drunk.

Lakbone ran his fingers through his beard. "You will recruit us back to strength, when you are emperor?"

"I sent a messenger bird a month ago," Gabriel said.

Derkensun sat back. "Good," he said. "We want a raven's feast for the old emperor. We want this dragon."

Gabriel knew that it was easy to treat Nordikaans as children, or caricatures of simplicity and violence, like their cousins, the Hillmen. So he thought for a moment.

"We will not get the dragon until very late in the game," he said seriously. "And we will only have one chance at him."

"But you will put our axes at the cutting edge of your shield wall," Whitehair said.

Derkensun brightened. "You have this war plan already?"

Gabriel nodded. "Friends," he said quietly. They were an odd audience, the Nordikaans. They had seen and fought almost everyone. In some ways they were more like creatures of the Wild than like men. It was hard to remember that Derkensun was young Mortirmir's best friend. "This is not a simple war."

Whitehair leaned back and laughed. "There are no simple wars," he said. "When Baldir Rotgut steals Lodir Fuckface's cow—even then, no war is simple. Many sides, many faces, many greeds, and many cowards."

Gabriel nodded. "So, then. This war is more like walking a path through a swamp than like..." Words failed him. "Like fighting a normal war," he said.

"So?" Derkensun asked.

"So, if I do everything right...if we win all the battles...if we make all the right guesses...then, in the end, we'll get one chance to get the dragon. One. It could all come down to one sword, or one axe." He looked around at their cold eyes, that shone like the northern lights.

"Ah," Goldarm said. "That's us you'll be wanting, then." He looked off into the far distance. "I'd like to kill a dragon."

"And get revenge?" Derkensun asked.

Whitehair laughed. "Revenge is for boys who've never kissed a girl," he said. "Kill a dragon and your name would live forever."

"What's that?" asked Bad Tom, coming catlike out of the dark.

"We are talking about killing the great dragon," Whitehair said.

"I'm in," said Tom.

"We drink to that," Goldarm said. He rose, and the other Nordikaans rose with him. Gabriel rose too.

They drank.

An hour later, Gavin was lying on his stomach, naked, and his brother was probing the edge of his skin where the scales began with a pricker. "Fascinating," he said. "Little tiny scales forming…"

Gavin drove a helpful elbow into his brother's side.

Gabriel yelped. "Stop that!" he said.

"Mary wants a great knight, not a scaled monster," Gavin said.

Gabriel nodded. "Well, you'll be a handsome scaled monster," he said. "I agree they're spreading. It is as if your body had finally come up with a mechanism to grow scales." He used the pricker again. "Better than chain mail, though."

"I admit I thought the same," Gavin said. "Damn it! I want to get married."

"I think this calls for Master Smythe, and perhaps for Harmodius. Brother mine, I agree it's a problem, but let's get through the plague first. The news from the Brogat is very bad. And Mortirmir looks ready to drop."

Gavin rolled off the bed. "I know," he said. "I feel like an arse. But… Christ, it's scary. I could accept one shoulder. Now…"

"I hear you," Gabriel said.

They were up at first light, and Gabriel didn't think his company had ever looked worse. He had knights on palfreys and riding horses, and the tack was a wreck; even Gavin had a mismatched saddle and bridle.

Gavin shrugged. "Leather just rotted away in the Adnacrags," he said.

"I'm not sure whether we're going to impress the queen or amuse her," Gabriel said. He was in borrowed harness himself, plain stuff from the inn. Toby and all his armour were travelling with the queen.

But the flags were bright, and the company's level of training had never been higher. Several dozen pages came with them—all volunteers—and a few dozen wine-sodden archers came out to wave them off and then stumbled back to their beds. The men-at-arms rode off by fours, and at noon, when they met the queen's escort, they divided neatly on either side of the road, wheeled by sections to the center, so that they sat in two ranks facing inward, and they saluted the queen and her baby king by dipping their lances as she passed.

She laughed with delight, pausing to stop and thank many of them—Sauce, for example, and Francis Atcourt, whom she kissed. He blushed as red as a beet.

"He'll never wash his lips again," Sauce said a little too loudly. Ser Danved roared and smacked his hip, and Ser Berengar glared at him.

Then she invited Ser Michael, Ser Gabriel, Ser Gavin, and Ser Thomas Lachlan to ride by her side. Ser Gavin was kissed, in public, by Lady Mary, to the cheers of a hundred knights and ladies; Ser Michael held his son and kissed his wife. Gabriel waved at Kaitlin and she, bold as ever, got her horse to his side.

"I've met Blanche!" she said. "Who is hovering with the servants in the baggage. Gabriel, I *know* better than most what it is like to be the trull."

Gabriel had a sudden desire to slip into the dust and vanish.

The queen smiled gently. "I will summon Blanche," she said. "You are Ser Michael's countess?" she asked.

The queen restored social order, and by the time Blanche came up, Ser Christos was describing for her the defeat of the emperor and the collapse of the imperial army.

"And yet many thousands were saved," the queen said. She winked at Blanche, who was riding—by the apparent conspiracy of half the nobles in Alba—at Gabriel's side, and blushing.

Ser Christos nodded. "A northerner—an imperial officer—formed a rear guard," he said. "With some Outwallers and the survivors of the Scholae, they prevented a massacre."

"I would like to meet this officer," the queen said. She gave Gabriel a look.

He bowed in the saddle. "Ser Giannis Turkos is still in the field," he said.

The queen rode along through the afternoon, asking questions about the magnificent, if unhuman, landscape of the Green Hills and the fells. Her brother came up and cantered into their group, admired a trout stream, and commented on the number of Occitan knights who had joined them, having ridden north for three weeks or more as a result of a mysterious summons.

They passed through the remnants of the drove, already off the main road and cresting the first high ridge of the fells, moving at a shepherd's pace for the byres and folds above the inn.

The queen turned to Gabriel while her brother and Ser Michael began to exchange challenges for the tournament. "It has not escaped me that you have gathered virtually the whole force of the alliance in these mountains," she said.

"Yes," he said. "I *think* that we now understand the nature of the threat and the scale. And now we must take council, and come to agreements. And act."

She turned. "And have a tournament," she said, with some amusement. "Your rest from war is to play at war."

He laughed. "Yes," he agreed. "Especially since there's little risk of life and a good deal more wine and sleep."

"Will you tell me what you fear, before I hear it in council?" she asked.

He nodded. "In short, Your Grace, everything about the plague now depends on Amicia, Harmodius, Lord Kerak, and Mortirmir. That is one problem for which I can contribute very little, unless they come to me for a little power." He shrugged. "Then, as to the other matter, and the war... there is so much to tell. I will visit you tomorrow, I think." He turned and smiled at Blanche.

She turned away.

"And you are doing what, exactly, about the imperial coronet?" the queen asked.

"Princess Irene is on her way to the inn," Gabriel said. "I think she must be consulted."

Blanche bit her lip.

"Of course," said the queen with some asperity. "I would not like my new emperor to immediately demand an oath of fealty from me, Ser Gabriel."

"Excuse me, Your Grace," Blanche said. She turned her palfrey and rode out of the royal party, her back straight. Gabriel could see she was angry.

He also knew that he could not follow her.

And then he decided that he could. "Pardon me, Your Grace," he said, and got his borrowed warhorse to a trot and then a canter. The knights of the royal guard waved, and then he caught her up.

"I'm sorry!" he said.

"You didn't just leave the queen!" she spat.

"I did. I'm not planning to marry Irene, my sweet. I cannot seize the crown she must regard as her own without some discussion." He reached for her hand.

"Everyone is watching us," she said.

"Yes," he agreed. "I think you should kiss me, the way Mary kissed Gavin. Then they'll know *why* they were watching us."

"Really?" she asked. "So that I can show them that you own me?" She turned her back, and rode away.

The queen watched Gabriel ride away. She pouted a moment, and Ser Francis shrugged, and she laughed. "I'm glad to see that in the midst of dire crisis, we still have the simpler dramas of court life," she said. "By our lady," she said. "It does my heart good to have you all about me. And sometimes, in these dark places, I begin to see some hope." Her eye again fell on Ser Francis.

He blushed. Again.

The queen's arrival raised the pitch of celebration at the inn, and she took the field prepared for her and raised her tent, a pavilion of red silk with a cloth of gold decoration and the royal standard flying from both of the peaks. A hundred royal servants, having travelled hard up the Albin from Harndon, arrived after the queen and began to lay out bake ovens and even a dance floor under the direction of Ser Galahad D'Acon, which the queen ordered tested immediately by her people. Galahad D'Acon danced with Lady Blanche, and there was a great deal of comment. The Red Knight watched from a distance and said nothing. Then he rode away with a heavy escort.

The next day, the Princess of Morea came in, escorted by her father's regiments and a hundred knights of Alba and Occitan, led in person, again, by Gabriel. She was settled in a large pavilion under the imperial standard, and her army, a couple of thousand men, mostly city regiments of cavalry, went into camp in streets laid out and prepared by the quartermasters of the army of the north.

From Gavin's room in the outer tower, Gabriel could see thousands of tents: white wedges, round pavilions, and more complicated wall tents and marquis and a dozen other shapes that covered the flat ground stretching away almost a mile to the north of the inn toward the lake.

"You think Ash knows we are here?" Gavin asked. He was lying on his stomach again, and this time, it was Harmodius tending him, with Master Smythe smoking by the window.

"I think he knows we're here, and I *want* him to see that we have a bigger, better army than we had when we faced him at Gilson's Hole." Gabriel was watching a beautiful woman down in the inner courtyard. He knew her—he was trying to place her.

Master Smythe was watching the same woman.

Gabriel watched him a moment, too. "If you crack the plague," he said.

Harmodius gave a grim smile. "If," he said.

"He'll feel it. He'll see this army." Gabriel shrugged. "Won't he flinch?"

Master Smythe threw his arms wide in a theatrical gesture. "I would flinch," he said. "Ash..." He shrugged again.

"That's the woman you took fishing," Gabriel said to Master Smythe.

Master Smythe smiled. "Yes."

Gabriel raised an eyebrow.

"I didn't eat her," Master Smythe said.

"Ouch!" Gavin insisted. He smiled, though.

Harmodius shook his head. "It's as if, rather than transferring to you some essence of an *adversarius*, instead, I unlocked some preexisting tendency for you to have scales." He swore in frustration and tugged his own beard.

Gabriel was still watching Master Smythe. He saw the dragon's countenance change at Harmodius's pronouncement—the rapid sorting of facial expressions with which the dragon marked moments of intense confusion.

"I'm missing something," he said aloud.

The dragon affected not to hear him.

Harmodius rose to his feet. "I don't see anything more I can do here," he said. "Amicia and Mortirmir are working together. I should be there." He shrugged. "I suppose I thought this might have some connection to the plague."

He seemed defeated, as restless, annoyed, and fatigued as the wreck of young Morgon Mortirmir, who'd just had a very loud set-to with a young Morean noblewoman in the outer courtyard.

Gabriel helped his brother get into his shirt.

"The funny thing is that I'm fine," he said. "Better than fine. I feel— unstoppable. Immortal."

Gabriel froze with one hand on the laces for Gavin's inner doublet. "That's an interesting choice of words," he said. He coughed, and the black flecks spread across his hand, and some lingered like spore in the air. "One thing I am not feeling is immortal," he said.

"You aren't afraid?" Gavin asked. He wasn't trying to be insensitive. He was genuinely puzzled.

Gabriel chewed on his lips, his latest tic. "Every day, I have less breath," he said. "I can't really practice at the pell. I'm growing weaker." He leaned on the frame of the window, looking down into the court- yard, where the dragon's girl was hanging washing. She was lithe, and athletic, and very attractive. "If they don't find a solution, a lot of us are going to die," he said. "I confess it was not the biggest matter to me at first. But every cough—those black flecks are the necrotic result of the decay of my lungs. It was supposed to happen in an hour. But..."

He paused. "She's pregnant," he said aloud.

"Who?" Gavin asked. "Blanche?"

Gabriel whirled, and for a moment they were brothers. The tussle went on for several rounds, and grunting was the only noise, with the exception of two "you bastards" and a sucker punch.

"You aren't so out of shape," Gavin said.

Gabriel was breathing very hard, wheezing. He could see spots in front of his eyes. On the other hand, he was on top of his bigger brother, straddling his chest.

"That was a little nasty," Gavin went on.

Gabriel tried, and failed, to hide a smirk. He got off. "Blanche thinks she's going to be replaced by Princess Irene," he said.

Gavin pursed his lips, manfully hiding how much his brother hand just hurt his hip. "Well? The betting says you take the empire over the laundress."

Gabriel nodded. "Eh," he said, rubbing his jaw. "If only it were that simple."

"I have a hard time imagining you with Irene," Gavin said. "She tried to kill you. Or that's what Sauce says. Not that I don't understand the temptation. She can hardly be the only woman who has tried to kill you."

"She's the only one who proposed marriage later," Gabriel said. "I'm guessing... never mind." He looked down. "I don't think Blanche is pregnant, thanks for asking."

Gavin laughed carefully, so as not to reignite whatever had just happened. "Mater wanted you to marry Irene."

"Exactly," Gabriel said.

"She could be fey. She knew things." Gavin shrugged.

"You in a hurry to see me dead?" Gabriel said. "Some amount of time after I marry Irene, you'll find me drowned in my bath, dead in a fall from my horse, or having somehow cut off my own head with my sword."

Gavin sat back on the bed where he'd ended up. "Ah. I confess, that puts a different face on the betting."

"I would marry Blanche, even without the queen's foolish interference..."

"Whoa!" cried Gavin. "That's... harsh."

"But if I say so before I meet Irene," Gabriel shook his head. "Anyway, Blanche is not speaking to me."

Gavin laughed. "Oh. That kind of trouble. Well... I'll face a dragon with you, brother mine. But I won't be helping you face down some spurned princess. By the way, Aneas is fine."

"Chasing Kevin Orley," Gabriel said absently.

"Chasing the man who killed our parents," Gavin said.

Gabriel shrugged. "No," he said. "Orley's as much a victim of all this as I am. Thorn and Ash killed our parents. If Orley would disown Ash, I'd grant him an estate somewhere."

"Christ, are you insane?" Gavin was up off the bed. "Clean wode?"

Gabriel shrugged. "None of it *matters*. Listen, brother mine: I have the plague, I'm the captain general of the coalition against Ash, we're bleeding people and losing revenue, there's a whole other kind of monster loose in Antica Terra, and when the stars align, we're going to be invaded by some new horrible menace. Oh, and my mistress has just walked out on me. And to me, right now, that's the worst of all. I'm not... big enough... for this. When I walk out of this room, I have to be the fucking imperturbable captain general. I have to crack jokes, look good, and smile while I cough out my lungs and watch Blanche dance with D'Acon like she did last night. In a few days, after crossing lances with you to open the tourney, I get to sit down with everyone who matters in the alliance and hammer out a plan to win."

Gavin didn't sigh. He grinned.

"So?" he asked. "I have scales taking over my body, my brother's dying of the plague, my parents just died horribly, and my girl does not want a rushed wedding. She wants to milk the queen for every prize, because exile to a convent hurt her feelings. And I live in the shadow of my brother…"

Gabriel looked up. "Did you ever read the plan?"

Gavin laughed. "After Michael and Tom. I'm sorry, brother. But I notice things like that."

"Well, it's all a dead letter anyway." Gabriel sighed. "Here's the new plan," he said, and took an imperial scroll tube from his shirt. "Give it back when you've read it. One question first. Would you rather have command of this army, or rule Morea for six months?"

Gavin had been about to scratch himself under his beard. Instead, he froze. "That's a real question?"

"Not only is it real, but you are getting first choice, brother." Gabriel smiled.

"Army," Gavin said.

Gabriel nodded. "I wonder how Aneas would do with Irene?"

"You mean, given that he prefers men to women?" Gavin shrugged. "He has a partner, and good luck to them both."

Gabriel smiled. "I don't really want to share all my thoughts, but if you do not want a woman to have a legitimate heir…"

"Oooh," he said. Gavin put a hand to his face. "Remind me not to try to kill you," he said.

"I find my reputation as a good man to be very handy when I have to do something nasty." Gabriel shrugged.

Gavin nodded. "You are going to try to have Blanche and the empire too," he said.

Gabriel nodded. "Yes," he said.

"You always intended to make yourself emperor," Gavin said flatly.

Gabriel shrugged.

"Damn," Gavin said. "That means you intend to have Irene killed."

Gabriel looked at him. Gavin nodded.

"Right," Gavin said. "You mean, I should shut up."

"I don't want to kill her," Gabriel said. "But I fear I have very few options."

*

Outside, in the courtyard, the dragon's girl had finished hanging laundry. She flashed Gabriel a smile even as Toby started across the yard to intercept him. But he was determined.

"I don't remember your name," he said.

"Don't think you ever asked," she said, lowering her eyes. It was not shyness, and she smiled, secure in her own powers. "You can call me Bess."

He nodded. "Well met, Bess."

She smiled. "I know you're a great noble, but could you just reach me down that wee peg, Ser Knight?"

He stretched up and got it. He handed it to her with a bow. "You are with child," he said quietly.

She laughed. "That ain't much o' a secret, Ser Knight! I can even tell you how it happens of a lass." She smiled again.

He bowed again and turned to Toby.

"Princess Irene will receive you. And there is a set of messages. Ser Michael says, 'now.'" He smiled at Bess. It was very hard for a young man to do otherwise. It was not that she was beautiful, it was that, a few months in kindle, she was just about the epitome of Hills femininity.

Gabriel blew out a long breath. "I'll be in the solar," he said, and walked through the edge of the common room, waving, smiling, and moving like a knight through a swarm of foes. He made the side stairs and in moments was in his own chambers. He had three; an outer office that was also Toby and Anne's room; a middle room with a fireplace and a superb window, that everyone called the solar, where Ser Michael sat writing and today, Kaitlin sat sewing on a bench by a purely honourary fire; and an inner bedroom.

"Messages?" he asked without preamble.

Michael looked up. "Nice to see you too. You know that if I succumb to temptation and commit patricide, I'll have precedence over you, and it'll be my turn to be rude all the time."

Kaitlin laughed. "I have missed the way you two talk," she said. "I've spent months cooped up with women."

Gabriel was already reading. "Good God," he said. "Oh my God," he said. There was a lengthy pause. "Holy—! That means..." He turned over the parchment to make sure there was nothing on the back.

"Kronmir?" Michael asked.

"Sea monsters!" Gabriel said.

"What'd Gavin choose?" Michael asked.

"Army," Gabriel said, reading a second sheet. "Damn! Perfect. Alcaeus, I love you."

"I told you so. I told you Gavin would take the army. You'll have to leave Milus in Liviapolis. But I'm going. And so are Tom and Sauce." Michael was growing increasingly bold. "And Kaitlin."

Gabriel looked up. "Good," he said. His eyes passed over Kaitlin. "You know the risks," he said.

She looked at the baby in the basket by the hearth. Sniffed. And, without apology, began to change him. A servant appeared, and Kaitlin, who had begun life as a scullery maid, had no difficulty in handing off the old linen nappie and accepting a new one, pressed, and the bob of a curtsy.

Gabriel wrinkled his nose. "Mmm," he said. "Smells like Umroth ivory."

"Ewww," Michael said. "That's my son."

Kaitlin raised one beautifully dark and beautifully arched eyebrow. "Captain, I feel you are old enough to tell that this basket at my feet is the natural result of a dalliance. Like yours with Blanche, for example."

Gabriel's eyes flashed.

But his voice was mild. "Have you spoken to Blanche?" he asked.

"Yes, and..."

"Kaitlin, you are one of my *very favourite people*. If you see Blanche, pass her my invitation to a private dinner. But please do not interfere." He met her eye squarely. "Please."

She sighed. "But you'll take me with the company?"

Gabriel nodded. "Unless Sukey recovers, you may be head woman, while also being Michael's wife. Can you manage that? There may also be times when you have to be a great lady."

"I'm getting better at the lady part," she said. "So is Blanche." She looked determined.

Gabriel had read the second document twice. "Alcaeus remains my favourite. Michael, send everything we know about the Odine to Kronmir. Numbers only from now on, no names said out loud, got that?"

Michael was writing furiously.

"Kaitlin, invite Blanche for dinner. Lest she think the worst,

perhaps the two of you would join us in the solar for wine afterward."
He bowed.

"Enchanted," Michael muttered automatically.

"Delighted," Kaitlin said.

"Ricard is becoming a master archer?" Michael said. He waved at
the ink to dry it and then looked pointedly at Kaitlin. "Your layabout
brother. He's off with Aneas."

"Dan Favour is up to be knighted," Gabriel said. "Aneas will need a
resupply. By air."

"Who'd have thought," Kaitlin said, looking down at her dress of
embroidered linen.

"Where are you going?" Michael asked.

"I'll drop in on Aneas, before I visit Princess Irene," Gabriel said.
"This is how I practice for fighting dragons."

Ariosto was ludicrously happy to see him. Gabriel led his great beast
out of a shed, walked him round and round a paddock, and then, with
Anne and Toby's help, got him tacked up.

All things considered, he preferred open-field take-offs to dropping
off towers. He was aloft in a few great wingbeats, and before the Inn
of Dorling was lost below him, he was in the *aethereal looking for his
brother Aneas.*

*Aneas was curiously difficult to find. He had always been adept at hid-
ing, with a childhood penchant for ambushes and secrecy.*

*He found the recent battlefield first, by the trace emanations of serious
workings. The line of curse trees and the devastation they wrought was visible from a thousand feet up, and he read the battlefield the way a scholar
would read an ancient text, coaxing meaning out of a corpse, the herme-
neutics of war.*

*Ariosto began to unearth a grave and Gabriel told him not to eat. It had
never happened before, but the griffon's taste in meat was catholic, and
Gabriel tried not to be shocked.*

What are these things? Ariosto asked.

Gabriel looked at a horned one, the corpse two days old.

"If you can cut it open, why can't I eat it?" Ariosto asked.

*Gabriel had an answer. "Please don't eat it," he said. "It has some dark
power attached to it."*

"Oh." Ariosto stopped. "Disgusting."

They had to walk a distance together to find a place from which Ariosto could launch, because of the trees and the undergrowth. Walking, the griffon was a figure of fun, and Gabriel had to keep turning his head to hide a laugh as the lion struggled to cooperate with the eagle. Running was better. Walking was not his best thing.

But it allowed them to follow the whole course of the battle, and find Fitzalan's grave. And his brother's hermetical trail, faint but palpable.

Then they were flying. He scarcely had time to be cold before they were over a campsite with a thin thread of smoke rising, and he banked carefully, going around as the camp went into a state of alarm.

He wrote his name in red smoke and landed in a small meadow a hundred paces to the south.

He was just dismounting when Aneas appeared in the distance, waving his arms. Gabriel was aware he'd landed in a great meadow of blueberries... the bushes were everywhere, the crop massive, and their landing had crushed the plants, so that Ariosto's feet were stained blue. The griffon, a carnivore, was eating berries with passion before Gabriel had made his dismount.

"Gabriel!" Aneas roared.

Gabriel waved casually. He was untying the sacks of flour.

"Gabriel!" Aneas called, this time with real urgency. Gabriel was pleased that Aneas sounded so excited. If army rumour was correct, Fitzalan had been very close to his youngest brother and...

There was a flick of movement to his right.

He dropped from the high saddle, and he and Ariosto turned together.

Aneas was almost close enough to touch.

The black bear stood almost as high as Gabriel's shoulder, and was angry at being interrupted in an orgy of blueberry eating.

"We almost landed atop it," Gabriel said.

Food?

No. Leave the bear, Ariosto. Sheep at the inn in two hours.

OK. Looks tough, anyway.

The three of them, two dangerous men and a large monster, backed carefully away from the black bear. The bear went back to browsing the berries.

"You brought *wine*?" the female irk asked.

Gabriel poured her some of the inn's best Etruscan. "I thought you might be missing it by now."

"And flour and butter," Aneas said.

"What riches," Lewen, the male irk, said. "Butter! Mankind's greatest invention."

Aneas sat back, wine in hand. "This is luck, brother," he said. "We made camp to have a swim and make a hard decision."

There was a slim young man who was brimful of power. Gabriel watched him for a moment, and was suddenly unsure—man or woman. But sure of their power. "I am Looks-at-Clouds," the man said. "You are?"

"Gabriel Muriens. This young sprite's brother." Gabriel smiled at Aneas. Aneas managed a sort of lip twitch. Far better than his usual careful passivity.

"Ah!" the young man said. "You are the Red Duke?"

Gabriel nodded.

Looks-at Clouds nodded back. "Well then." He looked at Aneas.

"About this time yesterday, Orley split his forces again. He's running north. Another party is running east." He looked at the older war leader.

Gabriel wished he had a pipe. He rose and bowed. "I am Gabriel Muriens," he said.

The big Outwaller smiled and rose and clasped his hand. "We all know you, Red Knight," he said. "I am Pine."

The other Outwaller captain proved to be the very Giannis Turkos that the queen had just been praising. Gabriel couldn't have told him from Tall Pine. He had the same eyes and wore a breechclout, leggings, and what might once have been a linen cote. Gabriel knew Turkos from the desperate days before Gilson's Hole.

Gabriel had learned that command often consisted merely of listening to the opinions of others and waiting to see which point of view held the most sense. He listened as they expounded their arguments.

In short, Tall Pine and Turkos wanted to go home, and by pursuing the eastern fragment, they could get closer to home.

Darkness was falling by the time they'd all spoken. He had to go. The waterfall to the east was increasingly attractive; a nice swim, a night without responsibility...

"I must go," he said. "There's a great council fire lit at the Inn of Dorling," he said to Tall Pine. "You should be there, and so should Captain Turkos, if Aneas can spare you."

Aneas sat back, relieved of responsibility.

Gabriel looked at him. "Ticondonaga is back in our hands," he said. "So the party running east can't change that. I agree that I'd sleep better if this Orley were in the ground." He shrugged.

Aneas looked bitter. "But you've moved on." He all but spat. "This is no longer the main effort."

Gabriel shrugged. "Actually, I meant nothing of the kind."

"Will you be emperor?" Turkos asked suddenly. "You've been acclaimed."

"Twice," Gabriel said.

Tessen laughed, and de la Mothe looked at his cup.

"By my faith," he said, "I'm drinking with the emperor."

"That's why the wine is so good," Tessen said.

Gabriel looked at the imperial officer. "You know what?" he asked in Archaic. "I don't know. I won't marry Irene."

Turkos might have been appalled to be addressed so frankly, but he was used to Outwallers. "So don't marry her," he said. "The army acclaimed you. It's an honoured tradition. And Irene tried to kill her father, or so I hear." He shrugged. "I don't think the army would ever support her."

"And you?" Gabriel asked.

Aneas was watching him like a hawk.

Turkos swirled his wine. "When you saved me and the fur trade last winter," he said, "you showed you knew more about being emperor than any of the last lot. I loved Irene's father as a man. As emperor, he was an empty vessel." He shrugged.

De la Mothe shook his head. "No one will ever believe I was hearing this," he said quietly.

Aneas looked at Gabriel. "You schemed for this from the first, didn't you? Even when you went to Arles. You were working on becoming emperor even then."

Gabriel shrugged. "Would it make it better if I said there are many things I will not do to be emperor?" he asked.

Tessen, the irk, laughed, and so did Ricard Lantorn. But the irk spoke.

"It is better for me, man," she said. "It is good you say this."

Lantorn just shook his head. "Christ, all I want is to be a master archer," he said. "This is all over my head."

Gabriel nodded to him. "They're giving you Wilful Murder's bow. He died. Plague took him."

Lantorn's tough face was crossed with a single pulse of obvious grief. He hid it. "Old bastard," he said, and looked at the fire. Then he looked back. "Giving me his bow?"

Gabriel nodded.

Aneas knew how to be a good captain. "Go back with Gabriel, Ricard. I can spare you. Go and take your promotion."

Lantorn shook his head. "Nah. Savin' yer pardon, Cap'n, I said I'd go wi' you to get Orley, and I won' go back now. I have a score ta settle fer my brother, too."

Gabriel leaned over so that his shoulder brushed his brothers. "He just called you *Captain*," he said very quietly.

He had a quiet conversation with Ricard Lantorn, and then he went back to Ariosto. On the way back, he paused and took the imperial officer aside.

Turkos looked shocked after Gabriel spoke to him at length. "You'd do that?" he asked.

"I don't want to kill her," Gabriel said.

Turkos shrugged. "I can't tell you what would happen," he said. He smiled. "Truth? I think you are postponing an ugly duty, like putting down a sick dog. But perhaps she'll learn to sing hymns, too."

"She's more a victim than a foe," the Red Knight said.

Turkos shrugged. "I could say the same of the Hurans I killed. Or of Thorn."

The griffon launched out of the blueberries, and Aneas stood waving at a brother he'd once despised.

Looks-at-Clouds put a hand on his shoulder. "If you allow," s/he said, "I will stay you. Let Tall Pine go home."

Tall Pine spoke in Huran and then shook his head. "I go to the inn," he said. "The Red Knight wants all the shamans, too."

Looks-at-Clouds shrugged. "Orley is more important," s/he said.

Now Tall Pine shrugged. "Good then. Now we swim, and then eat." He smiled. "And we have butter."

Gabriel landed in the slanting sun of late afternoon; still plenty of light in the sky. He didn't change into formal court clothes. Turkos had steeled his resolve, and the conversation in the Wild had clarified what he wanted, and what he might do.

He even managed a smile.

Alcaeus's mother Maria met him in the entry to the great pavilion of imperial purple. In truth, like the empire it served, it was a trifle threadbare; the central pole had clearly frayed the silk of the tent and been repaired a little too hastily, and the west side of the tent was faded from being left in the sun, or being badly folded. The gilt work around the door was tarnished and looked as if it had been pecked by birds, and inside, the tapestries were old and faded and the carpets were not as rich as they should have been.

Yet the central lamp that hung, burning clearly with seven wicks, over the gilded wood throne was solid gold, and the cup in Princess Irene's hand was solid silver, and she wore a magnificent, if somewhat boxy, gold brocade dress from Venike.

The Red Knight ignored court decorum and swept across the pavilion to kneel on one knee at her feet and kiss her hand. This gesture had no imperial significance whatsoever. He'd put a good deal of thought into it.

"At last, the Megas Dukas deigns to visit us," she said.

She was still beautiful. In fact, she had gone from being a merely attractive dark-haired girl with flawless ivory skin and a nose slightly too large for her, to being a stunning woman with the hawklike nose of her family, and on her, it was perfect.

He chose not to answer.

And so, silence fell. The two looked at each other, and she did not ask him to rise, and he did not rise.

Maria cleared her throat.

"Are you in touch with your son?" Gabriel asked her. It was a clear contravention of the protocol of court, but there were two silent servants of the Ordinary present and no other court. The guard outside had been Scholae. He knew them all. This was meant to be informal. Which was to say, as informal as a girl born to the purple could stand.

"You may only speak to me, and then only when I speak," Irene said quietly. She was reminding him, he thought. She thought he might have forgotten.

He smiled at her. "That is the etiquette of the court, and for the empress," he said.

"I am the empress," she said. "I have travelled to the very borders of my own realm to see you. Is this nothing to you? I cannot imagine such a thing happening in my father's time. You are my Megas Dukas. I require you in Liviapolis. My city is in turmoil. The plague is loose there. And there are men—horrible men..." She paused.

Gabriel looked back at Maria.

She gave a small shake of her head.

"Tell me of the terrible men," he said.

"Men with the heads of animals. They riot and kill. They kill *doctors*. And priests. And magi." Her voice trailed off. She was the very picture of the princess in need of rescuing.

"So I understand," Gabriel said. "I am in daily communication with the officers of the city."

Irene looked at him. "What?"

Gabriel shrugged. "There is a war party headed for the Morea even now; reinforcements for the partisans in your countryside. My officers will see to its elimination."

Irene paused, her mouth open attractively, her perfect teeth showing. She took in a surprised breath. "You understand?" she asked.

"Yes. From Ser Alcaeus. Maria's son." Gabriel was still on one knee and his knee hurt and he wasn't breathing well and he hated hurting people. And he knew—close up—that for no real reason, he felt a good deal for this woman.

"Where is he?" Irene asked, her eyes going to Maria.

"In the city," Gabriel said. "He has been for several days."

Irene understood immediately. "I have a safe conduct!" she said immediately. "You cannot touch me."

Gabriel stood up, ending all pretense. "I am going to be emperor."

"Over my corpse," she said calmly. "Unless..." She paused. "You were acclaimed. I accept it. In fact, the patriarch accepts it." She shrugged. "But you will marry me. And we will be acclaimed together, as in the ancient times."

He met her eye. He had seldom done so in his months as her military commander. Court etiquette forbade such eye contact, and the only time he'd really looked into her eyes was the night Kaitlin had married Michael, and Ser George had married his lady. So many crises ago.

She could not hold his look. "You may not look at me like that," she said.

He nodded. "I will offer you no insult."

She nodded. "Yes. I understood that as soon as you came in. You were born...for us." She smiled.

"I will speak frankly, Irene. You are a desperate gambler on her last throw. Despite which..." He raised his hand to intercept her protest, "Despite which, I will assure your place and not have you killed by the mutes or sent to northern Thrake. Or stabbed with a magical dagger. Or have your knees broken. Or, if all that fails, have you shot with a poisoned dart."

As he spoke, she writhed. It was a controlled writhe. Invisible to anyone who did not know her.

He had just told her that he knew, precisely, how she had tried to have him killed. And her father.

"I have all of Andronicus's correspondence," he said. "Including that part that went by imperial messenger. And Kronmir works for me, now."

They looked at each other, and time might have been said to have stopped.

She sighed, eventually. "Very well," she said. Empress to princess in one breath. "I would make a good wife. I *like* you, Gabriel. That was... a different time. With different pressures." She didn't shrug; she was too proud. "Surely you of all men understand the terrain of politics, and the battles I had to fight. How could I know you would be more valuable to me than..."

The problem was that he thought she was telling the truth. Telling a truth. Capable of believing what she was saying, anyway.

He smiled. "You know the odd thing, Irene? I like you too. That's why I am not publishing the letters, or simply killing you. I have a deal to offer you, which, from my perspective, seems very fair. You may reject it. But in this negotiation, I have almost everything, including the approval of the army and control of the city and your person." He was holding her eyes. He saw her flick a look at Maria. Maria looked away.

"Damn you," she said.

"Damn you," Gabriel said. "You tried to kill me, and you left enough loose ends behind that now I own you."

"Traitor!" Irene hissed at Maria.

Maria shook her head. "I loved your father," she said. Then she made a deep obeisance.

Irene's eyes went back to Gabriel's. "Very well," she said. She was a survivor. "Whom do I have to marry?" she asked.

"My brother Aneas," Gabriel said. "He's in the woods killing Kevin Orley just now. He is closer to your age than I am. He's quite handsome."

She looked at Maria. "He is a boy lover," she spat.

He had forgotten about how well informed she would be.

"A man lover, perhaps, sometimes," he said. "He likes power, too. I would make him Duke of Thrake."

She put a hand to her throat.

"I would leave you as regent when I went away, with Ser Milus as Megas Dukas and my brother on the throne next to you," he said. "Damn it, Irene, this is a very, very good deal I offer."

"You should just kill me," she said. Her ivory skin transmitted a flush very quickly.

"Is that your answer?" he asked. His voice was hard.

"You are too soft to be emperor. I am not. I will be empress over your corpse. I spit on your brother. And you." She rose. "Go."

Gabriel stood for a long time. Outside, horses chomped grass on the fells, and a red-tailed hawk screamed, and two servants had a tiff over who, exactly, drank the last of the lord's red wine.

Gabriel looked at Maria, and she looked away.

He had a war in his mind. He knew so many things Irene didn't. She was young, very young, and she hadn't done the things he'd done, and she was merely playing the game as she'd been taught, by ruthless experts, all but one of whom had failed. She was replaying their failures, while thinking them great.

It struck him that killing her was a terrible waste. He didn't want her death on his conscience. With all the other deaths, there was already an impressive trail of corpses following him.

But…she had it in her power to wreck all their plans, and she'd never even know why, and he didn't trust her enough to tell her. Master Smythe and Michael and Sauce all agreed that they could not trust her.

And any woman who could countenance her father's murder might sell out to Ash.

What Gabriel knew, what Maria knew, and what Irene, of course, did not know, was that if Gabriel walked out of the tent without his bargain, she was dead.

He stood looking at her.

She drew herself to her full height. "I hate you. I hate myself for once having wanted you. You are too weak to rule, and the empire will cheer me when I kill you, just as fiercely as now, they cheer you."

He kept looking at her. Almost everything in him cried out to tell her. To explain it all.

It was one thing to send men to their deaths in battle. He hated it, but he did it. Without much thought, really.

She was being sent to her death for being too full of guile and self-ishness to be trusted. A battle casualty of another sort.

"I will dance on your grave," she said.

Unconsciously, he ran a hand over his hair, and flexed the fingers of his silver hand, his latest habit.

He thought of his young brother, weeping for the death of his friend.

He didn't even shrug. The desire to speak to her was too great, and the equally balanced desire, almost sexual, to kill her himself, with the dagger at his hip. Political suicide, and yet, somehow, more honest. His real self.

He wondered for a moment how he would ever talk of this to Amicia, or, God help him, Blanche.

He found his right hand on his dagger hilt.

She flinched.

He took it away, and bowed.

He thought that it was odd that if she died, few would mourn her, but if he killed her here, in a welter of blood, men would think him a monster.

I am a monster, he thought. *In a good cause.*

"Go!" she shrieked.

He met her eyes again. "Irene," he said. "I would like you to live. And be powerful. This is what you want as well."

"Even if you kill me, I will triumph, because you will lose the trust of many men," she said.

Gabriel sighed. "You won't know," he said. "Because you'll be *dead*."

"I'll be queen in hell," she said.

He shook his head, admiring her courage and hating her foolish sense of drama. "You know the phrase, *Better the slave of a bad master than king of the dead*?" he asked.

"You almost speak High Archaic like a person," she shot back. "Don't quote the classics at me, you bloody-handed barbarian. Go—ride your servant girl; she's more your speed. And play at being emperor. The army will tire of you in time."

He raised an eyebrow. "That was a trifle arch, even for you."

He managed not to look at Maria, nor signal her in any way. He simply left, his shoulders square.

For more than an hour, he walked about the sheepfolds and the cattle fences as the summer sun plunged. And, naturally, he found thirty Hillmen in a small camp: close enough to the inn to get beer, far enough that they didn't need to mix with all the difficult foreigners.

Bad Tom was standing, naked to the waist. Donald Dhu was standing opposite him. Neither man had a weapon.

Both were bleeding.

David the Cow made room for Gabriel in the ring. "Cheers," he muttered, without taking his eyes off the two giants.

Gabriel was handed a mug of dark ale, which he drank off as he watched.

The two men circled carefully, arms out, weight forward.

Twice, they started to close—arms reaching—then did not, for whatever reason, slipping away from the decisive moment.

"Donald is down one throw," David said. "He's still fuckin' lit about his son. He thinks Tom's gone soft."

Gabriel nodded. He drank more.

He saw Tom's intention clearly, because he'd faced Tom enough times. The big man swayed once, and then another time. It wasn't much of a feint, because Gabriel knew he didn't need a feint. He just wanted Donald Dhu to come in range.

And Dhu did. Suddenly he powered forward, arms out. By chance, or intent, the two men's fingers meshed instead of sliding down one another's arms, and Tom kicked Dhu in the knee and thrust his right arm, almost as if he were punching the red-haired man, except that their fingers were intertwined and so he pulled Dhu's left arm across his body—the other man leaned to favour the knee injured by the kick, and Tom threw him suddenly over his own out-thrust shin, a casual throw, except that Tom followed him down, kneeling viciously with a knee between the other man's legs and slamming his one hand into the back of the other man's head, breaking his nose.

"Yield," Tom said.

Dhu rolled instead. Or rather, he tried, and it was a good try, and despite the pain, or because of it, he feinted, used his hips, and he moved Bad Tom, but he didn't roll him off.

Bad Tom broke his arm. It wasn't a long, drawn-out process. The big Drover simply used his purchase and broke the other man's arm and probably dislocated his shoulder, too.

Hill men were tough and had extravagant notions of how tough they ought to be, but most of the men in the circle flinched or looked away.

Tom got up. "I tol' ye to yield, and ye dinna." He shrugged. "Take yer tail and go awa' home. I'm done wi' ye. When yer shoulder heals, come back and say yer sorry, or come back and fight me to the death." He nodded to the men in the circle, and then he walked to the stone wall and took his shirt, a huge thing of bright yellow linen.

He saw Gabriel and nodded. Men were staying away from him, and Gabriel had the terrible feeling that he'd arrived at exactly the wrong time—the sort of outside interference that the Hillmen resented.

He drank the rest of his dark ale anyway. He didn't want to kill Irene. It made him angry. The whole thing made him angry. Being indecisive made him angry. For the moment, she was alive, and he knew he was avoiding a very real problem. Blanche was angry, and he didn't want to deal with that, either.

Tom moved away from him, talking to some men and avoiding others, until he'd made a circuit.

Gabriel got himself another cup of ale.

He was well into it when Bad Tom appeared. "An how long since ye have had a nice fight?" he asked.

"I fought Thorn to the death about three weeks ago," Gabriel said. He flexed his left hand. "Just before that, I fought de Vrailly."

"An' now yer resting on yer laurels, eh?" Tom asked. "I need a favour o' ye."

Gabriel nodded. "Anything, Tom."

"Good. I need ye to fight wi' me, right now, in a shirt, with a long sword. Do you a world o' good." He stepped back, all six foot five of him, and drew his enormous sword. The sword that had wounded Ash.

Gabriel felt all the lethargy of two large pints of dark beer.

"I have to piss first." He pointed. "And not against that sword."

"Fair eno'," Tom said. "Get me my old sword."

Behind him, some Hillmen laughed.

Gabriel went away two sheepfolds and came back to find the circle re-formed, and Tom waiting on his sword hilt, his point buried in the ground.

He stripped off his doublet, retied his points, drew his sword, and laid the scabbard, belt, and purse on top of his doublet.

"Ready," he said.

Tom opened with a massive swing, a monstrous thing that started with his sword hidden behind his right hip. He swung it up, over his head, and down at a diagonal that would have split Gabriel from eyebrow to hip.

Gabriel parried, letting Tom's blade slide down his, carefully avoiding allowing Tom's sharp edge to catch on his own. He countercut from the cover, rolling his own wrists and striking at Tom's, but the big man was too fast and too canny for such a simple play, and he flicked his blade up in a small cover. Then he cut straight at Gabriel's head.

Gabriel knew it was a feint, but the knowing and the sheer fear of the big man and his big blade almost cost him.

He raised his own blade in response—and read the feint.

As Tom's blade rotated—as Tom released the grip of his left hand on the pommel and stepped forward—Gabriel released his own grip with his left hand. But instead of doing the classic counter to the other man's classic attack, he simply crossed Tom's sword—one-handed. Not a winning proposition, except that he stepped in, something most men did not do to Tom Lachlan, and slammed his left hand into Tom's right elbow. And stepped through again, Tom rotating to avoid the blow, and tapped Tom on the forehead with his pommel. It was not a gentle tap, but neither, apurpose, was it a knockout blow.

"That for you!" Tom shouted as the Hillmen roared.

Tom came in again. This time the blades both licked out, right on center—thrust, parry, deceive, counterdeception.

Gabriel saw his moment and grabbed Tom's blade, but he'd been lured. Tom pulled the blade.

Gabriel's left hand was not made of flesh. His grip held, and Tom's eyes widened as Gabriel's point came up between his eyes. "Now that's cheatin'," he laughed. "Damme! I clean forgot that you had steel instead o' flesh on the left hand."

He came in again.

Gabriel was breathing like a bellows, his injured lungs not doing a very good job of supporting the fight, and he began to back away, ceding, he knew, too much initiative, and when he drew a deep breath and stood his ground, he chosen the wrong distance. Tom's heavy cut locked their blades, and Gabriel chose to put weight into his cover. Tom glided in with his left hand and got it between Gabriel's on his hilt, and in one powerful move, threw the smaller man to the ground... and took his sword.

Gabriel lay on the springy turf, his hip a little bruised from a rock, and a line of blood just starting on his left shoulder where Tom had tapped him with the sharp blade.

"Another shirt ruined," he said. He got to his feet with a hand from Tom, and they embraced. Some Hillmen cheered, and the rest just smiled. Some began to square off in fights of their own.

"There," Tom said, handing Gabriel back his sword. "Yer better already."

Gabriel had to breathe a while. Someone brought him more ale. Remarkably, it was the dragon's girl, Bess. She grinned at him.

"I'm not sure which one of us is the bad penny," he said.

Tom laughed. "Bess is no better 'an she ought to be," he leered. "Away wi' ee, lady." He leaned against the stone wall. "You looked terrible. Ye needed a fight an' a fuck. I can only give ye the fight," he went on.

Gabriel had to laugh, and he did.

Tom told him a little of the trouble between him and Donald Dhu.

Gabriel knew it all, but listened anyway. Then he told Tom about Irene.

"Oh shit, laddie. Just fewkin' kill her," Tom shrugged. "Or ha' it done."

Gabriel looked into the summer evening. There were superb flowers on the hills, and the warm early-evening midsummer sun lit the flowers like a promise of heaven. Even their fighting had served only to crush a few and raise their scent.

The flowers covered the hills for miles, as far as the eye could see, a riot of tiny buds in all the colours of the rainbow. Far off north, the waters of the lake seemed to burn.

"I have another idea," Gabriel said. "If it doesn't work, I'll kill her."

"Good lad," Tom said.

Gabriel shook his head.

"She dug her own grave," Tom said. "What now?"

"Dinner with Blanche." Gabriel nodded.

"Just pull her clothes off. Eat later." Tom grinned. "I told you. A fight an' a fuck."

"I don't think that would go so well just now," Gabriel said.

Tom looked at him, his black hair dripping with sweat and his beard tangled. "Don't ye, now," he asked. He looked away and smiled. "Well, ye'll know best, o' course. When do we ride?"

"Have you read the plan?" Gabriel asked.

"Every word," Tom said.

"Then you know," Gabriel said.

Tom nodded. "Well. I'm ready. Donald Dhu is beat and headed home, the poor bastard. I need him to see he's just sad and mad over his boy. I'd be the same. But..." He shrugged. "I can't have him making trouble for Ranald while I go wi' ye."

"I'd like to have had the same solution for Irene," Gabriel said. "Break her arm and send her home."

"Still eating at ye? Listen, boyo. Donald Dhu is a well-loved man, but he'll never get more 'an thirty loons in his tail 'cause he hasn't the name, and he's got nothing to sell to some giant fewkin' dragon nor a sorcerer but beef." Tom Lachlan spread his big hands. "Whereas, the mighty Princess Irene has more plots than a dairy farmer has milk pails and more good looks 'an any woman I know. I'd do her."

"You marry her. You can be emperor." Gabriel laughed a little.

"Nah. I'd kill her. I mostly kill anyone I can't trust. See, I can trust Donald Dhu. If'n he decides I have to go, I still trust him to come at me wi' a sword, in front o' the boys. Not she. She's a piece o' work."

Gabriel stared at the ground. Then he shrugged.

"I'm half drunk and I have to go eat dinner," he said.

Tom nodded. "I can fix that. Have more ale."

Gabriel took the refill of his cup. "What will this fix?" he asked.

"Ye won't be half drunk," Tom said.

Blanche sat in the solar, sewing.

He was late.

He was always late. He was more important than the queen, and she was baggage.

Thoughts like that made it difficult for her to breathe, but she was willing to face up to them. She was used to being very important, in her own way, and he had made her unimportant. With the queen, she was vital. With him, she was sport.

And he showed her how unimportant she was when he was late. Every time.

She thought of how careful poor Kaitlin had been in phrasing the invitation, and she bit her lower lip in vexation, and continued sewing. It was a simple overgown, something for herself, loose and baggy, something she could throw over a pretty kirtle to take a baby or do work.

She also thought that she had been very foolish to have danced last night. She had danced with Galahad D'Acon, and she had danced with Ser Michael, and she had seen his eyes and realized that he did not share, and she had hurt him.

At the time, that had seemed a very good thing indeed.

The more she let her thoughts go down that road, the more it seemed to her that she should, in fact, pack her things and go. In a year, her life would return to normal. In a year, the scandal of her open dalliance would fade. Many marriageable men would forgive her a dalliance with a man so powerful. Those were the facts of real life.

She began to gather her needles. She'd threaded a dozen to allow her to sew faster, and they were stuck into the velvet cushion on the fire rail. Needles were too dear to be left in the fire rail, and...

The door opened.

She saw him, and the blood on his arm and his disheveled hair. Toby was behind him, a hand out, reaching, and he slammed the solar door hard enough that everyone in the tower must have heard it. Toby's curse was just audible through the heavy oak door.

"I..." she began. She rose to her feet from where she'd been kneeling, and put out a hand. "You're bleeding."

"I stopped for a beer with Tom." His eyes were very bright.

"And started bleeding?" she asked.

"You know Tom. He decided I needed a fight." He shrugged. She had a hand on his arm, and was looking at the shirt, and the arm under it.

Despite herself, she smiled. "He is a curiously wise man," she said. "Did the fight make you feel better?"

"Much better," Gabriel said.

He was looking at her, and his eyes were very wide and preternaturally alert.

He passed the silver hand under hers, an unconscious parody of Tom's throw, and slipped it around her waist, and put his mouth over hers. He tasted of beer, and he smelled of fight, and her whole body responded to him, so that her body was like a runaway horse even as she herself wondered where she should be.

And he *had* learned how a side-laced kirtle worked. When his hand went onto her bare side—it was too hot for shifts—she let go.

"Kaitlin and Michael are coming for a cup of wine," he said.

She had her head pillowed on his shoulder, and she was naked. And her kirtle was ruined. It had blood on it, and it had been torn. The blood was his, but...

"I'd like you to marry me," he said. "I love you."

She rolled this around for a while. She didn't really have a thought in her head, and, in fact, it annoyed her that his mind was back to reality while she was still savouring...savouring...

"I'm naked," she managed.

He laughed. "Sweeting, Toby will not allow anyone, dragon or giant or Ser Michael, through that door. And this inn is full of lovely people who will run, *run* if asked, to get you a fresh kirtle and dress your hair."

She got up on one elbow. "You would marry me? What about Irene?"

Gabriel looked at her. It was a terrible look; not the look of a lover at all, but a look of fearful concentration. She didn't like it.

"If you are to be my wife," he said, "I think you need to know the truth, and the consequences." He took a breath.

"What truth?" she asked. She didn't like the way he looked.

"By now, Irene may be dead," he said. "If not, and it will be her choice..." He paused. "Her life will change."

Michael sat on the bench in front of the fire while Toby served wine. Kaitlin and Blanche—Snow White and Rose Red, straight from the tales—had their heads together over the baby, who was either spitting or giggling or just possibly both at the same time.

Michael drank his wine slowly.

Gabriel drank his wine more quickly.

"May we live to see old age," Michael said. "May we live to see our children grow, and in their turn, rise to life."

Gabriel lifted his cup, then handed it to Blanche, who drank.

Kaitlin met his eye and raised one eyebrow.

Gabriel smiled crookedly.

In the morning, Archer Gropf reprised his role as Master Tailor Gropf. Bales of wool and linen were arranged behind him in two bays of the great inn's stable block, which had been cleared of straw and manure and scrubbed. He had a number of wooden boards, which he measured, and then, after some thought, into which he drove iron nails at set distances.

Out in the stable yard, the full company was mustered, absent only the very sickest like Ser Phillipe de Beause. The holes in the company were vast—they had lost almost a third of the men-at-arms and a quarter of the archers, and Bill Redmede had made plain that none of his Jacks were marching with the company, no matter what financial inducements were offered. His brother Harald of the royal foresters had said the same.

On the other hand, a third of the population of the northern Brogat was now gathered under the Ings of Dorling, inside the circle of the Wyrm. People told themselves they had come for the tournament, but most had, in fact, come because the word was out that the Wyrm was taking refugees and that folk inside the circle were safe from the plague. And so far, the rumour had been accurate. Not a man or woman who had survived the trip into the circle had died. None seemed to contract it, either, and the distance that had developed between those who had it and those who didn't in the early days had largely vanished.

The yeomen of the northern Brogat and their sons were natural recruits: tall, hardy, and in many cases already veteran archers and soldiers. And too many men knew that the year's planting was already lost, and wages from some fighting would tide over a whole family.

There were tables outside the outer yard. Cully ran a table, and Sukey, even sick, managed another, and Gavin managed a third. But in the stable yard, there was a formation, holes or not. Tom Lachlan barked, and fifty-some battered lances found their places and stood attentively in full harness, as if ready to march away, with blanket rolls on their shoulders and food bags by their sides, and were mustered by name for subsequent paying, and then went, by name, to the head of the line.

The first table was a pay table. This improved the spirit of the occasion immediately, especially as the captain had declared the loss of horses to be "hard lying" and paid an allowance for men who had walked, and because the queen had announced the two weeks of the Gilson's Hole campaign to be "double pay days." Man by man and woman by woman, the company's archers, men-at-arms, pages, squires, laundresses, and wagoners passed the table, took their money or made their marks to place it on account in the company bank, and went on.

The second table was an immediate review of each man or woman's kit. Ser Danved stood there with Ser Gavin and Smoke, and they examined harness, looked at tack and saddles, fondled buckles, pulled on straps, and emptied food bags. Swords were drawn and presented. Lucky soldiers, like young Diccon and Petite Mouline, had everything. They received a silver leopard bonus and went on their way to the third table. Unlucky soldiers, like Cat Evil, who had sold his arrow bags and his sword, were "encouraged" to pay on the spot for new equipment. Some men vanished from the line altogether at this point, with chits for the armourers or the bowyers or the sword smiths, all of whom had set up as if the inn were a fair, which in fact it was. In a shed on the outer yard, Edmund Allen hammered away, taking dents out of a bascinet, while a dozen apprentices from Master Pye's shop in Harndon ran his errands, kept his fire hot, or sharpened swords for a penny a throw.

But after the third table came Master Gropf and his boards. Each member of the company, depending on role—but *everyone*, laundress, wagoner, or knight—received an issue of cloth. A pretty young woman in a low-cut kirtle who couldn't sew and did whatever Sukey told her, named Letty, got six yards of white linen, three yards red wool for a gown, three yards kersey for a cloak, one yard each red and blue fine for hoods, and hanks of thread and packets of valuable needles.

An archer like Cat Evil drew nine yards of white linen for shirts and braes, six yards of scarlet wool for cotes, a vivid tartan in red, yellow, and green for special occasions, yellow and green wool for hosen, and an assortment of boots, belts, and hats. Some things cost him money, but the cloth was measured out to the nail and cut.

Men-at-arms went to the second bay. The colours were the same; the quality was not. The tartan was knapped, soft, and made of the best wools, if the same colours; the linen was whiter and finer, the scarlet dyed with beetles rather than tree bark, for a better colour. But the measurements were the same.

Master archers and some women drew from the second bay, as well, and as the line moved, there were calls and occasional cheers. It turned out that every member, from slattern to knight, received enough superfine wool to make a dress hood, at the captain's expense. Letty giggled. "For wool this pretty, I'll learn to sew. Won't my poor ma be surprised?"

Tessa Gilson, who had watched her baby brother eaten by a wyvern and the remains buried in Albinkirk, who had now marched over half the Brogat in a month to come back to home, laughed nastily. "Your mama'd be surprised by a lot o' the things you've learned, Letty," she said. "Sure is pretty wool, though."

By the time the last names in line—Gadgy's Romany name was Zzhou—were getting their cloth, the most skilled needles had already run up the first garments, and the whole inner court was served dinner by the inn while the best sempters and seamstresses struck bargains and sewed, and the worst tried to learn to make themselves at least a shirt or a shift.

And the next day, the veterans were served wine and food all day while they ran up new clothes and the whole process was repeated under their eyes for the men and women who'd signed or marked at the three recruiting tables in the outer court. Not all the recruits were new men; Lord Wimarc, who had been Father Arnaud's squire and was a donat of the Order, had signed as a knight, but every man and woman in the company knew him and liked him as a serious boy and a deadly blade. A handful of Hillmen who had marched with the company signed on, and Angelo di Laternum brought three young Etruscan men who'd followed Princess Irene out of Liviapolis a month before as guards and now seemed rudderless since the princess had disappeared in the night and not included them in her plans. But most of the new knights were Occitans, knights who had followed their prince all summer and had his permission to go, or new men just come from the south, summoned by news of a tournament and eager for action. And the empty farmhouses of the Brogat and of western Morea provided pages and varlets, slatterns and laundresses, and forty new archers, and all those new men and women received a bounty, were armed and equipped with huge dents against future pay that made a few wonder if there'd ever be any to send home, and then handed cloth and linen, a fortune to any farm boy. New girls who could sew, and that was most, found that sewing paid better than fornication.

And the third day, a party came up the road from Harndon, led by Ser Gerald Random, and as soon as they arrived, guild soldiers and craftsman marching hard, they were put to work constructing the lists. And behind them came a flood of Jarsay knights and Occitans and westerners, and through the woods came bogglins and Golden Bears and even, cautiously, a solid company of wardens, crests deflated like berets on their long-beaked heads, to bow before Duchess Mogon and sit while the queen and duchess and Flint gave justice under yet another ancient tree.

Toward evening, Tall Pine and Ser Giannis Turkos came in with thirty Outwaller warriors and made camp with Nita Qwan, Gas-a-ho the shaman and Ta-se-ho, the old hunter, and their warriors. They sat and smoked together, and in time they were joined by the Red Knight and his brother.

Ser Gabriel didn't hesitate to share smoke.

Turkos held out a scroll. "As you know, we met Orley's force in the mountains east of the lake. Almost to Thrake," he said. "And we defeated them."

Tall Pine's warriors nodded. A few shook sticks with antlers newly cut from living flesh.

"Orley's men have antlers," Tall Pine said. He shrugged. "Had antlers."

"Many escaped west, and some east, and your brother continued in pursuit of those who went north," Turkos said. "Tall Pine and his people have been long from home. We agreed to bring messages here. Then we would all like to go home."

The Red Knight enjoyed his turn with the pipe, which was a magnificent one: a beautiful dark red stone bowl, with a long stem of some polished reed, wound in delicate porcupine quillwork. "I am glad you won," he said. "And I free you after a long summer's work to return to your villages." He nodded. "But not until we have beaten the plague. I cannot let you carry it home."

Several men were coughing.

Tall Pine nodded. "This seems wise," he said. "We have our own thoughts on this trouble."

The Red Knight nodded. He paused to cough, and to stare, as one did, at the ruin of his lungs. The smoke seemed to help, but some days he had his doubts. "Perhaps Gas-a-ho would join the council of our shamans," he said.

Most of the warriors smiled. Gabriel noted to himself...alliance meant inclusion in every council. It was a lesson he kept relearning.

He turned and passed the pipe to Nita Qwan. "I invite you to council with us after the first of the...ceremonial fighting, concerning matters that affect all of us. The Duchess Mogon has requested you. I ask you to represent, not just the Sossag, but all the northern peoples."

Nita Qwan looked around at his companions. "No man can speak for the free peoples of the north," he said. "A matron, maybe. Or maybe not."

Tall Pine nodded. "My brother speaks wisely. We are free. We have no princes or kings or dukes. If we wanted such, we would have them."

The Red Knight nodded, rocking on his haunches. "And yet, some speak in council, and others do not, or so I understand?" he said. In fact, when he was a boy his father had often taken him to see the Outwallers. He had a fair idea how the northerners, especially the Sossag, spoke.

"Each speaks as he will," Tall Pine said.

"Then let Nita Qwan come, and speak as he will," the Red Knight said. "And he can report our words to the Sossag, and the Huran, and any others who wish to listen. Because now is the time when all the free peoples must fight together, or be washed away the way a swift-running stream in spring washes away a sandbank."

The pipe passed, and no one said nay.

"What has happened to the Princess Irene?" Turkos asked quietly.

"I have sent her to school," the Red Knight said.

"What school?" asked Turkos.

"The Wild," Gabriel said.

The Tournament of the Dragon opened with a parade, as such things often do. Despite the plague, despite the great battle, despite the threat of the dragon Ash and the fighting in the Adnacrags, or perhaps because of all those things, coupled with the presence of the young king and his mother the queen, the tournament opened with pageantry and music and much fanfare.

The Queen of Alba led the parade, as was her right, with the royal standard borne before her and a sword, point upright. She held the baby king in her arms, just christened that morning in the chapel of the inn by the Bishop of Albinkirk, with the name Constantine.

Her ladies and her knights rode by her, and they were magnificent. Lady Mary was radiant, her deep chocolate-brown hair and pale ivory skin set off by silk-embroidered crimson velvet and white, white linen. She rode a fine eastern mare whose colour matched her hair exactly. She led a knight all in green by a golden chain from her hand to his neck. She smiled a great deal. On the other side of the queen rode Lady Rebecca Almspend in midnight blue, her light brown hair, the longest and most remarkable hair in all the Nova Terra, in a wondrous cascade down her back. A ring on her right hand caught the sun in a dazzle of light that made the crowd cheer, and she led a knight by a silver chain, and he wore a red-and-black tabard in the checky of the Hillmen. And close behind the queen, in a gown of sky-blue silk worth more than all the clothes she'd ever owned in her life, with an over-gown of golden yellow all embroidered in golden flowers and wearing a chaplet of wildflowers from the fields, rode Lady Blanche, and she led a knight all in red by a chain of gold. And by her side was Lady Kaitlin, and she wore a scarlet gown edged and accented in gold and lined in squirrel fur despite the heat of the day, with a short cloth-of-gold cloak and a long and pointed hat of peacock's feathers to set off her beautiful hair. Where Lady Mary's skin was ivory, Lady Kaitlin had the lightest dusting of freckles, and far more colour on her cheeks, and the silk brocade of her overgown in scarlet and dark gold matched her complexion. She held a silver chain, and led a knight in blue, whose bascinet was crowned with a great spray of blue plumes.

And behind this part came two teams of chivalric combatants. The first was led by the Prince of Occitan, and his co-captain Ser Thomas Lachlan. Their team was proceeded by two women on warhorses, and themselves dressed for court: Lady Briar and her daughter Lady Helewise. The other team was led on by Lady Natalia in a superb gown of gold and blue with a train that spread over the rump of her horse and another lady in an incredible display of crystal, lace, and flowers, whose elfin beauty brought roars of approval from the crowd—Queen Tamsin of N'gara, and they were followed by the Faery Knight with Ser Gregario, Lord Weyland, as his co-captain. There were eight knights on each team.

Behind the teams came a host of knights and ladies, or, in a few cases, knights and gentlemen; Ser Alison, often called Sauce, rode a superb jet-black courser, and Count Zac, on a spirited mare, led her by a chain of steel; there were two Occitan ladies in harness, and one lady from Jarsay. And a great host of ladies dressed in their very best, and young knights eager to prove themselves.

And behind them, the regiments. First, unquestioned, came the twenty-six surviving Nordikaans. They came in their full dress: mail that reached to their thighs, and gold decorated helms, and greaves of blued steel or shining bronze, polished matching vambraces, and carrying on their shoulders heavy axes.

Behind them came the Scholae, in the full splendour of their scarlet and gold, with armour of white steel. A year of constant war had changed them, and so had the horse plague, so that despite their terrible losses in the fields around them just a month before, they had half their number walking behind the mounted men. Ser Giorgos Comnenos led them, tall, ascetic, handsome as a saint on an icon.

Behind them came the royal foresters of Alba, who had served through the fighting in the deep woods, and whose smart red jupons and forest-green cotes were now offset with porcupine quill garters and sword belts from a summer with Outwallers. They swaggered with their bows on their shoulders, and behind them came the Armourers' Guild of Harndon in blue and gold, looking as rich as an imperial regiment with odd, new weapons on their shoulders, bronze maces on heavy wooden poles, and then, behind them, the scarlet-clad Vardariotes, with their strange eastern bow cases and short, soft boots and curved swords.

And then came the company. If less than half its people had worn its scarlet, white, and green uniform for more than five days, they appeared magnificent, led by Ser Milus and Ser Francis Atcourt. But many of the men-at-arms were dismounted, and more than half the archers and pages. Still, when the company's Saint Catherine standard appeared past the outwalls of the tavern, twenty thousand people gave the kind of cheer they'd only offered for the Queen of Faery and the

Queen of Alba. By the time the company appeared, the stands were full, and so were the roped-off areas for the crowd. Every effort had been made to see to the comfort of men and the Wild, too, but in the event, either by the dragon's hand, or by chance, or by the will of some higher being, the men and women of western Morea and northern Alba mixed freely with the bears and bogglins, wardens and irks. The cheers for the company were loud because everyone knew them, and perhaps, because there were now a pair of Irkish knights among the men-at-arms, riding horses, and three supernaturally tall forms paced along with the archers.

And behind the company, a few hundred archers and other contestants, entered in the lists but not enrolled properly, or simply people who liked to be in a parade and not in the crowd. There was Tall Pine at the head of his warriors, painted red and black, a stunning sight. He wore a solid gold gorget provided to his forefathers by some past emperor, and a great flowing robe of black squirrel fur and carried his pipe. By him walked Gas-a-ho with a pouch of badger decorated with quills, wearing a headdress of heron and eagle feathers that towered above the others. He had a single black bar of paint over his eyes. The Outwallers received a rolling cheer that sounded up and down the crowd, and when it swelled to a certain level, Nita Qwan let out a great scream and all the warriors joined him, a scream that cut through the applause of twenty thousand folk of all nations. A few warriors brandished the grisly trophies of recent victories, but they were the youngest; the rest walked with the dignity of senators and legates, breaking into broad smiles when a child reached for them or a woman blew a kiss.

By the time the company entered the ground around the lists, the queen had made her procession all the way around, dismounted to roars of applause, and been met by Ser Gerald Ransom and Master Smythe, who escorted her to her place in the stands, where two thrones had been prepared. Having greeted the queen, Ser Gerald walked away to a secret room under the stands...a secret room he had prepared for the first tournament, the one that ought to have happened in Harndon. And there, in privacy, the one-legged merchant became a knight in full harness, his missing leg cunningly hidden by Master Pye's best work. And Toby, loaned for the occasion, led Ser Gerald to his horse and got him mounted, and handed him up his visored great helm, and

Anne Woodstock buckled the helm to his back plate and tied his lace under his chin.

Ser Gerald was in the queen's colours, as was Ser Galahad D'Acon. And while the last of the parade was coming to a halt, and the crowd was still on their feet, the two of them rode out from behind the stands, to the center of the lists, and there, saluted each other and the queen, and rode to either end—and charged.

Both their lances shattered magnificently, and Ser Gerald breathed freely for the first time in hours, as he was a newly trained jouster and having begged the boon of opening the lists, he'd worried about it for weeks.

No sooner did Toby have his helmet off then the red knight and the green knight were at it.

Galahad D'Acon's helm came off over his head, and he favoured Ser Gerald with his beaming smile. "Look at them!" he said. "With war lances!"

Both men set their lances as soon as they began their charge—both expert jousters on expert horses.

Most of the crowd leaned forward, amazed to be offered such good sport in the very first moments.

The green knight's lance plucked the red knight's helmet right off his head.

The red knight's lance broke into a thousand splinters on the green knight's shield, and his lance head stuck deep, so that the green knight rode along the lists with the head stuck in the face of his green shield as the crowd roared, and he had been rocked in his seat. The knights were only running single courses, and the pennon went up awarding the point to the red knight, who pumped his fist in the air and rode along, saluted the queen bare-headed, and then cantered along the lists to where Toby and Anne were just ready to receive him. Ser Gavin rode up for the other direction, and his squire, Rob Salmon, had his helmet off his head in a moment.

Ser Gavin looked at his brother. "Some bastards will do anything to win," he shouted.

Up in the stands, the dragon turned to the queen of Alba. "I do not understand," he said.

She smiled brilliantly at him, clearly delighted with everything. She put a hand on Blanche's shoulder. Her former laundress had seen the war lances and the solid shafts, and she'd lost a year of her life when Gabriel's helmet flew off.

The queen looked out at the lists, where Ser Ranald and Ser Michael, also with war lances, flicked their salutes to the thrones.

"What do you not understand, my fair host?" she asked.

"As to that, if one of us is to be fair, it would be you, Queen of Men." Master Smythe had disconcerting eyes, and they bored into her. The queen smiled despite his eyes.

"But my confusion is about the helmet. Surely, the loss of a helmet is very serious. And the breaking of a lance, nothing." He shrugged. He looked at Mogon, who sat in her own splendour by his elbow. Mogon had a superb fan of griffon's feathers—feathers that seemed to have been made of gold—and she used it to fan herself even as she ate her fourth iced sherbet.

"I cannot pretend to understand human combat rituals," she said. "I can only promise you that ours are just as silly. And beautiful."

The queen smiled. "I can see, Ser Dragon, that you were not brought up in Occitan nor yet to the joust. The red knight left his helmet unlaced, expecting his brother to strike for it. It slid from his head, and he kept his seat perfectly, and thus, no point is scored against him. But his spear shattered and he rocked his brother in his saddle. Ser Gavin was too good a lance to be discomfited much, but the point clearly goes to Ser Gabriel, and the more so as it takes so much courage to leave your helmet unlaced. Don't you think?"

"And yet you use this game to train for war?" the dragon asked. "Would it not—"

The crowd roared.

Ser Ranald and Ser Michael had *both* splintered their heavy lances, and both men's shields were split by the impact, and yet neither was injured. Lady Rebecca and Lady Kaitlin were leaning on each other, but managed to laugh and wave their hands as if they hadn't a care in the world.

And then, in a burst of colour, the two teams entered the lists. It was too much—skilled jousters and veteran fans in the crowd were still trying to explain the Red Knight's trick and there'd been another pair and now two *teams* entered and the barriers, themselves on wheels, were being maneuvered out of the lists even as eight knights formed a solid line at either end of the lists.

Silence fell.

Most of the humble folk of the Brogat had never seen an irk or a bogglin, except under awful conditions of bondage or terror or war. Now there were several thousand of the creatures in the crowd. Perhaps out of sensitivity to fresh alliances, both teams had irks and men.

The two teams saluted the queen, and by then, Ser Gerald, master of the tournament, had shed enough armour to help Queen Tamsin dismount and lead her to her throne beside the Queen of Alba, from which Master Smythe departed with a stunning bow and flourish.

Tamsin turned and waved at her love, and the Queen of Alba gave the signal.

The two teams charged.

The melee was not fought with lances. Instead, each knight had a sword of staves of wood, loosely enough bound so that they made a very loud noise when they struck, and cunningly enough made that a blow from one could knock a man from his saddle.

The Faery Knight and the Prince of Occitan made for each other, but half a dozen knights on either team had the same notion. Ser Gregario unhorsed Ser George Brewes at the outset, and that knight rolled once and scrambled out of the lists, a veteran of other melees. Tom Lachlan knocked an irk clear of his saddle in one two-handed blow and managed a cut at the Faery Knight, but the canny Ser Tamio parried with his own wooden sword and cut back at Ser Thomas, and for ten long breaths the two champions cut at each other, blow and blow, and no one interfered. The Prince of Occitan unhorsed Ser Tancred and landed a good blow on Ser Gregario. But Ser Danved had the time and presence of mind to bide, and he came in close, locked the prince's sword arm with his own, and threw him from his horse. Then Ser Berengar put Ser Danved down, the smaller man appearing out of the dust and slamming his wooden sword into his friend's outstretched arm and riding through, until Danved fell, cursing, and Ser Berengar was in turn unhorsed by Daniel Favour, with a keen fire burning in his eyes.

And still Tom Lachlan and the Faery Knight traded blows, as fast as smiths working metal, and men fell all around them. The dust rose, Daniel went down at the hands of Ser Francis Atcourt, and for a moment, as horses panicked and Ser Christos burst from the melee, nothing could be seen.

Ser Christos had two swords, having disarmed someone in the dust. He bided, riding carefully along the lists. He threw the extra sword into the crowd, and people roared their approval. An Irkish knight rode out of the dust without a sword, and simply jumped his beautiful silver horse over the list barrier and then turned, pulled off a gauntlet and offered Ser Christos his hand, and both men opened their visors. Ser Francis Atcourt rode after them, realized that they had elected to end their fight, and bowed to the queens.

And then Bad Tom and the Faery Knight rode out of the dust. Both of them rode to the foot of the lists below the royal box, and the folk in the crowd closest could see that both still held the hilts of wooden swords in their hands. Both threw the hilts into the crowd, and tapped their right gauntlets together, and rode, side by side, out of the lists.

The people screamed their approval, even as the bells on the inn peeled for lunch.

The queen paused on her way out of her box to lean over and kiss Ser Gerald on the cheek. "It is already superb!" she said.

He grinned. "This is the tournament we was supposed to give Your Grace," he said. "Instead of that sad thing of Rohan's, God rest his soul." He looked at the swirl of dust. "People need such things in a bad year. And I thought we would start with a bang."

Duchess Mogon leaned in between the merchant-knight and his queen, her big head and inlaid beak delicate as a dancer. "May I ask if perhaps two of my... ahem. Knights? Might give a display of our game of war?"

Ser Gerald, who had planned every minute of the next four days, did not freeze or curse. He smiled steadily. He glanced at the queen. "Easily done," he said.

The Queen of Alba and the Queen of Faery both clapped their hands. "Delightful!"

Master Smythe leaned in. "You may want to let the Outwallers show you their form of jousting," he said. "It is done with a ball and sticks. There's always blood."

Behind them, the barriers were being wheeled back into the middle of the lists.

"You have more surprises for us?" the queen asked. She smiled at Tamsin, thinking that she had never seen such a beautiful person ever, even in a picture.

Ser Gerald bowed to the two queens. "I promise nothing *but* surprises," he said.

"I don't even want to sit with you," Gavin said to his brother, and aimed a blow at the air by his head.

Lady Mary kissed him. "I was not given to understand that you suffered from temper," she said. She looked at Blanche, and her eyebrows went up and down, and Blanche tried to hide a laugh and mouthed *Yes* back.

The Red Knight sat by his brother and was served, and he leaned over, kissed Lady Blanche to the delight of many, and then shook his head. "Brother, it was a cheap trick. What can I say? You are a better jouster. What else can I do?"

Gavin leaned back, rolling his eyes. "See? It is just like growing up. First he does something outrageous, and then he apologizes, so that no one..." He looked at his brother. "It was beautifully done."

"Ser Henri would be proud," Ser Gabriel said.

A little, very uncomfortable silence fell.

"You will have to get your revenge tomorrow, in the regular jousting," Lady Mary said.

"I won't even be here..." Ser Gavin stopped and laughed. "If Gabriel keeps hitting me, I won't even be here," he went on smoothly.

"Assuming any of us survive the council tonight," Ser Gabriel said, lugubriously.

The afternoon drew on. As soon as the day began to cool, the first of several hundred archers began to loft their shafts into round targets of straw.

"This ought to get Wilful to rise from the grave," Cully muttered. "Damn it, I miss him."

Smoke took his shot and watched it strike home fifty paces away. He nodded his satisfaction. "He liked a clout shoot or a long shoot," Smoke said. "But he was a gloomy bastard, and by now..."

Long Paw wasn't jousting. He was in a fey mood and when it was his turn, he placed an arrow on his string and pulled as if trying to throw the quarter-pound arrow into the next county. Instead, he shot high in the air. The arrow fell at a steep angle—and struck the target.

"Show-off," Cully said.

"By now, Wilful Murder would'a noticed that there's no duty roster posted for tomorrow," Long Paw said, clearly very pleased with himself. "No good will come of it," he said loudly.

"*Mark my words*," came the chorus.

Dozens of men and women laughed.

An Outwaller in red paint strode to the line and loosed his arrow. It did not appear that he had aimed or even prepared himself. He never set his hips. His arrow, however, flew true and struck the target very near the center. He grinned at the company archers.

They grinned back.

A pair of bogglins shot and struck the target.

"I know it's wrong," Cully said. "I can't abide their mouths. They go the wrong way."

Smoke elbowed him. "They got bows, they can shoot, and we're *allies*." He'd heard that bogglins were always hungry, and he waved a half loaf of bread at the pair.

Sure enough, they came over and bowed—itself an inhuman motion.

"Bread for me?" one said.

"Sure," Cully said.

"Eat bread, still try win," said the second bogglin.

Cully made a face.

Long Paw nodded. "He means, just because he eats your bounty don't mean he won't try to beat your shot." He made a saluting motion with his right hand. "That's alright, mate. Eat up and shoot well."

The bogglins bobbed their heads like extremely ugly children. Their bows were stubby and short, but carefully recurved.

"God help us all if they figure out how to make a hornbow," Cully said.

"Allies," hissed Long Paw.

Cully shrugged. He turned to the young Outwaller who had chosen to stand with them as they waited for the next distance. "Ever thought o' travel?" he asked casually. "Like to fight?"

"Fight?" the young man said, and his eyes burned.

"Speak Alban?" Cully asked.

The man made a face. "I speak this stone-house tongue," he said. He spoke in a slightly accented High Archaic. Cully had spent years in Liviapolis. He nodded.

"Ever considered coming along o' we as a soldier?" he asked.

Smoke stepped up to the line at seventy paces and drew and loosed. It was not his best arrow, but it hit the outside rim of the straw target... and stuck. He looked disappointed.

Cully looked at him. "A hit's a hit," he said.

The Outwaller stepped to the line. Again, he didn't even seem to focus. He loosed, and twenty warriors in the crowd shrieked. He turned away before his arrow struck. "Where do you go to fight?" he asked. "Who do you fight?"

Cully could tell the young man was excited. "We go far," he said evasively. "And we fight whoever the cap'n tells us."

The young man's arrow again hit the straw almost on center.

Cully shook his head and stepped to the line. To his left, the two bogglins loosed together. One missed, and one hit.

Cully loosed, and hit.

Long Paw loosed, and hit.

"How far?" the warrior asked.

Long Paw shook his head *no*.

Cully wanted this boy. "Across the sea," he said.

The warrior's eyes widened. He stepped close to Cully—too close, for most men—and took Cully's new red coat between his fingers, rubbing the fine wool. "This for me?" he asked.

Long Paw rolled his eyes. "Don't try to cheat him on the fine wool," he said in Alban. "He'll know."

"I'd put this one in cloth-o'-gold. You saw him shoot."

The targets were at a hundred paces. Now there were only two hundred archers left, and the shooting went much faster. Men and women stepped to the line and loosed one arrow, all or nothing for this range. One woman laughed when she hit—she was an older woman with two children following her, and she shook her head.

No Head, who had just missed, liked her smile. "What's funny, mistress? A fine shot."

She laughed. "I don't think I've ever hit a target at this range," she said.

No Head nodded. "Well, now you have."

"Mostly I shoot deer for the pot," she said. "The closer the better."

No Head nodded.

He smiled at a bogglin, who stepped up to the line and seemed to strain every limb to bend his bow. His arrow flew—and struck.

"Well shot, boyo!" No Head said.

The woman flinched when the bogglin moved closer.

No Head put a hand on her shoulder. "Allies," he said.

"I can't stomach 'em," the woman said.

"You know they only live twenty years?" No Head said conversationally.

"Oh!" the woman said.

Her daughter said, "That's terrible, mister. Mama's already older 'an that."

Her boy looked at the bogglin. "Do that mouth thing?" he asked.

The Bogglin split its four-part mouth sideways.

The boy tried to imitate him, and the creature spat a brown juice and shook.

"That's bogglin laughter," No Head said.

"You like them?" the woman asked him. The targets were moving to a hundred twenty-five paces.

"Spent most o' my life killin' 'em," No Head said. "But then," he said, "I found they ain't so bad."

No Head watched Cully strike home, and Long Paw, and an Outwaller boy standing with them. All three shot beautifully. Smoke had almost missed at a hundred, but at one twenty-five he struck dead center and got a hearty cheer.

"Better take your turn, mistress," No Head said.

"Never shot this distance," she said. "I won't even reach."

"Sure won't reach if you don't try," No Head said.

The bogglin pulled his bow carefully, as far as he could...and it snapped. The sound carried, and the crowd fell silent.

A tall irk, one of the judges, came over to them, looked at the bogglin's bow, and shook his head. "I rule thisss no ssshot. If anyone will lend it a bow?"

No Head smiled at the woman, wondering if she had a man. He got his bow off his back and handed it to the little creature, and he played with it a moment and then shook his head.

"Too many talls," it said.

No Head nodded. He watched Count Zac rifle an arrow effortlessly into the target and then waved to the man and borrowed his bow for the bogglin.

"Not my shot," the bogglin said to the irk, and loosed an arrow. It flew well past the mark.

Zac calmly handed over three more, and the little creature loosed two of them.

"Like," he said.

He seemed to gather all his limbs, pulled his bow, and loosed.

His arrow struck the target.

Zac looked impressed, and smacked the little creature on the wing case.

The woman stepped up to the line. She took a long time, rolling her shoulders. But when she moved, it was all grace, and her bow rose like a bird taking wing, and her arrows leapt…

…and struck.

"Oh!" she said with delight. "Oh!" she said again. Her daughter leapt up and kissed her, and her son laughed and went to watch the bogglin.

"I'm Fran," she said to No Head.

"Ever thought o' travelling, Fran?" No Head asked.

The targets were moved to one hundred fifty paces. There were twenty-eight archers left.

The Outwaller boy—Heron—struck the target. It was the first shot he'd taken with a stance and a careful draw.

Smoke missed. He shrugged and stepped out to fetch ale.

Long Paw missed and cursed. "I hate these one-arrow matches," he said.

Cully loosed and struck.

Zac loosed and struck, and then handed his beautiful jade-coloured horn bow to a bogglin, who loosed—and struck.

The tall, bony woman, Fran, at the end of the line, drew, pointed her arrow almost at the heavens, and loosed. Her arrow went high, and struck—fifteen paces *beyond* the target. She laughed a great deal and let No Head buy her a flagon of wine. Her boy was handing arrows to the bogglin, his arrow squire. Her daughter sat down with Long Paw and Smoke opposite her mother.

"Can ye fight?" Long Paw was asking. "No offence, mistress. It's a hard life. Can ye kill?"

"Kilt my man," she said. Her tone was not even flat, merely cool, as if women killed men all the time. "He had it coming."

"That counts," Long Paw said, his eyes elsewhere.

The distance was moved to one hundred seventy-five paces. There were eight archers, and everyone knew that at this stage, it was luck, skill, and *fortuna*. All the archers shook hands with all the rest, even the bogglin, whose name, it transpired, was Urk13, or something like that. One of the Exrechs came to watch.

Zac shot first. It was a bad shot, which wavered in the air too long, and seemed to fly short. But it struck the very distant target, and hung. It didn't go deep. But the head stayed in the target.

Cully made himself stand by the little bogglin. He was ashamed of himself for admitting he didn't like the creatures, and he had to prove himself to himself. That was how he was. That was how you got to be the captain's archer. He went and stood shoulder to shoulder with the little bug, and he gave the thing a nod, and then he went into the place he went when he was shooting well, and he loosed.

His arrow buried itself into the straw, and the crowd gave him a shout.

The bogglin drew Zac's bow with a lot of effort and loosed. He had declined Zac's offer of a bone-tipped flight arrow, and his release was perfect. The arrow rose like a falcon and fell like an eagle.

A hit.

Cully couldn't help himself. He put a hand on the thing's wing case. "Well shot," he said. Close up, the bug had a smell Cully remembered from combat . . . a salty smell. Not a bad smell at all.

The thing looked at him. The eyes were like a person's eyes. Cully decided to stay with the eyes. He managed a smile.

They *all* hit at one hundred seventy-five paces.

The range moved to two hundred paces. The three judges held a brief conclave and announced that the range would now increase by ten yards a shot.

Cully stepped up and loosed.

Hit.

The bogglin stepped up. Its whole body strained, and Cully was afraid a moment for the thing's chiton structure. There was a terrible creaking.

I'm worried for a bug, he thought. But the arrow struck home.

The crowd roared. Up until that shot, most of the bogglin's fans had been other bogglins, but now there were hundreds of bears roaring, wardens thumping armoured tails, and men of the Brogat cheering the little thing.

The duchess, Mogon, came up to the archery line. The archers all bent their knees, but she went to the bogglin and put a hand on its head.

It cried. Tears flowed down its face.

"What the hell?" Cully asked.

The young Outwaller's face was working with emotion. "She scent-marks him," he said. "She offers him her name. His fame will live forever in her nest. This is a good thing, and is why she is a good lord."

Cully wasn't really sure what that meant, but he could see what it meant to the bug.

Zac missed. It was just a freak in the wind, but he took it personally and walked away scowling.

The Outwaller shook his head. "Would you lend your bow?" he asked.

Cully considered the young man. "Yep," he said. He handed it over, and called a judge, who gave the Outwaller five arrows to learn a new bow.

The Outwaller warrior loosed them all, carefully, taking his time, apparently unaware of the hundreds of people watching his every move. Finally he drew his competition arrow to his ear and loosed. He shook his head and turned away, and indeed, he'd missed.

Robin Hasty missed.

The target was moved to two hundred ten paces. It was just Cully and the bogglin, Urk of Mogon, now.

"Far," Urk said.

Cully smiled. "My best range," he said.

Urk's two jaws moved. "Good," he said.

He shot. And hit.

Cully shot. And hit.

By now, people who didn't give a damn about archery were watching. Hundreds of knights, fully armoured and ready for various events, were standing in the sun to watch. The Red Knight and the Green Knight both stood at the edge of the spectators, and both queens had joined the duchess and the master and the Keeper.

The target was moved to two hundred twenty paces.

Cully shot first. He had a great release...he knew the moment the string left his fingers that he'd hit, and he was right. He was rewarded with a roar.

The Outwaller boy hadn't gone back to the line. He was standing, watching Cully shoot, and now he handed the older man an arrow. "Your best that is left," he said in Archaic. "Not the best arrows."

Urk walked up to the line twice with Zac's bow, and both times walked back. He asked for permission to try a flight arrow before his formal shot.

The judges looked at each other.

Cully nodded. "Let him have three," he said.

The bug loosed three arrows. The third clipped the target and bounced away.

The bogglin looked at Cully and bowed. "I thank you," he said. Then he took a flight arrow from Fran's boy who was helping him, drew it past his head, and loosed.

And hit.

The crowd was already wild. Cully's chivalry won him many new fans, and so did the bogglin's skill.

"We are over the time allotted," the irk said with a bow. "Our queens offer you a choice; share the victory, or move the target to two hundred fifty paces."

Cully had the winning arrow in his hand. He knew he could hit at two-fifty. He had a war bow and thirty years of practice. He thought about it. About the captain's admonition to make them allies, and about his own aversion.

The bogglin would never reach a target at two-fifty. Not even with Zac's bow.

The bogglin stood with his borrowed bow in his spidery fist. He looked at the ground.

"I say draw," Cully said softly.

The bogglin looked up, eyes shining.

"Ever think of travelling?" Cully asked the little fellow, after he'd embraced a bogglin for the first time in his life.

The Red Knight was in full harness, waiting his turn to fight on foot against the Green Knight, when the imperial messenger appeared overhead. He knew it as soon as it cried, and raised his fist, and the bird came in a rush of wings. It came straight to him, and he knew what that meant.

He stepped back from the railing of the lists and went to stand by himself. His breath came short. He read the cover letter from Alcaeus and then began on Kronmir's densely written report, scanning line after line and trying to work out the code.

Finally, he gave up. "Withdraw," he said to the marshal.

Ser Michael struck his name off the list.

"Like hell!" Gavin called. "Do you reckon knighthood so cheap?"

Michael flinched, but that tone got a sudden smile from Ser Gabriel. "Fine," he said. "Our fight's next, then. The world's about to burn."

Gavin nodded. "Ain't it always," he said.

Gabriel waved to Toby and got his helmet on his head. Gavin wore a bascinet and a long trailing green plume, and Gabriel wore his own bascinet. He envied his brother's plume.

They'd agreed to fight on foot with spears and arming swords. It was an Archaic combination, one that looked pretty and offered scope for drama, and which Gabriel had not actually fought before, although he'd certainly imagined it often enough, looking at ancient texts.

He didn't even spare a thought for the coded text that bird had brought. He was escorted by Anne, his page, to his corner of the foot lists and there handed a spear.

"Where's Toby?" he asked.

"Next up to fight, wi' the squires, my lord," Anne said with a look that suggested that he ought to know.

His marshal was Bad Tom, of all people. The big man grinned.

"I didna' think you'd miss a fight," he said. Then he raised his voice so that it filled the stands.

"Gentle cousins! The Green Knight, Ser Gavin Muriens, will here engage the Red Knight his brother, Ser Gabriel Muriens, in a contest with spear an' sword, fightin', they assure me, like the knights of the time of the Empress Livia, though I ha' a strong sense that they're full o' rope. But have it as they will! Salute the queens! And all those who do ye honour by attendin'! An' the Lady Tar, height the Virgin, on her day!"

Gabriel was not sure he'd ever been quite so hot.

"*En garde, mes amis!*" roared Tom in a passable Gallish.

"*Et allez!*" he called, and Gavin moved, his spearhead low in his left hand, his arming sword well back in the long tail garde, ready for a heavy swing.

Gabriel's head cleared, the heat fell away, and his sole thought was that it appeared his brother had been practicing this Archaic form. *While I command armies and learn to ride a griffon. Bastard.*

He parried the spear and the point of the arming sword went high over his garde and pricked him in the neck through two layers of mail.

The crowd roared.

Et allez!

This time, Gabriel was considerably more careful. But care couldn't replace practice, and his damned brother had practiced. He rolled the spear over Gabriel's spear—they were both holding the shafts in the left hand, where they could be used to parry—and *thrust with the butt spike*. Since, until that moment, it hadn't occurred to Gabriel to use the butt spike as a weapon, he overparried, using his arming sword—and his brother thrust, *stoccata*, a pretty thrust that struck Gabriel under the arm.

Ordinarily, Gabriel might have applauded the neatness of it, but Gabriel had a life of experience with Gavin, and he knew that he was being punished. For various things. And he had his usual reaction to his brother's aggression.

When Tom called the *allez*, Gabriel stepped off line and thrust with the point of his spear. Then, with a flick, he reversed the spear and swept it left to right, collecting both of his brother's weapons and then pushing an *imbrocatto* thrust across his own body, hand reversed, everything reversed, really. The blow was fast, and hard, and precise. It struck Gavin *just* under the right pauldron and Gabriel left it there, flaunting it for the marshal and the crowd, who roared their approval.

His brother grabbed his head. "Good blow!" he shouted, helmet to helmet.

Damn him and his chivalry, Gabriel thought. But he hugged his brother hard.

"One more!" Gabriel said.

This time, the two brothers circled after the *allez* for far longer than before. Both flicked little thrusts with their spears, and Gabriel considered changing hands—the spear in the right might actually have an advantage—not what the Archaics did, however. They probably threw them.

Gabriel sidestepped and even as his brother moved, Gabriel struck. It was a matter of timing, of tempo, and he could not have rationally explained why he struck. But he went forward onto his left leg and exploded forward again. The two spears met and crossed and both slid past their targets and both swords rose and cut diagonally, strong blows that met at the center and sparks flew, visible even in the blazing sun, as two sharp swords cut each into the other's fine edge.

Gabriel hammered his pommel into his brother's visor. Only then did he realize his brother was going for a wrestling throw and he lowered his weight. They were too close for anything to be visible—every part of a fight at this range was touch and feel and intuition. Gabriel stepped back, even as his brother's leg wrap went forward, but Gavin knew his response as well as he did himself, and Gabriel had to writhe like a snake to avoid being thrown in the reverse of his own arm lock, and then they were steel belly to steel belly, locked like two statues.

Gabriel went for his dagger. His hilt was *there* under his hand and his hand rose like Ariosto taking flight, the dagger gleaming in the brilliant sun, and no thought in his head that this was his brother and comrade of fifty fights. His brother's right arm was gone from Gabriel's left—he wrapped his own left around his brother's armoured neck and in that moment thought *brother* and placed the tip of his needle-sharp dagger lovingly atop the mail of his brother's aventail.

"Hold!" roared Bad Tom. "Och, the pair o' you. Yer both *that* lucky ye lived to be grown."

Gabriel's dagger was pricking at Gavin's throat.

Gavin's dagger point was under Gabriel's mail skirt, pricking something else.

The queens began to laugh, and then all of them were laughing.

The two men embraced, steel breastplate to steel breastplate.

There was chanting in the crowd, and the roar grew and grew. Gavin tried to say something to Gabriel, and then shook his head and let his brother go.

There were perhaps twenty thousand sentient beings watching, and the noise was incredible. It was like a living thing, or a storm, or a great monster of the Wild; it rose, and rose.

Eight Nordikaans appeared at the end of the lists, and there was Ser George Brewes and there was Bad Tom, and Sauce, and Giannis Turkos and Ser Michael.

They had a shield.

The crowd roared. The chant rose, intelligible for the first time.

"Imperator! Ave! Ave! Ave!"

Gabriel could see Derkensun. He could see them all, and he walked to the shield and stepped onto it as if by right.

This would be a bad time to fall over, he thought, and then they were raising him, and the storm of sound beat against him, all the approval he could ever have dreamt as an angry child.

"Ave! Ave! Ave! Imperator!"

He raised his hands.

The queen rose to her feet, and raised her arm to him in acknowledgment.

The sound lifted him, and for a moment he felt a thrill of joy, an almost sexual pleasure. And then, oddly, he heard Wilful Murder's voice in his head, as clear as if the man were by his side—more clearly, as the sound would have drowned a real voice.

Wilful Murder's voice said, *Here we go, then*.

Forty minutes later, Gabriel was in his solar, sitting in sweat-damp arming clothes, decoding, with Master Julius making a copy and decoding at the same time, and Lady Almspend doing the same—Rebecca could, in fact, write with her right and left hands at the same time.

All three of them paused to murmur from time to time.

Outside, the crowd roared.

"Toby, get Master Smythe," Gabriel said. "And Harmodius or Amicia."

"It's Anne, Your Grace. Toby is fighting," his page said from behind him.

He waved his hand.

He heard her footsteps going away. He kept writing, and some time later, Harmodius cleared his throat.

"Read this," Gabriel said, handing him a smudged sheet of parchment. "I want someone to get me Ser Payamides...the infidel."

"He's with the queen and Blanche," Anne said quietly. "He just fought."

"Get him," Gabriel said.

Harmodius was already reading. Gabriel felt, rather than saw, the dragon enter. Then Blanche—he knew her step. She put a hand on his shoulder and he squeezed it, surprised by how comforting it was to have her there, and he heard her working with Anne—fetching wine, pouring.

"Ser Payam," Anne said.

Gabriel raised his head. The room was full of people, reading, writing, working.

"Ser Pavalo," Gabriel said formally, rising to his feet. "Tell me, have you fought the not-dead?" he asked.

"Many times," Payam said. He did not smile, and his hand went to the sword he wore. "Many times."

Gabriel nodded, excited. "Do you carry... any of the drug that you take... there is a drug, is there not? That you take to keep the not-dead from taking you?"

Payam paused. He looked at Harmodius.

Harmodius frowned. In Askepiles form, the scowl looked very dangerous. "Al Rashidi would tell you..."

The black man shrugged. "It is not so secret," he admitted. He reached into his purse, and Harmodius, who had just finished reading, leaned forward in expectation. So did Gabriel.

"I know it is made with the powdered bones," he said apologetically. "From the Umroth."

Harmodius snatched it. He didn't even speak. He ran from the room.

Payam watched him. "What is wrong?" he asked.

Everyone was watching the closing door and then Gabriel. Gabriel wanted to speak, but was afraid—so afraid—to be proven incorrect, even as he was heartened that the old man had come to the same conclusion he had.

Gabriel looked around the room. "Give Harmodius time," he said. "We may have a solution to one problem."

He didn't say, *While the others grow deeper.*

A long evening, and archers lofted shafts, crossbowmen shot, swords danced and rang together, lances were lifted, and Ser Danved avenged his defeat in the melee by throwing Ser Berengar over his hip in a poleaxe fight that had the crowd on their feet. Toby won several matches with the long sword before going down to defeat at the hands of Francis Atcourt's squire, Bethany, and came back sweaty and glowing with pride. He was not a natural swordsman and had to work hard to do well, and Bethany, who went on to win the squire's prize, stated loudly that he had been her hardest match.

But Isabeau fought the prize match without either of the queens in attendance. The stands were full, the twilight still strong, but none of the great nobles of Alba, Morea, or the Wild were present.

They were in the paneled room of the old common room. Sauce, who was triumphantly wearing a crown of laurel, was pushed into an uncommonly small space next to Lord Kerak, whose large, reptilian bulk was, Sauce had to admit, very comfortable, smooth, and cool. And well muscled.

The table was no longer a long rectangle, but had been replaced with a big, round table, and the room itself seemed to have changed shape, although the crucifix in the niche was the same, as were the oak panels.

The Red Knight—now the emperor, at least to some—had a pile of parchments crackling under his right elbow, and he was covered in ink so that he looked piebald. Next to him was Master Smythe, who looked like a manuscript illustration of a great noble, with every hair perfect. On his right sat the Queen of Alba, and next to her the Faery Knight with his queen, and then Count Zac as the senior imperial officer present and Tom Lachlan as Drover and the Keeper and his son, and then Wayland as the Captain of Albinkirk, Ser Ricar Fitzroy as the queen's captain, Gavin as Earl of Westwall, Flint and Kerak and Nita Qwan for their people with Mogon. Ser Michael sat behind Ser Gabriel, and he, too, wore a crown of laurel, having bested both Tom Lachlan and Ser Gavin in the jousting. He had a pile of parchment too, and next to him sat Master Julius, scribbling.

There were four empty seats, for Harmodius and Mortirmir, Amicia and Gas-a-ho. And around the outside of the room, dozens of men and women: Rebecca Almspend, Blanche, Mary, and Natalia all perched on stools, Francis Atcourt and the Grand Squire and Giorgos Comnenos and many others. It should have been too close and hot to breathe, but it was not.

Master Smythe looked around and his face wore a look of pleasure.

"My friends," he said. "If goodwill and shared knowledge can triumph over ignorance and evil, then you are the very people to win the contest. I will encourage Gabriel to speak, because he understands most of what is at stake."

Gabriel didn't fidget. He rose to his feet. "The first and most pressing issue is the cough," he said. "Lord Kerak?"

Lord Kerak rose and bowed, forcing Sauce to fit into an even smaller space by the chimney.

"First experiments were successful," he said. "We have high hopes. Shall I speak on?"

Gabriel nodded. "Everyone here needs some hope."

"Perhaps..." The irk nodded. "Perhaps I am the right one for this. We believe we have solved the riddle of the plague."

The room erupted, and the irk held out a hand for silence but had to wait some time.

"Listen, the thing is not yet done." That got him silence. "But it is well begun."

"What is it?" Lord Weyland asked.

Kerak spread his hands expressively. "The cough, or the plague—it is a trident," he said. "It attacks the host three ways. Or rather, it uses three theories of hermetical working, all at the same time. It is green, and gold. And black."

As he said *black*, every person flinched.

"We do not usually speak of black," the queen said.

Kerak nodded. "Yet perhaps we should, loud and often. And in this case..." He looked around. "Black is the colour of death and decay. It is not particularly powerful. No, this is a falsehood. It is very powerful, so long as all you desire to accomplish is death and decay. It is useless else."

Gabriel leaned forward. "Black is the colour we ascribe to the workings of the Necromancer and his followers."

Mogon nodded. "Black was the colour of many of the workings of the Odine," she said.

Master Smythe said, "It was the emanations of the black, and the utilization of black by Thorn, that caused me first to take an interest in all of you."

Becca Almspend shrugged. "I have studied these matters all my life, and my first encounter with black was under the Old Keep in Harndon, with you, Your Grace." She nodded to the Queen of Alba, who frowned.

Lord Kerak waited for the comments to die away and then nodded.

"So..." he said. "We understood the basic animicule that attacks its host, although it is far too small to see, and that rendered any form of counterworking very difficult. Imagine hunting ants with a pole-axe." He shrugged. "On the other hand, far away in Liviapolis, schol-ars, including Mortirmir, rediscovered a technique of the Archaics. I confess I had never heard of it; human working can be very subtle. This working attacks the animicules. This green working should have given us instant control of the plague, but it did not, although Lord Morgon's potion both isolated and slowed the attack of the pestilence. Harmodius and I found a way to identify victims by means of a tag or trigger set off in every victim's body by the disease; with luck and some analysis, we were able to deconstruct the Archaic working and then, using the diagnostic working as a targeting solution..."

The queen raised her hand. "We understand that you have identified everyone affected and that, at an enormous cost in casting strength, most of the affected people, are stable."

"Stable, but decaying," the irk said, "because we don't have an answer to the necrotic portion of the working. We have all worked to slow it, and, hypothetically, any technique that slows any hermetical working should, at some greater level of power, cancel it, but this was not our experience. There was some component to the black working that was...not responding to our efforts. Like attempting to push oil against water."

He looked at Gabriel.

Gabriel stood up again. "We have agents in Antica Terra," he said. "One of them recently had to fight against the not-dead. In the pro-cess he discovered...no, let me start again. He was provided with an antidote to the not-death. He was told that of course, the Necroman-cer's power can be cancelled in the usual way. Like to like. Unlike to unlike." He waved at Kerak.

But the door opened and Amicia came in.

Amicia glowed with power. Her skin was not the smooth, browned skin of youth and vigour, but golden skin as if she were a living icon, and her eyes were lit with a fire too bright for most to endure.

"It is done," she said. Her voice sounded not like one woman's voice, but like the voice of *woman*. She went first to Blanche, who had the young king on her lap, and then Harmodius entered with a basket that any goodwife might use for her baking.

"One dose per person," Harmodius said. "It works."

An hour was spent planning the counteroffensive against the cough. It was loose throughout Alba and as far south as Harndon, and as far east as Liviapolis. The Prince of Occitan was justifiably anxious for his own lands, and the Outwallers feared the plague more than they feared Ash.

The queen summarized.

"We must raise every scrap of hermetical talent we have, train them to work these new patterns, and provide them with hundreds of pounds of powdered Umroth." She looked around. Many men wore Umroth ivory; the hilts of almost every baselard and rondel dagger in the room were of the stuff. But it was legendary for its value.

"Really," Lord Kerak said clinically, "any bones of not-dead will do."

Gabriel made a face. "That is an ugly picture," he said, and would say no more.

Harmodius looked at Morgon Mortirmir, who had aged five years. "I will stay and heal," he said. "Amicia too, as long as we have her."

She was sitting by the queen, glowing like a living statue.

"But one of us needs to go with Gabriel."

Every head turned. Most of the people in the room knew, at least in outline, the plan...the grand plan for the next few weeks. But not all, and one who did not was Blanche.

"Go with Gabriel?" she said aloud.

Morgon nodded. "I will go with Ser Gabriel," he said. "As long as I get some sleep first."

"Best go to bed now then, laddie," Bad Tom said. "Are ye the emperor now, boyo?"

Master Julius, notary and sometime advocate of Harndon, looked up from the gigantic tome of bound parchment he had brought in. "In my opinion," he said, a little portentously. Lord Gregario paused, in mid-description of an item of horse tack he wanted ordered; Amicia paused and looked up from where her golden skin illuminated Blanche's. Adrian Goldsmith, journeyman goldsmith and artist, sketched furiously, trying to capture that moment, and his charcoal was the only sound.

Master Julius was almost *never* the center of attention, and he swallowed. "Well. The precedents are...yes. But really. As far back as... never mind. There has been acclamation. Unless there's a counterclaim, you have been emperor since Gilson's Hole. Your...Grace." Pause. "Er, Eminence. Holiness? Majesty?" Master Julius subsided, looking annoyed with himself.

People laughed. It was a matter of relief—the plague, the war. The laughter went on too long and was too shrill, but it was laughter nonetheless.

Gabriel laughed with the rest, but when the laughter quieted, he looked at Master Smythe. "There's another thing," he said. "I assume that the fact that the Umroth ivory works as a specific against the cough means that Ash is in league with the Necromancer."

Master Smythe sighed. "I have to admit that is the most likely scenario," he said. "That means...a variety of things. Please tell me in detail of your encounter with the power of the black in Harndon," he said to the queen.

But it was Becca Almspend who told the story. When she was done, occasionally interrupted by the queen, Master Smythe steepled his fingers. "I see," he said, as if the words hurt him.

"Don't we think there is a gate in Harndon?" Gabriel asked.

Smythe shrugged. "Perhaps. There are, in fact, too many damned gates."

Gabriel produced another sheet of parchment. This one was a work of art, with the whole background a beautiful dark blue, and foreground figures in zodiacal signs and with tiny gilded stars; the night sky, in fact, although divided into seven portions.

He held it up for all to see. "This is the decoration of the ceiling of the gate chamber at Lissen Carak," he said.

Master Smythe half rose to his feet.

Gabriel went on. "It shows seven sets of constellations. My first theory was that it showed a single sky. My second theory was that it showed the sky from seven places."

Master Smythe put his good right hand on the Red Knight's shoulder. "This is not..."

Gabriel shook off his hand. "I thought these were seven night skies," he said. "But now I think that I understand the machine they've made of our sphere better. These are seven *situations* and each corresponds to an opening of the gates. And when the gates open, they go to that place. The place with the correspondence. Exactly like using a memory palace to build the codes for a hermetical working except on a larger scale."

Master Smythe sat down. He was shaken—his face registered a dozen emotions, some utterly *wrong*, as he sought for an expression suitable for his state.

There were people present who had no idea what the Red Knight had just said, but they were few. Most of the people present, regardless of race, had been present for the council at Albinkirk, or had heard what was discussed.

"So there are seven gates?" Kerak asked. He leaned forward. "Now this is interesting."

Master Smythe drummed his fingers. "There are at least fifteen gates, no two the same. A few are master gates that can be used at all the conjunctions. A few are single-use gates." He shrugged. "No one knows where they all are."

Pavalo Payam rose. "My master knows where all of them are. There was a scroll. I stole it. From the Necromancer." He looked around.

"Do you remember what it said?" Amicia asked.

"You stole it from the Necromancer?" the dragon asked. "I am impressed."

Payam bowed to the dragon's compliment and shook his head to Amicia. "I could not even read it," he said. "But my master will know."

Desiderata held up her hand. "There are some number of gates, and they go to different places. How many?"

Gabriel looked at Smythe. "Seven places in total. I believe."

Master Smythe looked pained, but he nodded affirmation.

Desiderata looked at the dragon. "Surely, we are allies, and you can tell us these things?"

Master Smythe took a deep breath and, for the first time any of them could remember, hesitated and released the breath without speaking. He looked around. He considered.

"Just tell us the truth," Gabriel prompted. He was standing, his painted chart from Lissen Carak in his hand, in sweat-stained arming clothes, and he had never looked more like an emperor.

Master Smythe waited a long time. Finally, slowly, he began.

"Imagine that there was a weapon," he said. "Imagine that weapon was so powerful that with it, you could conquer...anything." He looked around. "Whom would you trust with that weapon?" he asked.

Desiderata nodded. "I would be very careful in my choices," she said.

"Bless you, my lady. I understand that at this moment, we are allies struggling together to save ourselves and our perceptions of our world from Ash, and perhaps from his allies. Yet my kind—for good or evil—have charged themselves with making sure that this thing that we hold so precariously does not fall into the wrong hands. Once, so long ago that you possibly cannot imagine it, a single race almost eliminated all the others. In fact, it has happened three times. Not just here. Not just on the eight worlds. But...everywhere. And *everywhere* is vast."

He looked around. "When one petty baron fights another," he said, "children die and women are raped and crops are burned. The hate comes, and for some generations, those who survive are scarred. Is this not true?" He didn't pause. "And those of you whom I admire, you strive to prevent this. When you fight, you fight to minimize the loss, and the hate, to heal the scars as soon as they may be healed."

Some men nodded. Others looked as if they had never considered such things.

Sauce snorted. "Some knights, maybe," she said. "Tom fights for the hell of it."

Master Smythe looked at her the way a teacher looks at a difficult student. Sauce stuck her tongue out. "Sod off," she said. "You don't scare me."

Master Smythe shook his head. "But imagine there was an order... like the Knights of Saint Thomas...who fought only to prevent others from fighting? Ignoring right and wrong for a greater cause?"

Gabriel shook his head a fraction. "Sometimes there is only fighting," he said.

Master Smythe sighed. "I have lived longer than a hundred of you, and yet I will say that I have never, once, seen a situation improved by a war."

Gabriel scratched under his beard. "Yet you seem to want us to fight the Odine," he said.

Smythe gave him the same look he'd given Sauce. "That is a different matter entirely," he said.

Gabriel made no comment. His nasty smirk suggested that he thought he was right.

When Smythe stayed silent, Gabriel looked around. "That sounds very noble," he said. "Let me suggest an alternative scenario," he said. "Let's suppose that after the Odine, you see us, especially the race of man, as the next most dangerous. And you will stop at nothing to see that we do not gain control of the gates." He nodded. "Now, let me take that thought further," he said. "Let me suggest that if you did not need our help to suppress the Odine, we wouldn't know any of this."

Master Smythe frowned. "This is foolish," he said.

"Really?" Gabriel said.

They stood, eye to eye.

"You don't fear oblivion and defeat," Gabriel said. "You fear that we'll kill Ash and beat the Necromancer and the Odine and in the process, we'll win the gates. And because you fear us so much, you and Tar and any other surviving dragons are treating us as potentially hostile at every turn, and trying to arrange it so that we'll defeat your enemies but not understand anything…"

"Please stop," Master Smythe said. "You could cross a line that would force me to cease to support you at all."

"Seems to me we're supporting you, laddie," Bad Tom said.

Ser Gavin and Ser Gregario and a number of others nodded.

Sauce made a face as if she'd eaten something she disliked. "I hate to agree with Tom," she said. "But…"

Gabriel turned to the dragon. "I don't think anyone in this room has the least interest in the conquest of everywhere. I think it's all we can do to save ourselves. So I propose that while I follow the agreed plan, you and these ladies and gentlemen work out a … treaty. An agreement that satisfies everyone, or better yet, leaves everyone equally dissatisfied, about control of the gates. Would that not be the adult solution, rather than a massive betrayal of your tools when they've become too powerful?"

"Treaties can be broken," Master Smythe said.

"And so must be maintained. But I tell you, Master Smythe: we need to move forward in an aura of trust, and not an aura of lies. It is not so much that all of you struggle to keep the occupants of the other spheres out, is it? It's that you intend to keep us all *in*. Not just the Odine."

Master Smythe sat back and looked at the ceiling.

Gabriel shook his head. "And one of you has already betrayed your pact of dragons, hasn't he? Who is *Rhun*?" he asked.

Master Smythe's head shot round, and for a moment, his eyes glowed red and his expression was not human at all.

"So really, you need us, because you cannot, and do not, even trust the other dragons to do the right thing. Your allies are right here in this room. I think we need to be treated that way. As allies."

Master Smythe looked around.

"When you asked me if I planned to go to Antica Terra, you already foresaw this moment," Gabriel said, his voice grim and remorseless.

Master Smythe nodded. "Yes," he said.

There was a pause, mostly while people looked at each other and didn't understand.

But Amicia understood; the queen; Ser Michael, Bad Tom, and a number of others. They understood.

Morgon understood. He looked at his captain. "When are we leaving?" he asked.

"Where are they going?" Ser Gregario asked. "The tournament's just opened." He and Blanche exchanged a look, one suggested that people who didn't share their immediate plans were in a great deal of trouble.

Gabriel sat back. "I'm taking about a third of the army to Antica Terra," he said.

Bad Tom looked smug, and Ser Gavin looked annoyed, and Ser Gregario shot to his feet. "What?" he demanded.

Gabriel looked around. His own officers were prepared to obey. The imperial officers shrugged; Harald Derkensun didn't even look up. But most of the Albans were appalled, starting with the new Archbishop of Lorica, who had a hand to his throat as if he'd been attacked. He exchanged a look with Blanche, of all people.

He rose. "My lord; that is, Your Majesty, if I read today's events correctly." He was a tall, ascetic man, and a plain speaker. Well beloved by the people of Albinkirk already. He took a breath. "My lord, you are the sword and shield of the north. You cannot just abandon us. Your duty as a knight... I beg you to reconsider."

Gabriel looked around. "Friends," he began. He rose. "This decision was not taken lightly. But it was taken almost a month ago. And we began to prepare for it more than a year ago, when we started rebuilding the imperial fleet." He nodded at the looks of surprise. Master Smythe raised an eyebrow. "The game is vast, my friends. What Master Smythe and I agree on is that we have at least two enemies, and perhaps as many as five or six. All of them are playing for the same ends... to win control of some number of gates at the conjunction of the spheres. We have to guess at our enemy's next moves. But let me say this clearly. The fall of Harndon or Arles would hurt every one of us here as immediately as the fall of Lissen Carak. If we lose the gates...then the very best we can look forward to is an endless war against a rising tide of sorcerous foes."

"You're going to relieve Arles," said Ser Gregario, who saw the strategy clearly. And was annoyed he hadn't been consulted.

"Four days ago it still held against the undead," Gabriel said.

"You're sure? How do you know?" the archbishop asked.

Gabriel sighed. "I don't know. I don't know *anything*." He glanced at the dragon, and the dragon met his eye and pursed his lips. "I have to guess. But I believe that we have hit on a strategy that is sufficiently original to surprise all of our opponents, deceive them into believing we are following their lead, and has incidental side effects that are beneficial."

"Name one?" asked Rebecca Almspend. "You are taking a third of our army several thousand miles to fight an opponent who is not Ash and about whom we know almost nothing. I thought"—she tried not to sound arch—"I *thought* we were putting Du Corse and his people on ships to do this task." Almspend was looking at the queen, her best friend, who turned her head away. The final planning staff had been very small. Gabriel and the queen had known that feelings would be hurt.

"I can't risk Du Corse's failure," Gabriel said. "There are factors about which we had not been informed a month ago. Sea monsters. Eeeague. The Odine." He sighed. "Let me lay out three side effects that are beneficial. First, we will, if we succeed, save Antica Terra from domination by the Necromancer, if it is indeed he, and not some new force. Second, the merchants of Venike and Genua will underwrite the entirely of this year's campaign and probably next year's as well. Which is good. I am out of money; the queen is out of money. The empire is out of money. The costs of this war are...staggering."

The archbishop stared at him. "You are making the Venikans pay?" he asked.

Gabriel shrugged. "I will make them pay," he said, as if delivering a death sentence. "But this way, I can also visit Dar as Salaam. Or rather, Morgon can. It is Al Rashidi who holds most of the answers."

Harmodius nodded, and Master Smythe smiled. "I told you that you were going to Antica Terra," he said.

Bad Tom nodded. "And horses, don't forget."

Heads turned.

Bad Tom grinned. "The horse plague's bad here, eh? But there's no horse plague in Antica Terra, and we can remount the whole army."

"No ussse to usss if the army isss in Etrusssca and Asssh isss at our gatesss here," the Faery Knight said. Lord Gregario gave him a firm nod, happy to have an ally.

Gabriel nodded at Gregario. "Look. This is all very high risk. We have to win every battle, make all the right guesses, and even then... even then..." He looked around. "You and Gavin and Tapio have to hold here until I come back."

The Faery Knight played with his long chin. "My ssscoutsss sssay that Asssh is moving in the wessst. N'gara will be asssailed. Will thisss army of the north come to my aid?"

Nita Qwan looked around and rose, but Mogon shook her head and spoke herself, her voice deep and resonant. "Even now, Kevin Orley is raising men and Rukh to attack the Sossag country. Who will aid us?"

Gavin stood. "We won't even wait to be summoned, my lord and lady. We'll march the day after tomorrow." He looked at his brother. "We mean to surprise Ash with our temerity."

"We are all going to attack," Gabriel said. "West from N'gara, north from Ticondonaga, and east from Liviapolis."

An hour before dawn, and the morning star burned like a baleful eye. Kranmer's comet, a well-known harbinger of doom, shone red-gold in the dark sky to the west, his long tail extending back over the horizon.

Smoke was saddling his horse while Anne and Isabeau, who hadn't been to bed, laid out tack by lamplight.

"Son of a bitch," Smoke said. "Son of a bitch."

Farther along the line, Cully was looking over his kit, inspecting each item.

No Head brushed past him. "We're not fighting today," he said. "An' you can get any stuff you need in the city."

Cully watched the squires and pages. Angelo di Laternum's new squire pushed past.

"Cully?" the young man asked.

"How can I help you, young sir?" Cully answered.

"Is it true we're all getting cured of cough?" the boy asked. He coughed into his hand.

"On parade, in one hour," Cully agreed.

No Head helped Tippit with his bridle, and the older man spat. "Wilful would ha' loved this," he said.

"Oh aye," Cully said. "He'd be rubbin' our faces in it this minute." *Mark my words.*

Cully went to help Heron and Urk of Mogon. They hadn't even received their basic kit yet.

Sukey was already cured. She stood with Kaitlin and Blanche, counting things. Much had been loaded by those in on the plan during the last three days, but everything had hinged on the cure for the cough and until they were safe to leave the circle, some things could not even be packed.

The tents were being left standing. The captain claimed he had tents already made and loaded on the ships—ships none of them had ever seen, waiting in the city's military yard, ships he and No Head had designed and Milus and Alcaeus had watched built. So people said.

When Sauce rolled her eyes, the captain—now the emperor—laughed. "What do you think No Head and I were doing with all those drawings?" he asked.

There had been a great deal of secrecy, and Sukey, who had known most of it for a month, gave quiet orders and took the deepest breaths she could manage. And thought of her mother.

Morgon Mortirmir came down the steps from the attic of the stables, lacing his points.

"Magister?" Sukey asked. "You need a squire."

"Or an apprentice or both," he said. "Tancreda and I need to run a brief errand and then we will be any help we can manage."

"Can you answer me one question?" Sukey asked. "Will…I…get my breath back?"

Mortirmir nodded. "Yes. It will take weeks. But yes. Have you seen the chaplain?"

"Father David?" Sukey smiled. "He's asleep. And I'm letting him sleep. He waited on the sick hand and foot."

"Tell him I'd like a moment when you see him awake. Doesn't he have to pack?"

Sukey smiled. "I packed for him. You have no idea how hard he prayed for me when I was sick."

Another hour found the entire company, old veterans and new recruits, all gathered together, standing in neat lines in the outer yard with their surviving horses in their hands, along with Count Zac and Ser Giorgos and all the imperial troops. The horses looked bad, most overtired, and there were no spares. The morning star was just setting, and the comet looked like a splash of light against the last dark of night.

The captain rode out on Ataelus. He saluted Bad Tom and raised his voice. "In a moment, the company's hermeticists will deal with the cough," he said. "You're probably all wondering where we're going," he went on. "We ride today for Middleburg, and we'll go from there to Liviapolis. I don't expect any fighting there, but I might be wrong."

Silence.

"And then we'll board ships and sail to Antica Terra," he said.

Murmurs.

"And then," he said, "I'll be leading you to hell." He looked around. "I know you think I'm kidding," he said. He shrugged. "You'll see."

Mark my words...

Part IV
Antica Terra

Kaitlin, Countess of Kendal, swung in a hammock deep in the bowels of the great ship *Sant Graal* and tried to decide if she was pregnant again, which would be incredibly unfair given the infrequency of the combination of lust, privacy, and her husband's presence that would allow such a thing—or whether she was merely seasick.

They had been at sea five days. Sailors said the wind was fair. She had no idea. Every time she went on deck, everything seemed a chaos and a panic, with men running to bellowed orders, sails going up and down, and the constant rolling of the huge round ship.

The Red Knight, as she still thought of him, had ordered the three ships built. The emperor, now.

She lay, feeling miserable, and thought of the beauty of the imperial coronation, the magnificence of the cathedral, and the speed with which they had moved in...and then out...of the city.

She heard a great shriek, and she had to calm her muscles, a few at a time. She wondered if she was strong enough to find Blanche.

She wondered if there was some other way to get home.

And then she leapt out of her hammock, struck her knee on the floor, and ran, hand to mouth, for the main ladder.

On deck, it was worse. The sky was grey, not blue, and the charcoal-grey waves were tall, and seawater blew in a heavy wind and soaked her instantly. The big round ship—some people said it was the largest afloat—took the seas well, but it was called "round" for reasons, and what made for good flotation didn't help the seasick. The ship moved.

Kaitlin heaved over the side, and there was another shriek.

The door of the main cabin opened like a vision of heaven. Inside was light—a beautiful golden candle light. She suspected Michael might be in there. She threw up over the side again, cursing her lot, and finally felt better.

The emperor was holding her hair out of her eyes.

"Don't you dare laugh at me!" Kaitlin spat.

Gabriel laughed. "I think we're going to have some court ceremonial lessons," he said. An arm of spume off the nearest wave was blown over them, soaking her again.

He put her wet hands on the lifeline that ran down the waist of the big ship. "Go to the cabin," he said.

"I'm soaked!" she yelled. "I'll go below."

There was another wild shriek from the stern.

"I have to go," he said. "The cabin will be better for you. And there's wine. And Blanche is bored." He gave her a gentle push and ran aft, slipped on the deck, fell, and a wave came over the bulwark. It was not a big wave, and it only dragged him to the scuppers and pulled him against the side of the ship, but he hung on, rose, and ran the rest of the way to the door into the high stern castle.

She followed him as far as the steps, and then entered the door from which he'd come.

There were half the officers of the company, and their partners— Sauce and Count Zac, Bad Tom, her husband, and Giorgos Comnenos and his wife and Sukey. Sukey looked grey instead of her usual magnificent pale brown, and so did Tom. No one was well dressed.

Kaitlin got the door closed before the wind put out every candle.

Blanche rose from the coach, the long settee built into the stern of the ship under the great stern windows. On this ship, however, the stern windows overlooked a small platform, like a balcony, and a long, long heavy pole, as big as the mainmast, that pointed straight astern.

Kaitlin had no interest in looking at the vast majesty of the sea coming up astern, roller on roller to the grey horizon that seemed, today, far too close. But she was grateful for Blanche's warmth when the golden-haired woman wrapped her arms around Kaitlin. She led her into the alcove by the coach and stripped her shift over her head and replaced it with a dry wool gown. Kaitlin tried to resist the sisterly impulse to subside into Blanche's arms. The wool was luxurious.

"I'm so seasick," she confided. "Or I'm pregnant again."

Blanche embraced her.

Kaitlin worried about her son. *I can be away for an hour*, she thought, eager for adult conversation. She had a nurse, who seemed afraid of everything and yet completely resistant to the sea.

Her husband came and replaced Blanche's arms with his own. He put a cup of hot wine in her hands and she drank a little.

Sauce looked up from her cards. "Tom's been liking the chicken soup," she said kindly.

Bad Tom did not look like the monster of the battlefield he sometimes could be. Instead, he looked as if he'd just begun to recover from jaundice, and his eyes had red rims.

"I think I still have a touch of the cough," he muttered.

Sukey made a sound not unlike a kitten's pitiful mew.

"I'm in good company," Kaitlin allowed. "Let me try the soup."

Blanche watched him recover from the cough. He was very difficult to live with. He never stopped talking and he was far too intent and often distant. He would make love to her in the lightning-shot ecstasy of the stern cabin in a storm and almost immediately rise and begin writing, which made her feel small and possibly used. He would go to see his monster the moment the thing screamed, leaving her or anyone else. He came to bed at all hours, having spent time with the helmsman or fencing on deck by mage light with Michael or playing piquet.

But what she really missed was how much the queen needed her and how important she was to the queen's life. But the queen had sent her—had blessed her. Had offered her lands and a title, in fact, to go and represent her.

"Do not let him forget he is Alban, and one of us," she said.

Blanche was used to a life of work, and hard work: work at which she excelled. She had little interest in being a mistress, and she was quickly bored, although the lovemaking was, she admitted to her own surprise, very exciting. She had always assumed it was something women put up with to get children. Her mother had told her so in just so many words, dwelling on shame and dirt.

Her mother had never made love during a lightning storm at sea by a window of a hundred panes of glass and rollers taller than the stern of the ship.

But Blanche was determined to fit in, and to work. She suspected she'd perish of boredom, otherwise. Luckily, fate sent her a sodden and very seasick Kaitlin, and she spent two days caring for Kaitlin and for Galahad, her son, named for an old tale and the handsome servitor of the queen's too. If she had a daughter, she was going to call her Tamsin for the Faery Queen. Kaitlin had said so just that morning.

The first thing she found in Kaitlin's space belowdecks was that the other women didn't have fine hanging beds as she had in the stern cabin. Kaitlin had a hammock, hung in a range of hammocks with the other women of the company, and noblewomen and seamstresses occupied the same lines. Two men-at-arms stood guard at all times at the head of the range, and the archers of the household were in the next range: all men and women that Blanche knew. It was intimate to a degree Blanche had never seen; there was no hint of privacy, and the smell—the "fug" as the sailors called it—was like nothing she'd ever endured.

Little Galahad was not helping. He was loud in his protests against the sea, and his wet nurse was a slattern, more interested, already, in finding herself an archer—or two, or five.

The morning after the sodden Kaitlin had flung herself into the great cabin, Blanche went to visit her and found her work. The baby was crying because he was dirty, and Kaitlin was beside herself because the baby was dirty, and the slatternly nurse was indignant because she was being blamed for it.

It was surprisingly like life in the palace.

Laundry wasn't easy at sea. Blanche had noted that the food was dull, and sometimes bad, but she hadn't fully understood how afraid everyone was of fire until she went to the galley herself, carrying a naked baby on her shoulder. The cooks were all men, all survivors of bad wounds; Pierre had a peg leg, and Antoine had just one arm.

Oak Pew was there, still pale from the cough. Blanche had never encountered her sober before and was shocked when the older woman took the baby and made cooing noises.

"The wet wind makes me ill," she said, "but I love the sea. Oh, what a cute baby. What a fine little man you are," she said, running her rough hand over the baby's smooth thighs.

Blanche almost said something foolish, like *But you're lovely, sober!* but she restrained herself. Instead, she found that Oak Pew, being a regular in the galley, could be her intermediary to the rather scary men who were the cooks.

"I need hot water. I need a lot of hot water, to wash clothes. At the least, I need to wash all the baby's things." She shrugged. "I'm at my wits' end."

Oak Pew spoke to the cooks in Gallish. They answered with shrugs. "Antoine says he only has so many pots, and…"

Blanche laughed. "And he's not anxious to have baby shit in them," Blanche said. "I heard him. My mother spoke Gallish at home."

"They do laundry," Oak Pew said. "They do it in seawater and it's full of salt—bad for a woman and terrible for a baby. But they must have washbasins or wooden tubs." She rattled off a long string of rapid Gallish, which Blanche could just about follow.

Antoine nodded and Pierre led them out of the galley and down a short, very narrow passage, to a storeroom. There were washtubs of wood, all knocked down and stored with their hoops, like barrels.

Blanche sighed. "It's like the palace," she said. "You have to make the tool before you can do the job." Nonetheless, she left Galahad with Oak Pew, a daring decision in the eyes of many, and ran, barefoot, aft, to the small deck above the great cabin, from which the master mariner commanded the ship. Most of the ship's officers and trained men gathered there, and Gabriel stood with the master mariner, a Morean seaman of few words and vast experience.

She'd seen them all do the routine whereby they paused on the steps to the quarterdeck and crossed themselves to the crucifix, hung on the new aft cabin, built high on the castle, that the pranksters called the "eighth deck" because it was half the size of the quarterdeck.

Gabriel smiled when he saw her. Master Alexei bowed politely.

"Despoina," he said. "Welcome to my deck."

She curtsied. "Master," she said, "I've come to beg a boon."

He nodded, his eyes already flicking around his ship. It was interesting to watch him—every few seconds, he looked at the mainsail and the mast tops and then looked forward. "Yes?" he asked.

"I wonder if I might borrow your carpenter, and have a few of your washtubs knocked together," she asked.

He nodded, glanced around his ship, and smiled at her, possibly amused. "Leonardo!" he called. "Attend this lady."

Leonardo, it proved, was entirely competent. Blanche suspected, from what she'd overheard, that Gabriel had ransacked the imperial navy and hired Albans and Galles to fill out his crews, but everyone she met seemed thorough and professional, and Leonardo was clearly glad to have something to do. He built her three washtubs in a time that would have been considered miraculous in the palace in Harndon and then filled them with seawater to make sure they were tight. They weren't, but he kept filling them.

"That's why we use soft wood," he said. "It swells. Everything warps at sea. Best to just let nature do the work. Give her half a glass."

She went below and negotiated, for a little of Gabriel's money, that the cooks would give her six fills of her tubs in hot, fresh water. The rain had filled every barrel on the ship. She hadn't even considered the rarity of fresh water.

She collected all the baby's clothes—and all of Kaitlin's under-clothes, her own, and Sukey's and Blanche's and Sauce's. Sukey smiled and assigned her four young women, and they contributed their own clothes, and before the water was hot, she had all the shifts of all the women and girls aboard. This led to a certain hilarity belowdecks, as thirty-five women went about clad only in kirtles, to the delight of most of the archers and men-at-arms.

Of course they began to ask for their own clothes to be washed—seven days at sea, and men were wearing braes for the fourth time, some of them.

Sukey just shook her head. "This one's on me, Blanche. I run the laundry, and why I thought that the saints would do the clothes at sea...perhaps I thought we'd all run naked."

"The cooks can't boil any more water," Blanche said, "without affecting food."

There was an archer standing behind Sukey with his arms full of white smalls. Sukey took them and added them to the pile with a smile, and the young archer vanished.

"We aren't doing men's clothes," Blanche began, and then she got it. "Who's she?" she asked.

Sukey nodded. "Someone who shouldn't be here," she said. "But I'll hazard she's got the solution." Sukey left Blanche standing by her tubs with her new girls: four strong young women, all new to the company and all inured to work. She gave them her new-girl lecture from the palace about cleanliness, and when the first hot water came, she led them in washing her own hands, arms, and face with soap. Then she filled three tubs.

"I'll do the baby things," she said. "They're foul, and they will take some skill." She'd scraped the worst off over the side into the clean, fresh sea, and now she gave them a first wash, turning her water foul but the cloth whiter.

Work enveloped her, as it did. She did the dirtiest work, and her girls immediately liked her.

She'd done this all before. The first woman to teach her to wash laundry had told her, *Shit washes away*. It was her life principle.

Her girls were like girls. They liked to talk, none of them particularly liked to get their hands in dirty water, and all four managed to get water everywhere.

But the work got done.

She was unaware that Gabriel was there until he came forward. "Sukey told me," he said.

"You aren't angry?" she asked.

He made a face. "It is you who could be angry. I should learn to do this," he began.

"And then you'd try to compete with me to do it better," she said, hands on hips.

"What do you need?" he asked, pushing hair out of her eyes.

"More hot water?" she asked. "As you are emperor and everything."

"And emperor on a ship is only the second or third in command," he said. "But hot water I can do, and so can Morgon."

She never thought about using the hermetical.

He boiled her baby diapers in their second clean water, right in the tubs.

"You could find employment in any laundry," she said. "Lord, the time saving."

Sukey, close at hand, laughed. "Sweet Christ, if women ran the world, think of the magic items we'd build. Self-heating laundry tubs."

One of the girls, Kady, laughed, showing her strong teeth. "Magical stoves!" she said.

They all laughed. The smallest one giggled. "A charm against making a baby?"

Kady blushed. "That would be—" She couldn't stifle a laugh.

Morgon Mortirmir was just coming up the main ladder. He looked at young Kady. "Why would you want such a charm?" he asked.

Kady blushed again.

Sukey shrugged. "Because guessing your cycle is dull," she said.

"And it doesn't always work." She'd spent enough time with the young magister to know how literal his mind was.

Morgon shrugged. "It's not that complex a matter," he said. "Let me see what I can do."

He also boiled some water for Blanche, three tubs at a time.

She nodded to Sukey. "If Ser Morgon will repeat this trick another time or two, I can start on the men's clothes," she said.

Sukey pulled her aside. "You don't have to do this," she said.

Blanche grinned. "You work. Kaitlin works. I wish to work. I am very good at this."

Sukey hugged her. "It cracks my hands. I hate laundry."

"Lanolin," Blanche said.

"Is His Nibs going to let you do laundry?" Sukey asked. "The empress of laundry?"

The stream of imperial messenger birds was incessant. Gabriel had at least one a day and sometimes two, with Alcaeus and his mother sitting in Liviapolis; Kronmir's messages from Venike, and now, almost daily messages from Du Corse. The Galle was at sea, with his own company and several hundred borrowed Alban men-at-arms and archers. Gabriel was sharing information on the Necromancer.

Michael sat in the after cabin, writing.

"It's like old times," Gabriel said, coming in with a messenger on his fist.

Anne Woodstock put her head in the door. "Master Giannis says the *Mary Magdalene* and the *Joseph of Arimethea* are in sight."

Gabriel smiled. "Thanks, Anne," he said. When she'd closed the door, he took the message off the bird—Forty-One, a small bird. He read it and handed it to Michael to copy fair.

Michael copied it and looked up. "So nothing is attacking the Galles," he said.

"Another of my clever plans bites the dust," Gabriel admitted. "I was sure the Eeeague would attack them and we'd slip by." He frowned. "And that means we may be attacked. This is all so high-risk." He shook his head. "We're so close we could rendezvous. They must be just over the horizon—the birds are going back and forth in two hours."

"You said you were ready to fight," Michael said.

Gabriel raised an eyebrow, and Michael nodded. "This *is* like old times. You mean, it's always better to slip by than to fight," he said. "I'll be ready to be captain, any day."

Gabriel nodded. "Good," he said. He paused. "You know that if I go down, it's you."

Michael shrugged.

Gabriel scratched under his beard. "Birth matters. Sauce can command; Tom can too. But...only you and Gavin have the birth." His eyes met Michael's squarely. "And Giorgos Comnenos. He's for emperor."

Michael swallowed. "Don't die," he said. "I don't need to see how thoroughly you've planned my future."

Gabriel nodded, eyes on the next message. "I've done my best," he said.

Next morning was clear. The weather mages kept a breeze in the great sails. Otherwise, they'd have been becalmed. But they were not moving much.

Master Janos had a great sail lowered over the side for swimming, and the men went first, bathing in the clear water. Most could not swim, but the sail kept them safe, and the lookouts were watching for sharks. There were big sharks in these waters. The master mariner assured them they were just a day or perhaps two from the Elbow and the coast of Iberia. Indeed, the lookouts spotted a few sharks, but none came close enough to provide sport for the duty crossbows.

The *Mary Magdalene* was so close that they could see people's faces craning over the side, and Michael waved to Master Julius and wished that the man were aboard the flagship and available to do all the clerking. The *Joseph of Arimethea* was a ghostly presence, pale and almost white, on the horizon to the north, and making a long board to close them.

About noon, when Michael emerged from the water, salty but clean of ink, the lookout hailed the deck that he'd seen ships.

Gabriel was still in the water. But he came up the side naked, water dripping off his beard.

Master Giannis called into the tops, "Where away?" in Morean Archaic. The lookout, also Morean, answered in the same language.

Gabriel turned to Michael, naked, and Sauce, not quite naked in a man's shirt. She had been lounging on the deck, creating havoc among the sailors.

"Arm," he said.

Naked, he ran up the steps to the quarterdeck, even as Anne, very damp, and Toby, just as naked, converged on the day cabin.

Gabriel paused, just above them. "Flying armour," he said. "Master Giorgos?"

Master Giorgos was looking east under his hand.

"The Elbow is visible from the top," he said. The Elbow was the promontory of Iberia, out-thrust into the sea. Galle and the Eagle's Head were equidistant, the one to the north, the other to the south, two days' sail on a good wind.

Gabriel nodded. "And the Galles?"

"Alexei can see two or three round ships out to the north," he said. "And the *Joseph of Arimethea* is signaling."

"Fighting?" Gabriel asked.

"Hove to," Giannis said. "And he thought he saw something under us."

Gabriel leaned over the side, aware that it was wasted effort. "Very well. We are not defenceless. Rig the gonnes."

Master Giannis looked aft. "Already done."

Gabriel bowed and went down the steps and into the cabin. There, Anne, now in an overgown of Blanche's, and Toby, in a shirt, began to dress and arm him. He got wool hose, despite the heat on deck, and a linen doublet under his fur-lined and collared jupon. Thigh-high boots.

Mortirmir came in without knocking.

"I'm going to try our little trick," he said.

Gabriel nodded. "Be my guest," he said.

Mortirmir went aft, into the little passageway by the coach, and reappeared outside the stern windows under the overhang of the griffon's box. He had to stoop. He leaned over the side and dropped something that looked like a heavy spear with a silk rope attached, and then another.

He put a dozen of the javelins into a leather bucket and went out the door.

Time passed. Gabriel's heart was thudding in his chest and there was no reason.

The cabin door opened and Blanche appeared, in a damp shift. "Master Giannis says that there's a dozen or more ships all hove to," she said. "And that something huge is well beneath us." Her voice was steady, except that on the word *huge* it quavered.

"Tell Master Giannis that whales are friendly," he said.

She blew him a kiss.

He took his helmet and gauntlets. He was shaking, and he knew it was just fear of getting the griffon aloft, of all the things to be afraid of.

"Best get armed," he said kindly.

His squire and page nodded.

He ran up the quarterdeck ladder, giant spurs threatening to tangle his feet every step. Spurs and ships were not friends.

Ariosto was very glad to see him, and the great head with its mad eyes came around and he was head-butted.

We are flying. Right now.

Love you! Great!

The griffon was very cramped in its cabin, which smelled very strongly of old griffon dung, a nasty business.

Somewhere, a winch began to wind, and the heavy back wall of the cabin cracked open, revealing the calm sea aft, and the long pole that rose and fell with the ship's motion, like a horizontal mast.

Ariosto writhed and hopped onto the pole before the back walls were fully open, and immediately spread his wings and gave a great cry of happiness. The mage wind caught under his wings, and he leapt away in a turning flash of muscular grace and vanished over Gabriel's head.

Both of us! Gabriel said.

I know, brother. But I need a stretch.

Men were leaning down from the eighth deck. Morgon Mortirmir leaned down. "Problems?" he asked.

Gabriel shook his head. "No," he said.

"I have a contact, deep beneath us," Morgon said. "Thirty paces long. That's all I can say." He shrugged. "Except that it is alive, as you and I are alive."

Gabriel nodded. "Release a bird," he said. "Tell Du Corse I'm coming over."

Ariosto appeared, far astern, coming out of a long curve, and he matched speed with the ship and came down on the perch as neatly as a bird landing on a pole. The sailors had raised most of the roof of his cabin so that he could hop straight back in, and Toby and Gabriel began immediately saddling the great animal. His wings were in the

305

way everywhere, and the lion end seemed unsuited to the sea, and his most recent dung smelled strongly of fish.

But they got his tack on, and Morgon's bucket of javelins. Today, Gabriel had his *ghiaverina*, also in a leather case, and a bow.

Too heavy?

Lighter than grain. We fight?

Maybe.

He checked the buckles on the complex, tripartite girth one more time.

You could just mount here, instead of on the perch, Ariosto said.

It seemed like a good idea.

He got his feet in the stirrups and got the belt across his heavy saddle, through the keeper on his cote, and it clicked home...

Ariosto was facing astern. He took one long, dainty step with a taloned forefoot onto the perch—and leapt into the air, twisting his body through half a circle and very nearly catapulting his beloved rider into the depths. As it was, Gabriel's entire weight hung by the thread of his waist belt for several terrified beats of his heart, and he was lying far out over the crupper, as if a better jouster had almost unhorsed him.

But they were rising on Morgon's mage wind, moving straight astern and almost directly above the ship.

Gabriel got himself erect.

Stop screaming, Ariosto said.

Gabriel got his visor down, and the world became silent and tranquil, and his heart rate began to slow. They were still rising, well above the topmasts now, and when he turned his head over his right shoulder, he could now see the Gallish fleet to the north. There were twenty ships there, including almost every heavy ship out of Harndon.

He got into his *memory palace and found Morgon waiting for him. The young Alban had a mirror on the floor by Pru's pedestal, and there, in the dark mirror, swam a great shape.*

"The master mariner assures me this is a great whale," Mortirmir said. "It is almost directly beneath our ship. I can only say that it is very agitated."

Gabriel noted the golden shield waiting where he'd left it. He began to prepare other workings, and he made them in the shape of jewelry and bedecked Prudentia with earrings, a pair of rings, a brooch. It was all symbolism, anyway.

When he was done preparing defences, he built some spears. Morgon faded in and out, reporting very little.

Gabriel emerged into the real to find that they'd come two-thirds of the way to the Gallish fleet, and they were both very high and moving very fast. It was a beautiful day, and the rollers of the calm sea were now a near perfect carpet of sun-dazzle.

At this height, the twenty ships lying under bare poles close to the Iberian coast were clearly embattled. Several ships had been totally destroyed; the sea was littered with wood, and a great spear-pointed tail emerged from the water near another and struck the ship a heavy blow. At this altitude, the blow was silent and appeared to do no damage.

Ready, brother? Gabriel asked. *Now we fight.*

Who? Ariosto asked.

The serpents.

Oh. I don't swim so well, the ships look easier to attack.

Serpents. Please dive.

Here we go!

Ariosto folded his wings.

Gabriel took the Lord's name in vain.

They fell, if an arrow shot from a bow could be said to fall.

I need to pass just over that one . . . the one on the surface . . .

Which one? Ariosto asked.

In fact, as they dove, Gabriel could see three sea monsters.

Gabriel pulled very slightly on the right rein until Ariosto lined up his dive with the triangular head just emerging from the water.

That one, he said, realizing that they both had a great deal to learn about fighting from the air.

Ariosto's wings came up, cupping the air and slowing them. Gabriel thought that they were going to hit the water and the speed of their approach astounded him, and he prepared his working . . .

. . . and missed his moment, and they were turning west over a sea littered with wreckage.

"Damn it!" he said out loud. Ariosto had clawed the sea monster's head beneath his booted feet and he'd almost lost his lunch in terror, and the great griffon had skimmed away having left bloody furrows over the sea monster's eyes. Gabriel looked behind him, and the thing was thrashing in the sea and men were dying.

I know you said not to attack . . .

No, that was beautiful. I wasn't ready. It was all too fast.

You want me slower?

No, I want me faster, Gabriel muttered inside his head.

They rolled to the right and he saw another serpent, this one ripping along the surface, racing up on one of the Alban ships.

This one.

Got her.

Ariosto's turn became tighter and Gabriel *got into his palace and took one of the spears in each figurative hand. To Morgon's slightly insubstantial figure, he said, "I hope we have this right."*

"*Du Corse received our bird. That's all I know,*" Morgon said.

Gabriel emerged to a shallower dive. The serpent was a hundred paces aft of an Alban round ship, moving fast enough that its head-up posture left a huge wake. As Gabriel watched, the head lowered to smash a ship's stern.

Match speed, Gabriel asked.

Easy.

The wings fluttered and they seemed to halt in the air.

Gabriel tossed his first working from fifty feet above. It struck the broad, scaled, armoured back in a burst of red light and blew a foot-wide hole into the thing's body, exposing the spine.

The whole serpent *rolled* and the head shot up out of the water. Ariosto responded perfectly, like an eagle flowing around trees in the woods, and his foretalons and hind claws raked the head casually as he passed, wings vertical, body slewed out and Gabriel horizontal, but this time, Gabriel had the presence of mind to lob his second spear of red light at the head from almost arm's length.

And then they were gone. Ariosto was climbing, his wings straining for every inch of altitude as the head thrashed beneath them.

You hit hard, brother, Ariosto sang out. Gabriel had the curious feeling that the griffon viewed him as the junior partner.

Perhaps he was, at that.

Then they were turning, running south across the grain of the battle. Below them were eighteen surviving ships, and there were Eeeague on some of the decks. On others, ballistae were rigged, loosing bolts into the sea or at serpents, but they scored few hits.

The ships closest to Ariosto were cheering, though.

Gabriel got a glance back over his shoulder. There, on the surface, was the monster he'd struck. It had blood *pouring* from it, staining the seawater red-brown at its head and midspine. It lay half afloat, half submerged, and a sperm whale struck it in the head as he watched, dealing it a heavy blow so that more of its body sank. Its counterblow was feeble and the sperm whale danced aside, and then Gabriel was turning again and he saw a second serpent, a long and sinuous shape, rising swiftly.

That's one, Ariosto said. *No idea we're up here.*

Gabriel was surprised at the catlike cruelty and joy in his mount's tone. "Here we go," he said out loud.

This is fun. Why didn't you tell me we'd kill things together? Pause. *By the way, I'm hungry.*

This time, Ariosto turned in lazy circles descending, and Gabriel watched the water as the opaque shadow rose from the depths and became more clearly defined.

Something is happening here, Morgon said.

Gabriel looked south. His squadron of three great ships was closing, but still six miles of water lay between them. The *Joseph of Arimethea* was closest, but was hovering, her sails backing and filling, awaiting her consorts.

Our whale is gone. It went down. Something is lingering just at the edge of my perception.

Gabriel was attempting to keep part of his consciousness in the real and part in the *aethereal*, without much success.

Bide, he muttered to Morgon.

The triangular head was almost distinct. He had his *ghiaverina* in his hand, and his last red spear.

It was going to broach. He had half expected it.

It knows we're here, he said to Ariosto.

They snap-rolled to the right.

The head broke the water in a titanic explosion of water and its mouth opened, row on row of slightly crooked, spiky teeth running away into its gullet like an organic cavern. Its breath reeked of fish and ocean and rot and its tongue reached...

Gabriel moved with Ariosto into a left bank, wings vertical, and he felt it coming and didn't fight it, trusting the force of the turn to pin him to his saddle. He loosed his red bolt as the head, faster than he'd imagined, tracked them and closed, the tongue reaching...

His spear of light struck inside the cavity of its mouth against the roof and burst...

The head staggered...

The tongue snapped like a whip and Gabriel's left hand shot out and the *ghiaverina* cut through the tongue and up, and Ariosto seemed to wriggle in the air as the jaws closed, and the last eight inches of the *ghiaverina* passed through the outstretched upper jaw without slowing them in a spray of red-brown blood.

The head began to fall away.

The broaching had run out of energy.

But Ariosto's dive was still full of power and he followed the falling head, talons raking the eyes as they plummeted, turning, a blow from the *ghiaverina* to the back of the head and then the head hit the sea and the rising water tore at them—they were upside down—all airspeed lost—and then the lionlike back legs touched down on the rising coil of the serpent's midsection and gave a galvanic leap, and the magnificent wings beat, and they were aloft again.

Gabriel reached into the basket at his side and drew forth one of Morgon's javelins and waited for Ariosto to turn. Already they were working better together...already the great griffon could read the change in his weight and move under him. Ariosto turned as the serpent gained control of its length. It lay just below the surface, and Gabriel threw a javelin and missed.

But Ariosto turned as the head came up, giving him a second throw even as the first vanished in a thousand fathoms.

He leaned out and dropped the javelin, using Ariosto's speed in the air to give it impetus, and it penetrated the scales and sank to the middle of the shaft.

Get out of here, he told his mount.

The serpent dove, the head dropping and the body following in a single, smooth bending like a bow, and watching it was eerie.

Ariosto's wings swept out, up and down.

Tired, brother.

Me too.

I wanted to kill that one.

I think we have. Watch.

Gabriel, safe in a climb, went *into his palace and waved at the insubstantial Morgon.* "I got one. Number two. Number one was a miss."

Morgon *played with the strings on his fingers.*

On the quarterdeck of the *Sant Graal*, Morgon Mortirmir stood watching the water without expression. The waist was full of archers and men-at-arms, and the crews of the two gonnes, tubes loaded by specially trained men and women with the silver-grey powder that burned, stood by them with lit matches.

Michael was watching Mortirmir while trying to urge the great ship through the water with his armoured hips.

Suddenly Mortirmir's eyes focused. The magister smiled. He raised a hand and snapped his fingers.

Ariosto leveled off and the Red Knight looked down into the sea.

Something happened.

He could not have said that he felt it, or heard it, or merely sensed the passage of power in the *aethereal* but he knew the moment.

Four hundred fathoms under Ariosto's feet, the javelin served as a conduit, and Morgon Mortirmir's fireball burst forth like a wicked bloom in the icy depths.

Gabriel passed over the water and began to throw fire into the Eeeague, whose sixfold living pods were climbing a Gallish great ship. His fire drove a pod back into the water and Ariosto turned and Gabriel had the satisfaction of seeing a man in Du Corse's arms wave, and then Ariosto's wingbeats slowed.

Very tired now.

Go for the ship, brother, Gabriel said.

They turned lazily, just above mast height. Gabriel could see, off to the west, a great slick of blood rising to the surface, a funnel of the stuff in the water, and sharks were coming in—an incredible tide of sharks, hundreds, perhaps thousands of them. From three hundred feet they were like flies attracted to dung, like ravens on a more natural battlefield, except that as the broken half of the serpent rose, uncontrolled, to the surface, eyes blasted from its head, ripped in half and still somehow alive, the sharks hurled themselves at it in an insane fury, driven mad by the great rising helix of blood in the water.

Ariosto shrieked in appreciation. *And you thought you'd eat* me, *you son of a bitch*, the griffon said, or something very like. *Meat. Prey animal. Weakling. Mine!*

And as the tired wings carried them south, something else came rising on the sea—another serpentine shape, this, too, with a triangular head. But it was not a beast, but an appendage, and one tentacle writhed home around the serpent's neck and then another, and the vast titan began to be dragged *down*.

What in all the spheres was that? Ariosto moaned.

Oh God, Gabriel thought. His sense of scale had just received yet another kick in the head and he was trying to think of a sane world where there were trees and deer and perhaps giant beaver or something normal. *I guess that's a Kraal.*

Aaaiiieee! Ariosto moaned again.

Far out over the water, they flew, and the tired griffon nonetheless rose, because he feared the water.

But nothing interrupted their return flight.

This could be rough, Ariosto said. *I'm really tired. Hungry.*

Love you! Gabriel said.

In his memory palace, *he found Mortirmir.*

"*Turn the* Sant Graal *into the wind,*" he asked.

"*On the way. How was my fireball?*" *the young man asked.*

"*Everything that could be asked. Scratch one sea monster.*"

"*Very gratifying,*" *Mortirmir said.* "*Here we go. Ready about.*"

Under Ariosto's talons the round ship, aided by mage wind, began to turn west into the wind. She turned well, and Ariosto coasted west on an updraft that gave him several minutes of much-needed rest.

When the *Sant Graal* had her head into the wind, all her sails down but a single driver forward that was full of mage wind to keep her steady, Ariosto gave a great cry and began to descend. He flew alongside the *Sant Graal* as she ran west into the world's wind, and then Ariosto crossed the wind, coasting, descending, crossing the ship just above the mainmast and now descending downwind, and then the griffon turned, a few hundred paces aft, gave two mighty heaves of his wings and began to descend into the wind, the west wind passing over his wings and slowing his descent. Gabriel could feel the great beast's fatigue, and he could sense the griffon's fear for the first time.

You're fine. Look, almost there.

The griffon began to waggle—left, right, its body moving, wings adjusting, pinions rippling in the sun.

Down.

Down.

Down.

Fifty paces from the stern of the ship, and Gabriel could read *Sant Graal* in letters of gold under the stern windows and there was Blanche, standing on the stern with Mortirmir and Michael and all the crew in armour.

They waggled again.

Damn, said Ariosto.

His wings gave more of a heave than a simple beat.

For a moment they skimmed the water.

But even if his wingtips touched on the downstroke, the great avian powered himself *up* in the last ten paces and got his talons out, a little low, the catch a little desperate, and the pole swayed wildly and the whole ship fell off course two points, the stern driven round by the weight of the monster landing. Masts creaked.

Don't talk when I'm landing, the griffon said. He shuffled once and gave a little leap, and they were in his cabin.

Feed me, he said.

The ship rocked from the leap. But people were cheering, and Gabriel sat a moment, unable to move.

Gabriel gathered his wits to hug his beast, and then he slipped from the saddle and Toby and Anne and Blanche, of all people, were there, pulling the saddle away, and two of Sukey's girls had a sheep—a terrified live sheep. It had every reason for its terror, and in seconds it was gone.

Gabriel didn't stop to watch, even though he had a little trouble with his feet. And a very urgent need to relieve himself. Toby got the gauntlets and then the helmet and he stumbled up the ladder to the eighth deck. He saluted the cross and nodded to the master mariner.

Mortirmir crossed the deck.

"Our whale is back," he said. "Nothing else."

Gabriel was having trouble breathing. Someone put a cup of wine in his hand, and he drained it before he tasted it. "Water," he said. "I'm going to guess that someone nasty just got the surprise of their eons-long existence," he said with the smug satisfaction that made him easy to hate.

Mortirmir nodded. "We expected this," he agreed.

"I think our adversary just lost several thousand years' worth of sea monsters in an hour." Gabriel gulped water, spit over the side. Looked up at the sails. "Of course, the dragons didn't warn us, and now they'll fear us more." But he couldn't stop the grin.

Two hours later, and the unarmed women were moving about with water buckets again, and the hard edge of preparedness was wearing off. There had been no attack; the gonne crews had practiced shooting at barrels, with their long bronze pieces, and they had crept north toward the other fleet, which lay at anchor, just a few hundred paces from the Elbow, in the curve of the cliffs.

Gabriel watched as they came up. There was no fighting. Boats were moving over the water, and there were cheers.

"Du Corse had a head on his shoulders," Bad Tom admitted. "Covered his flanks, an' shallower water, and all his bowmen could concentrate on yon." He nodded his approval. "I couldna' ha' done better."

Gabriel looked under his hand. "Nor I," he said.

On the deck of the *Jesu e Maria de Harndon*, the largest ship to sail from that city, Gabriel found Du Corse in his arming clothes.

"I'm not sure I ever thought to embrace you," Du Corse said. "But then, I'm not sure I expected to find you riding a monster."

"The Eeeague are gone?" Gabriel asked.

"Fled as soon as…" Du Corse shook his head, struggling for language. "As soon as the one great *thing* dragged the serpent down."

"You were holding them," Gabriel said.

Du Corse tilted his hand: *comme ci, comme ça.* "Perhaps. They were very wary in shallow water, like trout on a sunny day."

"Trout fear herons and eagles," Gabriel said. "For good reasons." He smiled. "And now, their fear is renewed."

"You still mean to land in Galle?" Gabriel asked.

Du Corse blew out his cheeks. "No," he said. "I do not think my people are ready to face that again. We lost four ships. They were just working out how to fight us when you came. It was…" He looked at the floating wreckage. "It was terrible. They went for the ships at the ends of the formation first, of course. Men started to know they were next." He frowned. "I will land in Iberia."

"You have all my messages about the not-dead." Gabriel was looking at the sky. The wind was changing.

"I have them. And I understand you are the emperor." Du Corse paused to kneel by a young man who had received the full blow of an Eeeague's acid in his face. He was blind, and very brave.

There was nothing to be done. But both men knelt by the boy, helpless before his helplessness.

Gabriel had plenty of time to consider that he had used the Galles as stalking horses for his own fleet. And what that cost was.

"Yes," he said. "I have taken the iron sceptre."

Du Corse nodded. "Well—I warned Rohan about you, and my king. Back in Arles. What, five years ago?" He shook his head. "I confess I didn't expect to find you my liege lord."

"Who is the King of Galle, now?" Gabriel asked.

Du Corse took a breath and rose to his feet. "The Duke of Arles, if he is alive," he said. "And then I suppose his daughter, Clarissa."

Gabriel looked out at the gulls, who were gathering in an ugly flock over a piece of the carcass of the sea serpent. "Do you ever think that there is a higher power?" he asked the Gallish knight.

Du Corse frowned. "I'm sure of Satan," Du Corse said. "God is harder for me."

Gabriel was watching the sun set in the west. "Five years ago, we faced each other in Arles."

"And you saved the duke and his daughter," Du Corse said. He shrugged. "It was a large and convoluted circle, Your Grace." He bent his knee.

Gabriel, unused to such things, stepped past him. "Oh, a plague on it, Du Corse. Our war is over. Go save what can be saved. But for the love of God, if a God there is...be cautious. This *thing* we face is more puissant than anything. It *takes* people. And uses them as puppets." He took Du Corse's hand. "You know?"

Du Corse's demeanor cracked, and the man smiled. "I know, my lord. We will take care."

Then the emperor was away, in a heavy longboat crewed by very scared Alban and Morean oarsmen who rowed very rapidly through a sea flecked with bits of sea monster and the floating wreckage of ships and men, all harried by scavengers.

Back on his own ship, Gabriel ordered the fleet to turn south on the new breeze. "We will not anchor for the night," he insisted.

Then he watched the great bay of the Elbow until the sun set and the moon rose.

When Michael brought him wine, he drank it and turned back to watching. "It's the Wild," he said to everyone and no one.

Blanche, who had never seen him in such a mood, put a hand on his shoulder. "What's the Wild, love?" she asked.

Almost at their feet, over the stern, a floating mass of blubber was savaged by a dozen sea creatures.

"All of it," he said. "Apparently, the whole universe."

She paused. "This ship," she said. "You and No Head were drawing it, two months ago in Albinkirk."

He nodded.

"How long have you planned all this?" she asked.

He shrugged. "Two years," he said. "Or my whole life, depending."

She led him below. She had never seen him so tired, or so open.

The Galles coasted with them all night, but dawn revealed the entrance to Laluna Bay, and with several signals the Galles turned for the land.

As soon as the sun was well up, Gabriel was mounted on Ariosto and aloft, but there was little to see beyond the clear blue sea and the coast of Iberia. He made another landing, a much more comfortable landing, and went out again before last light. They suspected that they had companions deep beneath them, but they didn't have spears to waste, as Morgon's workings were complex and took him hours to prepare. But each day, dolphins sported off their bows, and blue whales, rare in these seas, were seen to spout off to seaward.

Lying with Blanche, watching a whale spout far astern through the gallery, her head on his shoulder, Gabriel stroked her hair. "The wonders of the deep," he said.

"I may never cross so much as a stream again," Blanche murmured.

There was a silence.

"What are you thinking?" she asked.

He took a breath. "I'm thinking that I'm an arrogant fool, Blanche. I didn't really plan this. I'm thinking that there are many, many heroes.

That many hands shaped these events. I'm wondering what effect it has on the *aethereal* when so many minds desire the same thing. I'm thinking that the great beast coursing through the water behind us is something's son or daughter, and that even the sea serpents..." He shook his head. "I'm thinking a great deal of nonsense. Because I'm..." He ran out of words.

She rolled off him and sat up. "I'm not the captain-general of a great alliance," she said. "But I think that you are in a black mood, and it has to do with the sea creatures." She waved a hand at the darkening sky astern. "You watched them for a long time."

He lay back and scratched his beard. "I confess to some dark thoughts," he said.

"Tell me," she said.

He shrugged. "I watched the sharks eat the serpent. I listened when Ariosto called the dying thing prey." He paused.

She was listening intently.

"And I thought, *That's us*." He shrugged again. "That's all. It's all the Wild. Even us. *We are the Wild*. How old do you think the sea serpents are?"

Blanche wriggled. "No idea," she said. "Old."

"Hundreds, maybe thousands of years, according to Mortirmir." Gabriel sat up. "Never mind, love. Black thoughts. Nothing to them."

"That's crap," Blanche said. "Don't fob me off. You didn't sleep last night."

Gabriel drank some wine from the cup next to the bed. "What if this is all there is?" he asked. "A war inside a war, inside a war? Things eat things, and other things conquer things, rape things, eat things, enslave things..." He was breathing hard.

Blanche was looking out the stern windows. "I think you are tired of fighting," she said. "For me—I confess to have eaten a great many fish the last days. But..." She rose, and stepped up next to the long table in the coach, so he could see her lithe figure silhouetted against the stern windows. "But for me, the last tenday has been an adventure, a terror, a few days of boredom, a little triumph, the fun with Kaitlin's baby and the miracle of his pudgy thighs and then more terror during the battle. And some other kinds of fun." Her voice was almost disembodied in the half dark. "Love, you fight, and you see war everywhere." She shrugged. "I am coming to find the sea beautiful, and yet I know it is full of fish and sea serpents." She turned. "That is all my wisdom."

Gabriel laughed for the first time in two days. "That was—amazing."

She slapped his naked chest. "You only say that because you think I'm an empty-headed laundress," she said. But her voice was playful, not angry.

"I think you are the most confident person I have ever known," he said.

"Me?" she said. "That's a laugh. You just like that I'm afraid of different things to those *you* are afraid of." She lay down.

"Now you're cold," he said.

"Make me warm, then," she said lazily. "Really, sweet, there's more to life than fighting."

The next day saw them raise the Eagle's Head and all three great ships were at arms, the gonnes loaded and run out amidships, and the crews and passengers armed. Gabriel was aloft on Ariosto.

Toward noon, with the Eagle's Head on their port side and the *Joseph of Arimethea* leading the turn into the straits, Gabriel saw shadows on the water to starboard, in the deep water off the north coast of Ifriquy'a.

He circled in the fierce winds that exited the straits and the ships waited, rising and falling on the choppy water, waiting for the change of tide that would take them into the Inner Sea against the wind. Until then, they were saving their magisters for fighting. The effort of moving three heavy round ships against the wind and tide would have used up even Master Morgon.

It was a long, hot day, and tempers were short. Blanche did laundry again. It was not so exciting the second time, and the girls cursed and mumbled, but the baby needed clean clothes, and so did Blanche.

Morgon boiled water, so casually that Blanche tapped him on the shoulder. "I thought," she said, privy, as usual, to the emperor's inner thoughts, "that you were being kept in reserve?"

"Oh," Morgon said. "It's so little *potentia*."

Then he froze. Blanche had enough experience of them all to know the young man was in his memory palace.

"Of course," he said aloud. "I boiled water," he said.

A thousand feet above the straits, Gabriel saw the serpents move, a hundred fathoms deep.

Did someone just do a weather working? he asked in the *aethereal.*

Morgon shrugged. "Of course," the magister said. "I boiled water."

"The sea serpents can see or feel or hear your emanations," Gabriel said. *"They're coming."*

"Drop a spear," Morgon said.

In the real, Gabriel used his knees and gentle pressure on Ariosto's beak to turn the big avian a little west. They descended rapidly, trading altitude for speed, running west a few long heartbeats, and then Gabriel lobbed a small spear with a float attached by a silken cord.

It vanished into the deep sea, a mile west of the sea monsters.

In the water, he reported.

Mortirmir played with the strings on his fingers. "Let's try this," he said. "In the name of philosophy."

A pulse of pure *ops* flashed out of the spear, which was held fifty feet below the surface by its float and tether.

All three of the sea serpents turned as one and began racing west.

In his palace, Gabriel and Morgon watched together.

"Fascinating," Morgon said. "I wonder if they prey on the little fish. The ones we use in school."

Gabriel shook his head, amazed.

"Drop another farther west," Mortirmir said, *and* Gabriel turned Ariosto and flew west again, this time several miles. He expended another spear.

Behind him, Mortirmir cut the first spear and it plunged into the depths, now silent.

And lit the new one.

The sea serpents turned once and then, like dogs picking up a scent on a deer hunt, turned west again.

They were now miles to the west of their true prey, and the tide was changing.

Ariosto grumbled, and Gabriel turned for the ship, having learned his lesson about staying aloft too long.

I wanted another fight! Ariosto said.

We have other business first. I promise you, there are many fights ahead.

Two days later, and they reached Dar as Salaam in the evening sunlight. Blanche and Kaitlin both thought it was the most beautiful city they'd ever seen, and they stood at the railing in relatively clean kirtles, watching the minarets and the superb onion-shaped domes rise out of the sea with an incredible, heady array of smells, human and exotic, a staggering olfactory feast of spices and sewage and seawater. Morgon Mortirmir came and leaned on the railing with them, and one of the archers. The girl archer.

Kaitlin took a moment, but she knew the archer. She shifted a little. "*You are Tancreda*," she whispered.

The smooth-faced archer turned, flushed.

But then she smiled.

Kaitlin shrugged. Out loud, she said, "You danced at my wedding. With this fellow."

Blanche looked blank. Mortirmir looked offended that his cleverness had been penetrated.

But then, as was his wont, he lost interest and looked at Dar as Salaam. "Now," he said, "we will see something. How I wish Harmodius were here."

They approached the port in late evening and a pilot boat visited them. Blanche stayed in the aft cabin, but she saw the men in their baggy trousers, and she saw how they fawned on Pavalo Payam, treating him like a great lord.

He came aft to her Gabriel, who was sitting in braes and a shirt, reading. He'd seldom looked less like an emperor.

"My lord, I beg your leave. My master will want to see me."

Gabriel got up and pressed Payam's hands between his own. "We are friends, and I am not your lord. Come and go as you wish," he said. "Only carry my respectful salutation, and Magister Harmodius's…"

"Yes, yes," Payam said, a little impatient.

Gabriel grinned. "There's a girl," he said.

"More than one," Blanche added.

Payam bowed, all mock ceremony now. "It is possible," he said, in his deepest, most reverent voice. He winked at Blanche, who winked back.

"Go, then. Send us word," Gabriel said.

When he was gone, Gabriel kissed her, and began various other preliminaries. It was incredibly hot. Blanche liked his attention but was almost completely uninterested, although she knew that if she let his hand continue, her interest might recover.

"Will you really marry me?" she asked.

Gabriel's hand didn't even pause. "Yes," he said.

"When?" she asked.

Gabriel's eyes met hers. "Now? In fifteen minutes?"

"I'm fairly certain I'm pregnant," she said.

His smile was a great reward, and a great relief. "I wonder how that happened?" Gabriel asked.

"I wonder," she answered.

"Venike, if I can arrange it," he said.

"Oh!" she said. She knew that she had just been slotted into a military logistics program.

He looked at her carefully. "Actually, it will be useful in many ways," he said.

"Oh, that's a relief," she said. She was daring to be annoyed at him.

Gabriel propped himself on his elbows. His chest was on hers, and she was, damn him, starting to be interested.

"Sweet, you know..." He shrugged. "Now is as good a time as any."

"So kind," she murmured, considering murder.

"Listen! If you marry me, this *will be our life*. Every act is on the public stage. You were a laundress. Everyone will know. If you had lovers before me, everyone will know. When you get married, it's a matter of public policy. I will use our marriage to draw the Venikans to me. I need them. I need their banks to finance my wars. You think you are a laundress, but when I look at you, I see the same talent that I see in Sukey and Michael. You can organize. You can plan and execute. I can't fight Ash alone. If you marry me, you marry the war against Ash. You get promoted straight from bed warmer and queen's laundress to Planner of Everything." He shrugged. "And marrying a commoner is excellent policy just now, and God help us if I entangled myself with someone like the Earl of Towbray."

"Michael's father," she said, just so he'd know she was keeping up.

"Just so," he said, with the patronizing smile she despised.

"Do I get to read the plan?" she asked.

He ran his slightly rough tongue across the palm of her hand, and then across one of her nipples. "Right now?" he asked.

She sat up and pushed. "Yes," she said.

He sighed. "Couldn't I just explain?" he asked.

He left her reading the plan when he, fully dressed in velvet, silk, and wool, went down the ladder to a waiting boat and was rowed ashore to meet the sultan and his great magister. He made it clear that this was not a city where women went on diplomatic missions, and she accepted that, without arguing, although it came into her head to mention that Pavalo had had no trouble taking her seriously. It might have been a spat, and she didn't mean to inflict them on him.

Not too often.

So she listened for him going down the side, and began to read.

Before she finished the first page, her hands were locked over her belly in fear.

The sultan awaited them on a divan, and Al Rashidi lay on a daybed piled high with pillows. The sultan rose as they were escorted in by twenty turbaned knights in magnificent mail and plate armour covered densely in silver-inlaid verses of the Koran.

Gabriel went forward and bowed deeply, and Pavalo Payam spoke for him. To save time, he was approaching the sultan only as the Red Knight. Emperors and sultans could waste weeks on protocol.

But the sultan's Etruscan was strong and accurate, and so was Gabriel's, and after a few stiff exchanges of remarkably flowery compliments, they were on the meat of the matter: sea monsters and war.

The sultan was remarkably well informed.

After several more exchanges, Payam bowed. "In the name of my master, I say, our M'bub Ali has met your Kronmir. They are two of a breed. Need I say more?"

The sultan glared, but Payam looked like a warrior who had faced the not-dead without flinching and could handle a sultan.

Gabriel breathed deeply and settled into the cushions that had been brought.

Al Rashidi never rose. And whenever Payam looked at the old magister, tears came into his eyes.

But when the formal interview was over, they were escorted across the city; that is, Ser Michael, Ser Giorgos Comnenos, and Gabriel Muriens and Morgon Mortirmir. They entered a fine courtyard of a set of low buildings that appeared to have been constructed of white marble, and heard the call to prayer from a minaret. The faithful went to pray, and Gabriel laughed to Michael.

"Here we are the infidels," he said.

"*You* always were," Michael said.

And later, after sherbet, they were led into Al Rashidi's chambers by Payam, and seated in good Venikan chairs.

"I'm afraid this is for those who can enter the *aethereal*," Al Rashidi said.

Michael and Giorgos bowed and went out into the yard with Payam, to practice together one more time.

Al Rashidi's palace was as magnificent as any Gabriel had seen, and he had, thanks to the alliance, seen more than most. It was an endless vista of inlaid surfaces, floors, walls, and ceilings in an endless profusion of parquetry, intarsia, ivory and ebony and every colour in between.

The magister himself awaited them with a bow in the center of a court-yard whose flags were inlaid marble. Every stone was different, every symbol different.

Morgon was almost unable to speak, and he gawked like a tourist.

"You are like a god," he said.

Al Rashidi's head snapped around. "Blasphemy," he said. "But the flat-tery is still sweet to me. And you will become greater than I, unless you are killed. Now come. My time is short."

"Why?" Gabriel asked.

The magister turned. "That is worth answering," he said. "I should have been dead a long time ago—perhaps a year." He shrugged. "Unlike my brother Harmodius and this young phoenix, I have studied the necroman-tic arts." He smiled bitterly. "I took one of the parasites to keep me alive. This morning, I killed it. Now I will be gone by sunset."

Gabriel, who seldom swore, said, "Sweet Christ," aloud.

Al Rashidi shook his head. "No oaths," he said. "What I did is a great sin. I can only hope that what I did is reckoned against what we must do."

Gabriel thought this way every day. "I'm not the one to make that call," he said. "But I too hope that we do is reckoned against what we must do."

Mortirmir was too young, despite his intelligence, to understand. "Why not keep the parasite?" he asked. "If you can control it?"

Al Rashidi nodded and stroked his hermetical beard. "Payam asked the same," he said. "First, because I lack your arrogance, and I'd never be sure that the Odine were not tricking me. Even now, it seems possible that my every word is known." He shook his head. "Tell me no plan. I will show you one thing. It is my gift to you and your allies. And I offer one piece of advice, from my own master, whom they killed." He looked at Gabriel. "When you have defeated the Odine, kill all the dragons."

Gabriel nodded.

Mortirmir nodded too. "This is what Harmodius says."

"You hesitate, Red Knight, and yet I tell you that I see into their minds, and they plan the same against us." The old magister did not appear to be dying. He appeared to glow almost white with vitality.

Gabriel shook his head. "We would not even be ready to strike without the dragons," he said.

Al Rashidi nodded. "Listen, then. You are the culminations of more than a hundred years of planning, you and your friends. We have known the dates since Dame Julia plotted the stars and the gates, almost a hundred and sixty years ago. You say the dragons have helped us, and I say..."

Gabriel almost lost his concentration. "You know the dates?"

Al Rashidi waved a hand as if this were of no moment. "Please," he said.

He paused, and led them into the room. It was his palace, and there was no passage; one moment they were in his courtyard, and the next, in a room.

The room was covered in tiles, and each tile was a magnificent shade of blue with gold letters and devices, and no two tiles were alike.

"... I say that if the dragons were our allies, they would have already given you what I am giving you now, as my last will."

And with that, he began to unravel a working of such complexity and puissance that Gabriel, who knew the workings of Harmodius's innermost mind, was staggered, and Morgon moaned aloud.

He taught them, symbol by symbol, until the whole magnificent tiled room and all its workings were fully installed in their palaces, and all the meanings of all the tiles explained.

It was not just a single working.

It was a set of nested workings that contained a great many substrata of knowledge about the necromantic, and a whole library of knowledge on the Odine. In learning, Gabriel learned the dates on which the gates would open, and even a simple map of where they led.

Gabriel read it, imbued it, gnosticated it. He swallowed it. As there was no time in the aethereal, he and Morgon did not hurry.

And finally, in the dying light of the great man's life, he asked, "If this is the great working against the Odine... where did it come from?"

Al Rashidi nodded. "It is another good question, Red Knight. Once there was a man who sought to cheat death. And even as he sold his soul to them, he sold them to us. Always, every side has a double agent. Always, there is division in the enemy camp. Every race has a traitor. Every camp has spies."

"And the dragons defeated the Odine ten thousand years ago?"

Al Rashidi shrugged. "That's what they tell us."

Morgon thought differently. "How much power does this require?" he asked.

He seemed eager to try his hand.

Al Rashidi bowed. "A very large amount of ops. You cannot be interrupted while you cast. The result has an effect on the texture of reality. Of course, this is true for every great working. But in this case..."

Gabriel looked at Morgon and then opened his memories of Master Smythe at the standing stones. Al Rashidi played the memory several times, examining the flaws in his recollection.

"It is, as near as I can see in another palace, the same working." He rubbed his long beard, as if stroking a cat. "Now I am truly puzzled, Red Knight."

"Is there any way that I could have ... researched this working, based on what I witnessed?"

Mortirmir interrupted. "Yes, by the rood!" he said. "Look at this, and this!" And he played back Gabriel's memory, a disorienting experience inside Gabriel's own head.

There was a brief hiatus, as Mortirmir, in a tone almost insufferable for its arrogance, explained how, exactly, his team had cracked the cough and the coded workings they'd built to defeat it.

Al Rashidi did not attempt to slow him, but listened to the end.

"This method you have developed is not just trial and error," he said.

"No, Master. All hermetical workings begin in theory. We attempt to identify the theory, and once that is identified, we eliminate hypothesis until we are left with ... actuality." Morgon looked at them as if they were both students. "The theory here is obvious, is it not?"

Al Rashidi managed to smile and not be offended that a seventeen-year-old student was lecturing him. "Go ahead. Show me."

Morgon shrugged. "I confess I'm aided by knowing that Kronmir's lady friend, who was taken, refers to the taking in the plural. And this... the theory is that there is no Odine. There are merely a myriad of the worms, each of which must be dealt with as an independent entity. As if the whole, while greater than the sum of the parts, loses power in being identified as parts. In this lies the theory."

Al Rashidi was looking at the edifice of his magnificent tiled working. "Yes," he said. He had begun to burn a bright white, and his face was losing shape. "I leave this effort in good hands," he said. "That you are infidels is of no matter. We must rise and fall together as humans. I have planted the tree, and look, it has already grown mighty. I will not cross Jordan, but by the thousand names of Allah, let the Odine tremble. Let the dragons tremble. Let the Kraal and all the creatures of the Wild tremble. Morgon Mortirmir, I charge you with my dying breath—accept my blessing and all that goes with it. In your hour of triumph, remember that there must be justice. And perhaps even mercy."

The old man's face shone like the moon, and almost like the sun. He turned to Gabriel. "I am sorry," he said.

Gabriel shrugged. "I know what is to come. Even if we triumph."

Al Rashidi spread his arms. "Is it possible?" he asked, not Gabriel, but something indefinable. A broad smile crossed his face, and his whole being turned to light. It seemed to Gabriel that his last sound was a laugh of pure pleasure.

But Gabriel was already running from the dying man's palace, towing Mortirmir by an aethereal *hand.*

"Wait!" Mortirmir cried, like a looter in a burning treasure house. "Wait! Everything is here! Hundreds of years of work are about to be lost!"

Gabriel had been trapped near the collapse of a palace before. It was the most frightening end he could imagine, but even so, Mortirmir's plea had effect.

Like looters, with little knowledge of what they were taking from a great galley of art, each of them took the room closest. Gabriel's was a niche, and he stripped it and duplicated it inside his own palace almost without analysis, although he noted that it seemed concerned with water.

And then, exactly as with Father Arnaud, the place gave a flare of light and began to dim, and things began to move in the corridors.

Mortirmir stood, stricken. "I do believe..."

Gabriel didn't have time, even in the timeless aethereal, *to explain.*

"Shut up and follow me," he said, and the corridor dimmed again.

He reached out for Blanche. Even in another palace he could feel her, and even as he found her, he also found the golden cord that attached him to Amicia, even now. He laughed even as the walls grew faint.

"Your turn to save me," Gabriel said, holding the golden lifelines of love and pulling Morgon after him.

*

Amicia was in the abbess's garden, which was full of beds. In fact, every open space in the fortress had beds; the beds of hundreds, thousands of suffers from the cough.

Amicia was not *working*. That is to say, she carried bedpans and smoothed brows, she helped clean pus, she brought cool cloths and read aloud and said the office of the dead. In fact, in the two days since the army had marched from the inn to Lissen Carak, she had not slept. But neither was she working hermetically. Harmodius and her own abbess had begged her not to, and she obeyed.

But it was hard, watching weaker practitioners with vastly smaller stores of *ops* work the cures until they ran out of any form of Umroth ivory or any other bone of the not-dead. Every knight with an ivory dagger hilt had turned his precious weapon in, and those hilts, rigorously tested, had then been ground fine. The resulting powder formed the basis of complex, tripartite hermetical workings that unraveled the cough and allowed the patient's own body to complete the work of healing, if the sufferer was not too far gone.

They were just about keeping pace with the plague. New cases came in as fast and they sent people, healed and immune, back into the world. The cured people were themselves part of the plan, because they took the tidings home, so that village after village knew that a cure was found and knew where to send the sick, and where to send every scrap of ivory from Ifriquy'a, every needle case and every sword hilt and every pricker and every eating knife and every sewing awl . . . every tool ever made of the stuff and sold in Harndon; but people were still dying, and the northern Brogat was the worst hit.

Harmodius himself was already in Harndon. The city had stores of ivory.

None of it was going to reach her in time. Gabriel had promised to send from Ifriquy'a, and Harmodius from Harndon, but she knew that Miriam's supplies were exhausted, and that in a day or perhaps two, people were going to die just because Lissen Carak was too far away.

And still she restrained her powers. She knew that her skin now glowed all the time; that her access to *potentia* seemed to increase every day whether she used it or not.

The queen and Miriam begged her not to pass into apotheosis, because they needed her powers.

Harmodius begged her, because he said that in the moment that she began to pass, Ash would attack her.

He'd held her hand and said, "You are the most valuable of us." He smiled. "But you would be the first to tell us not to sacrifice the Brogat and Jarsay to save you."

It was a strange existence. She ate a hurried supper of fish, watching her luminescent skin generate light even as she wondered why her digestion was suddenly so bad. Bad digestion seemed the very antithesis of apotheosis. The thought made her smile, and wish she had Gabriel to tell it to.

And then he was *there*. Pulling at the tether that bound them.

"Your turn to save me," he said, so clearly he might have been sitting at the refractory table.

She *went into her palace and took the golden thread bound to her finger and pulled gently, and she felt him come.*

Even in the real, she could see him for a moment, and Morgon Mortirmir behind him in a long dark tunnel.

"Thanks," he said cheerily. "Where are you?"

"Lissen Carak," she replied.

Gabriel nodded. "And my brother?"

"Passed westward with the Faery Knight, Tamsin, and the army," she said. "Why did we never consider communicating this way before?"

"I hadn't imagined love as a strategic commodity until now," Gabriel said.

"Ash is attacking N'gara," she said. She was fading already.

"Gavin will stop him," Gabriel said cheerfully.

And she was gone.

Gabriel came to his senses in Al Rashidi's study. He was ravenously hungry and it was dawn and he had been under for almost a full day. A servant gave him water.

Mortirmir went to the sofa, but Al Rashidi had been dead for long enough that servants had taken the body to be washed.

"He was a great man," Mortirmir said. "Harmodius came to him when he was my age. Al Rashidi was old even then."

Gabriel, who held most of Harmodius's memories, smiled.

Forty years before, in this same room, Harmodius made a gesture—

Al Rashidi turned and raised an arm—

328

Both men were suddenly hidden in glowing hemispheres of sparkling light. The master's was the deep green of the true religion, and Harmodius's was the sickly golden-yellow of pus. Or the bright colour of new-minted gold.

All of the slaves and students threw themselves flat on their faces or crouched under tables.

"Truly, I mean no harm," said Harmodius.

The master laughed. "You are most powerful," he said. "Why have you come in this way? You had only to knock on the door and declare yourself."

"I have had a particularly annoying few days," said Harmodius, annoyed and amused at once. "I had not planned to arrive as a beggar at your door," he continued.

He lowered his hemispheric shield, and the master instantly lowered his own.

"Be welcome in my house," said the master. "What is your name?"

The young infidel smiled. "I'm called Harmodius," he said. "I understand you have a copy of Maimonides's De Re Naturae?"

He shared the memory with Mortirmir.

Mortirmir laughed. "We share this, Your Grace. I have many of his memories too. When he occupied me, he left a great deal behind, even though he was only here a little while." The young man shook his head. "He was as young as I, when he came here."

"And laid the basis of the plot in which we are still raveled." Gabriel shook his head. "The fate of the sphere hung by some awkward threads."

Mortirmir nodded. "And still does, my lord," he said.

The two of them reminisced about Harmodius and talked about how old the alliance to fight against "the powers" must be. Gabriel knew that the legendary astrologer Dame Julia had been born more than two hundred years ago, and Mortirmir had never read her works, a complete set of which occupied a whole wall of the Chamber of Secrets.

The great magister's Islamic funeral occupied the whole of the next day, and the sultan was unavailable, and so was Payam, and even Gabriel began to fray about the edges. But he and Michael and Giorgos Comnenos and Morgon Mortirmir put on their best western finery, minus the furs, and went. Morgon was stunned to find that he was called to help carry the master's bier. And to see the number of mourners. They walked out into the desert, and walked back, in silence.

Gabriel had the impression of vast wealth, of a riot of perfumes, of deep mourning for a man who had protected his people. Rather unexpectedly, he wept.

After the procession, Ser Giorgos took him aside. "Walk with me," he said, and the two of them, almost unnoticed, walked among the procession of thousands.

"Why am I here?" Giorgos asked.

"When I am dead, you will be emperor," Gabriel said.

Ser Giorgos stopped walking and stood perfectly still, and women, weeping and raising their hands to heaven, went around him as if he were a pillar of stone set in their way. He stood there for many beats of his own heart.

Gabriel kept walking.

His appreciation for the Garden of Gethsemane was increasing by the moment, and he didn't really want to talk to anyone. Except perhaps Blanche.

It was a very quiet evening in the home of the dead magister.

The next day, Gabriel and Morgon practiced the great working they had been given. The understanding of it was the understanding of eons of history, and the casting of it was like moving the earth, and it had components that were themselves advanced workings, one of which was a sort of locator, except that having located even as much as a single entity of the Odine, it provided the caster with a kind of link that savoured, to Gabriel, of the same kind of link that bound him to Amicia.

"What are we manipulating, here?" he asked young Mortirmir.

Mortirmir shrugged. "You understand, my lord, that although we see them as foul little worms, as parasites in the physical body of a man or a horse…" The young man stopped.

Gabriel sat back. He had seldom felt so empty.

"That is but a metaphor. It is a metaphor we use to frame our attack, which is itself a set of symbols trying to inflict themselves on reality."

Gabriel leaned his chin on a fist. "Go on, scholar," he said.

Mortirmir opened his eyes, realizing he was being mocked. "I never know what you know and what you don't know," he said, accusingly.

"If I told you all I know, you would beat me with whips of fire," Gabriel said.

"You are a most uncomfortable companion, my lord," Morgon said.

"I have my reasons." Gabriel sat back.

Morgon shrugged. "The Odine do not even exist on exactly the same...plane...that we do," he said. "Their power over us..." He shrugged again. "To be honest, I think there's another, entirely unexplored set of options for attacking them. Dragons are vast, dangerous predators, and they design vast, dangerous workings to overawe all other creatures. This working is one such. It is magnificent." He shrugged. "I digress."

"Always," Gabriel said.

Morgon smiled. "Almost always. That's what Tancreda says."

"Tancreda, who is masquerading as an archer on my ship. Does her brother know?" Gabriel asked. "I may not see everything, but the Comnenos family are soon going to be a very important family indeed, Morgon. And you aren't hiding her very well."

"I am not? By Saint George, my lord, she is more arrogant than I!"

"You have that in common, then. Ser Giorgos is her cousin. He'll have to know, and soon. I recommend the two of you marry. In Venike." Gabriel waved his hand. "Now tell me the answer."

"The Odine are not like us. They exist differently. Even the dragons used remarkable weapons against them. Will. Love. Hate. Not everything can be fought with a scholar's rationality." He looked into the distance. "I do not think they considered these ramifications strongly enough, nor did enough research on the emanations of...what I suppose we would call soul, or spirit. These are dangerous waters, my lord. I'm a hermeticist. This is for a theologian or a philosopher."

Gabriel sat back. He was thinking of his communication with Amicia. He was thinking of how the strength of his golden link to her allowed them to communicate...an emotion rendered in the *aethereal* that has power in the real.

"Even dragons and wyverns and wardens cast wave-fronts in the *aethereal*...of fear and terror, of panic." Morgon steepled his fingers. "It is my contention that humans can do the same, but we do not, mostly because of our more settled thoughts. I would have to experiment."

"But how would..." Gabriel had meant to ask the young magister how he'd use such a weapon, but he saw it.

"We find Odine by projecting a web of emotional energy and seeing what gets eaten." Gabriel could see it. Could see why so many creatures had evolved wave fronts.

"That is a clever, gross simplification, my lord." Morgon rubbed his beard. "What you call emotions are not always emanations of spirit, and I have no idea which ones the Odine... appreciate."

Gabriel sighed. "Let's try again," he said, and the two of them went back to casting.

The second day after the procession, magnificent clothes were sent from the palace, and when the four of them were fully dressed, they proceeded to the sultan's throne room in palanquins, where Payam greeted them. With the sultan were a dozen men wearing swords, and in the harbour there were now more than twenty heavy galleys.

"The sultan has declared a war of faith against the Necromancer," Payam said, "and however unworthy I may be, I will command a portion of his army of the faithful against the common foe. And all the bone we can spare is being readied to ship to Harndon."

"This is glad news," Gabriel said. "Gladder still if one ship at least is sent to Liviapolis." Gabriel bowed. "I pray there is enough."

Days on dry land had healed Tom Lachlan's seasickness. He grinned. "I know where to get more," he said.

Every head turned.

"Defeat the Necromancer's army. Kill the not-dead. Grind their bones." He grinned, eyes sparkling.

A little hush fell.

Gabriel slapped Bad Tom on the back. "Sometimes you make me doubt that we're the side of light," he said. "But... it's a point worth considering."

And when the preliminaries were done, Gabriel and his friends sat with Payam and a dozen officers of the sultan around a great table filled with charts and itineraries, and began to plan the invasion of southern Galle. He was introduced to Ali Ben Hassan, the Sword of the Sultan; his commander of ten thousand, and a veteran of fighting the not-dead.

Thanks to a stream of birds from Liviapolis and Iberia, Gabriel was able to map out the progress made by Du Corse's army, which was just crossing the spine of Rolandi, the great mountains that divided Galle from Iberia. He marked Du Corse's progress for the Ifriquy'ans, and then, with M'bub Ali, they chose their own landing area.

"We have raided here many times," M'bub Ali said without any apparent sense of irony. "We know the beaches and the ground to the north."

And again, it took a day: a day none of them could spare. But there was no point to planning badly; no point to an uncoordinated attack. And the Ifriquy'ans had the most experience fighting the not-dead, and defeating them, of all people, and much of the day was spent outlining tactics and strategies that had been used in siege and in battle. Gabriel had not considered that the not-dead did not always need to breathe, and could sometimes go through rivers or across lakes. He had not considered the collapse of morale that could happen when men faced what appeared to be their own friends. He had not fully appreciated how limited the Odine were by site and emanation of power alone, so that night attacks without magic could be very successful against them.

Payam shrugged. "It takes a very brave man to attack the not-dead in the dark," he said. "But in truth, we are better at fighting in the dark than they are."

And for the first time, he faced the question that would haunt the next four weeks.

It was Mortirmir, looking at the careful drawing of Ibn Salim's *Perfect Battle*, a carefully coloured picture of the kind of earthworks that could best funnel the not-dead into prepared killing fields—it was Mortirmir who first asked it.

"How many of the people of Arles and Galle are we willing to kill to achieve victory?" He looked around. "I mean...even if the Necromancer or his lieutenants can be trapped onto one of these created battlefields—we're not killing our enemies. We're killing taken people."

Ali ben Hassan shook his head. "You must harden your heart," he said sorrowfully. "Even if it is your sister's husband or your own brother, he is dead, and must be killed."

Gabriel rubbed his beard. "Even leaving aside the question of killing the not-dead," he said, trying to raise a smile, "our officer on the spot says there must be more than a hundred thousand people taken by the enemy. Killing them all could leave Arles and northern Etrusca too weak to be viable. The Wild…the real Wild…is still there, in the mountains. Hovering. Waiting for weakness."

Ben Hassan shook his head. "These thoughts will not help you," he said.

Gabriel nodded. He looked at Ser Michael.

Michael could see he was planning something.

"Very well," Gabriel said. "I will come over the mountains from Etrusca and you will land at Massalia along the coast, and we will march to the relief of Arles."

"If it has not already fallen," Ben Hassan said. "I'm sorry, Your Grace, but the Necromancer has every advantage in a siege."

"He may. But I think he has sent a mighty lieutenant to do his bidding, and he is still eager to break in here himself. Tell me, Payam; or ask the sultan. Is there a gate here?"

Men looked away. Other men frowned. Pavalo Payam gave a wry smile.

"Perhaps we do not know what you mean by a gate," he said.

"Perhaps you do," Gabriel said. "A supernatural exit from this sphere to other spheres. Your master, Al Rashidi, would have visited it from time to time."

Payam went and spoke to the chamberlain and the sultan for some time, and then returned.

"Come," he said.

He led them down under the palace. As at Lissen Carak, they went down a considerable distance through tunnels that rolled up and down as if carved by sinuous worms through the naked rock of the earth; the sides were often perfectly smooth, reflecting light like polished glass.

And deep in the earth, where no natural light had ever come, Payam lit a hermetical lamp, and there was a great curtain of power, and set into the ceiling by it, lit by the golden glow of the hermetical workings, all crystals and jewels, was a night sky of constellations.

Gabriel went to the curtain, found the lock, and inserted the key from Lissen Carak.

It fit.

"Eureka," he said softly.

Michael put a hand on his shoulder. "What does it mean?" he asked.

Gabriel smiled, and there was no bitterness there. "It means we're still in the fight," he said. "It means we haven't lost yet. In fact—" He shrugged. "In fact, I begin to think..."

But he would say no more. He carefully copied all the jeweled constellations. And he whistled and hummed a great deal.

The next morning, as the ships were loaded, and after kissing Blanche enthusiastically and giving her a small fortune in silk and cotton, Gabriel mounted Ariosto. He had Morgon behind him, and Ariosto was none too happy with the double weight.

It took them a long time to climb away from the harbour, so they had time to savour the sun on the waves, to see the long spit with the ancient lighthouse, and the superb crescent of the harbour, with palaces and houses side by each, a display of tiles and golden opulence that beggared anything that Harndon had to offer. The beaches were superb, with fine white sand, and the sun glittered on a thousand minarets, and as they climbed, the voices of the muezzins climbed to the heavens with them.

"Incredible," shouted Mortirmir.

He's not that heavy after all, muttered Ariosto, wings pumping heavily, his red and green and gold pinions rippling in the morning breeze.

The desert stretched away to the south, and the higher they climbed, the greater, vaster was its presence, a sea of sand. The grave ground to which they'd walked a few days before was virtually in the city, when seen from this high, and still the desert rolled away south to the very rim of the world, and air currents rose off its heat.

In the *aethereal, the city glowed with power, the same sort of ancient, nested workings that protected the palace in Harndon and the fortress of Lissen Carak, except that here they covered the walls from end to end and several outwalls and fortifications. Indeed, beyond the strip of farmland that sustained the city and ran forty miles in either direction and up the great river a few miles, there was no human habitation. There were no villages.*

"*The Necromancer is close to victory here,*" Morgon said. "*Look at how vast the habitation of man once was.*"

They flew along the coast and saw whole cities washed by the sea, temples thrown down, piers empty of ships, all white marble and brown stone fading into the sand.

And finally, high over the desert, Morgon began the opening sequences of the great working Al Rashidi had taught them.

Gabriel concentrated on Ariosto. He had no idea what counterwork a titanic alien sorcerer might throw at them, so he wove shields and hung them on Prudentia's outstretched arm and waited.

And waited.

This is as high as I can carry you, Ariosto said.

They were as high as Gabriel had ever been. The sea appeared to be a dark blue sheet, and no waves showed, but a little sun-dazzle in the delta. The sand dunes were like lines graved by an apprentice, and trees were not even dots. The air was thin, and Gabriel, who was not exerting himself in any way, found himself breathing hard.

We are high enough, he said.

He *went into Morgon's palace carefully, so as not to interrupt. Morgon was in two places; one watching a mirror, and one moving pieces on a chessboard that itself seemed like a labyrinth.*

"Ah," Morgon said. "Either I've made a mistake, or the praxis does not work, or the Necromancer is not within the circle of our attempt. Of the three, the last seems the most likely."

Gabriel pondered this. "Several hundred miles?"

Morgon shrugged. "At least a hundred in all directions. No army, no emanation."

"Damn," Gabriel said.

They landed at midmorning. The sultan had come out to watch, and he embraced Gabriel, but Gabriel had to tell him, in stilted Etruscan, that they'd had no success.

The sultan inclined his head. "It is no sorrow to me that the Necromancer has found other prey," he said. "Six hundred years my people have borne his assaults. I will not waste this respite."

"What is on the other side of the desert?" Gabriel asked.

The sultan looked south. "Once, there were other kingdoms," he said. "Now nothing comes out of the desert but the not-dead. Someday, perhaps..."

They embraced again, and the imperial ships departed without ceremony.

Four days more. Gabriel couldn't raise Amicia or anyone else; the moments when all the powers aligned sufficiently to allow such a communication were rare. The thread that bound them was still there. It was heavy with potency, but something had changed and he'd missed it. He had no real idea what.

Barring miraculous communication with Amicia, he went to his most precious asset: the imperial messengers. Blanche found him on deck talking to a dozen of the black-and-white birds, or waiting anxiously for the next one to arrive. She wanted to cry, because he was so tender; he stroked one bird for a long time, and then he began to speak. She hid herself.

"You, my friends, are all that's keeping me in the game," she heard him say. "Did Livia have you from the first? Did Livia know what the stakes were?" He muttered something she didn't catch.

"If we win, I'd free you all, except that I suspect you like this life," he said. "Maybe we're related," he went on. "Because God knows I like it. There, eat that. Nice bit of mouse. Oh, don't be like that. That mouse is completely fresh." Silence. "Swallow the tail, you look ridiculous."

She moved off because he would have heard her giggles, and saw that Anne, his page, was standing close by. They exchanged looks, and both had to cover their mouths.

He did, however, collect a dozen messenger birds and send them off in all directions, and at least two of them left for Venike with carefully written directions for materials and space for a wedding. Two weddings.

Other birds went to his brother, now nearing N'gara far to the west; for Jules Kronmir, who was with Il Conte Simone and Magister Petrarcha at Berona; for Harmodius at Harndon, for the queen, for the Faery Knight and Tamsin, for Pavalo Payam and his fleet, for Du Corse who was now heading north in Galle, marching on Lutrece and swimming in a sea of refugees and terrified survivors.

In the great stern cabin, looking at maps, Michael shook his head. "Three armies coming from three directions, all much smaller than the enemy?" he asked. "Doesn't that invite defeat?"

Gabriel blinked once. He shrugged. "It does," he admitted.

"Why not all our troops together in one place?" Michael asked.

"Many reasons," Gabriel said. "Above all, the amount so many men eat. The Necromancer's forces will have stripped the country. They are a plague of locusts, and their enemy will outnumber us whatever course we take. And because surprise remains our best weapon. I intend to make the Necromancer's lieutenant as uncomfortable as possible. So he'll make mistakes."

"You think the Odine make mistakes?" Mortirmir asked.

"They lost to the dragons," Gabriel said. He smiled at Blanche, who was rereading his master plan for the thirtieth time.

She looked up. Everyone in the cabin knew the plan, or at least the outline of it.

"And N'gara?" she asked.

"My brother will attack into Ash's preparations. That should hold Ash." Gabriel was still writing.

"Because?" Michael asked.

"Because Ash is a cautious beast at heart. And a little like a house cat and other predators I've known. He really doesn't like to tangle with anything his own size. He wants the other big players to finish each other off. He will not expect an attack."

Michael blew out a breath. "Risky," he said.

"It's all risky!" Gabriel spat. He shook his head. "We can't afford a single defeat."

Michael winced. "We'll get one, though. Everyone loses sometime."

Gabriel frowned. "You're cheerful," he said.

"I'm just being honest, Gabriel, and you'd better think about it." Michael shrugged. "You are developing a...fatalism. I don't think that's a winning mind-set."

"I am. I'm trying to build a world where everyone works together. We only need one nice defeat and some of our allies will start thinking about slave soldiers and alliances with evil." Gabriel shrugged. "We not only need to keep winning, we need to appear invincible. There's people in Etrusca and Galle who've allied with the enemy. The Patriarch of Rhum is almost certainly working against us. He has enormous influence *and* an army."

Sukey made a face.

Michael shrugged. "I understand why you think it is important. I'm merely saying that there's very little butter spread very thin over a great deal of toast."

Gabriel tugged his beard. "Yes," he said.

"I don't think Gavin and the Faery Knight can stop Ash at N'gara." Michael shrugged.

The emperor was leaning on the chart table looking out over the sea. He put his face in his hands a moment. "They don't have to win," he said patiently, after a deep breath. "They just have to keep Ash busy."

Michael crossed his legs and looked at Kaitlin a moment. "And, in the meantime, what are we doing about the dragons?"

"Nothing," Gabriel said. "If we beat the Odine, by a miracle, then and only then can we talk about the dragons. Not my enemy! Not my problem." He shrugged. "I need a swim."

"Don't get eaten by a sea monster," Michael said. "If Ash isn't what you are worrying about and the dragons aren't your problem, why do you look so grey?"

The emperor had very quickly become a young man wearing nothing but linen braes.

"Where is the Necromancer?" he asked.

Michael froze.

Gabriel paused, his eyes on Blanche. Then his gaze shifted to the map, and then his eyes met Michael's. "I've bet the farm on meeting this threat here," he said. "And thanks to Al Rashidi, not only do we have a chance of winning, but I have an insanely nasty plan to win the whole tournament. But... what if the Necromancer has done what we've done? Gone off to Occitan? It's only four hundred leagues off his west coast."

"Oh Christ," Michael said, and crossed himself.

"Harndon? Liviapolis?" Gabriel said.

"Stop," Michael said.

Gabriel nodded. "I was happy when I thought that whatever the greatest evil sorcerer of our time was doing, it was directed at Dar as Salaam." He shrugged. "Now we don't know where it is." He nodded softly. "So I confess, I've been in a panic since we left Dar. As far as I can see, the Necromancer is betting everything on Arles. But I could be wrong." He shrugged. "If I'm wrong..."

Blanche was trying to put her unruly hair up. She stopped, arms over her head. "So what do we do?" she asked.

"Swim," Gabriel said. "However I worry, we're committed, and we can't change now."

When he left the cabin, Blanche looked at Michael. Michael shook his head. "He's changed," Michael said. "He's... desperate."

Blanche had tears in her eyes. "No, Michael," she said. "He's fey. He knows when he'll die."

Kaitlin put her hand to the cross at her breast. "Blessed Saint Anne!" she said. "He does?"

Blanche nodded. "Yes. At least since Dar. Perhaps before." She shrugged, and then began to cry.

They raised the south coast of Etrusca in the dawn, and Michael found Gabriel on deck. He and Tom were playing dice.

Michael was wearing only braes and a shirt, like a peasant at harvest time. But he went and sat with them. A pair of sailors were sitting close by, wagering on the side.

"Tom says I'm a fool," Gabriel said.

"I said you were a loon. I ha' always said so. It's no news." Tom cast the dice and grunted.

Michael wasn't sure what game they were playing, and his slightly sleep-addled brain made him feel as if perhaps this were a dream. "Isn't it early for dice?" he asked.

Gabriel shrugged. "I had a bad dream," he said.

"Christ on the cross, what do you call a bad dream?" Michael asked.

Gabriel gave him the grim smile he remembered best from the siege of Lissen Carak. "Is this part of your lessons?"

"I don't know," Michael shot back. "Is it?"

Gabriel nodded. "Very well. I was on a throne, sitting above the world. Spread at my feet was a chart—and the pictures that Miriam drew us from the chamber at Lissen Carak. I could see them clearly. And a woman came...not a woman I know, but I knew who she was. You know how dreams are?"

Tom laughed. "He didna' tell me this bit," he said. "But aye, I've had a dream or two of a lass."

Gabriel swatted at Tom.

"She was *Tyche*," Gabriel said. "The Archaic goddess of fortune."

"Tar," Tom said.

Gabriel shrugged. "She was fortune," he said. "And while I was looking at my picture and my chart, she said, '*Would you be lord of all the worlds?*'"

Michael nodded. "Sure, this happens all the time in my dreams. What did you say?"

Gabriel laughed. "I said *no*. And she took me and put me on a great wheel, like a mill wheel, and it rolled, and I, who had been so high, came down with a crash, and the wheel rolled over me. And a gate opened...and there were the Odine, waiting." He looked around. "And I woke up."

Tom nodded. "Well, aye, the meaning is as plain as the nose on my face. Ye ought to ha' said *yes*."

Michael put his bearded chin in his hand. "What was on the chart?" he asked.

Gabriel shrugged. "It's funny. I haven't made it yet. I mean to make a chart of the gates. But on the chart, there were arcs, as if each gate..." He stood up.

High above them, a lookout called that he could see Neroponte clear on the port bow.

"As if each gate..." Gabriel said again.

Time seemed to freeze.

Tom laughed and Michael put a hand to his shoulder. "Shhh," he said.

"*Would you be lord of all the worlds*," Gabriel said softly. "Damn, damn, *damn*."

He was gone so swiftly that Michael couldn't even catch his sleeve. But both men followed him into the day cabin. Both men stood at the table, ignoring Blanche's soft snores.

Gabriel had his copy of the ancient parchment that Pavalo Payam had stolen from the Necromancer. He unrolled it and Tom pinned it with a thumb.

Blanche raised her head off the tasseled pillows. "What?" she asked.

Gabriel started to draw. He began to draw the formation of stars from Lissen Carak. "Our sky," he said. "Damn, damn, damn. It's not about gates. It is not about the gates here. It's about *all* the gates. Look; six of these don't seem to bear any resemblance to any constellation here. Harmodius thought as much; Al Rashidi suggested they were far to the east. But they're *in another sphere*."

He sat suddenly. "Oh God," he said.

A month before, Michael had seen this man grin at his brother in expectation of nothing better than a fight. A dare. Now he wore the same grin, a look that might have given any sane man pause.

"There's my loon," Tom said.

"You have no fucking idea," Gabriel said. "I'm going to be the loon of loons."

Blanche cleared her throat. "Could someone demonstrate a little chivalry and hand me in a kirtle?" she asked from her closed bed-tent. "What are you talking about, my sweet?"

Gabriel was scribbling rapidly. Michael could read. His heart was in his throat. Tom understood too.

"You said you'd lead us to hell," Tom said. He laughed. "Oh, we will make such a song!"

Michael put a hand on the parchment. "You're serious?" he asked.

Gabriel shrugged. "Mayhap I have it all wrong. We won't know until we win through to Arles and rain war down the Necromancer or his lieutenant. But by God—and I mean to include him...by God, Michael, if I put the key in the gate and see this constellation..." He looked around.

Michael shook his head. "Would you be lord of all the worlds?" he asked.

Venike rose out of the sea like a bride waiting for her groom, her magnificent churches towering amid a forest of ships' masts. Everything was built of stone, and hundreds of statues adorned every facade. Like Dar as Salaam, there were tiles, but also frescoes, richly painted on every wall, a riot of colour and image covering the bride of the sea, and the sea's highways, in the form of canals, came to almost every doorstep.

Blanche loved Venike from the moment she saw the first towers.

She and Kaitlin and a now-revealed Tancreda Comnena had worked for three days to sew garments to add to those they'd brought from Harndon and Liviapolis. The silks and cottons of Dar as Salaam were the most magnificent materials Blanche had ever worked, and the three women, along with Master Gropf and a dozen archers who had the most advanced sewing skills and a handful of Sukey's girls, had turned the after cabin into a riot of satin and brocade and netting, small jewels and seed pearls.

Oak Pew had come in the second morning at sea, sat next to the master chart of the military campaign, and set up an embroidery frame. Kaitlin had never imagined that Oak Pew—Sally, when she was sober—could embroider, and yet, sober and meticulous, if a little shaky in her hands, Oak Pew proceeded to edge a silk-tissue veil with imperial eagles and dragons in alternating gold and black thread with a speed and skill and that suggested that her youth had been spent in a very noble house indeed, or perhaps a childhood indentured to an embroiderer. Whichever had been her point of origin, Oak Pew would not say.

Regardless, when the company began to disembark, the ladies were dressed as befitted their status, at least in the eyes of the richest mercantile city in the world. And as Blanche watched the company disembark, she understood why the captain had been so careful to uniform them in the best available cloth a month and more before. Despite almost three weeks in the holds of ships, they emerged with armour polished like mirrors and swords that shone like white light itself, in spotless red and white and green, to form four neat ranks along the edge of the sea.

A thousand men and women. Two hundred full lances, plus the *casa*, which now, as the emperor's mailed fist, was fifty lances commanded by Ser Michael with Ser Francis Atcourt as his ensign.

And with them came another four hundred of the emperor's Vardariotes, and a hundred of the Nordikaans, and all the surviving Scholae. And from Alba, a hundred royal foresters and almost two hundred of the Harndon Armourers' Guild, the elite of the city's trained bands, every man armed with the new bronze tubes on heavy staffs, the tubes themselves glowing like a golden haze in the sun, and four heavy, wheeled carts that held a further array of them in white iron and ruddy bronze.

It was not a great army. But it was a beautiful one, in the very best equipment, and the Duke of Venike and his councilors received it with some trepidation and some relief and a great deal more concern.

The Duke of Venike was a very old man with a face like a death's head. But even his skull-like jaw opened in a grin as he watched the company and the imperial regulars file down off their ships onto the broad, paved square. Blanche thought that it might be the largest paved area she'd ever seen. It was as big as the heart of Harndon, bigger than the palace there. And it was surrounded by tall buildings, as good as anything in Liviapolis: a magnificent basilica with nine tall towers; a long, low palace with hundreds of glass windows, unlike anything she'd ever seen; a library with arched porticos and a long stoa of ancient columns saved from the wreck of cities lost in the east. Venike was like a temple to the arts of mankind, but it was also a terrible reminder of all that had been lost.

The emperor was the last man but one to come down the gangplank of his ship. He wore a harness in the newest style, and only a very few men knew that most of the pieces had been made for the former King of Alba to wear in a tournament.

It was entirely plated in gold. Three *lacs d'amour* surmounted the imperial eagle and dragon in enamel on his breastplate, and Ser Michael, behind him, unfurled the imperial standard that had not flown openly in the Antica Terra in more than a hundred years.

The Duke of Venike bent his knee.

Every man and woman in the vast square did the same, although there was a hum of surprise and many muttered comments. Venikans did not often bend their knees.

All of the company's trumpets sounded, and the heralds of Venike played a fanfare in return, and Gabriel Muriens avoided tripping on his spurs and managed to come down the gangplank to the edge of the square, where Ataelus, more than a little upset by three weeks at sea, waited restlessly.

He mounted in one explosive display of strength and horsemanship and rode along the ranks of his small army, and they cheered him, and then he rode to greet the Duke of Venike, who shocked his own councilors by kneeling again and placing his hands between the emperor's.

If the emperor was shocked, he showed nothing of it. Rather, he put a hand under the duke's elbow and raised him, leaned forward, and whispered in his ear, and the duke smiled. Ten thousand voices cheered.

The emperor introduced his standard-bearer, the women of his party, and his officers, and the duke introduced his wife. People cheered again.

"That's all the troops you brought?" the duke asked. "I expected... ten times as many. Pretty as they are."

"I hope you have the five thousand horses you promised," the emperor replied. "I only brought one."

Blanche awoke the morning of her wedding to find that nothing was actually ready.

While she sipped kahve and listened to Kaitlin outline where they were on all the lists the two of them had made, and Tancreda Comnena insisted that her brother was *trying* to humiliate her, Blanche looked out the great open windows, pane after pane of clear glass, at the magnificent canal that flowed almost at her feet.

"By Saint Mary Magdalene," she said. "Who would not want to be wed on such a day and such a place?" She laughed. "I'll marry him in my shift, with flowers in my hair," she said. "Let us start ridding ourselves of what is impossible." She sat with her lists and used a lead to put lines through things that were not ready and, in her view, were not worth the time to look into them.

Jeweled garters vanished, and a head net of Hoek lace, half finished, was left. Stockings of sheer Dar silk were abandoned as needing too much time to finish, although Kaitlin thought they'd be the most beautiful adornment her friend could imagine...

"No," Blanche said. "And no," she said, putting a line through a silver water bucket for the ceremony. The emperor, by which everyone meant Gabriel, had one in his camp equipage, and no one had the time to unload it all and look for it. The local Patriarch had to find his own.

Kaitlin frowned. "You aren't getting enough fun out of this," she said.

"Who says?" Blanche allowed. "I like lists."

The Duchess of Venike was announced. Blanche had been introduced the day before, and her magnificent brocade skirts had hidden the trembling of her knees. Now she was in an old shift with a slightly torn shoulder, seven hours from her wedding.

Her eyes met Kaitlin's.

Tancreda, bred to the highest etiquette, stood up straight. She had on an archer's shirt with a short robe of emerald silk over it.

"I don't have time to receive someone in any degree of formality," Blanche said, a little desperately.

Tancreda was like a native guide. "No," she said firmly. "She must be here informally. No woman would intrude on the last hours before a wedding. Let me talk to her. For me"—Tancreda's chin thrust out— "I will marry mine in this shirt and, as you say, flowers." She grinned. "Married!" she laughed. "My cousin is delighted and my brother is appalled."

"Your brother now knows what you've been doing all that time you said you were studying," Kaitlin said. "He's teasing you."

Tancreda looked first surprised, and then delighted, laughed. "He always knew? Now he has to admit it." She swept out of the room.

"You need servants," Kaitlin said.

Blanche laughed. "I had servants in the laundry," she said. "I know how to give orders. I'd love to have six girls from the palace laundry. Goodness, do you think I could wash linens this morning?" She giggled, and the other girl returned her giggle.

"I never had servants," Kaitlin admitted. "I'm still not good at it. Tancreda can help us."

"She's here unofficially, and she has twenty women with her!" Tancreda said. "Seamstresses! Four embroiderers. A glover!"

Blanche found herself embracing the slim young woman who was the duchess of the great city. She had muscles like Gabriel's. Blanche, no weakling, knew muscles.

"Call me Giselle," the duchess said. She had the hard hands of a man. She threw herself into a chair like a man, too, and despite her kirtle and simple, elegant overdress edged in fur and pearls, she wore a sword and a dagger at her hips. "When I understood you were to be wed in the midst of this…" She shrugged and smiled. "My husband did the same to me. He insisted we wed immediately."

Blanche sat, suddenly unafraid of her slightly ragged shift. "Why, Excellency? If I may ask?"

Giselle frowned. "He's much older than I, and he said that he'd be dead soon enough." She shrugged. "There were other reasons. But that was the true one." Giselle stretched out her legs like a man and began to play with her dagger. "I assume that your man feels the same?"

"I think he feels that this is the last moment before the…campaign commences," she said.

The duchess nodded. "It seems an odd choice," she said. "Unless, pardon my bluntness, you are pregnant, and he does not expect to survive the campaign."

The two of them locked eyes.

Blanche framed the words, *That is none of your business*, and then let them go with a sigh.

"Something like that," she said.

Giselle's beautiful, hard face cracked. "Damme," she said. "That was asinine even for me."

Blanche looked away.

"God knows, you are beautiful enough," she said. She laughed. "Good. I'm sorry, but my husband and I are betting everything on

346

you and your husband. So I have brought you an army of tailors and sempters and the like. The least I could do." She laughed. "Having bet our city on your Red Knight, the cost of a few embroideries is nothing."

Blanche leaned over and kissed the Duchess of Venike. "Did you find Gabriel five thousand military horses?"

Giselle's eyes narrowed slightly. She sat back and nodded appraisingly. "Ah," she said. "Not just a pretty face."

Blanche shrugged.

"The marketplace rumour says you were a laundress," Giselle said.

Blanche stood up. "The Queen of Alba's laundress," she said. "I'm a very good laundress. The emperor needs someone who can keep his linens *really* clean."

Giselle also guffawed like a man. "I had that coming."

Kaitlin, silent until then, nodded. "I was a laundress too," she said.

"It's a new fashion," Blanche said.

Tancreda shrugged. "I'm not a laundress, more's the pity," she said. "My grandmother was empress." She looked at Blanche. "Although, to be fair, my earliest memory of her was lecturing someone on how to get linens really white."

"It's a useful skill," Blanche said.

Giselle leaned over and kissed Blanche. Her lips lingered a little too long and Blanche's heart moved a little faster and she flushed.

"If the emperor jilts you, I'll marry you myself," Giselle said. "When I'm a widow." She guffawed again.

Tancreda rolled her eyes and started marshaling lists. Again. And Blanche discovered that Giselle liked lists too.

Pencils flew. Sailors were drafted as runners; the silver bucket was found.

Before nones rang, Giselle was one of them.

In a separate apartment, by immemorial custom, Gabriel sat with his officers, forbidden to see his soon-to-be wife. His clothes were ready; indeed, he'd chosen his wedding suit and had it made before they left Liviapolis, as a small wager with himself.

"The royal army is west of N'gara, and already engaged," Kronmir said, pointing at a rough map drawn on the marble floor in charcoal.

Mortirmir was lying on a daybed, head pillowed on cushions

covered in embroidery and probably not meant to be actually used. He was already dressed for his wedding. In fact, when he rose he had donned his wedding clothes, and he clearly thought that Gabriel was a fool for waiting. "Fighting Ash?" he asked.

"Better to fight west of N'gara than at Lissen Carak. If we must, we can trade space for time," Michael said.

"You mean, if we lose at N'gara?" Mortirmir said.

There was a small silence.

"Yes, Morgon," Gabriel said.

"Why not just say so?" Morgon insisted.

"Naming calls," Sauce snapped. "Christ on the cross, Master Mortirmir, must you always spit out whatever thought enters your head?"

"My thoughts are important," Mortirmir said. "I feel you might value them."

Sauce looked around, met Gabriel's eye, and shook her head. "I need a breath of air," she said, and pushed out of the crowded room.

Gabriel followed her out. "He *does* have important thoughts."

"It's as well," Sauce spat, "as otherwise I might kill him."

"He's better with Tancreda around," Gabriel admitted. He was watching the horizon. They were on a balcony, and he could see up the last curve of the canal and over a great bridge to the open sea. A pair of war galleys were coming in. "No dissent today, Sauce. Or over the next two weeks. I'm out of..." He paused.

"Money?" she asked.

"Everything. But money most of all. Patience, energy, spirit, gold, fodder, knights, and archers. I'm out of all of them." He smiled, but it was not much of a smile.

She put a hand on his shoulder. "The army is ready to march. Company has never been better."

Gabriel was still looking out to sea. "This is the easy part," he said.

Sauce shrugged. "So you keep saying. Sometimes, I'm tempted to tell you to stop taking yon so seriously. You know what I think? I think that the great ones, the busy ones—like you and your mother and Thorn and Ash...you always think it's the end of the world, the one great chance, the last desperate throw. And you know what this little whore of South Liviapolis says? It's never the last time. It's one day at a time, all the way. Never the last battle. Just *another* goddamned battle. You used to think you was cursed by God. An' now, I note, you think mayhap you was *chosen* by God. An' I say... mayhap you're just another one, and the last, desperate throw is all in your wee head." She met his eyes the way she had not in a year or more. "Wed your lass. I like her. Make some babies. Drink some wine. Fuck the end of the world. It's overrated. Let the dragons and the little wee worms go hang. No matter what we do, some git like your Morgon Mortirmir will stick his pissle in the crack of doom and our kids will have to do it all again."

She stood on her toes and kissed him on the lips, as she had not in a long time. "I love bein' a knight, and a captain. But I learned a few things as a whore." She smiled, and swept her sword to her side and passed him, leaving him looking out to sea.

And then, when most men might have been drinking with their friends, or contemplating wedding vows, the emperor and several of his officers were sitting in one of the duke's great halls with a dozen Venikan noblemen and as many bankers.

The duke was present, unofficially, but his presence probably did something to attenuate the dismay of the bankers at the foreign emperor's extortionate demands for money.

"You bring fewer than three thousand men and you want five hundred thousand ducats in gold?" asked one of the gold-haired Corners.

"Yes," Gabriel said.

"You expect us to fund the whole war?" Theresa asked.

"This year, yes, Next year, perhaps." Gabriel nodded.

"We will be broken by this. Who will repay us?" Corner asked.

"The combined revenues of the empire and of Alba, with some new taxes, over the next forty years," Gabriel said. He had done the figures, with Michael and Master Julius and lately, again, with Sukey and Blanche.

"Forty years!" one of the bankers, a Niccolo something or other, shrugged. His smile was patronizing. "I do not think I can see any advantage in this."

"Your other option is to be dead or taken by the enemy, all your goods rotting, and your gold winking in the sunlight." Gabriel's smile was at least as patronizing.

The banker frowned. "I am told there are ways of reaching accommodations with this... enemy. I think it is time we investigated them, instead of this absurd pretense of defiance that belongs to another age." The man sat back, and two other of his peers nodded.

Theresa leaned back and motioned with her hand, as if bored and demanding wine, or coffee.

A pair of Venikan marines seized the banker under his armpits and hauled him from his chair. A third man pulled a bag over his head.

"Any accommodation with the enemy is treason," Theresa said over the sound of the man's begging. "The Council of Seven has spoken."

The banker was carried away, feet dragging behind him. His demands became pleading, and the pleading became increasingly high-pitched, and the door opened—the door to the passageway and stairs that Kronmir had used, weeks before. They could hear his feet bumping against each step as he was carried relentlessly away.

The Corners looked at each other. "Niccolo Variner was a trusted friend," the nearer said.

"No," Theresa said. "He was a despicable traitor." She nodded. "Pray, continue."

The emperor raised his hands.

"It appears we have no other choice but to grant you these moneys," Corner Primo said.

The emperor frowned. "No," he said. "You don't."

Seven hours and much bell tolling later, the emperor, in red satin worked in gold thread, and the soon-to-be empress, in white and green, passed between the serried ranks of the company, through the Scholae's ranks, under the sabers of the Vardariotes and finally under the axes of the Nordikaans. The people of Venike cheered them to the echo, and the soldiers cheered, and under Oak Pew's magnificent veil, Blanche Gold wept a little, and could not have said why.

Or perhaps she could. Perhaps she might have wept for the past and the future. For what she had already lost, and for what she would lose. Perhaps even for what she gained.

But she never missed a step. Her shoulders stayed back, her head stayed up, and she bowed to saints, made reverence to the Patriarch, curtsied to her husband, and knelt to receive a crown.

None of it had any real impact on her. It was all at a distance until the red figure at her side, currently wearing a flame-coloured cloak trimmed in ermine that clashed terribly with his doublet, leaned over.

The crown on her head had nine golden spikes and was as high as his own. She had watched him crowned in Liviapolis and had wondered then what he was thinking.

Now she seemed incapable of thought. And he leaned over, lifted a corner of her veil, and said, "And now you take precedence over the Queen of Alba."

And then the reality of it descended on her, and for a long moment, she could not breathe.

The duke might have had reservations about his new allies, and the banking families might have been a state of near revolt, but the city did not stint.

Blanche surfaced from her thoughts and her internal confusions to find herself at a table set in the immense square in front of the magnificent Basilica of Saint Mark. She smiled at her husband and savoured the word.

"Husband?" she said aloud.

"Wife?" he said, looking at her. He put a hand on her hand and *she was in his palace.*

"I am not sure I ever thought you'd do it," she admitted.

He grinned. Even in the aethereal. *"There really weren't a lot of rivals,"* *he said impishly.*

She laughed and released his hand and turned to Morgon Mortirmir, because she was herself again, and Mortirmir needed help on social occasions.

But he was besotted with his Tancreda, and he never seemed to take his eyes off her. She wore a pale ivory silk embroidered with hundred, possibly thousands of pearls. She'd had another dress, but when the duchess had offered her own...

Tancreda laughed.

Ser Giorgos came over and offered a long toast to the happy couples. Ser Michael rose and made a few barbed comments, but not many.

He needn't have held his tongue.

Bad Tom rose, five tables away, and roared the crowd to silence. He walked to the center of the tables: tables spread with gold and silver plate, where six hundred noblemen and noblewomen of the city sat with knights and ladies from Alba and Morea and Dar as Salaam.

He had a heavy gold cup in his fist, and he raised it high.

"Gentles all!" he roared. "I've known this loon wha' you call emperor for nigh on six year, and I expect that I know him as well as any man born." He looked around.

Gabriel groaned.

"An' the lass he wedded," Tom said with a smile. "I don' think I'd be takin' me role too far to say that I ga' him the advice that brought us all here today when I tol' him..."

Sauce, who had risen from her seat to make a speech of her own, kicked Tom adeptly behind the knee, and he stumbled, whirled without spilling a drop...and paused.

"Ach, aye," he said. "So there's stories best not told in fine company. Mayhap...So I'll leave my stories for another day. Here's to a loon and his lady. When they..." Tom's fingers began to entwine, and Sauce, a foot smaller, inserted herself in front of him and seemed to eclipse him.

"We wish them every happiness!" Sauce called.

"In bed and out!" Tom roared, and ladies in the crowd swooned... or shrieked with laughter. A few began to measure Tom with their hands.

The crowd laughed, and many "*Vivats*" were shouted. Many Venikans wished them long life, and there were some raucous requests.

"Uh-oh," the emperor said.

Blanche was laughing under her veils and wondering if she had to wear them to the very end of the evening. She saw Tancreda kissing her new husband and smiled. Beyond them...

Forty veteran archers of the company marched in step along the path between the tables and halted in front of their captain.

Smoke and Long Paw stepped out from the ranks. Long Paw bowed deeply.

"The which we promised Wilful Murder," Smoke said.

"Oh my God," the emperor said, and tried to hide his head under the table.

"I think you have to take this like a man, sweet," Blanche said.

"We promised him that if you did wed Mistress Blanche"—Smoke paused and realized he was probably on dangerous ground—"which I meant to say as *when* you wed."

Some of the archers could barely contain themselves.

"Which Wilful and the rest o' we wrote ye a wedding song," Smoke continued. "A month ago an' more."

"Afore the battle," Smoke said.

Cully cleared his throat.

A hundred paces away, Bad Tom turned to Sauce. "An you wouldn't let *me* speak, lass?"

Sauce shrugged. "You I can control," she said. "The ghost of Wilful Murder is beyond me." She got up and walked across the square to join the archers, and so did fifty other men and women, including Ser Michael and Kaitlin and George Brewes and Francis Atcourt.

Sauce put her hands on her silk-clad hips and sang a single clear note.

There's a red cloak by the fire where the lad and lassie met,
And it would not do to do the do they're doing in it yet,
But now they're bound and wedded and we're very much impressed
To know at last the captain's found her cuckoo's nest.

There were verses of the same, and the empress decided that if her charms could be described in song, she could remove her veil, while people who could translate Alban were suddenly in very high demand in the crowd, and the emperor put on a brave face and beamed at his soldiers.

Mortirmir turned and looked at his captain. "I swear they're implying that you didn't know how people copulated until recently," he said.

Blanche dissolved. Kaitlin pretended she was having a fainting spell, and, in fact, three hours later, the worse for drink despite the baby she now knew lay in her womb, and still given to fits of giggles, the two of them and the Duchess of Venike were sitting on the empress's wedding bed, singing...

But now they're wed and wedded and we're very much impressed
To know at last the captain's found her cuckoo's nest.

Giselle shook her head. "I don't even understand the verse about the horses," she said.

Kaitlin explained.

Giselle fell to the floor, clutching her sides. She kept trying to speak, and there she lay, blowing like a gaffed fish.

"I'm not sure what I think of knowing that Wilful Murder thought my breasts were the finest he'd ever seen," Blanche said. She smiled, remembering the man.

Mark my words...

Giselle laughed. "I'd have to agree," she said, and they all roared and more wine appeared.

And later, the emperor walked in. Michael had fallen in the corridor and was now sitting on the beautiful silk carpet, entranced by the patterns. The Duke of Venike was sitting in the courtyard of the palazzo with Bad Tom and Long Paw and the Corner brothers. They were singing. The old duke turned out to have a hoarse voice but every idea of how to carry a tune. He was teaching them to sing *Che cosa e quest d'amor* in a remarkable falsetto. Tom was trying to sing falsetto.

Sauce was what she called *fuzzy*. But she picked up the duke's tune faster than the others, and she didn't need to sing falsetto to reach the notes. She was just trying a harmony when Gabriel put a hand on her shoulder and slipped away. He walked up the outside steps to the second floor and then into the candlelit corridor, where he stopped and put a blanket over Michael. Anne Woodstock appeared from one of the rooms and beckoned him, and pointed him to the end of the corridor, where the windows looked over the Grand Canal.

He went into the bedchamber, which was hung, at least for the night, in a fortune's worth of borrowed tapestries and carpets. The bed-hangings alone were embroidered in gold and were probably the property of the state.

Blanche was sitting on the bed, braiding her hair. Kaitlin smiled. She had the duchess by one arm and was just trying to get her down off the bed, which was quite high.

Gabriel laughed, and with Blanche and Kaitlin and a little help from Toby and Anne and Master Nicodemus, Gabriel's steward, they moved the duchess to the next room.

When they had her undressed and tucked in, Toby reappeared from the corridor.

"Jules Kronmir," he said. "Sorry, Captain. That is, Your Grace."

Toby was slightly the worse for drink. But behind him, Anne Woodstock was sober as a judge, still in her livery, and armed.

Gabriel sighed. He was still dressed.

Blanche stood on tiptoe and kissed him, biting his upper lip lightly. "I'm not drunk anymore," she said. "Mostly sober." She smiled. "Just saying." She looked back over her shoulder with a cool confidence that Gabriel loved in her. "If'n you take too long, the duchess will try an' take your place."

Gabriel nodded to Toby and passed into the corridor.

Kronmir bowed. "Your Grace," he said. "Congratulations on a brilliant wedding."

Gabriel smiled. "It was rather good."

Kronmir nodded.

"And unless you're about to say that the enemy is at the gates," Gabriel continued, "and frankly, perhaps even then..."

Kronmir bowed. "I expect we can hold the hordes a few more hours, my lord," he said with a rare smile. "But Magister Petrarcha is now sure that the Necromancer is here. At Arles." He held out a tiny slip of parchment. "Thirty-Four made it into Arles and out again."

Gabriel leaned over and kissed the startled intelligence officer. "My favourite wedding present," he said. "Oh, Jules Kronmir, you are a pearl beyond price." He laughed. "Give Thirty-Four a whole chicken, or a peacock, or whatever she fancies. Live mice!"

Kronmir bowed, but he was bowing to empty air.

Blanche found that she was still drunk, and that a little drunkenness made her quite bold. The results were spectacular.

She lay atop him. She had surprised him, and that pleased her.

"We're married," she said.

All the candles were still burning, a hundred wax candles, a reckless expenditure of beeswax and gold. All so that they could both be witnesses to their own lust.

Blanche grinned.

Gabriel grinned back. "So we are," he said.

"Do we live happily ever after?" Blanche asked.

Gabriel's look grew distant, and then sad. "No," he said. Then he thought of what Sauce had said. "Damn it. Maybe yes."

They were both silent a long time.

"You aren't as light as you might think," he said.

"That's the most amorous, elegant thing you could think to say to me?" she asked.

He shifted. "Yes?" he said.

"Why are we married?" she asked.

"Because I love you," he said.

"People like you sometimes love people like me. We're kept in nice houses and our babies are raised in the best homes." Blanche had him pinned, literally. She wrapped her legs around his to make her point. "We don't get married. We don't become empresses."

"The old king married his Sophia," Gabriel said.

Blanche wriggled, and when he didn't speak, she blew softly on his eyelashes, which he hated.

"Do you know who Clarissa de Sartres is?" Gabriel asked.

Blanche sighed. "No."

"She may, right now, be the Queen of Galle," Gabriel said. "Her father was the last Prince of Arles. She is still holding the castle of Arles, as of yesterday, and we are going to rescue her."

Blanche wriggled. "Is this about our wedding?" she asked.

"Yes. Be still, woman. I'm your lord and husband. You have to obey my every whim." He tried to tickle her.

Blanche moved her slightly sticky bare thigh in a way that suggested that her knee knew the location of his testicles.

He subsided.

"If Clarissa holds Arles. If we defeat the Necromancer and relieve Arles, and save the gate. If, as we have reason to believe, both her father and the King of Galle died fighting the Necromancer..."

Blanche shook her head. But his eyes were without deception.

"The pressure on me to wed Clarissa would then be immense, sweet. Even people like Michael would want it." He shrugged. "I wanted to wed you. By wedding you now...I have closed certain doors." His eyes met hers. "Listen, it'll be a wild ride, but Bad Tom follows me because *I am a loon*. In a year, I will probably be dead. I have to take risk after risk. There is no holding back. We can't lose, or rest, or fail."

She raised herself on her elbows so that she could look at him.

"All I can offer you is a place on the ride," he said. "And that if I make it to the end, I'll hand the crown to Comnenos and *then* we'll live happily ever after."

Blanche laughed. "I don't believe it," she said. "I don't think you have *happily ever after* in you. I think you are all strive and struggle every day."

She leaned over him and kissed him.

She was completely sober, and she found that she could still surprise him. But being who he was, he had to surprise her, and the two of them, the top mattress, and the richly worked bed-hanging, all ended up on the floor.

"Sleepy?" he asked.

She laughed. "No?" she answered.

"Let's walk," he said.

He really could surprise her. "Walk?" she asked.

"I've been filling out lists for two days," he said.

"I could teach you a few things about lists," she said.

He nodded. "So I gather, from the duchess, your greatest admirer. After me, let me hasten to add."

She bit him.

"I'm about to fight a four-week campaign. And live. Or die. I don't want this night to end, and honestly, I'm not sure I can do that again." He smiled at her.

They both laughed.

He opened his campaign trunk and threw her braes and hose and a doublet.

She went behind a screen and threw him a towel.

In front of their door stood Anne Woodstock. She had a bare sword in her hand.

Gabriel was clearly touched. He bowed, knee to floor, as if he were the squire and she the great lord, and the page girl blushed.

"We are going out," he said. "You may retire, and get some sleep."

She smiled.

"I'll borrow your sword, if I may," Gabriel said.

And then they were out in the night. Just the two of them. No Toby, no Anne, no string of servants, no Master Nicodemus, no Bad Tom or Sauce or Michael or Kaitlin.

Blanche realized she was seldom alone anymore.

It was dark. The moon lit the canals, and the narrow alleys and walkways had lanterns and torches in iron brackets.

It was all very beautiful.

Everything smelled of seawater. There was no garbage, no refuse, no dung carts.

Blanche was wearing a pair of plain leather shoes, and the stone beneath her feet was smooth and cool and bare of dirt. She began to understand how the people here often wore only hose with leather soles on them, instead of shoes.

"Where are we going?" she asked, after a while.

He shook his head. "No idea," he said.

They slipped through alleys so narrow that they had to pass one at a time. One alley was a tunnel that dipped low under a wall and came up on the other side. They emerged into a small square that seemed to be lined in lights. A church rose in splendour, the front covered in statues and carving that rendered stone like frozen flame, and high above them, the candles in the church backlit the rose window of coloured glass, a beacon of beauty.

"That's where we were wed," she breathed.

Gabriel squeezed her hand. "They must have decreed that the square be lit all night," he said.

The pinpoints of candlelight all around were like a flight of faeries.

He led her across the square.

There was a low bridge of one of the small canals, and there was a boat.

"Let's take a boat!" she said.

"I didn't bring a purse," Gabriel said. He was obviously sad to disappoint her.

She rose and kissed him on her toes. "Silly," she said. She had his purse on her borrowed man's belt. She found a rose noble—an enormous sum.

He laughed. "I carry them to give rewards, not to pay boatmen," he allowed.

She held the coin up and the boatman took it, bit it, and shrugged. He spoke Etruscan.

She didn't.

But of course, Gabriel did.

And then they were seated together, and the boatman was poling them along. They went up one little canal and down another, and at one point he bent low and they passed under a whole house, or perhaps a block of houses, and emerged to a wider canal and a forest of masts, twenty or more Venikan warships all docked together.

"The duchess is a soldier," Blanche said. "She fancies me."

"Everyone fancies you," Gabriel said. "Don't let it go to your head."

She poked him.

"I'm not coming, am I?" she asked.

"You are, at that. At least until Berona," he said. "If you don't come, who will do all the laundry?"

She poked him again.

"But I think you are coming all the way," he said. "I'm going to take a momentous risk. If it works..." He paused. "Well, if it doesn't, the end will be very quick indeed."

And later, the sun began to rise, and after a whispered discussion with the boatman, the boat turned.

"What did he say?" Blanche asked.

"He said that if I wanted to use the curtains, we could make love," Gabriel said. "I said we'd rather have breakfast. I think he fancies you, too."

Blanche ran a finger down his jaw. "Sometime, I think I'd love to make love in a little boat. Right now, food is my sole passion."

They landed on another square, this one with a little fortification on its seaward side. Behind the fortification, which was manned, was a tavern or an inn. A dozen people in the wreckage of magnificent clothing sat or lay about at the outside tables.

"The city never sleeps. That's what they say, and here it is true. I believe these are survivors of our wedding." The two of them clambered out of the boat. They were fed eggs and little cakes, and drank hypocras. The sun was rising, and the last of the magnificently costumed musicians had "one last cup" and stumbled away. The boatman shared a cup with them.

"Your boy's a beauty," he said to Gabriel, who laughed.

"He thinks you are a boy," Gabriel said.

"No, he doesn't," Blanche said. "I'll wager he even knows who we are."

Gabriel sat back.

Blanche smiled.

The boatman smiled back.

The hundred candles hadn't even burned out yet.

He went to the balcony over the canal and they stood, his hand around her waist, as the red ball of the sun came up over the east and the strong red light poured over the golden domes and smooth grey-and-white stone of the city and turned the canals orange as it rose.

"That's as happily ever after as I can manage," he said into her neck. She laughed.

Three weeks earlier, and two thousand leagues to the west

Princess Irene had expected to die when the Red Knight left. She knew she was a fool. In fact, she was unable to stop herself from speaking, because she felt shamed, humiliated, abandoned. And guilty.

So she sat on her throne for a long time after he left, and stared into space, and thought about her choices.

Maria came to the foot of the throne, and bowed. She had a cup in her hand.

"So you were always his creature," Irene spat.

Maria looked at her, her face grave, but serene.

Irene wanted to explode. Except that she'd been trained better. And she'd had enough of her own foolishness for one day.

"Is that poison?" Irene asked.

Maria curtsied. "No," she said. "It is a drug."

"And if I drink it?" Irene asked.

Maria shrugged. "I cannot promise you life," she said. "It is not mine to promise. But..." She shrugged. "I do not think he seeks your death. A nunnery is not so bad."

Irene cried a little, dismissed thoughts of suicide, and drank from the cup.

When she woke, it was morning and she was lying on the ground. She had a moment of extreme disorientation. She was lying in a wool blanket. She didn't know where she was, and for a moment, she didn't know *who* she was. Her hips hurt, and she was deliciously warm, and her head hurt.

There was a face close by hers, covered in tattoos. Irene might have screamed, except for the extreme lethargy that seemed to possess her.

She twitched her toes, and moved her fingers, and a little at a time gained control of her body. Her mouth felt as if she'd eaten sand, and her eyes were crusted. Slowly she raised an arm and rubbed her eyes.

The eyes in the tattooed face opened. They were a brilliant green and appeared unearthly.

Irene took in a sudden breath. Beyond the beautiful eyes, the sun was rising over trees, and a great beast was rising away on wings of red and gold and green. She took in a great breath as if she'd been long under water, and then exhaled, and took in another.

"I am not dead," she said aloud.

"You are quite warm," said the tattoos. "If you were dead, I expect you'd be cold."

Irene lay another moment, comforted by the press of bodies to either side. When it was cold, in the city, she slept with her maids. She never dared say so, but the press of warm bodies on either side was one of her favourite things in the world. She let the moment linger.

And then, resigned to whatever brutal fate the Red Knight had allotted her, she sat up.

It was dawn. The sky was a warm pink and no more. A fire smouldered in a neat fire pit at her feet, and twenty huddled shapes lay under blankets. The air was brisk, even cold, and the two upright men were in wool cotes and hoods. They had bows in their hands. Neither paid her any attention.

At her feet, a familiar face was stirring a pot over the fire.

"Gabriel?" she asked. Even as she said his name she knew it was not he; and she knew, too, that she would have been ashamed if it had been.

The young man turned. The face was different—his eyes were slanted like a cat's.

"I'm Aneas," he said. "And you are Irene."

She looked at him for a long time—perhaps a hundred beats of her heart.

She looked briefly at her soft hands and took in one more long breath. Then she rose, carefully, from her blanket and threw it over the tattooed figure next to her. There was a purr of pleasure from underneath, as if a giant cat lay there instead of a tattooed man. Or woman.

She considered various options. In fact, she was silent for long enough that the emotional warmth of the body heat drained away, and she discovered anger.

"What am I doing here?" she demanded.

Aneas Muriens—the family resemblance was obvious—studied her a moment longer. "That will largely be up to you," he said. "I didn't ask for you to be here. This is my brother's doing." He played with the fire.

He was angry, too. She wondered if that gave her something on which to build.

"I'm not going to run screaming, if that's what you expect," she said.

"No screaming?" Aneas asked. He dipped a horn cup into the mixture he was heating and handed it to her. His Alban-accented Archaic was flat. He overpronounced almost everything.

Barbarian.

She took a sip. It was mostly honey. She drank some. It was like a dark, tart hypocras. She'd had kahve. This seemed stronger.

"No, my screaming's done," she said. "If you mean your brother, the usurper."

Aneas shrugged. It was very like his brother's shrug, and just as infuriating. "You don't ever want to be in a contest for people's affections with my brother," he said. "Everyone always loves him."

"I hate him," she said.

He smiled condescendingly. "Really?" he asked. "Is that why you called his name when you awoke?"

She felt herself flush. She hated that loss of control. But she was a princess of the oldest royal house in the world. She took a steadying breath. "I'm awake now. What am I doing here?"

"We are following Kevin Orley. Do you know who he is?" Aneas asked. When he said the name *Orley* he said it as if it were imbued with eldritch power.

"Yes," she said. "Thorn's apprentice. A claimant to the name of Orley, as yet unproven. Lived for some years with the Sossag." She nodded. "I am a princess of the line of emperors. It is my business to know these things. Why are we following him?"

Aneas gave her a nod, as if of recognition, or approbation. "We don't have the numbers to defeat and destroy his forces. In fact, I'm going to guess that he's already found new allies as he moved through the woods. Gabriel or Gavin is going to send a major force against him. We have to track him until then."

"But he outnumbers us," Irene said.

Aneas grinned wolfishly. "By an order of magnitude."

"And we'll follow him anyway," she said. "So your brother sent me here to die or be captured."

"Ever lived in the woods?" he asked. He had stopped listening to her when she had turned sarcastic, like a dancer turning on one foot and changing direction.

"I've hunted boar," she said. "With twenty huntsmen and some cousins and a lot of big tents."

"Can you maintain a fire?" he asked. "I have other work I should be doing."

She looked at him. "Your brother suggested that I marry you. He said he'd make you Duke of Thrake."

"Did he?" Aneas smiled. "I'd rather like to be Duke of the North. I think I'd be good at it." He looked at her. "He mentioned it to me, as well."

"I can maintain a fire," she said.

Aneas nodded. "Fair enough," he said. "Keep the fire just as it is now, Irene."

He began to walk away. She caught his arm.

"I'm here for you to woo me, I assume?" she asked, more boldly than she felt.

He shook his head. "I think you have to woo me," he said. "This is one of my brother's idiot japes. I'm always the butt of them." But his smile was not as nasty as his words.

Then he left her, and the fire.

An hour later, and everyone was up and fed, and they were walking. Her soft fingers still burned from washing the pot that had held some noxious pudding of ground grain. She'd eaten her share.

One of the men had told her that the pot wasn't clean enough.

In fact, as the pack straps dug into her shoulders, she thought that it wasn't the work she resented. Work was itself good. And being a princess had always been work. A day's correspondence, dancing lessons, some theology, some basic magery, and a long set of pointless meetings and audiences... her daily routine was nothing but work.

It was that everyone gave her orders. Most of them were polite about it, as if she were a child.

But the tone was clear. She was the lowest-ranking person there.

She thought about what a nunnery might have been like.

She thought of how pretty Aneas was.

She thought she might try harder to kill the Red Knight. She

363

wondered, just for a moment, flirtatiously, if she could marry Aneas and arrange for both Gabriel and Gavin to die.

She smiled to herself and kept walking.

They walked. No one asked her how she was all morning, although the strange tattooed boy looked into her eyes from time to time in a way she found intrusive.

Twice they stopped. The first time, she slumped to the ground. She didn't rise until one of the Outwallers grunted at her, and she had no idea why they'd stopped or for how long. She was in a haze of mild pains…her hips, her feet, her shoulders. The perfume in her hair attracted hordes of small, biting insects. The neckline on her shift allowed them access to her neck and the tops of her breasts, and by the time the sun was high in the sky, her misery had reached a level where she could no longer tell herself she was lucky to be alive.

But she was tough. She had danced every day, practiced dagger fighting with a master, ridden her horses and hunted. She was not soft. It was merely that this walking in the Wild required a kind of hardness that she lacked.

The second halt was more sudden, and lasted longer. She slumped with her pack against a tree, and her mind was working. She was thinking of that pack, and how the Red Knight must have packed it himself. She was thinking that his brother must have been involved.

She was thinking that the painted man they called *Lewen* must be an irk. He spoke pure, unaccented Archaic because it was his own language, not because he was one of her subjects. She wondered if she could appeal to him. That she might just suborn him, if she played him correctly.

And there were half a dozen Outwaller warriors who spoke some Archaic, as well. Their war chief had already gone east to Ticondonaga and the inn, but they had stayed to track the enemy. They were certainly her subjects, she thought. She heard two of them talking about serving alongside Turkos, and she knew that name.

Except that the Red Knight had rescued Turkos, in the Winter War. When everything had come apart. When the barbarian mercenary had proved first an able ally, and then a cunning plotter. That he was now going to make himself emperor was like gall on her lips; that her father's army had acclaimed him burned her like fire. He was a barbarian.

There had, of course, been other barbarian emperors. In fact, there had been a dozen such, and most of them from Alba.

She wanted to comfort herself that the Patriarch would refuse to crown him, but in fact, she knew that the Patriarch preferred him.

Everyone preferred him.

She let the ends of her futile, vengeful plots fall away. The captains were gathered around a spot on the trail; the tall Outwaller captain in his red paint, and the shorter imperial officer in his buckskins, and young Aneas, who looked like a boy next to the other two. He *was* a boy.

She thought he might be seventeen.

She remembered that she was only just eighteen.

Aneas surprised her by walking back from the little huddle on the trail and kneeling by her.

"How are you doing?" he asked.

"I'm alive," she said, looking for the right combination of pluck and pathos.

He smiled. "So am I, so far. We have a thorny problem to solve. Take your pack off. Rest." He rose and left her.

The odd boy with the tattoos came and sat by her tree. He didn't ask but put his back against the same tree, so that his muscled arm was touching hers. Irene glared at the boy, who met her gaze evenly and offered her some garlic sausage on a knife so sharp that the edge glowed in the sun filtering through the trees. The knife was close enough to her throat...

"What's your name?" she asked. The boy had the beautiful green eyes to which she'd awakened.

"Looks-at-Clouds," he said, but Irene was already reevaluating gender. It was a woman's voice. "You are very beautiful. May I teach you a thing?"

Irene blushed. When you are a princess, very few people tell you that you are beautiful, even if you suspect it. "You may," she said with dignity.

Looks-at-Clouds snapped a fern off at the stem. S/he held it out to Irene. "Fan yourself with it. Tonight I will teach you to wash." The shaman bent over, far too close for Irene's comfort, and sniffed at her neck. Irene shuddered.

"Rotten meat," Looks-at-Clouds said. "And musk. Smells that attract every predator from tiny to huge." The shaman's Archaic was not courtly, but it was very correct, with a little too much emphasis on consonants. Irene bit her lip in consternation.

"It's perfume!" she hissed.

Looks-at-Clouds blinked. "Not here," s/he said. "Here, this says *prey*."

"I am *not* prey," Irene snapped.

Looks-at-Clouds rose bonelessly, like a dancer. "Prove it," s/he said. The shaman loped off and knelt by Aneas.

Her next visitor was a bogglin. He crouched by her and offered her a carrot. It was fresh. It must have come with the Red Knight when she was left, drugged, in a camp full of barbarians and Outwallers....

The thing was mottled green and grey and brown, and smelled a little like cinnamon. It had moss growing on its back.

She took the carrot. It was kindly meant. And she was not afraid of a bogglin. In fact, she was fascinated.

"Do you speak Archaic?" Irene asked.

The bogglin shook his head. "No," he said, in what might have been Alban.

She had some Alban. "Thanks," she said.

The old bogglin nodded. His face split in four.

Irene was a young woman who had faced assassins and courtiers and public performance of duty. She straightened her shoulders and managed a broad smile.

"My, my," she said. "Those are a great many teeth."

"He's smiling," said another man, in Alban. "We calls 'im Krek."

"Good day to you, Krek," she said, in her court-greeting Alban.

The bogglin nodded. "Gut day to you, Eye-reean," he said.

"I'm Ric Lantorn," the man said. "I'm to keep ye alive."

"Or kill me if I go wrong?" Irene asked.

Lantorn shrugged. "Ser Gabriel didn't say nothin' about killin' you," he said. "He'd a' mentioned that."

Irene looked at the man steadily. "I know you," she said in Archaic.

He shrugged. "Wager 'tis my sister you know, lady," he said in Alban. "Looks-at-Clouds says you need to wash off the perfume and the bugs is gettin' you." He handed her a small clay bottle. "This stinks like shit, but it'll give ye peace from the little bastards." He smiled and even gave her a nod, as if she mattered. "Call me if'n you need help."

She managed her court smile at his back as he walked away.

Two miles later, she tried the oily stuff, which was brown and smelled more like turpentine than feces. With the help of the fern as well, she was less troubled and began to look around her.

They crossed a little stream, and then another, and she began to perceive more. The little column moved steadily along, but there were pairs of rangers well ahead and off to the right in the deep green of the leaves, and at least one more pair reported back in late afternoon, and Aneas loped off with Looks-at-Clouds, as if the weight of his pack didn't trouble him at all.

She knew a great deal about military operations for a young woman. So she had to assume that only one or two rangers at a time were actually in contact with the enemy, or watching them. And that pair would rotate.

They walked up a shallow slope to the top of a low hill. The stream ran along its base on three sides. Without a word said, everyone began to drop their packs and blanket rolls. Lewen, the irk, seemed to be in charge, but he didn't actually say very much. He used a stick to scrape a shape, and Lantorn produced a shovel, a very small one, from his pack and began to dig a trench. The others began to cut boughs and some went farther afield and began to stack up firewood. They made more noise than she'd heard all day, but still they didn't speak much.

Irene had seldom felt so useless.

But soon enough, Lantorn grinned at her. "Fill all the kettles with water," he said. "Find a clean place wi' a bit o' hole to dip it out."

She nodded, took the four copper kettles that had appeared out of packs, and carried them to the stream below the camp.

Suddenly, she was alone, in the woods. She could hear the others up above her, building shelters from branches, but she was alone. It occurred to her that she could escape. Of course, they were all woods people, chosen rangers; she'd be caught in minutes. And if she did escape, she'd be alone in the deep Wild. It was a foolish idea.

Still, she looked off into the trees.

After a little while, she filled the kettles and went back up the hill, two kettles at a time.

Lantorn came and built tripods of green wood, and hung the kettles with light chains, so that the water began to heat over low fires in the fire trench, almost invisible even a few paces away. The smoke went up between the trees.

Lewen noted her interest. "We cannot afford to be seen by the enemy," he said in his fluid High Archaic. "Some days we do not cook at all."

"I can hardly wait," Irene said.

Two Outwallers came in with a dead fawn. The fawn was beautiful—its corpse pained Irene somehow, and she flinched every time she looked at it. Lewen, who seemed to be watching her, smiled his wicked Irkish smile. "You may help Master Lantorn break up the animal," he said. "Butchering is a difficult job."

Irene was revolted. "I…" she began. "I thought irks ate…no meat."

Lewen opened a mouth full of sharp teeth as if mocking her.

Lantorn ignored the byplay and drew a short, heavy sword that looked almost like a meat cleaver. It was the length of his forearm, and the blade was as wide as the palm of her hand.

He grinned. "Good for making kindling. And cutting bogglins, when required."

Krek rustled his wing cases. "Good for taking a man's head off, I think. If I wanted eat one." His strange four-sided mouth moved. Irene hoped that was a smile.

Lantorn bobbed his head. "Right you are, lad. Just as good fer butcherin' a man. Not much for fancy fencing. Now, first, we get the little thing's skin off…"

What followed was perhaps the most terrible and disgusting hour of Irene's life. Somehow the fawn was like a child; with her own hands she helped skin it, carefully separating the disgusting stuff that bound the hide to the muscles with a knife handed her by an Outwaller, who gave her a smile that had to have been meant as flirtation, except that just touching the dead fawn made her writhe in horror. But she was a princess of the noble house, born in the purple birthing room, and she did not show her anger or her disgust.

Or she tried not to.

When Lantorn ripped the last of the skin free—after cutting the poor thing's feet off—it was time to open the fawn's belly, and again the archer made her do it. She held her breath as long as she could, and when she breathed in she felt polluted by the dead thing's warm and earthy intimacy, the smell of its intestines, the evidence of its last meal.

"Careful, lass, that's the liver, and we'll be wanting to eat that. Nice bit o' meat," Lantorn said. He laughed at her tentative strokes. His laughter drover her to cut deeper, to get the noisome job done, and he put his clean hand on her bloody, ordure-covered hand.

"Nay, lass. Not so 'ard. You puncture that little sack and we ha' deer piss on all our meat, eh?" He nodded. "That's a fine meal. In your city, rich fucks will pay right well to have fawn. We ha' it for free, or for a shaft or twa, eh?"

She shuddered. She couldn't tell if he was mocking her or if he took genuine pleasure in dismembering a dead animal. She cut again.

"Na!" he said sharply. "Na. Not sa' hard. I told ye."

She found herself pushing against his hand. It was too much—the blood on her hands, the juices of the dead thing, his words. Cut, but not hard? He made no sense.

"Stop, damn yer eyes!" he spat, closing his hand on her wrist.

She burst into tears. It hit her suddenly, and she was powerless to stop it, which only increased her rage, her frustration—appearing weak was the antithesis of her approach to life. Now they all thought she was weak. She rubbed her eyes and got the foul mess on her face and her gorge rose.

Lantorn stripped the knife out of her hand and finished the cut deftly. "Nowt for tears, missy," he said.

She knelt and sobbed, hating it all.

The rangers were more considerate than she would have thought of such hard men and women. Most turned their backs. None mocked her further. She used the hem of her plain, short linen kirtle to wipe her face of the gross mess and then her hands. Some she rubbed on the top of her moccasins.

The creature's intestines came out in a single wet plop onto a carefully arranged pile of leaves, and Lantorn made another skilled cut around the creature's anus to release the last coil of intestine. Then he slid his hands under the leaves and lifted the whole glistening, horrifying mass and threw it hard, two-handed. His throw was so powerful that she saw the dead fawn's guts fly, spreading as if alive, to fall into the stream with a soft *splash*. Immediately something moved, and then something else; the water didn't precisely boil, but the deep pool where she had filled the pots was alive with something.

"Snapping turtle," Lantorn said. He grinned. "The Wild, eh, lass? Don't let it get to ye. Things eat things. Best to be the one eatin', and not the one et."

She swallowed hard, several times, and managed not to retch.

"Now we cut the meat off the bones," Lantorn said, as if teaching some useful skill.

An hour later Aneas and the tall man-woman returned from wherever they had been. They were solemn, even somber. Irene, who felt filthy and wretched, noted that neither of them had done any work. The camp was modest but complete, with small shelters on frames, deep fire pits, and venison stew. Most people came and filled their bowls. Aneas waited and watched.

He came and squatted by her. "You are not eating," he said.

"I... don't want any," she said carefully.

He frowned. "Please eat. I cannot take food until you have eaten. And despite your... concerns, your body needs fuel."

In fact, the food did smell delicious. Irene sat there, hating the food and desiring it. It pleased her that he couldn't eat until she ate. "Why don't you just eat?" she asked.

"I'm the captain," he said. "I eat last."

"That's a foolish rule. The emperor eats first." She met his eyes.

"Perhaps the emperor has different principles of command than my master-at-arms," Aneas said. "Or perhaps when you are emperor, you don't need to worry that there's not enough food." He smiled.

She refused to smile back, although her lips twitched.

"She is playing with you," Looks-at-Clouds said. S/he smiled at Irene and handed Aneas a wooden bowl heaped with meat. "She enjoys the power she has over you. Just eat."

Irene glared at the shaman.

Looks-at-Clouds met her eyes and smiled. "You have so much to learn," s/he said. "I cannot wait to teach you."

Irene took breath to make a hot reply, but she bit down on it. This was not the time or place. Instead, as there was no longer a point in resistance, she took a bowl of food and ate it.

The fawn was delicious, which angered her more, in a distant way.

Later she rolled in her blankets and slept between Looks-at-Clouds and Lantorn. For an hour, she lay trying not to touch either.

When she woke in the morning, she was nested between them and warm. The sentries had built up the fire.

"Another beautiful day," Looks-at-Clouds said, and kissed Irene before she could flinch away.

Irene snapped her head away.

Looks-at-Clouds smiled.

The camp vanished in moments. Irene had noted that there were other women, at least a pair, but she had assumed them to be trulls, but this morning they had bows on their backs. The two blackened their faces at the morning fire and moved off into the woods.

She wished she were going with them. She allowed herself a brief fantasy, wherein she became a mighty ranger, a queen of the woods...

Today she had to pack her own things, and she struggled to make her pack as small and tight as Aneas or Gabriel had done before her. She grew frustrated with her blankets; there were two, and they seemed huge, and covered in leaf mold.

Looks-at-Clouds came and watched her.

"Shall I help you?" s/he asked in his/her oddly accented Archaic.

Irene considered the fluffy mass that was her blankets.

"I would appreciate your help," she said with all the dignity she could manage, and some utterly false cheer.

Looks-at-Clouds seized the blankets and shook them so hard they snapped in the still air, and then laid them down. S/he folded them in thirds and rolled them tight, kneeling on them. It took no time at all, and s/he was reaching for the ties that Irene had, with some forethought, looped over the roof pole of her shelter.

"You understand, yes?" Looks-at-Clouds asked. "You are very quick."

Irene wasn't sure what the green-eyed shaman meant. "I feel very... stupid."

Looks-at-Clouds shrugged. "Really?" s/he asked, and smiled, showing too many teeth.

There was a final whirl of activity, and a bronze cook pot was strapped to the bottom of Irene's pack, adding substantially to the weight.

"Your turn," Aneas said, at her elbow. He was apologetic.

She favoured him with a smile. "Of course," she said.

They were on the edge of a lake. It seemed to run south to north, but she couldn't see the head or the tail of it, because it didn't run straight. Twice they walked on broad gravel beaches, but the trail always wound back into the deep woods, so that the lake was merely a glitter of light to her left.

The trees were incredible.

They were huge. There were giants whose tops she could not see; towers of wood that rose sheer and vanished, straight as huge arrows, their bark almost smooth, so big around that five or six warriors would not have stretched their arms around the trunk. The ground between them was covered in leaf mold and otherwise fairly open, although stands of raspberry cane or scrubby pines and firs dotted the forest floor where a great lord of the woods had fallen at last to age and decay and the depredations of the woodpeckers and the ants. Where ancient giants had fallen, often there was a low rise, straight as a ruler and fifty paces long, the wood long since rotted away. Ferns grew everywhere like a wild crop of some kind.

From time to time they crossed rivulets coming off the high ridges to the east. The first few times she'd walked carefully to keep her feet dry, but as the day advanced and her fatigue increased, she'd been less careful and her feet had been soaked.

And it felt wonderful.

Someone had made her Outwaller shoes of light deer or moose hide, and they dried as she walked. She began to put her feet into the water apurpose; it was cooling, and curiously restful on the feet, and they dried quickly.

In late afternoon they stopped for the third time. One of the Outwallers, Mingan, who was tall and very solemn and remarkably like his name bird, bent over the trail and sounded his horn, and all the war leaders came at a run. Irene realized for the first time that the party was larger than she'd thought, and there were men and women she hadn't seen before, moving to the east and to the west.

There were irks.

One of them sat with her. She smiled, and Irene smiled back.

She didn't move like a person.

And the two human women she'd noticed earlier. One of them was Alban, and gently born, with better manners, and she curtsied and spoke in halting Archaic.

"Cynthia," she said. She was pretty, despite a shirt of mail and a deerskin jupon. Irene had finished her little canteen of water and Cynthia took her to a stream to fetch more. They filled almost thirty canteens, which took them the better part of an hour. Irene was becoming accustomed to the *idea* of work. There was so much work, and almost everything was done as a team—while they filled canteens, others were looking at tracks, standing guard, scouting ahead.

Looks-at-Clouds came to help. "They are in council," s/he said. The shaman—Cynthia called her/him a *bacsa*—smiled and shrugged. "The enemy has divided and divided again. And also been joined by new enemies. Rukh. What you call giants."

Irene didn't really understand. "What are we doing here?" she asked.

Cynthia shouldered a dozen canteens. Irene shouldered the rest. She was not afraid of work, but of humiliation and degradation. Carrying canteens with Cynthia seemed . . . normal.

Even in her present state, Irene was beginning to sense that they were not trying to humiliate her.

Looks-at-Clouds picked up the canteens left on the ground, a mixture of military copper canteens, gourds and pottery bottles wrapped in leather. The three of them walked back to the trail. Irene watched the woods carefully. The other two seemed to know where they were.

Cynthia shrugged. "We're running Kevin Orley to earth. Before he does any more harm."

Irene sighed. "Because he is an enemy of the Muriens?" she said bitterly.

Looks-at-Clouds laughed. "Orley is an enemy of all people," s/he said. "And most of the Wild, too." S/he did that curious thing with his/her eyelashes. "He is the new avatar of Ash."

Irene dismissed her vague thought that Orley might be an ally against the Red Knight. "Ah," she said.

Again, the leaders were kneeling by the trail. They accepted their canteens with thanks and Irene withdrew, but whatever they had decided, they were finished talking.

Irene had always imagined soldiers as ignorant; tools to perform needed actions. The way these rangers discussed things suggested that they viewed themselves as participants, not tools.

That was interesting,

The sun's rays began to lengthen, and the woods went from hot to cool.

Aneas sounded his horn softly, and the whole party turned west and walked to the edge of the lake. It was only a few hundred paces away and her heart quickened in hope.

She was not disappointed.

As soon as they halted, everyone dropped their packs. Lantorn and the irks and a man she hadn't met yet loped off into the woods. Aneas tapped two of the Outwallers and spoke to them in a fluid language, and they grinned and vanished into the trees.

Then everyone began to work.

Looks-at-Clouds took her hand and led her into the trees. "Can you use an axe?" s/he asked.

Irene bit her lip in vexation. "No," she said.

"Learn, then," Looks-at-Clouds said. The shaman was patient. S/he had a little axe and used it carefully.

"What are we doing?" Irene asked.

"Stakes for shelters," Looks-at-Clouds said. "We need thirty-two stakes and nine long poles. Look—a stake is this long. Sharp at one end. This size. No, that is dead pine. Look, I can break it with my hands. No, that is rotten. See this? It is ash. It grows straight. My people say that Tar made the ash for man, because all the other tree kindreds were too weak."

Irene watched the *bacsa* fell the ash sapling in three blows. S/he began to trim the branches like a ruthless executioner.

"Take all the little branches away," Looks-at-Clouds ordered. "Good. This is how you take off branches. Cut this way. No, not into the crotch. Like this. It is very sharp. Do not put your foot there. That is foolish. Here. One hand. Like this."

Irene was not patient with herself. She cut and apologized, cut and missed.

"Stop and breathe. You know nothing. This is no sin. Only stop and *learn*." The shaman showed her again.

Irene cut a single small branch off the trunk.

"Good," Looks-at-Clouds said. "Again."

She began to move along the trunk. At first, slowly, and then with growing confidence.

"Already you take no care," Looks-at-Clouds said. "The axe remains sharp. A little knowledge does not dull it. Be more careful. Breathe. Learn. Be slow now, so later you can be quick."

Irene stopped. She took a deep breath, her intention a little mockery, and her eye lit on a flower.

It was the first flower she had seen in the forest. It caught her eye and her breath and her heart.

"Ah!" Looks-at-Clouds said. "Yes."

Irene reached to pluck it, and the *bacsa*'s hand closed on her wrist. "It is beautiful where it is," s/he said.

Irene burst into tears without any thought or reason.

The shaman wrapped both arms around the princess. S/he smelled of tall pines and sweat. Irene was not in control of herself for several moments.

"I'm sorry," she said.

Looks-at-Clouds laughed. "I never know what you people mean when you say this," s/he said.

When all the stakes and poles were cut, they carried them to camp. Looks-at-Clouds taught her to make a travois and pull them in one load. And then she went with Aneas and Cynthia to gather ferns and pine boughs for bedding.

If she was surprised to see the youngest Muriens working so hard, his shirt off and his body shining with sweat, she didn't show it.

Shelters were going up rapidly in the little clearing by the lake. Three fires were started in a long trench. There were tripods at either end of the trench, and poles laid across the tripods, and bronze and brass pots hung on the poles by chains. They were full of water fetched from the stream.

She had never seen anything quite like it. It was as if a house had grown from the pine needles.

Aneas paused, his arms full of pine boughs. "It is a lot of work," he said. "Most nights we simply bed down on the ground."

"But?" she asked.

"We think it will rain—hard. And we have decisions to make." He began to walk away.

"May I use your belt axe?" she asked.

He grinned. "Of course. Be careful..."

"It's sharp," she said for him, in Archaic.

He smiled and went off, and she began to use his razor-sharp belt axe to cut the soft boughs from stunted pines.

An Outwaller warrior she didn't know came and stripped the weapon out of her hand. He was angry. He shouted and she forced herself to stand up to him.

Looks-at-Clouds appeared from the trees and took the man by the shoulder. He spat.

"You are cutting too many branches," Looks-at-Clouds said. "Look. The tree will die."

Irene frowned. "There seems no shortage of trees," she said. "And it is so small."

"It may be as old as these giants," Looks-at-Clouds said. "And the same might be said of people. There are so many. Who will miss a small one. You, perhaps?" But the shaman smiled agreeably and handed the belt axe, haft first, back to Irene. "Take a few branches from each little tree, and walk wider."

Irene sighed, fighting the urge to return anger with anger, and did as she was told.

When all the shelters were floored in pine boughs and ferns, every ranger put her pack into a shelter.

Irene watched with something approaching horror.

Aneas picked up her pack. "You get the width of your pack for sleeping," he said pleasantly. "You are between me and Lantorn. When we trust you, you can choose your sleeping partners."

The thought of touching Lantorn made Irene pause. She saw a flash of the fawn, its guts . . . "Not him," she said. "Please."

Aneas thought a moment. "Very well," he said. He called something, and the shaman whistled like a bird and did an odd thing, almost like a caper by a newborn lamb.

"You may have the *bacsa* on your other side," Aneas said. "The *bacsa* is delighted to be your companion."

Irene flushed.

Aneas smiled and she could tell he was annoyed. "Looks-at-Clouds likes you," he said. There was a complex tone to his words.

She was still considering what he might mean when she was asked to stir a pot, and she did, watching as men sewed and women sharpened weapons. Two men she didn't know asked if they could use "her" fire for a pot of pitch.

She laughed. "Not my fire," she said.

That seemed to puzzle them.

Cigne, the Occitan woman, appeared in a shirt and nothing else. "Hey, Moth!" she yelled in Alban at a big, well-muscled man who might as easily have been a knight as a ranger.

The man so addressed came and sketched a bow. He was wearing a loincloth and had a flower in his hair.

"Women bathe," Cigne said. "Take her pot."

"Bertran de la Mothe," the handsome man said with a bow. Irene wasn't sure she'd ever seen a man her own age so nearly naked. She flushed.

"A pleasure to take your pot," he said.

"Don't let his hands within reach of your boobs," Cigne said. "It's not your princess-ness he's after, eh, Moth?"

"You entirely malign me, cruel lady," de la Mothe said.

Cigne nodded to Irene. "Coming?" she asked. She led the way, and they caught Tessen, the irk woman, and Cynthia, also wearing a man's shirt and no more. They walked through open woods where there was no trail, and emerged onto a beach screened from the campsite by a rocky headland and a turn in the lake.

Cynthia and Cigne stripped their shirts off and ran into the water.

The irk was slightly more shy. She walked a little way apart and stripped in the trees. Irene was eager to emulate her, eager to wash away the sweat and the peculiar, sticky grime on her hands and apparently her eyelids. She stripped off her linen kirtle and her shift, which was not nearly as brown with dirt as she'd expected, and the halter she wore to support her breasts. She folded her clothes carefully and walked to the edge of the water and...

...it was very cold. She gave out a little scream as her feet touched it and she froze, arms crossed over her breasts.

Cigne was floating a few paces away. She laughed. "I'd tell you it gets better," she said, and Irene could see her lips had a blue tinge. "But I'd be lying." The Occitan woman stood up in the shallow water and began to wash herself.

Tessen was swimming. She was already far out in the lake.

There was another head there, swimming strongly.

"Ah," Cynthia said. "Tonight our *bacsa* is a woman. Soap, Irene?"

"Christ Pantokrator!" Irene said, forcing herself into the water. "Does the *bacsa* change?"

"All the time," Cynthia said. "Oh, Judas-it-is-cold."

"They call it Cold Lake," Cigne said. "For reasons." She smiled.

They were all trying to be friendly.

Looks-at-Clouds swam up to the beach, arm over arm like a racer, and rose to her feet. Even in the evening light, she was obviously a woman, albeit a very slim, flat-breasted woman with hard arm muscles and an abdomen of iron. Her tattoos were impossible to read and spiraled down her arms, and she had a cuff of tattoo on each thigh just above the knee and a girdle of runes around her loins.

The *bacsa* found Irene's eye on her and laughed, and Irene flushed from her navel to her throat in the cold water. The Outwaller kept laughing, and Irene, moved by a happy childhood memory, cupped water and splashed the Outwaller, and in seconds all four were casting arms full of icy water into each other and screaming like girls.

But the cold water was oddly exhausting. Cigne gave her soap and she washed, very thoroughly, under Looks-at-Clouds's direction, especially her neck and face and hair. The tall Outwaller came and put a hand on her waist and pulled her close, so they touched, and she froze, but the shaman was only smelling her.

"Good," the shaman said. She was released, and blushed again.

The sky was still clear. The women—and whatever the *bacsa* was—dried themselves with their linen shirts and then used them to dry their hair a little, and then put them on. Cynthia washed hers.

"*Honi soit qui mal y pense*," she said, putting on her now-transparent shirt.

"She wants the Moth," Cigne said.

Cynthia shrugged.

Cigne laughed. "I rather fancy Lantorn," she said. "But I can't tell if he fancies me, or anyone besides his bow." She smiled at her partner. "And I won't wet my shirt to see what he looks at, either."

"Perhaps I just wanted a clean shirt," Cynthia said.

Irene was afraid to appear so naked in front of men, and the comments of the women made her writhe, but no volley of catcalls greeted them in camp. In fact, most of the men were newly bathed too, and they sat on logs, combing out each other's hair with horn combs.

"We don't get to bathe every day," Aneas said. He was seated on a rock, and he was also naked except for a shirt. "But we're safe enough here, and we have guards out. We don't have to hunt today, thanks to some luck." He smiled at her. "Sit. I can comb hair."

Irene sat on a mossy log and discovered that it felt lovely on her legs. She smiled. She tried a little bit of flirtation, learned by watching maids.

"Mine is a mess," she said with a smile she thought might be winning.

"Yes," Aneas said. He turned and began to talk to Mingan in another language, as if she were not there.

Lewen, the irk, came and sat opposite her. His hair was already braided, and he lit a pipe from his fire kit and drew deeply on it.

"I think we have to move faster," he said without preamble.

Aneas was invisible behind her. This was confusing to the princess. Each time Lewen spoke, it was as if he was speaking directly to her. And then Aneas Muriens would answer.

"I understand," Aneas said. He wasn't agreeing. He was pulling the comb too hard through her hair.

"They will come at our settlements this way, and the southern Sossag villages. There aren't patrols out of Ticondonaga to stop them anymore." The irk shrugged and passed the pipe. Again, it wasn't passed to her, but to Aneas, who took it and drew deeply.

"Without you, I won't have the swords to make a fight of it," Aneas said.

Lewen shrugged and took the pipe back. "You don't now, my friend. Six or more Rukh?"

"I can't let it go. He's headed for Squash Country." Aneas paused. He wasn't braiding her hair anymore. "I think he's headed for Thorn's Island."

"Tessen says the same."

Aneas grunted. "I only know because of Looks-at-Clouds. Who seems to know Orley better than the rest of us."

"The *bacsa* does what the *bacsa* does. It is a saying among the Huran." Lewen inhaled his smoke again. "I can be at N'gara in five days." He shrugged. "The first two times Orley sent men—or whatever he has now—west, I let you talk me into staying with you. But now there's four or five hundred of his dark creatures lose in the north woods." He blew out and a smoke ring formed. "Or more. I cannot fathom how his adherents gather."

Aneas touched Irene's shoulder. "Do you have a leather thong?" he asked.

She resented being touched. She lost her flirtatious smile and writhed.

Lewen cut a thong from the top of his leggings. His knife was very sharp.

Aneas took the thong and put it in his mouth. Then, when it was wet with saliva, he put it in her hair. She wanted to cry out with disgust.

Lewen read her well. He laughed. "When the deerskin dries,

it shrinks," he said. "Otherwise, they fall out of the hair, even hair as spectacular as yours." He was laughing at her. "I confess I never thought to meet the *porphyrogenitra* by Cold Lake."

She turned her head away so as not to look at him. He was alien, and ancient. His Archaic was flawless. He should have known better. All of them should.

"Perhaps among your kind insolence is normal," she snapped, before she could think.

He stood up. "No, Irene. I recollect how to bow and what to do at a court. This is a different kind of wilderness. You did well today. Why spoil it?"

Aneas waved. "Never mind all this. I'm thinking that you could get Gavin to send me..." He looked at her.

He was wondering whether he could trust her, and it stung.

"Never mind," she spat. She stood up. "I'm just a cook. I don't need to be included in your councils." She took a step away, head high...

An owl hooted.

And another.

The reaction was instant, like a fire catching on birch bark. Everyone in camp lunged for something. She saw de la Mothe throw a haubergeon over his bare skin, and Cigne was stringing her bow.

Thunder rumbled.

Lewen was gone when she turned her head.

"Damn. I've been had." Aneas paused only a moment, snapped up his belt axe, and looked at her. "Go to your pack and lie down," Aneas said. His voice was very clear, low, calm.

He was speaking to her as if she were a child.

"Go now," he said.

The owl hooted, and right in front of her, Lantorn made an animal sound and a dozen of Tall Pine's warriors who had stayed with them followed him at a lope. They were silent as predators, and they ran north. Somehow, their painted silence and animal ferocity chilled her.

To her left, Cynthia shrugged into her mail. And then carefully buckled on her sword belt, which also held her quiver.

Nothing else seemed to be happening. For a moment, Irene wondered if this was their idea of a practical joke. She turned her head to look at Aneas.

He was gone.

She looked back for Cynthia, who had been nice to her, and the Alban girl was also gone. The air was calm and warm, and thunder rumbled again in the west, and the sky there was unnaturally dark.

She turned all the way around.

Nothing moved. No birds sang, and no squirrel chittered. There was no breeze.

Then she was *afraid*.

She went to the shelter and lay down where she'd been told, with the packs.

She didn't even have a knife.

But Looks-at-Clouds's axe was on a strap by the *bacsa*'s pack. Irene took it. It made her feel better.

She could see the fire, and the pots, simmering away.

Beyond the fire, she could see the next shelter, and to her left, a narrow patch of woods. Her eye was drawn to it.

It sparkled. The woods *sparkled*.

She looked away and looked back.

It still sparkled.

Then the patch of woods flashed white, like a scene lit by lightning.

And went dark.

She blinked, rapidly, but the woods were the same.

Thunder rolled, very close. The black clouds from the west were piled very high, and the still air was heavy, warm, and felt like danger.

Somewhere to the north, there was a scream.

Irene discovered that she was biting her own arm. She grew angry with herself.

There was another pulse. This one she felt. She had almost no hermetical talent, but she knew when there was *potentia* in the air, and the air was rich with it, like the smell of fish in a fish market.

Suddenly there were more screams. Or perhaps war cries. They were high-pitched and desperate, and went on. It sounded like hundreds of voices, and they were very close.

And then a loud bang.

And another.

She saw the bogglins before she heard them. They stopped at the first fire trench to eat the pot of food. They were spindly and dark brown, and their wing cases were slick and shiny as if they had been oiled. They looked very small, to her, after two days with Krek.

Irene knew they were not on her side.

Even then, a few feet from monsters who would eat her, she wondered what her side was, now.

Another scream.

And then a horn note.

She could feel her heart thudding in her chest. She was lying on her side, and her body felt heavy. When the bogglins stepped around the frame of the structure, they would see her. She wished she had a dagger. She knew how to use a dagger, and she knew how to quickly and neatly end her own life. That was basic training, in the palace.

She drew in the most silent breath she could manage.

The nearest bogglin upended the bronze pot, and the four quarters of his head divided, and he sprayed something at his mates. He made a noise, like sniffing.

And then he had an arrow sticking out of his abdomen. He took several steps, with an extra leg out to catch himself each step, and then he was facedown, with the bronze pot incongruously on his head like a stew-filled helmet.

And the bogglin behind him saw her. It threw down the hardtack it had in its two upper hands and drew a long knife and chittered.

The other bogglins—hitherto just legs, to Irene—whirled, and one grunted and fell.

There was chittering *behind her*. She heard it through the shelter wall.

A sudden darkness fell across the camp. A wind hit—an immense gust, strong enough to drop a tent.

All the little wigwam shelters held.

Thunder crashed, very close.

Irene got to her feet. She was not going to die lying down. She had the axe. And they were all around her. She didn't think bogglins could swim.

She darted to the right, out from between the shelter and the fire, just as the sheet of rain hit the camp. It was like a living thing, visible, fast as a snake, tall as a palace, and the trees swayed before it. A few fell, and their crashes were lost in the sound…

Where, just moments before, all had been silent, now all was noise. There was noise everywhere, a soundless sound—of rain, thunder, high wind, and terror.

Irene swung at the first one she saw, despite her disorientation. She hit something and then she was past. Something cut her—she felt the cut and swung again, and lightning pulsed to complete her sensory overload. More pulses than she could count.

Her feet were on sand, and she kept going, although movement was difficult. She had forgotten how cold the water was, but she cared nothing for it. She ran a few strides in the water and leapt.

The shock of the cold went through her despite her shock.

She swam anyway. She swam for what seemed like a freezing eternity, and the force of the rain backed away, and the lightning pulsed more slowly, and the thunder was merely loud.

She still had the axe. She held it near the head, and swam, even as the cold began to chew at her, and she wanted to let the axe fall from her increasingly numb fingers.

She heard a horn, and another.

Something was very wrong with her. She felt tired—too tired. Too tired to swim.

She turned in the water and a wave of pain struck her from her lower left leg.

I'm cut. Badly cut.

Another horn blast.

She swam.

And swam.

It was cold and she knew she'd lost blood. Too much blood, and she had time to be afraid...of the blood loss, of whatever lived in the water, of what blood attracted, of the men and monsters and everything that was against her.

But then she thought, *By the Imperial Purple, I am not going to die here.*

She focused her not inconsiderable will on swimming. The storm was moving away with amazing rapidity. There were stars to the west, and directly overhead, a little orange light.

Nice light by which to die.

She was not going to die. She managed to get herself back into shallow water. She had never been so cold. She was only fifty paces from the camp, and a long, almost beautiful curl of blood, lit by the last sunlight, trailed away from her left leg and out into the lake.

She turned her head away.

She had a shift on.

She had garters.

She knew what to do.

She made herself ignore the blood. And the sleepiness—it was corrosive. That was the end. She knew it. She had never been closer to death, not even with assassins killing her maids.

I will not die here.

She unbuckled the garter despite her numb and curiously unwilling hands. She moved it lower on her left leg.

God, or the Virgin, sent her a stick. A healthy, strong piece of oak, under her rump. She pulled it out—flotsam from some old beaver dam—and slipped it through the garter, and twisted.

It hurt.

Sweet Mary, mother of God, Holy Virgin, pray for us now and in the hour of our death.

The blood flow all but stopped.

Her heart was beating very, very hard.

The garter was stretching. But it was woven silk—one of her own things, scarlet silk from home. That thought strengthened her, that here, in the Wild, she had the imperial red of her home to save her life.

Porphyrogenitra.

I will not die here.

She sat in the icy water, and the rain fell on her. She was ten feet off shore.

The blood stopped.

The horns sounded again.

Maybe ten paces away, a monster burst from the lakeside undergrowth. It was naked, with enormous, almost caricaturist testicles. It was more than ten feet high, and it had a dozen arrows in it. It roared its rage.

Bertran de la Mothe stepped out of the woods behind it and shot it from very close.

It turned.

Ricard Lantorn shot it from the other side, a range of perhaps twenty feet. The sound of his heavy quarter-pound arrow going home was the meaty sound of a man's fist striking another man in a boxing match.

The giant's head turned from de la Mothe to Lantorn.

He took a great stride.

Lantorn looked startled. Afraid.

De la Mothe put another arrow into the giant, and it stumbled.

Lantorn drew an axe from his belt and threw. It was not a small axe, and it struck just above the groin and the axe head went deep into the thing's vitals. They exploded out of his abdomen, a cascade of guts where its severed abdominal muscles no longer held them in.

Irene kept hold of her garter and the stick. But she found the axe under her where she'd dropped it in her fumbling for the garter. She was trembling—shaking.

The giant fell.

A bolt of lightning fell from the sky and immolated de la Mothe. It left an imprint on her retinas.

Lantorn winded his horn immediately, and three more horns sounded back.

"Help!" whispered Irene.

There were bogglins moving in the brush, just a few yards away.

Lantorn sounded his horn again and ran.

A second bolt of lightning sliced through the rain and blew a tree to fragments, but Lantorn rolled like an acrobat. He pulled his axe from the writhing giant's corpse and threw it again in one step, killing a bogglin. Then he drew the short, broad-bladed sword and cut straight from the draw into a second bogglin, and the others broke. They skittered back.

Strong hand came under Irene's armpits and she was hauled to her feet.

A heavily muscled Outwaller pulled at her. She slumped—and the Outwaller swept her off her feet and threw her over his shoulder.

She screamed.

Lantorn was ten paces away, and every one of those paces was filled with brown bogglins.

From her position on the Outwaller's shoulder, she could see the horns growing from his head. She opened her mouth to scream.

She awoke with a fire almost by her face.

She was naked. Lying by a fire.

Her injured leg was dead. Not even pins and needles in it.

She fought the whimper in her throat.

There were horned men all around her, and she could smell the bogglins, and she was cold, and terror went all the way through her.

Irene feared rape and degradation. For herself, and because she was *porphyrogenitra* and degradation of her body was degradation of the empire, or so she saw it.

I will not let . . .

One of the horned men came and stood over her. He didn't laugh, or mock her. She had never seen one of them close, and he was big, his muscles curiously twisted as if in a mockery of the way a strong man might look. Like a tree that had endured too many storms.

Despite the terror and blood loss, her head was clear. Or perhaps because . . .

The antlered man's head was too small for his frame. The antlers were incongruous, and there was dried blood where they sprouted from his head.

His face held no expression. His eyes were dead.

He knelt and put a hand between her legs.

She spat at him. It was the only resistance she could make.

He hit her.

And then he was gone. He was on his face, lying with his arms spread in the wet pine needles, an arm's length away. He still said nothing, but merely lay at the feet of a taller, bigger antlered man. Worshipping.

"No," the Stag said. "Mine."

Irene's gorge rose, and she vomited into the fire. The Stag was a foot taller than his creature, with slabs of flesh that might have come from different muscled animals and the rack of a great hart of sixteen tines atop his head.

She was so weak she simply slumped back. Somewhere deep in the recesses of her head, she thought, *I have lost so much blood; perhaps if I open the tourniquet, I will die.*

The antlered men were all bowing to the Stag.

Irene's left hand went slowly down her thigh to her knee.

And her left hand found the buckle.

My curse on you, Gabriel Muriens. And on you, Stag man.

Perhaps she whimpered.

He crossed the clearing in two strides and his vast, naked foot came down on her hand, crushing her wrist.

"You are mine," his voice said. It was a chillingly normal voice. The sort of voice of a councillor or a wise soldier. "Your life is no longer yours." He knelt slowly by her, as if his knees were stiff.

386

He wore armour—good armour, the steel of Mitla with precisely rolled edges. She had time to notice it all, because everything moved so slowly. His armour was all brown and rust at the edges.

Close up in the firelight, he stank like carrion.

Her gorge rose again, because close up, she could see that the armour was *fixed to him*. There were pins into his flesh and bone, and they bled in rivulets onto the steel.

His eyes were like any man's eyes. They were brown, and sad, and full of pain.

He leaned closer. She could smell the blood, smell fear and old meat and dead things.

"Who are you?" he asked. He put a hand on her face. There were iron plates fixed to the back of the hand. With sinew.

She screamed.

He put a hand on her mouth. And another over her heart, on her breast. He was kneeling on her broken wrist and the pain was excruciating and then . . .

He stood up.

He looked down at her.

The pain was *gone*.

And there was something in her head. Something black, like an egg.

"A princess of the empire!" he said. "Oh, Lord Ash, you have sent me a wife."

The morning after the attack on the camp. Aneas had healed the wounded, and they had buried the dead.

His dreams were unpleasant, but that had happened before. He wished for the comfort of veteran captains like Turkos or Tall Pine, but they were far to the east by now, or so he had to hope, and he made do with Mingan, who was as young as he was himself. He knew that he had *won* the ambush by Cold Lake. But the loss of Irene made him feel that he had failed, and his hatred of Kevin Orley now seared him with a burn of personal failure.

Mingan laughed and suggested that perhaps youth made them stupid enough to succeed.

Aneas took no comfort in that, but he didn't stop the pursuit.

They had been climbing for so long that Aneas had lapsed into the pure misery of moving too fast for comfort. He knew he was moving too fast. He knew that he didn't have the swords to face the horned men. He *knew* he had made all the wrong decisions.

He knew that he had lost Irene. Lantorn had seen her taken.

Since the loss of his mother, nothing had affected him like her loss. It was a failure of his knighthood.

He had begun to like her, and had been responsible for her.

He came to the first opening in the trees and stopped.

Lantorn came up behind him and gave a grunt.

They were high. How high was hard for him to say. Below him, the Adnacrags rolled like a carpet—a wet and bumpy carpet, but it was all laid out below him.

An eagle turned circles, and it was below him.

Aneas opened his chart, and looked at it, and a tiny nimbus of hermetical power flickered over his sweaty eyebrows.

Lantorn made a face.

Looks-at-Clouds put a hand on his shoulder. "Look there," s/he said. "The Inner Sea."

And indeed, beyond the line of cloud, and the eagle, and the lower mountains and the farther lakes, there was a ribbon of blue to the west and north, a ribbon that faded into the horizon. The Outwallers exclaimed at the wonder of it, pointed, offered tobacco to the sun and the cardinal points.

That night they had a cold camp. They ate dried food, and not much of it. They worked no *potentia*.

In fact, Aneas had brought them up so high to watch the earth for other workings. And not to reveal themselves.

So he sat with Looks-at-Clouds for hours as darkness fell and the stars rose and filled the sky. The stars were superb. He had never seen anything like it. He laid out his blanket on dry grass and lay on it and watched the stars move in the heavens. And suffered for the depth of his failure.

If only...

In fact, the fight in the old camp had been a victory. He'd lost two of his own, and hurt Orley's party far worse, killing five of his Rukh and decimating his bogglins with a single working.

But at the moment that mattered, he'd been too far from the camp. He didn't even think Orley had *planned* to take Irene.

Looks-at-Clouds lay down next to him. "She is alive," the *bacsa* said. "I feel her. Something bad is in her head."

"Christ," Aneas muttered.

Then he felt the prickle of power, off to the north.

He was out of his blankets in one motion, and he was suddenly freezing.

He stood there, under the stars.

"I feel it," Looks-at-Clouds said.

Aneas made his way to the little ledge from which they'd watched the north country, kicking someone's horn cup in the thick darkness and breaking a heavy stick. It sounded very loud in the night, but it was a distant enemy they feared.

Looks-at-Clouds rolled clear of the blankets. And looked out.

"Got him," Aneas said. "Damn it. We are gaining!"

Looks-at-Clouds grunted. "He casts much power."

Aneas laughed grimly. "He's looking for us. And mayhap his missing Rukh."

Looks-at-Clouds watched in the *aethereal* for a long time. "He is seeking to break her mind," s/he said. "To make her one of his antlered men." S/he smiled. "I can work with that."

Three days of walking, a prisoner, a slave. The only humiliation not offered was sex; otherwise, she was chattel, ordered to fetch, to carry, struck casually. At first, she'd expected Orley to protect her, but he made no move to, and when he smiled to see her struck, his antlered men became bolder.

Her leg, where he'd healed it, had a long black scar, like a tattoo. It bothered her, that something of him was now part of her, and it bothered her more when she saw one of the antlered men naked, and saw that his body was crisscrossed with black scars.

And he'd put something in her head.

And she had bruises. Nothing more, yet, but she feared...everything. And she was polluted by the thing in her head.

At night, in camp, he assaulted her mind. For this, she was prepared; although she had no hermetical powers, she was, as a princess of the empire, fully trained in self-protection. She had high walls of white marble, and although he stained them with blood and ordure, although he burned them with fire, and sent disgusting *things* to climb them leaving trails of acid that burned at her walls, she held him back...the black thing in her mind was like a traitor inside the castle, but she walled it off, cocooned it in other thoughts.

The second time that it sent emanations into her white walls, she almost succumbed. The images were dark and seductive, not repulsive. But still far from overpowering her.

In the end, she could build her walls as fast as or faster than it could belch black. And in the morning, she felt less—afraid. It was difficult to explain, even to herself, but the victory inside her head—her resistance—was *helping*.

But to resist him, she had to be awake, and every night left her weaker.

She found herself sleeping as they walked. Antlered men struck her to wake her, or jabbed branches into her legs. She no longer had her pack or her light shoes, and everything hurt.

Still, her mind ran on. She even went so far as to imagine open alliance with Orley, or outward surrender. But she could not imagine submitting to him; the smell, and the armour that was somehow part of him, raised her gorge. There was no one with whom she could negotiate, and nothing palpable she could offer.

There were other captives. At some point, the war band had struck a settlement, probably off to the east, near Long Lake and Ticondonaga. There were a few children and as many women, and they did all the camp work. When any of them angered an antlered man, they were struck. On the third day, one of them was beheaded, and her body was left in the camp, the head nearby, gathering flies. Another of the antlered monsters stuck a little knife in her, as if trying to prod her to work. He grunted, and moved the knife. The woman, dead, did not move, and the antlered one spat on her in anger and perhaps disgust, and rose. He sniffed, and walked back to the fire.

After three days of abuse, it was the casual murder of the woman that spurred Irene to action. She decided that she had to escape, even if it resulted only in her death. She knew how to take her own life. And the knife in the dead woman would be her release. She moved boldly, or as boldly as her swollen feet and bruised arms allowed. She went to the corpse and tried to pull the knife free. It was caught in bone— perhaps the reason it had been abandoned in the first place. She waited for a shout, for discovery, as she worked the knife back and forth, twisting it carefully in the corpse, striving not to break the blade.

Her back was to the fire. She could only imagine that they were all looking at her. That her death or worse was on the wing.

Out in the woods, a Rukh bellowed. Orley had all the allies he could want...bogglins, Rukh, even a few dozen irks, as well as his antlered men.

The women watched her. Two with dull, dead eyes, but the other pair whispered to each other.

The knife moved. It moved perhaps the width of a fingernail, but that promised her everything. She had no plan, but her determination was now absolute.

She forced herself not to look over her shoulder.

She moved the handle back and forth, back and forth. She thought of the fawn.

Lantorn seemed like a hero to her, now.

I will do this, she thought, and lo, the knife came free, slipping from the dead woman's flesh like a scabbard.

Personal cleanliness was no longer on her objectives. She slipped the knife, sticky with another woman's blood, into the garter she'd used to tie off her leg three nights before. It was warm against her skin. As long as she had it, she could arrange her own death in three or four beats of her heart, and this alone raised her spirits.

The two whispering women watched her.

She fell asleep as soon as she sat down while the captives gathered firewood. She awoke to pain—Orley stood over her with a stick.

"Go work, wife," he said. "That's what women are for. Work."

She grunted, still incoherent with the pain of the blow he'd struck to her side. And then her panicked mind seized on the knife. Her single stained shift was rucked up around her. Was it above the garter?

"But in three days," he said, and he licked his lips. "I'll find something else for my wife to do." He laughed. "My empress." He nodded at her, his eyes neither mad nor bestial. "You are the fit wife for the Orley of Ticondonaga. But you must be mine absolutely. I would not share you, not even with my master, but he insists. And to be fair, he is in my head, too." He laughed again, and this time he did sound mad.

He turned, his armoured skin silent, and walked away over the forest loam.

The knife was still there.

When they cooked that night, one leaned over. "You gonna run?" she asked.

Irene met her eye and pursed her lips. She didn't have a smile in her. The woman nodded. "Take me."

"They'll catch us," Irene said carefully.

The woman shrugged as if indifferent.

By then, Irene had her plan. It was absurd and desperate, but the knife made her bold. She could triumph in death, and she knew what the future held. It was never going to get any better.

Orley's assault began late, and caught her asleep. But this was the fourth night of his attacks, and she was learning. Tonight, she lay as quiet as possible, allowing his infiltration, hoarding her forces, waiting.

All or nothing.

She imagined his darkness storming her citadel. She imagined what she would become... perhaps he would augment her flesh as he had done to his antlered men.

She happened to think of the *bacsa*, Looks-at-Clouds, and the image of the changeling came unbidden before her, as if she had summoned the shaman.

S/he kissed Irene on her dream lips. *We are coming for you,* s/he said. And suddenly Irene was flooded with something, some power like young love, like hot, pure anger, like carefully nursed rage, like untrammeled joy. She lacked a word to express it, but it came with the words and the kiss, and she took a deep breath and attacked the darkness.

She carefully reinforced the internal walls that surrounded the darkness, and then she attacked, and her new allies drove Orley's slime from her walls and routed his sludge and his dung and his black blood. His images were tired, banal, the chaos of disease and putrescence feared and sometimes loved by children, and she had to hold her hand from annihilating them, for fear that she would provoke a new attack, but on other nights he had only come at her once.

She lay in the cool air, feeling the bodies of the two women on either side of her. The stars wheeled overhead, cold and uncaring. She yearned for their distance, and she reached for them with her thoughts

just for a moment there was some sort of slipping

She snapped back. She had scared herself. She lay a moment, shaking, trying to imagine what had just happened to her.

She conjured the image of Looks-at-Clouds. Closed her eyes and all but clenched them shut.

And there...

I'm running. Now Help I

She couldn't hold the image.

She lay still again. Opened her eyes to watch the stars.

The stars were gone.

Just for a moment she choked, mortal terror flooding her.

And then her rational, trained mind told her that there were clouds coming in, moving fast, covering the moon and stars. In fact, when she turned her head, she could see the last stars winking out...

...and the woman next to her, awake.

The camp was not quiet. The antlered men were not quiet sleepers, and whatever had been done to them came at a cost. They moaned, or screamed, or talked, or, in some cases, whimpered.

Something was happening. She could feel it, with a tinge of joy at her victory, and a secret pleasure in having reached the shaman. She wanted to believe... to believe...

"Now," she said. She got to her feet. They hurt, and her hips hurt, her neck hurt, and she cared not.

She rose to her feet and walked. It was utterly dark, and the air suddenly smelled of rain.

The other women were moving behind her. She heard them, too loud, and she kept going. She had very little altruism in her; she knew that if they were pursued, the other women could slow the pursuit merely by being caught and tormented or killed. But another part of her thought about what it would be like to present herself to Looks-at-Clouds with two women rescued from this hell.

She paused. "This way," she said with the icy assurance of sixty generations of absolutism.

In the morning, they ate cold sausage and berries. There were only seven of the original rangers left, and Mingan's dozen warriors of all the Outwallers who had started.

Aneas had his pack on before the rest of them were fully up.

"Orley is going to make it to the Mille Isles unless we can catch him. He will cross to the Squash Country," he said. "He'll go to the Sacred Island and raise a new army."

Lantorn cleared his throat. "He 'as more critters now 'an when he started," he said.

Aneas looked around. "If we keep tracking him," he said, "and if Gabriel or Gavin send us aid—then our effort isn't wasted. If we break contact now, it's all to be done again." He didn't say *and we will doom Irene*.

No one spoke.

Aneas nodded.

"Why track him, then?" Tessen asked. "We know where he is going."

Wart, the Jack, nodded, but then shook his head. "'Cause he might go for N'gara to link up with his master, or go agin' the folk of the Squash Country." He raised an eyebrow at Aneas. "I'm an old Jack, mister. No one's a lord to me. But I'm wi' ye. If there ever was purpose to bein' allies, it's now. To keep this critter out of the Adnacrags, an' off all the people."

The bogglin, Krek, nodded. It made a noise with one leg and a wing case.

Cigne smiled. "I don't even know where we are," she said. "In the old Smokes west of my home, I know the leaves and the names of the squirrels. Here?" She brushed a scrubby mountain pine. "It's cold at night in *August*." She made a face. "But I'll follow you, Ser Aneas."

Lantorn shrugged. "Only seven o' we," he said. "But I tol' Ser Gabriel I'd watch the princess, and I reckon to have her back. I should na' ha' lost her."

Cynthia smiled and Lewen, the irk, laughed.

"I don't want to go back," Aneas said.

Looks-at-Clouds looked at Mingan.

The young war leader shrugged. "Tall Pine told me to help you," he said. "I will stay to the end. He gave a hard smile. "I don't want to be the one who says: don't go."

Looks-at-Clouds shrugged. "None of us do," s/he said. "Let's go."

The next day they moved fast—so fast that they all regretted their brave words, and spent the day in head-down, trudging, footsore misery. It rained in the afternoon, and in early evening they came to a wide road that ran along the base of a broad valley. Lantorn and Wart and Aneas all knew it.

They decided to go all night without any discussion. The road aided rapid movement, and apparently it was a spur of the north road from Ticondonaga, and only went their way a dozen miles. The seven put their heads down and walked, and the stones in the ruts cut their moccasined feet, and the only sign each of them could see was the pale shape of a pack in front in the near-perfect darkness lit only by stars. Lewen and Tessen took turns leading.

After midnight, when the moon began to set, Looks-at-Clouds stopped, suddenly, and hissed. The chain of rangers broke and became a huddle in the trees just north of the road.

"Ha!" Looks-at-Clouds said. "I have her!"

Aneas made a small working, and lit a small candle that Lantorn put in a wrapper of birch bark, and most of the rangers lit their pipes while Tessen walked off to guard them.

"Have her how?" Aneas asked.

"She is walking in the cloud country," Looks-at-Clouds said. "Hah!"

The *bacsa*'s eyes opened. "I must go back," s/he said, and this time s/he went far and deep, so the shaman's face by candlelight was blank and still as that of a corpse.

"Why did she call you and not me?" Aneas asked.

No one answered.

Time passed, and more time, and then:

"Now. We must move. Aneas!" The changeling's eyes were wide open. S/he took Aneas's hand and suddenly he was as blank as s/he.

And then both of them rolled to their feet.

"Too far to reach her tonight," Aneas said.

"We must trust to Tar and her daughters," Looks-at-Clouds said.

Aneas paused. "Wait," he said. He cast, and then cast again.

"Ah!" Looks-at-Clouds muttered, clearly impressed.

He piled on his third working and cast.

"Tell me when to release it," he said. "How I wish I could fly."

"Noon," Looks-at-Clouds said. "And better...if she comes toward us, every step is a gain."

Aneas nodded, and they were off.

"You found the princess?" Lantorn said.

Aneas nodded at Looks-at-Clouds.

"Ambush?" Lantorn asked. They were jogging.

Aneas grunted, and they ran on.

The rain struck almost immediately after they started, and it pounded them, a thunderhead as bad as the one the night of the fight in camp when she had been taken.

But Irene had a beautiful sense of direction, which was to say, she could sense where the shaman was as if there was a light burning in the forest. She continued in that direction, occasionally hitting trees and once ploughing into a small swamp ringed with alder that all but imprisoned her and the two women in her wake. On the other side lay two Rukh, huddled miserably in the rain, their huge shapes silhouetted by lightning, and she passed so close to the nearest that she swore she could feel the heat of his body, and then she was gone into the rain.

And the rain fell like hail, like pellets of metal. It fell like a physical force, obliterating sound, washing her skin. She was cold and wet, but free.

There was no way to measure time, and they communicated by shouts. At some point she decided they must be free of the camp, and she paused, looking back, and the woman who had spoken to her at the fire bumped into her. Lightning flashed.

"Irene," she said.

"Joan," panted the other. "Where's Polly?"

"Polly?" they both shrieked.

And then they were moving again. They didn't wait for Polly, and when, some time later, lightning showed Irene a third woman, she could claim no credit.

At some point Polly screamed and they turned. She was down, rolling in the flashes, and they lost too much time finding that she had stepped on a sharpened stick—they were at the edge of a beaver meadow, in full darkness. The sky was lighter.

Irene shook her head at no one. "We must keep going. Follow me."

Polly got up as if she were conjured and hobbled, and Irene led the way into the cloud of alders at the edge of the meadow. She couldn't see individual stems, but the mass was visible and she clawed at it, pushed, slid, and the two women followed her, passing over and then under, so soaked by the rain that the alder caused them no hesitation.

She burst through the alder just as she heard the roar behind her, an inarticulate cry of rage from the other side of the ridge.

That pushed her as nothing else had, and she began to cross the meadow. She got three steps and her left leg sank in up to her thigh and she was down in the muck, pulling herself along, and the other two women were no better off. The rain was filling the meadow.

She crawled, got upright again, and there were three mighty flashes of light, two a natural white and the third a malevolent red, but the combination gave her almost a full second of light and she saw the beaver dam to her right and called, "Follow me!" and got her feet under her. She was on the dam, and then crossing it, suddenly aware of how huge the dam was, and Polly, or perhaps Joan, screamed, and she turned. She placed her foot wrong, and in the darkness and rain, she fell straight into the deep water off the dam.

It closed over her head, and she thought, briefly, of staying down in its embrace and ending it all, safe and clean.

She thought, of all people, about Joan and Polly. After all, only she could see the shining beacon of the *bacsa*.

The bottom under her feet was thick, sludgy silt, like Orley's mind, and she overcame it and rose into the night. Her head broke the water and she struggled back up onto the dam.

She knelt a moment, looking back. It was lighter; somewhere far away, dawn was coming. She could see movement, and she guessed it to be Joan, who seemed bigger and more competent now.

It was then, curled up, coated in mud, atop the dam that she realized that she'd lost the knife.

Her breathing grew shallow, and she had difficulty controlling the racing of her heart, and there was a staglike bellow from the ridge behind her, and a gout of red fire.

For a moment, she paused and prayed. She wasn't even sure to whom she prayed—perhaps the Virgin Mother, perhaps the *bacsa*. Perhaps Saint Aeteas.

It was better than the whimper that might have escaped, and then she spat.

"Follow me," she said.

They could only run so far, and by the false dawn they were walking. Thunder rumbled to the north, close, and lightning flashed, but nothing fell on them.

"Orley is awake," Looks-at-Clouds said. As if to confirm her words, red light flashed to the north and west.

Aneas raised an eyebrow. "I'll try," he said, and released his castings. There was no palpable effect, and no one had any breath to ask, and they kept walking.

*

Irene had to force herself not to look back, and the three of them crashed through the alders on the far side of the meadow. The growing grey light revealed it as wide, and the river that flowed through it was substantial, and Irene wished she had some means to destroy the dam.

She did not, so she ran on. Light, and widely spaced beech trees on a ridge, gave them the chance to run, and all three women did, but days of torment told, and the running came in bursts punctuated by tortured walking. The bursts of speed became more infrequent, and the malevolent red light came on faster.

"You got that knife?" Polly asked.

"Lost it," Irene panted.

The other women didn't even curse. But they did seem to deflate.

From the top of the ridge, they could see in every direction despite the late-summer foliage, and Irene risked a glance back, where she expected to see Orley towering in his rage, but there was nothing to be seen. The meadow was broad and deep and most of it was hidden in a fold of the earth.

But suddenly, red fire rose from the meadow, burning like the light of a falling star, and shot past her to the south. And then again, and again.

"Come!" Irene said.

"Fuck it," Joan said. She slumped.

"No," said Irene. "We will win free. By God and Saint Aeteas, I will see you free. Follow me."

"Who are you?" asked Polly.

Irene paused. "No one," she said. "But your guide. Now shut up and *follow me.*"

They walked through the dawn, which was beautiful despite Aneas's growing despair. To the north and west, thunder rolled on, and just at dawn, three massive gouts of red fire rose like false sunrises and fell to the south, and they felt rather than heard the huge workings detonate far behind them.

Looks-at-Clouds slapped Aneas on the back and grinned.

"Two leagues," he said. "Stop. String your bows. Get ready. This will be ugly."

All of the rangers stopped.

Lantorn dropped his pack. "Fuck it," he said. "If I don't die, I'll come back for it."

Tessen nodded and dropped hers, took her bow and strung it, and Lewen did the same, bending it against the ground, a slim bow of a wood that seemed as hard as metal.

The woods came alive with the first true light, and there were flowers by the banks of a stream; a meadow full of beaver who stood on their lodges and cursed the intruders, and then a flutter of faeries, burning in the morning mist like jewels.

Looks-at-Clouds walked down among them when the others held back.

"Unseelie things, faeries," Lantorn said.

But the *bacsa* had them land on each hand and each shoulder, and was bathed in their pastel light. S/he seemed to be singing to them, crooning tunelessly.

And then they were gone, and the meadow was grey and empty.

"We are closer than I thought," Looks-at-Clouds said. "The faeries hate Orley. They call him the soul thief. The princess is still herself. She has strong walls and a tall castle. He has not broken her yet."

Aneas looked tormented.

Looks-at-Clouds shrugged. "Women are far tougher than men think," s/he said.

Aneas looked around at his people. Swords were loosened, and every ranger put arrows through their belt, ready to hand. The irks put poison on theirs, carefully, and the time seemed to pass like honey dripping, and ten times, a hundred times, Aneas considered going, leaving them.

But the odds were insane enough already. They needed to be prepared.

He filled the time building webs and hanging them in corners of his palace, ready to hand, and Looks-at-Clouds did the same, his/her face serene.

Then Tessen stripped the deerskin gloves from her hands and threw them into the water to her right. "Ready," she said.

"Ready," Lewen said.

The others nodded.

"She is still free," Looks-at-Clouds said. "I am about to…"

Thunder crashed, quite close.

"Deep V," Aneas called.

In a moment, the rest of them were gone, spreading in pairs to the right and left, so that Aneas was left with Looks-at-Clouds in the center. It was a formation they had practiced many times, and the Outwaller warriors went to the west while Lantorn led the rest of the rangers to the east.

Aneas gave them a few more long minutes, and then started forward, with Looks-at-Clouds pointing directions to him.

Irene decided to stay on the ridge. It didn't run directly to the moving point that was the shaman, but it was like a paved road compared to the valleys full of beaver swamp and alder hell.

She kept going. But now she made herself pause for the other women, even when her whole being cried out for her to run. She was sure that she could outdistance Orley, though. Something had slowed him.

But the other two women were slower and slower. The ridge petered out and they had to descend; one more ghastly marsh, with deep mud and cattails.

"We are close to rescue!" she said, a dozen times, dragging them out into the open. They were most of the way across the open, falling from one hump of dry ground to the next, coated in mud and bits of rotting bark. Irene dragged herself up on the far bank, eyeing the next ridge for the easiest approach through the alders

Joan sat down on a log and burst into tears.

Irene struck her.

Joan cringed, and Irene hated her—and herself, for striking the wretched woman. "Damn it, Joan!" she said. "We're *that* close! Come on!"

"Leave me," Joan said. She was weeping.

"Fuck that," Polly said, "Grab her, Reen."

So the two women went some hundreds of paces, crashing through the alders, ignoring the cuts to their faces and the backs of their hands, and behind them they could hear what seemed like the baying of hounds. The antlered men were hot on their scent.

They ran on, holding Joan between them, until the woman was shamed into running, or perhaps something changed in her heart, or the terror slipped a little away.

"This is the last!" Irene said. "Almost there!"

"Almost where?" Joan moaned, but Irene conveyed enough hope that the three broke into an exhausted stumble.

And then everything happened at once.

Joan fell. When she fell, she lay still, and Irene started back for her. She hadn't looked back for a long time, and there were a dozen antlered men, close enough to touch.

She had time to draw herself upright.

Arrows came from every side, and Irene fell flat before she became a pincushion. She got a glimpse of one antlered man hit a dozen times, and another turning to race away.

She lay in the leaf mold and panted. It did not seem that she could do any more, and it took time for her to realise what the arrows meant.

Polly was behind a log. "Friends of yours?" she asked.

Suddenly the forest was quiet. No bird sang, no one moved.

She felt the pulse in her head.

"Down!"

Red fire burned. A ball of pure flame struck close enough to cause a flash through her tightly closed eyelids, and a wash of brutal heat that seemed as if it ought to dry her shift or burn it off her body.

The heat didn't go away.

Orley had lit the forest.

A stand of spruce caught immediately, almost exploding into a pitch-filled fireball despite the recent rain, and Orley cast again, searching for his foes, and another explosion rocked the woods, blowing age-old trees off their roots and igniting them like sticks tossed into a big winter camp fire.

Irene could feel him casting.

"Run!" she called, her voice all but lost in the roar of the swelling fire. But she was up, and Polly saw her, and she had Joan's arm, and then Joan was up and the three of them ran south.

Another gout of fire, this one to the right, very close, and Irene was blown off her feet by the wind off the fire, and sticks and splinters hit her. She didn't pause. She rolled to her feet and ran.

The woods were catching fire all around her. And the trees, as they caught, blew sparks and burning cinders into the air and they burned her and still she ran, with energy she hadn't imagined she had just a few heartbeats before, and Joan and Polly ran with her, stride for stride.

She looked up, and there was Aneas, shoulder to shoulder with Looks-at-Clouds. He was glowing a bright green, and even as she watched he threw and disk of green and gold into the air where it spun like a child's toy.

Calm as a statue, Looks-at-Clouds leveled two fingers and made a click with her tongue, and a slim missile of blue fire shot between the women and vanished over Irene's shoulder.

Then she smiled at Irene. "Welcome," she said, as if she had time and nothing better to do than greet her lost friend.

Irene felt the pressure in her head, and then a red flash, and fire fell on Aneas's spinning disk and slid off, exploding into the woods to the west.

The line of fire now covered the whole ridge.

Aneas put his horn to his lips, and Looks-at-Clouds put his/her hands on the two women. Both women's eyes widened, and they exhaled together.

Aneas winded his horn, long and loud.

Then he put a hand on Irene's shoulder, as if to steady her. "Try this," he said, cheerfully.

Then he turned, and ran, and she followed him as if she'd had food and sleep and love for days.

The rest of the day was a blur of hellish running punctuated by draughts of raw *ops* from Aneas. They ran south for what seemed like an eternity, and stopped only while all of the rangers and most of the Outwallers hugged her.

Irene, to her own consternation, burst into tears.

Looks-at-Clouds embraced her, pressed his/her heat into Irene's body, his/her *ops* into Irene's soul. "Well done, love, well done," the *bacsa* said.

Despite the praise, Irene felt empty, neither afraid nor triumphant. Polly fairly burbled with energy when she knew that she was free; Joan never fell to the ground again. Irene felt that she was the one who was defeated, for a while, and then she let the feeling go and ran.

They paused again when the Outwallers called something, and everyone gathered. Irene's fatigue addled mind puzzled through their actions; they had downed their packs to fight, and now were recovering them.

"He can't still be following us," Looks-at-Clouds said.

"I can't even find him," Aneas said. "So we keep running."

Hours later, darkness was falling as they crossed another river on a big dam so old that most of the beavers' work had turned to hard mud and spring logs.

The Jack pointed upstream.

"Giant beaver," he said. "Beautiful critters, but no friends o' man."

Aneas looked at the dam and then at the river.

"We must," Looks-at-Clouds said.

"Get across," Aneas ordered, and the little column trotted to the edge of the riverbank. The "pond" above the dam was vast, extending for three-quarters of a league or more, and the beaver house in the middle looked like a castle of firewood and brush, and green grass grew like a small yard on the roof.

One by one, the rangers and Outwallers ran across the dam. It was narrow enough on top, and it was clear that Lantorn, at least, did not trust the riverbanks, and neither did the Jack, who put an arrow to his bow. But Mingan was the first across, and waved.

And then something moved from the beaver castle, and the water in the middle of the lake seemed to swell and stretch.

Irene found herself the last person on the wrong side of the river except Aneas. Looks-at-Clouds was casting something on the far bank, forty paces away, eldritch fire at her fingertips.

"You first," Aneas said. "I need to talk to the master of this place."

Irene didn't wait or make a quip, because her head was so empty of thought. She'd had little sleep in six days, and her knees and legs shook with exhaustion, and each jolt of *ops* helped her less, and for less time.

She took a dozen strides and fell, at full run, into the water.

She sank over her head, but she was wearing only a torn shift, and had nothing to catch on the dam or hold her down except fatigue. She kicked once, and then strong hands gripped her and pulled her out of the water.

She found she was laughing.

"It's easier if you stay *on* the dam," Aneas said.

"So you say," she managed.

She lay gasping, and then the mistress of the pond exploded out of the water by her dam. She stood on the muddy bottom, her tusks as long as a man's arm, and chittered.

Aneas held his arms wide as if he were addressing a council of Outwallers, and he spoke, or rather, chittered back.

She lay on her back and looked up at the deep, rich fur of the great beaver. She was as big as a house, or a Rukh. Beautiful, her eyes deep and yellow.

Her great tail slammed into the water. The sound of the slap was like a crack of thunder, and echoed off the hills.

Aneas chittered again.

"Get up and go," he said. "Please."

Irene wanted to lie there, looking into the beaver's eyes, forever, but she got up heavily, with no grace at all, and hobbled across the dam.

She looked back, where Aneas stood alone.

"This is the Black River," Lewen said. "There is no good crossing for twenty leagues.

"Bless this good creature," said Tessen. "She listens to him. She is angry, but not out of all reason."

"And he has the way of it," Lewen said approvingly.

Twice more, the beaver slapped the water, but each time, it was with less ferocity, and the ripples lapped against the banks of the lake. But her tail summoned other beavers, and the sun was sinking.

And then she turned and slipped into the water and was gone, and Aneas seemed to slump. He stood a moment, with the sun setting behind him, and then he turned and trotted over the long dam, as if every pace hurt him.

"Keep going!" he shouted.

Even as he managed the last dozen paces, two beavers struck the center of the dam.

Irene raised her weary head to watch.

The third time the beavers struck the dam, the whole center bulged, and then the old mud cracked…

…and the river burst through.

"Old Mogon had best make good on my promises," Aneas said. "Come. One more mile."

It was dark when they lay down. Irene was between Lantorn and Looks-at-Clouds, and her last waking sight was Aneas, awake, lighting his pipe at the fire. He and Lewen were standing watch.

Looks-at-Clouds wrapped long arms around her torso and pressed into her from behind and she fell asleep, and any darkness in her was buried deep.

Two more days. They slept on the ground, with tiny fires, and they walked as fast as they could, sometimes running, a confused welter of advances and retreats as they sought to maintain contact with Orley's forces without being overrun. The mountains began to flatten into long ridges and swampy plains. To the west, the Inner Sea began to loom with banks of clouds, and to the north lay the Great River. The Black River was always present, just to their left, in the next valley or two as they followed a series of narrow trails that led north and west, north and west again.

The second day, they lost all trace, even hermetical, of their quarry.

"He must be going north," Tessen said, and Looks-at-Clouds agreed. But they became ever quieter as the day wore on, and Aneas made them keep a cold camp.

Aneas had begun to wonder if Turkos had lost his way, or if all his messages had failed. He was so tired that every choice seemed the wrong choice. Twice, crossing low ground entangled with alder and pits of black mud, he considered ordering them to turn around. Admitting failure.

He owed his brother nothing. Or so he told himself.

On the third day, they came to a deep gorge, with a rocky stream running at the base.

"Woodhull Creek," Lewen said. "Or perhaps Little Woodhull." He nodded, as if satisfied.

The Outwallers dropped their packs and one lit his pipe and handed it around. Mingan dropped his pack on a log and came forward, dropped to one knee, and looked out over the valley of the Woodhull. "We must cross it to go north," he said.

The rest of them slumped to the ground. Most didn't even take their packs off; they just sat.

Irene dropped her pack with Mingan's and walked forward, massaging her hips. She wondered if this was how old age would feel.

But the valley of the Woodhull was beautiful in the August sun. A hummingbird came out of the brush below them and visited an ancient rosebush.

"People lived here," Irene said. Now that she saw the rosebush, she realized she was looking at an entire farmyard; there was the old foundation, and there, an apple tree with the fruit, not quite ripe, hanging down. Two Outwallers and Cynthia were plucking the unripe fruit and putting it in their packs.

Aneas raised his head, and Irene had the impression he'd fallen asleep sitting on the ground.

"Yes. Not so many generations ago," Aneas said. "Perhaps two hundred years ago."

"What happened?" Irene asked.

He just looked at her. Then he bent his head and took his axe from his belt. On the back of the axe was a small pipe bowl, and he reached in his belt purse and took out a case made of tortoiseshell. Inside was a bare dusting of tobacco. He tapped the shell until he gathered the tobacco, and tenderly nursed it into the bowl.

"War," he said, without looking up. "My ancestors. And yours. And Orley's." He shrugged. "My mother used to tell us that the Wild was gradually taking Alba back from mankind. Myself, I wonder if we aren't just defeating ourselves."

"You could let Orley go," she said.

"I should," he said. "I'm out of tobacco." He looked out over the Woodhull. "I hate to lose."

"So do I," Irene said. "But Orley did not keep me, and I am grateful for that."

Aneas smiled at her. "At best, we broke even there," he said.

Irene thought of the thing in her head and considered wallowing in pity, but instead she shook her head, mostly at herself.

"My feud with Orley is personal," Aneas said. "I admit it. I acknowledge that he didn't personally kill my mother or my father; that compared to the likes of the Great Dragon or Thorn, he was merely a foot soldier in an evil service. And I'm wise enough to see that his hate for the Muriens is the product of hundreds of years of atrocity and counteratrocity. The very wars that returned all this beautiful land to the beaver and the moose and the bogglin." He took out his tinderbox. "But he did kill my . . ." He paused. "Friend," he said weakly.

She was fascinated by the assurance with which he found things on his body, took them out, used them, and returned them. Tobacco, tinderbox, stele, flint, knife . . . And by his weakness. *Friend*. She had never had a lover, but she knew how people valued them.

He was paying her no attention. "But when Wart, a Jack, and Krek, a bogglin, and Tessen all agree that Orley has to be defeated..." He paused, and his hands moved quickly, the flint snapping against the curved stele in his left hand until sparks fell on his char cloth. "The one thing that Gabriel has right is that we have to do this together, or not at all," he said.

"I want to learn to do that," Irene said.

He dropped the fragment of burning cloth into the top of his pipe and inhaled.

He sat back, put himself against a gnarled tree, and smoked.

Irene stood watching the valley below. Mingan continued to kneel a few paces to her left, and when she turned her head, he flashed her a smile.

"May I try your pipe?" she asked.

Aneas raised an eyebrow. Then he handed it to her, wiping the stem. "I guess you've earned it," he said, and she couldn't tell whether he was jesting.

She drew in a little smoke. All the Outwallers smoked; most of the rangers. No one in Liviapolis had ever smoked, except one master at the academy.

She tried to trickle the smoke out of her nose. It was bitter, somehow, and yet sweet, and she gave a short cough at the end of her efforts. The axe in her hand was the one she'd been using to cut boughs, what seemed like a year ago: razor sharp. A contrast to the pipe on the back. The steel was beautiful, with a grain like wood.

She handed the pipe back, wiping the stem as he had.

He took it and drew in more smoke.

"Why would we turn back?" she asked.

"We are about to run out of most of our supplies," he said. "Tobacco, wax, sugar, flour for biscuits. Dozens of other things. Most of us have fewer than a dozen good shafts left for our bows. You, Polly, and Joan are in rags, and have to share blankets, and really, Polly and Joan have no business out here."

She felt as if her eyes were especially wide open. Was that the tobacco?

Polly and Joan have no business here. But I do.

"Aneas," she began, and paused.

He looked at her.

It was perhaps the longest time their eyes had met since she awoke next to Looks-at-Clouds.

"Orley put something in my head. You know that?" she asked. She hated that her voice caught.

He exhaled smoke. "I know," he said. His voice held sadness, pity...

"Everyone knows?" she asked.

Aneas nodded. "They have to."

She reached for the pipe, and he gave it to her. She took a deeper pull on it, and thought, inconsequentially, about running...running on exhausted legs. Looking back, for Joan. The thought made her smile. She breathed out. "Do you think..." She looked back at him. "Do you think that actions count more than thoughts?"

"I'd like to think so," he said. His smile was bitter.

"I wanted to leave those women. I actually thought to use them as...decoys." She handed him the axe. "But I didn't."

Aneas smiled. He put the pipe in his mouth. Then he looked up and waggled the stem at Mingan, who came and took it gratefully and puffed away greedily, eyes on the horizon. Irene noted that he kept his weight low, and didn't stand erect, as she had done, on the cliff edge.

There is so much to learn.

She smiled at Mingan. He openly admired her, and she enjoyed his admiration. There was something clean and simple about his attentions. And he was relentlessly dignified. And he spoke Archaic.

He grinned—just for a moment—and then handed her the pipe and slipped away.

"I think we should keep going," Irene said.

Aneas looked at her a moment as if he'd never seen her before.

"I have commanded a city under siege," she said. She shrugged. "These people love you, and if you say go, they'll go."

"They are exhausted," he said.

She smiled. "I feel better today than I have in a week," she said. "I have Tessen's perfectly good spare wrap skirt. Ricard Lantorn made a joke this morning. If it were my decision, I'd at least give it another day."

Aneas looked at her, raised an eyebrow, opened his mouth, and then thought better of whatever he was going to say. He could be a very awkward boy at times, and this was one of them. He was at a loss for words, and he showed it. Gabriel would not have shown this confusion.

But then Aneas rose and tapped his pipe axe against a tree. He did so until the dregs of the ash and tobacco fell out, and then his moccasined foot crushed the dying ember. He thrust the axe back into his sash.

"Thanks," he said.

On the fourth day since Irene's escape, they turned back east, hunted, took a deer, made a fire, and ate him. Looks-at-Clouds cast about in the *aethereal* for Orley.

S/he took Irene.

You know where we are? S/he asked.

The princess looked around. I know, and yet I know I have no gift for this.

Looks-at-Clouds in the aethereal *was a hermaphrodite; naked and beautiful.*

You think so, but then, so many things you think are untrue.

I was tested.

Not the way Orley tested you. You are made of very strong steel indeed. Let me see your dark egg. Ahh. A terrible thing.

She reached deep into Irene, which was, itself, terrifying.

Blessed Tar, Looks-at-Clouds said. This is an abomination.

Irene didn't want to breathe or move.

But . . . the hermaphrodite seemed to laugh. But . . . let's see.

There was an infinite pause.

And there he is, s/he said, and they were back in the real.

"Did you remove it?" Irene asked.

Looks-at-Clouds shrugged. "No, I cannot," s/he said precisely. "But I followed a thread to its maker, and it is a thing of Ash. I need another kind of working to defeat it. Someone . . . gifted. Differently." S/he frowned. "I used it to find Orley."

"What is it?" Irene asked. She had thought that the fear was over.

Looks-at-Clouds looked away. "It is a trap. An egg. And when it hatches, what emerges will consume you."

Irene felt her knees fail her. The *bacsa*'s strong arms held her up.

"Can it be removed?" Irene asked.

Looks-at-Clouds took a breath. "Perhaps," s/he said.

"Oh God. I should go away." Irene found it difficult to breathe.

Looks-at-Clouds squeezed her and wrapped long arms more tightly around her waist. "No, my sweet. Until we heal you, we will hold you very close."

"And if . . ." Irene could say it. It was inside her.

Looks-at-Clouds sighed. "Then Aneas or I will kill what emerges." S/he smiled. Her face was very close. "He did not kill you, and you escaped. Live. If the worst happens"—s/he smiled, and his/her Irkish teeth showed—"it will be quick."

Irene shivered.

On the fifth day after the escape, the wyverns came.

There were four of them, and Lewen spotted them a great ways off, so that they hid in a dense clump of old pines. But the wyverns were not fooled and landed in the meadow hard by.

Only when the old female began to call Aneas by name was he convinced. Still, there were fourteen bows bent and fourteen arrows on bows as Aneas went out of the trees to meet the old wyvern.

But the clear sound of his laugh carried. He talked to the wyverns for several exchanges.

"Come out!" he called.

He came trotting back, quivering like an eager terrier.

"Make camp. There is a great deal of news. And we are back in touch with the army. Tall Pine made it to the inn. They will bring us more supplies, and there is a war party coming by canoe up the Black River." He nodded. "Damn!" he said. He grinned like the boy he often was. He was clearly pleased.

The wyverns were terrifying. Even when they smiled, or ate blueberries.

"And the Long Dam Clan bears are coming up from Lissen Carak," Aneas said, pounding one fist into the other. "Ah, it wasn't for nothing. Count your days, Kevin Orley." He dropped to one knee in the sun and drew his sword. "By God and Saint George, I will have you," he swore. "Or I will die in the attempt."

The largest wyvern dropped a bag of flour on the ground and gave a screech.

Aneas got to his feet, looking a little self-conscious after his oath, and his glance caught Irene's. He smiled.

She smiled back.

"You were right," he said. "I won't forget."

Part V
Arles

The day after the captain's wedding, the company slept in.

Most of the officers knew the schedule. The men and women slept, but there were boats being loaded along half the wharves of the city, and across the narrow lagoon to the north, a huge herd of horses was assembled.

The city was busy. There were arrests: the sudden intrusion of soldiers into houses, and in one case, a foreigner was killed in an inn.

No boats were allowed to leave Venike, nor had been so allowed since the three great round ships landed.

And in the darkness before the dawn on the company's fourth day in Venike, they rose, put on their less spectacular uniforms, and formed in small squares. Corporals and knights with darkened lanterns read from slips of parchment and led men to boats, and they filed aboard with hardly a curse.

By the time the sun was rising, the emperor's entire force had landed on the mainland to the north.

The Venikans were efficient. The horses were waiting, already picketed by lance; a warhorse and a riding horse for every knight and squire, and good riding horses for every archer and page. The company carried the tack of long-dead horses, steeds and sometimes friends, across the muddy beach and up the duty path to the horse lines, and there Bad Tom and Sauce assigned them to their mounts.

And they tacked up.

Etrusca had been stripped of horseflesh for them. The Duke of Venike had emptied his coffers to buy remounts. Horses had been imported huge distances so that archers could complain about the colour of their new horses.

The duchess, it appeared, was coming along to protect her investment. She rode up with Jules Kronmir and a hundred of her own rangers. They wore green like the royal foresters.

"Where's the emperor?" she asked.

415

Bad Tom laughed. "Still abed, I'll guess."

Kronmir nodded. "He will join us at Berona," he said. He handed message scrolls to Michael and Tom and Sauce, and the duchess.

She smiled her brilliant smile. "They deserve a honeymoon," she said.

The army marched as soon as it was mounted. Kaitlin and Francis Atcourt had almost no work to do on the baggage, because the Venikan officers were used to war, and they had collected everything on Sukey's lists and they were moving it by water.

To Ser Michael, it was like learning to make war all over again. He rode by Sauce in a constant state of amazement.

"Why did they want us to help?" he asked. "I've never seen aught like this. They know more about war than..."

"This" was a baggage train of barges, eighty barges long. Every barge carried two long, high-wheeled military wagons, themselves fully loaded. Michael could see the gonnes from the ships being loaded by heavy cranes driven by winches, the winches worked by teams of mules and one giant crane powered by oxen.

The *proveditores*, the officers in charge of provisions, were meticulous. They had tablets, and while the men were landed to find their horses, the Venikan officers were moving along the barges with tally sticks. Checking the loads.

"What's the plan, Michael?" Sauce asked. They were riding over the dusty plain. Even the trees were different. The trees in Etrusca seemed to either rise like drop spindles or have odd, blobby tops. The occasional stand of oaks reminded her of home.

"You know the plan," Michael said.

"I know His Nibs says we're riding north until we make contact and joining hands with the locals and the Ifriquy'ans if they are in time. And Du Corse. And then there's a great battle." She looked behind them. "It's a bloody daft plan and I don't believe a word of it."

Michael laughed. "Well, for that matter, neither do I and neither does Tom."

"Is he making it up as he goes, while he tomcats with his blondie?" Sauce asked.

Michael, whose pavilion often lay close by Sauce's, was surprised at her tone. "Do we begrudge him a little...fun?" Michael asked.

Sauce looked away. "We're a long way from home, Michael. I don't think his head is on this. I think he learned somewhat he didn't much like, back at Dar." She shrugged, her breastplate flashing in the brilliant Etruscan sun.

Michael looked out over the plains of Mitla and returned her shrug. "It's a fine place to make war," he said.

"If only we had people to fight, and not monsters," Sauce said. "What's he playing at?"

"Be careful what you wish for," Jules Kronmir said from Sauce's left side. When he rode away, she turned on Michael.

"I can't like that bastard," she said.

Michael didn't know and didn't care. He waved at Kaitlin, who was riding like a noblewoman born to the saddle now.

Sauce followed his eye and frowned. "Tom and I are the only ones taking this war seriously," she said.

But the army camped near Vadova, and everything about the camp made Sauce happy. The latrines were already dug, and the food all but cooked itself.

Bad Tom found her standing by a cook fire where three of Sukey's girls, now Kaitlin's girls, were busy cutting cabbage.

"Look at this, Tom," Sauce said. She held up a large ham.

"Tar's tits. I could use that as a club," he said.

She drew a baselard from her belt and cut him a slice, and as he chewed, a glorious smile came to his large-nosed face. "Like bacon!" he said. "That's a pleasure and no mistake."

She cut him a piece off an enormous wheel of cheese. He ate it and again beamed with pleasure.

"Now that's a fine cheese. Hard, salty..." He grinned and cut another wedge.

"That there is military rations. Made special, just to feed armies. The cheese will keep for weeks. So'll the ham." She looked around. "These people know more about making war than anyone I've ever met."

"More to war than cheese and ham, Sauce." Tom tapped his sword hilt.

Sauce grunted. "Really?" she asked. "Oh aye, I suppose there's firewood an' sleep, too."

Tom grunted.

Sauce looked around. "We ha' food for three months."

Bad Tom stopped chewing. "What?" he asked.

"Whatever His Nibs is planning," she said, "it ain't quick."

Tom went back to chewing.

Sauce led him along to the next barge. "What do you see?" she asked.

"Barrels?" he asked. "Big ones." He paused. "Ale?" he asked, wistfully.

"*Water*," she said.

Bad Tom cut another slice of cheese and ate it. "Ach, weel," he said. "Maybe he fancies good water. Maybe the Darkness poisons wells."

"Maybe pigs fly," Sauce said.

Thursday, and the towers of Berona rose ahead of them as they marched east. The baggage train was two hundred sixty wagons, and there were as many again coming up a second river somewhere to the south and west of them.

Michael, who commanded the vanguard, met the Count of Berona, Simone, and a party of his knights as soon as they came over the hills. Heralds exchanged trumpet blasts, and Michael dismounted and clasped the count's hand.

Simone was tall, handsome like a dark-haired angel in a magnificent red cote-armour over his brilliant steel armour. Behind him were a hundred lances, all bearing his badge of a ladder, in yellow, on red.

"I am Ser Michael de Towbray, and..."

Simone bowed in his saddle. "Ah, you are all famous men, you and Il Grand Tomaso and the others in the songs. Welcome to my small city. Ah, and La Dogesea." He, in turn, dismounted and bowed to the Duchess of Venike, whose rangers were nowhere to be seen. He kissed her hand and she leaned down and kissed his lips. "Beautiful and deadly lady," he said.

She smiled at him. "Handsome and deadly man," she said.

"Zachariah, Military Count of the Imperial Seal, commanding the Vardariotes," Michael said. Count Zac bowed in his saddle and saluted with his mace.

Michael introduced his wife, and Sauce, and everyone else who was to hand. Count Simone's manners were beautiful, and although he spoke little Alban, he remembered each name, and made compliments to each that the duchess translated.

He told Bad Tom that he looked like Saint Michael.

Tom Lachlan blushed.

Michael had to restrain himself from laughing aloud, and Sauce looked elsewhere.

They never reached Berona. Just west of the city, guides directed them over a narrow road between two steep hills. They came to a gate, and when the gate was opened and trumpets sounded, they rode down into a huge field where a dozen of Kaitlin's outriders were already laying out streets for the camp.

Sauce rode in before Michael was dismounted. She flirted a little with Count Simone, who seemed delighted with her, and then she reined in by Michael.

"You know what the count just told me?" she asked. "This area is kept like this just for armies to camp. Look at the hills!"

On every hilltop was a stone tower.

"It can't be surprised. It's like a second fortress, outside the city. A very nasty nut to crack in a siege." Sauce was staring at the nearest tower.

Michael nodded.

"And you don't let the soldiers into your town." Sauce shook her head. "These people make us look like amateurs," she said.

"Perhaps because they are the descendants of the legions," Michael said. Even as he said it, he was imagining a place near Towbray Castle that would make just such a large, fortified camp, and another near Albinkirk, just south of the city.

The Beronese had another thousand cavalry and almost three thousand infantry already encamped, and the northern field army of Venike was there as well, five hundred knights and almost a thousand of their marines, half armoured infantry with bows or crossbows and poleaxes. Camp chatter had informed Sauce that the Beronese and the Venikans had already fought twice that summer, against armies from the east; one of men, and one of the Wild, although they were clearly hesitant to speak of the creatures of the Wild to foreigners.

Michael was just enjoying the sight of the Venikan marines doing drill when he saw a familiar red pavilion rising in the center of camp. He sent his squire, Alexander, to inquire, and the younger man was back in ten minutes.

"My lord, there's to be a meeting of all the commanders after complines," he said.

"With the captain?" Michael asked. "By which I mean the emperor?"

Alexander bowed. "Yes, my lord." He shrugged. "I saw only Master Nicodemus."

Michael nodded. "I'll just make sure the Primus Pilus knows, as well," he said.

Michael and Sauce went to mass together in the small church at the end of the valley. The priest seemed surprised at how many men and women came and sang. When mass was over, they walked back to find Bad Tom watching archers shoot. Half the camp seemed to be there, watching as a bogglin and a pair of irks shot against an Outwaller and Cully.

"I'm of a mind to make sure them o' Venike don't kill our bug," Tom said. "I dinna think they ha' a high opinion o' bugs."

But the shooting ended without incident, and the arrival of full darkness prevented any more shooting. One of the Venikan master archers presented himself to Cully, and there was talk of a challenge and a tun of wine. But the two didn't have enough of a language in common despite a fair amount of goodwill.

The darkness deepened. The red pavilion glowed like a lantern.

"Don't bother," Kronmir's voice came out of the darkness to Michael. "He's not here yet."

Michael walked through the camp with Kaitlin by him and young Galahad in his arms. He checked his sentries and looked at the horse lines and then kicked a few tent pegs and finally walked along the fire lines, looking in pots while Kaitlin listened to the women.

There was a long scream, like a predator high in the air taking prey.

Beyond the horse lines, a string of fires sprang up, forming a box.

There was a rush of wings and a sound like the wind before a storm, and then Michael saw a flash of red, green, and gold wing by firelight. He grinned. He couldn't help himself.

"Let's go see," he said to Kaitlin.

"Galahad doesn't need to be up any later," Kaitlin said.

Michael squeezed her hand. "He has a nurse," he said.

Kaitlin growled, but followed him. "A nurse isn't a mother," she said. "Or a father."

"I was raised by nurses," Michael said.

"And look at you," Kaitlin said. "You had to marry someone with sense because you didn't have any of your own."

Ariosto was being hurried under cover. The company had been warned not to talk, and most of them did anyway, but the captain's steed was known to be a military secret.

"He brought Blanche!" Kaitlin said.

Blanche was, in fact, both cold and elated, having just flown for the first time, launching in the last sunlight from a bay in the lagoon far from prying eyes and then flying over a darkened plain with the mountains, the very high mountains, higher than anything in the Nova Terra, still sun kissed to the north and west. She was wearing a tight-fitting jacket of leather and fur and a hood of the same and contrived to look both beautiful and practical. She embraced Kaitlin, and then the duchess, and was borne away to meet her new servants, recruited locally.

Michael was a little surprised to find that all the Etruscan men were on one knee.

So he bent his knee. Sauce followed him. Tom glared.

Gabriel came out of the covered pen where Ariosto was kept. He saw them—twenty of the best knights in the world—and he swept off his arming cap and bowed in their direction.

"Gentlemen, and ladies," he said. "No formality in camp, I pray you."

Everyone stood.

Michael noted that the Etruscans took his rank very seriously, and that he needed to play along or feelings would be ruffled. Sauce had been as slow to kneel as he. Tom had never knelt.

Michael made mental notes to discuss this in his morning orders group.

Then they all walked to the red pavilion, where Toby had erected the great table that Count Simone had given him, a round table that seated thirty. And many had to stop to applaud the table, and its indications of equality. Count Simon gave a small speech in Archaic and welcomed the emperor.

The emperor thanked him for the table and for his alliance and his chivalric virtue, and ended with a few lines from a romance.

It was all very nicely managed, Michael thought.

The Red Knight sat with the Duchess of Venike on his right and Count Simone on his left. Master Nicodemus, having returned from the cough to his usual role, bowed deeply. "It is His Imperial Majesty's pleasure that all his commanders sit as they please," he said.

Thirty seats meant that there was one for the commander of the Venikan marines and one for the Beronese captain of infantry and one for Master Pye, who had come in person to command the Harndon Armourers' Guild. Sauce sat between Tom Lachlan and Ser Michael, and Francis Atcourt sat by Count Zac and the emperor designate, Ser Giorgos Comnenos. Morgon Mortirmir sat by Master Kronmir and Magister Petrarcha. Kaitlin de Towbray sat between the empress and the duchess.

Wine was served.

Master Julius had his own table, and he was already writing, even as the emperor was already reading from a stack of messages provided by Kronmir while he sipped wine.

"This is like old times," Sauce said.

"The wine's better," Tom said. "An' I miss the little nun." He grinned. "But I do like the round table."

"And the queen," Sauce said. "I miss her."

Michael drummed his fingers on the table in impatience. "That was only ten weeks ago," he said.

Tom Lachlan sighed. "Aweel, lad. It seems like months and months." He looked around. "An' many absent friends, eh?"

The three of them drank to all the ghosts they shared.

It was a somber moment.

And then Blanche laughed.

Tomaso Lupi, who was serving wine to his count on one knee, was invited instead to a seat at the round table by Toby. One of Nicodemus's servants served wine.

The Red Knight rose to his feet, and silence fell. Just in that moment, Michael thought that it was interesting, and perhaps a measure of something, that men who had never met him fell silent. He was not an imposing figure, with his hair all windblown from flying and wearing a red wool coat that any merchant might have worn to market. He had his gold knight's belt at his hips, but no other badge of rank.

"Friends," he began. He spoke in Archaic. The duchess translated fluently into Etruscan and Master Julius into Alban. He smiled. "Thanks to Count Simone, we have this beautiful table, which perfectly expresses my views on rank. We must be a single army with a single will. Not my will, but *our* will. Let no man or woman hesitate to speak at this table."

No one spoke.

He took a deep breath. "Events are moving very quickly," he said. "There is news, some good, some bad."

Michael could see how tired he was.

Just for a moment, he thought of the captain, two years before. He'd aged. It wasn't just maturity. Some of the rough edges had worn off, but some of the joy was gone, too. *Did he still think that God didn't give a fuck? Would he even say such a thing now?*

Michael shrugged to himself, because he was merely reflecting his own views on his friend.

His friend, the emperor.

"The Sieur Du Corse will not make a rendezvous with us near Arles," Gabriel said. "He has had to retreat after two engagements with the enemy." The emperor did not speak of Du Corse's encounter with the *taken* host of the former royal army, led by the King of Galle, or how narrowly the routier had avoided disaster.

"He is now west of Lutrece, covering the withdrawal of refugees. The greatest city of Galle is lost to the foe, but its population has been saved." Gabriel paused to let the translations roll by.

Michael unclenched his stomach muscles.

"The paladins of Dar have landed a little east of Massalia," Gabriel's voice went on. He shaped a little *ops* between his hands and the table was illuminated from above by mage light, and a set of mountains grew out of the table. The Etruscans, far less used to open displays of magery, muttered, crossed themselves, or, like Count Simone, merely swore in delight.

"They are roughly here," Gabriel said. "We are roughly here," he said, placing a red dot on Berona.

"Arles is here," he said, and placed a burning green light. "As of last night, Clarissa de Sartres was still in command of the citadel. On the one hand, they are desperate and hard-pressed." He nodded. "On the other, they now have hope. For some days, the Necromancer told them that they were the last people in the world, and twice he has put... worms... into the castle."

The translations rolled on.

At the word *worms* every face wrinkled in the same distaste. But everyone knew what the enemy was.

To emphasize the point, and with the help of Magister Petrarcha, who now stood, he cast an illumination of a trio of the worms coming like a hideous hydra from the mouth of a captured enemy. The illumination was played from the duchess's memory and the worms came very close indeed. Everyone flinched, except Tom Lachlan, who leaned closer and grinned.

"Not so big," he said.

No one else spoke.

"In the west," Gabriel went on, "my brother has fought two battles outside N'gara and is now retreating to the east. N'gara is already besieged." His great map expanded to include Alba and Morea. Harndon was lit orange. Dar as Salaam was lit green.

A steady blue light burned to the north of the inland sea.

"Ash has raised all the Wild of the west," Gabriel said calmly.

Michael's back was rigid. "So what are we doing *here*?" he asked aloud.

Gabriel met his eye. "Pissing on one fire at a time, the hottest first." He looked around the table. "Gavin and Tapio are trading space for time. We know the timetable now."

"We could lose Alba while we save Arles," Michael said.

Gabriel shrugged. "We absolutely could," he said.

Michael sat down, abashed.

Count Simone raised a hand. "Timetable?" he asked.

Gabriel pointed at Mortirmir, who rose. "We are fighting a war on many fronts," he said. "We have two, or perhaps three, main opponents. The dragon Ash, the being we call the Necromancer, and possibly a third force." He shrugged. "And we must assume that Ash and the Necromancer will only quarrel among themselves when they have beaten us."

Mortirmir, interrupted by Petrarcha, outlined what they knew of the sides and the locations of the gates.

Count Simone stood. "So, which is it?" he asked. "Which gate is the one they want?"

Gabriel shook his head. "That's just it, *messire il conte*. I cannot say. My gut says Arles or Lissen Carak, because the enemy has worked so hard to take those two. But... there are gates in many places. The ones we know are marked with lights. Harndon. Liviapolis. Rhum. Dar." He shrugged. "Harmodius thinks there is, or was, one in the north of Alba. Destroyed with Castle Orley? Or maybe on Thorn's Island? Under the sea?" He shrugged.

"By the risen Lord," Simone said. "This is very…complicated."

Kronmir rose to his feet. "On the subject of Rhum," he said.

The emperor nodded.

"The Patriarch has suffered an unfortunate accident," Kronmir said.

Tom Lachlan laughed. "You mean he annoyed the loon," he guffawed. "And Kronmir offed him?"

Sauce slapped him. "Do ye always ha' to say the first thing that comes into yer fool head?" she asked.

Kronmir nodded. "The Patriarch may have been host to a worm," he said. "Accounts of the moments after his death conflict." He smiled benignly, like a priest giving a blessing. "The situation is being…stabilized."

"By professionals," Tom said with a laugh.

Even the emperor glared at him this time.

He shrugged and tapped his sword hilt. "I say what I like," he said.

Michael smiled.

Sauce smiled.

Even Toby smiled.

More wine made its rounds.

"So," the duchess said. "Now what?"

The emperor laughed. "Now we see if the Odine can beat two organized armies who aren't afraid of them," he said. "Duchess, I am often accused of arrogance. But in terms of military strength, unless we're surprised on the march, the Necromancer is no match for us."

Even the duchess was surprised.

Sauce laughed. "That sounded like you," she said. "I like it."

The emperor rose from his seat and walked around the table. "I think you expected a desperate battle speech. I'll save it for when I'm desperate. Friends, this is our feint. The only questions before us are about how thoroughly we can deceive our enemy, and then, how many innocent peasants and taken former soldiers we have to kill to defeat him."

Sauce growled. "Feint?" she asked.

Michael was grabbing the edge of the table.

Blanche was smiling.

Gabriel leaned forward and put his hands on the table. "I told you I was tired of reacting," he said. "Always dancing to Ash's tune."

The duchess frowned. "We are a feint?"

Gabriel smiled. "I exaggerate for effect. We will relieve Arles and save Etrusca. That is not a feint."

"You guarantee this?" she asked.

Gabriel smiled. "Nothing in war is sure," he said. He looked at Mortirmir, of all people, and Mortirmir nodded. Smiles broke out around the table.

Kronmir raised a finger.

Gabriel glared, and Sauce laughed.

"He hates to be interrupted in full blow-hard," she said to Michael, who stifled a giggle.

"Yes?" the emperor asked in haughty annoyance.

"The Duke of Mitla," Kronmir said. He shrugged.

Gabriel tubbed his beard in annoyance. "I was told..."

Kronmir shrugged. "There are food riots in Mitla," he said apologetically. "An effort *has* been made."

"I was given to understand that the duke was not infected," the emperor said with a wave of his imperial hand. As if dismissing the darkness and the Necromancer.

Kronmir rose to his feet. "Your Grace, one of the reasons I so enjoy working with you is that you do not insist on being told what you want to believe." The intelligencer raised an eyebrow.

The Red Knight deflated. "Damn," he said, and sat on his chair.

Kronmir spread his hands. "We have a saying, Your Grace, in my work: Never ascribe to hidden conspiracy or the dark supernatural what can be explained by ignorance, greed, and lust." He shrugged. "The Duke of Mitla is using the situation to further his own ambitions. He has enticed the pro-patriarchal city of Fiernce as an ally." He shrugged. "Mitla was scheming with Galle before this began. To the Duke of Mitla, nothing has changed."

Bad Tom laughed. "By the balls of Saint Peter! Do ye mean that there's a purely human bastard who's going to help the Necromancer for purely human reasons?" He looked at the Red Knight and thumped the table. "A fight."

Kronmir remained standing. "A not inconsiderable enemy," he said. "He will not offer battle. He will build earthworks and fill them with soldiers and demand an enormous payment in land and money to pass."

The duchess put her head in her hands. "I should have foreseen this," she said. "He is ever our foe."

Kronmir looked at her with something like disappointment. "Were you not planning to use our expedition to seize Mitla's northern marches for your state?" he asked. He shrugged. "Or so I'm told."

The duchess glared at him.

Kronmir shrugged.

Michael thought, from her look, that she might stick her tongue out at Kronmir, but she kept her composure and said, "The Duke of Mitla is, if nothing else, an experienced player at this game. He will seek to frustrate us simply because he can."

Gabriel looked around the table. "Well, that's my pretty timetable wrecked," he said. "So much for God-like invincibility."

The duchess shook her head. "But you can fight the Darkness?" she asked. "And what of the great flying thing that tracked us?"

The emperor looked at her, and then at Kronmir. "The company excels at killing wyverns," he said. "I assume we can take a giant carrion bird."

Kronmir raised an eyebrow. "It's very big. As big as..."

"A war galley," the emperor said.

"It could be a dragon," Morgon Mortirmir said.

Men looked at each other, except Tom Lachlan, who laughed.

"Now we're talkin'," he said.

The emperor and his magister were looking at each other. If they were talking in the *aethereal*, none of the others could tell. Blanche wrinkled her nose.

Gabriel shook his head.

"Regardless of the Darkness and the giant carrion monster and the Duke of Mitla, Your Grace, unless the skies fall or all the human magisters are *dead wrong*, we hold the balance of terror here. Not the Necromancer. He's been used as a stalking horse by Ash, who assumed that if we moved to rescue Arles, he'd have a free hand in Alba."

"And the armies?" Sauce asked.

"I'm showing the Necromancer what he expects to see," Gabriel answered. "A half-arsed counterattack. With armies." His grin might have been described as feral. "I just showed Ash's spies, and the Necromancer's spies a *wedding*."

"Aren't we doing that, though?" Michael asked. "Wait. What?"

"Oh yes," Gabriel said.

Michael looked at Sauce and shook his head. "Do you understand?"

Tom Lachlan laughed. "Tar's tits, laddie. *I* understand, and I'm not the witty one."

The duchess laughed. "I think you are quite mad. I would like to be infected by your madness."

Gabriel snapped his fingers and the map returned. "We will go this way, over the Cenis Pass," he said. "Payam and the paladins go this way, along the coast road." Coloured arrows flowed like snakes. "I expect there will be some fighting, and I'm sorry to say we must be ruthless. Our foe needs to know that we've made the choice to kill every one of his slaves."

All the Etruscans nodded.

Sauce looked uneasy, and so did Michael and Blanche.

"The imperial troops will cover the army, mostly because they will not be fighting their friends and neighbors and brothers," the emperor said. "If we have to turn and face the Duke of Mitla or anyone else, we'll use the Etruscan troops backed by some hermetical talent, and we'll try to defeat them before they all join together. Either way, we'll focus the *will* so ably scouted by Master Kronmir and the duchess on us."

Michael nodded. He could see it.

"And then, somewhere here, the enemy will be forced to concentrate his slaves," Gabriel said. "If we can get past Mitla."

"He can hold the passes forever," Simone said.

"Not even a single week," the emperor said. "Hordes of taken slaves don't have wagons and foragers. The whole only acts where the *will* is." He shook his head. "There's no food in the passes. The food is in the plains of Arles." He looked at Kronmir. "I didn't think of Mitla."

Simone nodded. "Your logic is attractive," he said. "I confess to having wondered why the Genuans made it over the passes to Arles. Now I understand." He made a face. "So. We cross the passes, and the enemy concentrates all his forces. If we can defeat the Duke of Mitla."

Where the high mountains gave way to the upper pastures of Arles and the streams began to swell into the rivers, the emperor made a mark in *ops*. "Yes."

"And then?" the duchess asked.

"And then we roll some very crooked dice," Gabriel said.

"You make it sound easy," Count Simone said. "When to us, it is the *Darkness*."

428

Gabriel came and stood by the count. "Please," he said. "There are many things that can, and will, go wrong." He shrugged. "It is war. But fighting the Necromancer is *not* the hard part. Harmodius and our ally, the Wyrm of Ercch, and the magister Al Rashidi have given us the weapons to fight the Necromancer."

Many cups were raised.

"But..." asked Sauce. "But then how do we get back to Alba?"

Gabriel smiled. Right at her.

"That's the hard part," he said. "First, let's plan for the Duke of Mitla."

They moved east at first light, a long column tipped with steel, and they had boats on the river and a second column on the south bank. Dan Favour led the green banda in a wide sweep on the north side of the river, and his patrols found the Mitlese first, near Astua. A thousand peasants were digging earthworks.

The emperor came in person and sat on Ataelus in the shade of a huge oak tree, watching them dig. They had a superb natural position, a long ridge with two high ends that dominated both the valley and the river.

"Maybe two hundred men-at-arms behind them. Zac says there's dust on the road behind." Favour pulled off his helmet and used a linen towel to wipe away the sweat and dust.

"Sure could use that griffon of yours," muttered Sauce.

Gabriel shook his head. "Ariosto is being saved for a special occasion," he said. "Mortirmir is using the imperial messenger birds as conduits. I gather that you Etruscans frown on the use of the hermetical in war?"

The duchess was in head-to-toe green. She shrugged. "With the exception of myself and Master Petrarcha and a dozen others I could name, there aren't enough practitioners to use in a war. It is Nova Terra that makes the hermeticists."

Gabriel looked out over the heat-rippled plain at the ridge. "I predict that will change in the next generation," he said. He frowned. "This is going to be bloody."

Bad Tom grinned. "Send me in," he said.

"Go," the emperor said. "Take the ridge."

The men and women of the green banda had prepared many times for a fight like this, but they'd never had one.

They rode to the base of the ridge, and some went north, into the woods there. Most, however, dismounted at the base of the ridge and slipped into the broken ground at the base.

And began to loft arrows.

A dozen peasants died. They were noncombatants, merely diggers of earth, and they were shocked at the attack. And they ran.

The greens, in a long skirmish line, in pairs of archers with ten paces between them, went up the hill. Even as they climbed, they moved to the flanks of the hill and used any cover they could find. The peasants had just been clearing the brush to make the fields of view perfect, and they'd left a few trees and bushes, and the greens tended to vanish into them. Women with crossbows lay prone.

They moved steadily forward.

By the time they reached the top of the ridge, they were in three widely separated groups.

The Mitlese men-at-arms didn't try to hold the half-built earthworks or the palisade, but lowered their lances and charged.

Bad Tom sat on his great black charger at the base of the ridge, at the head of the whole red banda. His visor was open, and he watched the greens clear the hill with a simple smile on his face.

"Straight up the hill," he said to the men-at-arms of the red banda. "We clear the whole ridge."

Those were his only orders.

They didn't dismount, despite the steepness of the ridge, and the reds spread out a little into a more open order, but the line kept coming. High above them, the greens were now fighting in three ragged clumps.

The Mitlese commander committed his reserve straight from the road behind the ridge. His first battle of two hundred lances made no headway against the skulking archers, lost many horses in the attempt, and then was ridden to ruin by a massive attack of men-at-arms who had the effrontery to *ride* up the front of the ridge. The commander was annoyed by the waste and threw in his second division.

It was the first time Gabriel had ever watched a battle. It was not a big battle, but the men and women who died in it were going to be just as dead as men and women in any other fight. He hated watching.

Gabriel spent the first part of the action writhing. His stomach muscles climbed the ridge with the greens and then with the reds. He feared to lose Sauce, and he feared to lose Daniel Favour, and he feared to lose Tom, and he feared to lose Smoke. And any of them.

"I'm a poor excuse for a soldier king," he muttered.

Almost without being aware of it, he was riding closer and closer to the ridge, and the *casa* followed him, and the Duchess of Venike.

Zac's Vardariotes trotted up. The count saluted his emperor with a flourish of his little mace. "Fight well, little brothers!" he called. "Caesar is watching!"

The Vardariotes gave a great shout and rode on, sabers flashing and red coats shining in the brilliant Etruscan sun.

They, too, rode straight up the front of the ridge. And vanished into the dust at the top.

At the top, Sauce opened her visor, cursed Tom Lachlan, and spat dust. She took a canteen from her squire and drained it.

All along her front, men and women in green surcoats opened helmets and tried to breathe. And drank water.

The reds crashed into the enemy and swept them away down the ridge in a swirling cavalry fight.

Sauce turned, handing the canteen to her new page, Romney. "Drink some, lad," she said. "Where the hell is Favour?"

Her curse was rewarded by a sparkle of sun on steel from the wooded valley to her right. She nodded.

"Right! Horse holders!" she shouted.

The captain of the Mitlese came forward with a white square of linen on his lance. They were all the way at the east end of the ridge, and Dan Favour's troop of the green banda was visible *behind* the captain.

He came forward with a dozen men-at-arms. They were big men.

Tom Lachlan went forward with Michael. Behind him, the company archers were already stripping the dead.

"We have come to offer terms," the big, dark-haired captain said.

Tom shook his head. "No. Lay down your arms. Or fight. No terms. No parleys."

The Mitlese captain shrugged. "Fuck you," he said, and charged.

His lance caught Bad Tom in the center of his breastplate. Tom went down over the back of his saddle and left Ser Michael alone with a dozen enemy men-at-arms.

Michael was openmouthed at the enemy's stupidity, but he drew his long sword and snapped it up from the left side of his saddle, straight from the draw into the oncoming lance, brushing the enemy weapon by like a whisper of mortality and then the full weight of his back cut. His sword couldn't bite though his enemy's helm, but the force of the blow unhorsed the man.

Michael was hit twice, parried another blow, and was through them.

In front of him, the Mitlese men-at-arms—or rather, the survivors of the last hour—were forming for a charge, but Michael guessed they were as surprised by their captain's treachery as he was. And behind *them*, Favour's greens dismounted and restrung their bows.

Unseen in the dust behind Ser Michael, Canny and Robin Hasty exchanged a look—and loosed.

"What the fuck is they thinkin'?" Skinch muttered. "Crazy fucks."

He feathered a warhorse fifty paces away. The Mitlese didn't have horse barding. They hadn't faced longbows before.

Bad Tom got to his feet.

"Someone's for it," Canny said, with a nod. "Cease!"

"The redoubt on the river would like to surrender," said the herald. He swallowed. He was scared.

Tom Lachlan's dagger was red, and so was the armoured fist that held it. He hadn't allowed the Mitlese sell-sword captain a chance to be ransomed. And he was still kneeling on the dead man's chest.

The whole troop of men-at-arms had been killed. The greens and the reds had shot into them until the last man fell, and the knights had finished the survivors. No quarter was offered, and no ransoms taken.

"No quarter," Tom Lachlan said.

Ser Michael was still mounted, and not in a combat rage. "Tom," he said, and tapped the big Hillman chief with his war hammer. Hard. "Tom!"

Lachlan rose to his feet.

Thankfully for everyone, including the herald, the emperor came over the top of the ridge with his household. Then came forward at a fast trot, even as the Vardariotes were passing through the greens.

The emperor was in his gilded armour, with a red velvet surcoat atop it. He had a sword by his side, but the only weapon in his hand was a baton of white wood. He waved it at Tom and then reined in. Around him, the Nordikaans also reined in, and Harald Derkensun barked an order in his own tongue and they all dismounted together, pulling their axes off their saddle bows.

The emperor's eye swept over the lines of corpses.

Michael locked his visor up. "Your Grace," he said. "Their captain attacked under a flag of truce."

Gabriel grimaced. "What?"

The Duchess of Venike leaned over and looked down at the corpse Tom had been straddling. "Castigliore," she said. "The Duke of Mitla's favourite thug." She smiled at Tom. "You grow on me," she said.

Bad Tom got heavily to his feet but managed a very passable courtly bow. His battle rage faded, leaving him with a very red face.

The herald fell on his knees. "I beg quarter, great lord!" he said, in passable Archaic.

"Granted," the emperor snapped, and rode on. "Zac! Go!" he roared.

The Vardariote officer waved his mace, and the Vardariotes burst forward onto the open road west.

Lachlan put his arm around the waist of the terrified herald. "Sorry, laddie. The de'il was in me." He scratched under his jaw and a patch of dried blood came away from his beard. "O' course the fort can surrender."

An hour later, the barges rowed by the earthworks of a fort that might have blocked the river when completed, by means of the fire of two heavy trebuchets.

The wagon train rolled along the base of the long ridge, unmolested. It had never stopped rolling.

The Scholae swept by in the rear guard, eating dust and cursing the emperor. Ser Giorgos cantered his fine Ifriquy'an mare up the flank of the ridge to convey the feelings of his regiment to the great man in person. He saluted, and the emperor nodded. He was looking west, along the line of the Terno River. The mountains were already visible to the west and north, a long line like the teeth of a monster of the Wild.

"I ate a great deal of dust today, for a man who is the heir to the empire," Comnenos said.

Sauce had her harness off and one of her arms was being bandaged. Behind her, Ser Danved was naked to the waist and having something stitched. He looked calm. He swore a great deal.

Sauce grinned evilly at Ser Giorgos. "Bet eating dust beats fighting," she said. "Fuck! Ow!"

"Your turn tomorrow," Gabriel said. "Ahead I see a long, funnel-shaped valley where the duke can do this to us every day until he runs out of sell-swords."

Michael nodded. "That's what I see," he said. "It's like Gilson's Hole, except we're on the other side, and we're the ones in a hurry."

Gabriel dismounted from Ataelus. He hadn't fought anyone. He leaned in and talked to his horse for a few moments.

Then he took the reins of Srayanka, his riding horse, a steppe mare. She was big and powerful, and yet appeared a pony next to Ataelus.

Bad Tom was lying in the grass, oblivious of any form of court etiquette. "What I see," he said in agreement.

Gabriel went and sat next to Tom, and Michael came up, and Kronmir, who dismounted, and Mortirmir, and the duchess. They had a view for ten miles up the valley.

"The Ifriquy'ans fought yesterday," Kronmir said. "It was just a brush, but Payam says that the will is turning on him."

"And we're two days behind," Gabriel said.

"We didn't lose any time today!" Tom said defensively.

"No, you were brilliant and the company was brilliant," Gabriel said. He shook his head. "Sometimes I'm just the captain. Tell the boys and girls that they were . . . brilliant."

Tom grinned. "They were fine, eh?" he nodded. "Like the book."

"Like the book," Gabriel agreed. "But it won't be like that tomorrow."

Michael looked away.

"The duke's troops will know better tomorrow. They'll have covering parties. They'll hold every trench line." He shrugged. "How many did today cost us?"

"Phillipe de Beause," Tom said.

There was a moment's silence. He had been one of the company's finest jousters. "Six men at arms. A dozen archers . . . Hugh Course. Dook, for the love o' God. I didna' think the man could die."

"Christ on the cross," muttered Kronmir.

The emperor shook his head. "And that was a cheap victory won with speed and determination." He frowned. "Five of those and we'll lose the edge of good leaders that takes us up ridges. Sauce or Tom. Or me." He shrugged. "I'm losing my love of this."

"Do you know the name of every soldier?" Giselle asked.

The emperor looked surprised. "I try to," he said.

She shook her head. "Then when you lose them, you will be broken. Best to let them remain faceless."

He looked at her with distaste. "The way the duke let you remain faceless?" he asked.

She shrugged. "I see your point," she said. "But I am right, nonetheless."

That night, they dug in. Toward morning, the pickets were attacked. The attackers had the worst of it and withdrew.

In the morning, the army was slow starting. It couldn't be helped; many had fought the day before. Muscles ached and wounds stiffened.

Armour was painful even to strap on over tired muscles.

"Stay with the river as long as we can," the emperor said, and the army marched, late, but in good order. The Vardariotes had swept all the way up the valley, overrunning two more positions with the coloured flags all laid out for peasant diggers who never arrived. They swept north and west into the high ridges, taking terror with them. A trickle of prisoners came back, including the duke's second son, Antonio, captured on the road, unaware that a battle had been fought.

They made twenty miles, and dug in again.

"Tell Payam we'll be six days late," the emperor told Kronmir that night. Master Nicodemus handed him a silver cup full of wine.

He was so quiet that Blanche was afraid.

"I hate to be late," he said to her. The camp bed was like a little tent inside the pavilion, and gave them the illusion of privacy. "I'm sending you and Kaitlin back to Venike."

She lay there, silent.

"We're a day or two from the Darkness," Gabriel said. "When we reach it..." He shrugged, wriggling in the bed. "I told you about Helewise and the Odine."

Blanche nodded, miserable. But silent. And with her jaw set.

The next morning, Count Zac was back to report that they faced a towering escarpment on the shores of a lake, fifteen miles farther west.

"Ten thousand men," Zac said. "I scared the piss into their breeches, but there they are."

"Lake Darda," the duchess said.

Kronmir wore what Sauce called his sour-milk look. He had a stack of flimsy parchments. Six birds had come in with the first light.

"More bad news?" Gabriel asked.

"Yes, Majesty," Kronmir intoned.

"Speak then," Gabriel said. "Let's get it over with."

Kronmir's eyes went to his servant. "There has been a new election of a Patriarch of Rhum," he said.

"That's speedy," Father David allowed. As a follower of the Patriarch of Liviapolis, he didn't pay too much heed to the politics of Rhum, but he had studied there. "These elections can go on for years."

"They have chosen Lucius di Bicci," Kronmir said. "He was the old Patriarch's legate for Etrusca. A warlord, not a churchman. They say he has five thousand lances to command and that he is marching already."

Gabriel pursed his lips. "Twenty days behind us, even if he could march the way we do," he said.

Giselle frowned. "He can threaten Venike, especially if he allies with Mitla and Genua," she said.

The emperor took a slow breath. "Twenty days from now we'll be in a very different kind of war," he said. "Can the Beronese and the Venikans stop them?"

"You would abandon us?" the duchess demanded.

Gabriel took another slow breath. "Giselle," he said quietly, "what the legate and the Duke of Mitla do is nothing but a distraction."

"Not to the farmers on the borders. Not to our ships on the seas," she said.

The emperor looked out over the camp. It was a quiet summer evening, and a thousand tents stretched away up the beautiful valley. A gurgling stream fell down from the lake above them, and the late-evening sky was pink and blue, the whole forming a sort of tapestry of a military paradise.

"If we stop to fight this legate, we might lose the war," Gabriel said. "Trust me."

Giselle sighed but did not dissent.

Gabriel turned to Kronmir. "Can we cut across the Darkness?" he asked.

Kronmir shrugged. "I have no idea," he said. "For one man on his guard"—he looked at Giselle—"and one woman, it was possible. For an army? I'm not even sure what form an attack would take."

Giselle shuddered.

Michael tapped his teeth with his thumb, and so, in fact, did the emperor.

He puffed out his cheeks. "We must try," he said. "Or we lose the Ifriquy'ans. They are fighting every day."

Kronmir nodded. "And retreating," he said. "They are farther from us today than they were yesterday."

"And Du Corse?" Gabriel asked.

"Far to the north and west. West of Lutrece." Kronmir shrugged.

Gabriel sat back. "Well, I suppose it was always too complicated," he said. "West, into the Darkness. That's why we brought all the supplies, after all. Everyone knows the drill."

Michael shook his head. "That's why we brought the supplies?" he asked pointedly.

"Being emperor is not as much fun as I expected," Gabriel said. He sighed. "No, I brought them for something else, but let's take one horrifying decision at a time, shall we?"

"We could just outflank this position," Zac said. "And emerge from the darkness here, west of Mitla."

Gabriel tapped his teeth again. "Hmmm," he said. "I hate to think what we're about to learn. All pregnant women are to go back east to Berona. Today."

Blanche met his eye. "Are you still marching to the gamble you said?" she asked quietly.

"Yes," he said, without hesitation.

"Then I will not go back," she said.

The two of them locked eyes.

People looked away. Servants turned their heads, and Bad Tom, of all people, left the pavilion. The silence went on too long.

"Very well," the emperor said. His eyes made a loop of annoyance. "I rescind the order. Pregnant women are warned that they and their unborn babes may be at risk from this point onward."

Sauce lingered with the emperor's chart when the others left, and she found herself looking at it with the duchess and the Count of Berona and Kaitlyn and Sukey.

No one went back with the convoy of empty wagons.

The Red Knight flooded the plains along the Terno with his light cavalry, who pushed on recklessly all the way to the Vale of Darda on a ten-mile front, and they burned every village and hamlet they came to, leaving more destruction behind than an army of the Wild.

But behind their screen of fire and brutality, the company turned west into the Darkness. Almost two hundred heavy wagons rolled west on two roads. Only those few soldiers dead to empathy failed to feel the frisson of fear as they crossed the river into the Darkness, and even in full sunlight, most of the soldiers shivered.

Camping was worse, and worse yet for Kaitlin, as problems of supply were rendered dramatically more difficult by the emperor's demand that no man or woman eat or drink anything in the Darkness that they had not provided themselves. But the Venikan *proveditores* were ready with lists, and food—clean, reliable food and water—flowed from the wagons into the hands of the soldiers. Mortirmir and Petrarcha set themselves to testing everything, and Gabriel joined them, reduced from mighty emperor to sorcerer's apprentice by circumstance.

By his order, no man or woman was to be alone. In fact, they moved in fives—even to latrines. Every soldier, every outrider, every page, every servant, every slattern, carried a weapon.

The whole camp sprang to arms in the Darkness, and a Venikan marine was slain by one of his own. In error.

The emperor went out into the dark with Harald Derkensun and Bad Tom and a trio of Nordikaans, and went from fire to fire. He began to learn the names of the Venikans and of the Beronese, and he took Tomaso Lupi with him as he walked through the cook area of the count's foot soldiers. Lupi spoke the dialect well, having lived as a peasant for a year, and he introduced his father-in-law at one fire and the headman of his village at another.

Relentlessly, Gabriel repeated his mantra: This had to be done, and they could do it.

The second time he went out into the Darkness, he took Blanche and Kaitlin and Galahad and Ser Michael with him. The sound of women laughing was a better tonic than his words, and many a farm boy smiled to hear them and stiffened his spine, and everyone smiled at a baby.

But despite all, in the morning, a young Venikan volunteer was found to have committed suicide, falling messily on his sword like one of the Archaics.

Gabriel refused to let the army march. Instead, he rode back along the ranks with the duchess until he found the man's captain.

"Where were the four assigned with him?" Gabriel demanded.

The captains shrugged. "Asleep?" he asked.

"You are relieved," the emperor snapped.

Mortirmir looked at the body. But the boy had merely had enough: too much terror of the dark. Or of war, or of his captain.

"Ye can't hang the other four," Tom Lachlan snapped at the emperor.

"I can," Gabriel said petulantly.

"Nah, yer just acting like me. An' no one's hit ye. Leave it." Lachlan leaned close. "Yer scarin' folks."

"How could those four let a boy kill himself in a camp where everyone is supposed to be watching each other?" Gabriel spat. "If the *will* went for that boy, we'd have an outbreak right now."

"Aye," Tom said. "Let it be a lesson to ye, the next time ye bite off more'n you can chew. But don't blame they." Tom looked at his captain, and there was no humour to him at all. "Blame yerself."

They stopped marching early, after only twenty miles. The emperor ordered all the wagons circled, and then he personally ordered the three banda of the company to march off half a mile with the Nordikaans and the Scholae. He put out a handful of pickets, and then he climbed up on a big barrel and told them all to gather round. Almost two thousand men and women packed in.

"Friends," he said. "I've brought you to a bad place. But you know how to do this. Our allies don't. So stop mocking them, and help. Tell them about all the monsters you've put down. Tell them that this isn't half bad because there aren't wyverns or barghasts."

"Or fuckin' imps," shouted Cully.

"Or fucking imps. Tell them about facing Thorn. But by all that's holy, friends, I need you to help them through this Darkness, because we have ten more days of it and I need them."

Most of them didn't have any more Etruscan than it took to order wine or get a girl, some not even that much. But there were men like Angelo di Laternum and Ser Berengar and Master Julius and Father David who spoke the language well, and there were others like Oak Pew who understood the captain's intention, and simply went and stirred a pot, or sharpened a sword, or helped with some firewood. Suddenly, the Nova Terrans were everywhere, in their groups of five.

And Ser Gabriel and his knights and ladies were everywhere too, all evening.

And in the morning, no one was dead.

And they were all awake before the trumpet sounded.

"Two more days," the emperor said. "Or ten," he muttered.

And that afternoon, the light cavalry came up behind them, a cloud of dust visible by midmorning. By noon, they were moving on the hillsides either side of the road.

In the late afternoon, after carefully testing a fast-flowing mountain river with water cold as ice, the *proveditores* began refilling the water barrels. Pages watered horses.

Ser Michael had been awake all night the night before. As ordered. Now he rode along the column until he found the command group lying in an otherwise empty olive grove, and most of them sound asleep on the ground. Only the Nordikaans, who seemed made of metal, were awake.

Michael lay down by the emperor and went to sleep.

He awoke when Gabriel moved. The great man had one eye open.

"I assume we're moving through the night?" Michael asked.

Gabriel nodded.

"Christ," Michael swore.

The sickle moon rose on a landscape empty of movement, except for insects and birds. It was too still, and the pickets and vedettes were constantly too alert.

No one had slept much for several days.

They moved fast, nonetheless. The road was good, and they'd been spared rain, and the wagons moved almost as fast as horses, rolling along the flat plain. Even when they began the long, slow climb onto the first ridge of the growing mass of the mountains that could no longer be ignored, the plodding heavy horses kept the pace, halting only to feed from bags and drink water before moving on with their wagons.

For the cavalry, it was a hard night.

For the armoured infantry, it was the stuff of nightmares, and as men's fatigue grew, so did their fear and their perception of threat, so that the woods on either side of the road seemed full of menace. Crossbows were loosed into the woods on several occasions, the third leading to a lone Vardariote berating Master Pye's Armourers' Guild.

But at dawn, they were in the foothills of the largest mountains any of them had ever seen. Above them, the road up the pass wound around like a snake. There was no cover at all. Smooth green meadow and loose rock rose, hummock after hummock, to an incredible height above them. A single waterfall fell in rainbow splendour, almost five thousand feet over their heads.

Ser Gabriel rode to the head of the green banda. They were at the rear of the column, in reserve.

Gabriel rode to Sauce, who was commanding them. She was sitting with Dan Favour and Long Paw.

"I bet we're not halting," Sauce said. "Your Greatness."

Gabriel nodded. He pointed to the heights towering over them, the two incredible ridges that dwarfed the pass between them.

"I need the Greens to seize the high ground," he said.

Sauce looked at Long Paw, who made a face.

"You are out of your wits. My lord." Sauce spat. "No offence. My mouth is dry." She looked up, and she had to crane her neck. "Can't make it up that in harness. An' you said the Necromancer couldn't hold these passes."

"I'm wrong all the time, as you are always the first to tell me," Gabriel said. "There's no one else I can ask. If you like, I'll go myself."

Long Paw grunted. He looked up and flexed his hands, as if he were about to box or wrestle. "Son of a bitch," he said.

Sauce shook her head. "It's two miles," she said, gazing almost straight up.

"Think of it this way," Gabriel said. "If you can do this, you can do anything."

"Where's yon beastie? The one with wings?" Sauce asked.

"I'm saving him for the hard part," the Red Knight said.

"Blessed Virgin," Sauce said. "All right. Let's get at it. Armour off, you lot."

The army halted and slept where they sat. Soldiers started fires at the edge of the wood line and made tea, which boiled very easily. A meal was served, mostly hard bread and cheese and ham.

At midmorning, in lowering cloud, the Scholae started up the road. A handful of Vardariotes rode ahead of them.

About nones, a handful of Vardariotes came back led by Kaliax, their war-leader.

"We've found them," said Kaliax. "The taken. The not-dead."

The emperor sat up. "How many?" he asked.

"A thousand. With spears, standing on the road, blocking it. There's a bridge." The steppe woman shrugged. "No one moves." She made a face. "They are very young. I rode close."

"Here we go," Gabriel said. He shook his head. "This will be as bad as they can make it."

Three thousand feet above him, the Scholae began to shoot with their horn bows. Sixty or eighty mountain peasants were dead before they reacted in any way, and then they all leveled their spears in one motion. One of them, pushed by another, fell from the bridge, a hundred feet to the rocks below. The rest started forward.

The Scholae butchered them with archery, trotting away a few paces down the steep pass. It was an exercise in horsemanship, and occasionally in discipline, and always, in volley control.

It took only a few minutes.

Count Zac waved his riding whip in irritation. "We are very good at this," he said, as if in apology for the butchery.

"We're very good at killing peasants," Gabriel said bitterly. "This is the war our adversary wants." He smiled grimly. "Our adversaries. Very well. Let them see how fast we are."

Shortly after nones, the army was up and marching, and the Scholae came to the second blocking force. They had built a low stone wall, waist high, across the middle of another arched bridge. The chasm under the bridge seemed bottomless.

The *casa* came up while the Scholae were still trying to clear the barricade by archery. The emperor looked up above, where he could see the tops of the two ridges now, and a chapel, only half a mile above him.

The bridge was packed with the not-dead. Because the bridge over the chasm had a high arch, they were mostly safe from arrows.

"Glad they don't have bows," Michael muttered.

Ser Gabriel went and looked down into the chasm. It was hundreds of feet deep. The rivulet at the bottom was scarcely visible.

He whistled.

Harald Derkensun stepped forward. "Allow us," he said.

The emperor nodded, then saluted gravely. "Go," he said.

The third blockade was the most imaginative. The *will* had prepared an ambush, and an avalanche. But Long Paw came down on it from above, an hour before sunset, with half the green banda. Sauce stormed the abbey at the head of the pass, sword in hand, and the not-dead scarcely resisted. Later, they decided that the *will* hadn't had time to focus on them.

She stood in the bell tower, ten thousand feet above the plain of Mitla, and raised her sword.

The cheers of the army rang back and forth, an endless echo.

"Camp," Gabriel ordered. "Wake me when everyone's fed. Tonight, the *casa* and the Armourers' Guild will mount guard."

Harald Derkensun groaned.

The emperor embraced Long Paw and Sauce. He turned to Daniel Favour.

"Kneel," he said. "My sword," he whispered to Anne Woodstock. She whipped it from the scabbard and put it naked in his hand.

There, at the top of the highest pass in the world, the emperor knighted Daniel Favour before the whole army. Blanche gave the young man a kiss on each cheek. He blushed.

"Glad no one was here to defend the pass," Sauce muttered. "I all but sprouted wings, and Dan Favour gets knighted."

Gabriel managed a smile.

"You said easy-peasy," Sauce said.

Behind her, a great cage covered in tarpaulins came up the last of the pass, drawn by sixteen heavy horses, and the occupant let out a loud scream.

"We're not to the hard part yet," Gabriel said. "And I'm wrong all the time. Pray I'm not wrong again."

Morning, at the top of the world. It was bitter cold, and men and women sharing blankets after three days without sleep and a brutal climb simply snuggled deeper.

The watch changed. Hundreds of exhausted Albans collapsed into sleep as the white banda came on duty. A long convoy of wagons was already snaking up the pass.

Father David and two Etruscan priests said Matins in the abbey chapel. Below them, in the pass, the smoke of burning and the stench of roasting meat rose. The rear guard, and Petrarcha and Mortirmir, were disposing of the now-dead.

A huge pulse of used *potentia* went out across the world from the top of the pass.

Gabriel was just going off duty. His pavilion consisted of a space of stone floor six feet long by two feet wide, and Nicodemus had padded it with a straw mat that the steward was sharing, his mouth already open in a snore.

But he felt the pulse of *potentia*.

And had there been anyone awake to see him, they would have seen his face crinkle in what might have been a smile, if it hadn't been more like a snarl.

Here we come. Let witchcraft celebrate.

Even at noon, men were still asleep. But the abbey was supremely defensible and had huge stores of unburnt firewood. A human army could hold the pass until their food ran out.

The emperor rose only to eat and hear messages. Kronmir looked twenty years older—they all did. Sauce looked like she was fifty. Michael looked as if he still had the cough.

Gabriel consumed a hard-boiled egg and a sausage and drank a cup of hypocras. While he ate, Mortirmir came in, and Petrarcha. They examined their map, and every message Master Kronmir had. And in the end, they agreed to wait another day. Messenger birds were launched.

In the evening, most of the soldiers awoke and ate dinner. Two hundred miles west and north, Pavalo Payam held his fortifications until he'd driven off a fourth attack, by which time the sun was rising like a bloody streak in the eastern sky. Then, as he rallied his army, his philosophers set fire to the forests on either side of his position, and he slipped away into the morning and the smoke.

The *will* was slow to react. Its focus was elsewhere, and its armies were too late to spring their trap.

The rose-coloured sky heralded the rising sun, and then it burst, a crescent of winged fire, on the mountains. Snow sparkled, close enough that Sauce had collected a little as her half of the green banda traversed the glacier that hung above the monastery at the top of the world.

But the emperor's army was already gone. They had marched in the darkness. It was autumn in the high passes . . . winter was close. But the sun rose, triumphant still.

The emperor came down the Cisna Pass. To say his army was well rested would have been an exaggeration, but the army was moving as swiftly as three thousand men and women could move with horse-drawn baggage.

A hundred leagues and more to the north and west, another army of men moved as swiftly, as Payam and the sultan's army raced toward them.

And messenger Thirty-Four, riding the thermals six thousand feet above the plains of Arles, could see tens of thousands of subjected slaves marching west. Thirty-Four could see men and women, horses and cattle, moving with precision, between the two armies that they dwarfed utterly. The emperor rolled north to Arles, out of the passes and down the single road along the edge of the great glacier. The army of the sultan abandoned its baggage train and raced east.

Between them, the darkness gathered and pooled, and prepared its malice.

Two hundred leagues to the south, the army of the Patriarch of Rhum marched slowly northward.

Toward the Darkness.

Zac swept wide, hoping for deer or cattle or sheep, and found nothing. In the middle of the white banda, No Head, unstrung bow on his back, cursed and gnawed on some dry bread.

Uruk of Mogon was looking around himself. "No meat?" he said.

No Head nodded. "No meat," he said.

Uruk's horny, ovoid head wobbled on his carapace. "Hungry," he said.

"You and me both, brother," No Head said.

"Too many rocks," Uruk said.

No Head nodded. "Have some bread."

Gabriel gathered all his captains again at sunset. Nicodemus and his people, all combatants now, prepared the round table, and this time, they sat in a circle on stones and drank warm water. There was no wine, not even for the emperor. There was bread, and not much more, in the hundred wagons that now formed the very heart of the army.

"It is possible that I won't survive the next few hours," he said. He held up a hand. "I'm not going to explain. If I fall, you have sealed orders. But if I do what I have set out to do, you must march as hard as you can. You must march until you drop. Until you reach Arles. It's about a hundred miles that way."

"What of the not-dead?" Giselle asked.

Mortirmir nodded. "There won't be any," he said.

"Or that's what we hope," Gabriel said. "We've done all we could to make our enemy put all his eggs in one basket. Now they are all together, as best as we can tell, about fifty miles from here."

"And you?" asked the duchess.

"Mortirmir and I are going to challenge the Necromancer for the possession of his slaves," the emperor said.

"Single combat?" Tom Lachlan asked.

"Nothing so chivalrous," Gabriel said. "Murder in the dark, if I can manage it."

"An' you ain't takin' us?" Bad Tom shot back.

Gabriel shook his head. "No," he said. "Not unless you can get on Ariosto. You must have noticed I haven't had him in the sky since we were at sea."

The officers nodded.

"We have fifty leagues of mountains and valleys between us and the plains of Arles," Gabriel said quietly. "Pavalo is a day's march to the south, and the Necromancer knows he's been fooled. And like any general, instead of pouncing on the Ifriqu'ans, he's circling his wagons. He lost contact, and now he just has to hold on. It's twenty-five days until the conjunction of the stars and the opening of the gate, or so our astrologers tell us."

"We only have food for five more days, and that's not going to be a life o' pleasure," Sauce put in.

"Three days, when we feed the Ifriqu'ans," the emperor noted.

They groaned.

"And at our backs, the Legate of Rhum has an army and a fleet." Gabriel looked at Kronmir, who looked pained.

"It appears that in toppling the Patriarch we have unleashed a more dangerous man," he said.

Tom leaned back far enough that it appeared his stool might collapse. "So we go back an' fight 'em?" he said.

Gabriel nodded. "Yes. Almost certainly. But Arles first. Only Arles matters."

Duchess Giselle slapped an angry hand on the table. "Berona and Venike will not feel that way when the full weight of the Patriarch and all our foes in the north combine against us, my lord."

The emperor rose to his feet, forcing his whole council to rise with him. "Madame, if I am here in the morning to discuss strategy, we will probably decide to send the Venikans and the Beronese back over the Cisna Pass. If Pavalo can be induced to join you, we will have more than enough soldiers to cow the legate." He gave her a smile that Sauce knew well, and Gavin. "If I don't return," he said with a malicious grin, "you'll have to rely on Michael." He nodded.

"I'm his apprentice," Michael said.

No one laughed.

One by one they came and wished him luck, and then he knighted Toby.

"Ser Tobias is a mouthful," he said, as he delivered the buffet to Toby's shoulder.

Toby burst into tears.

And last, he went to say good-bye to Blanche. But she forestalled him, and she came out to the round table with Kaitlin and Lady Tancreda. They were all dressed finely, and wore smiles on their faces. Tancreda raised her veil and kissed Morgon, and Blanche bit the emperor's lower lip. Gently.

"Come back to me," she said. "And no nonsense." She smiled, and he admired her, because she betrayed nothing.

He'd always admired her courage.

And then he was in his flying cote and his gauntlets, and Toby settled his helmet on his head even as Anne belted the sword around his waist. Blanche gave him his *ghiaverina* when he was mounted, and Morgon scrambled up behind.

Now we do this hard thing? Ariosto asked.

Now we do, the Red Knight said.

It took them almost an hour to climb into the very last light, the dying light of the end of day. As fast as the sun lipped over the far western horizon, so they rose to catch a little more of the pink and orange light. And still the great peaks of the mountains to the west and south towered over them, and even at this great height, the mountains to the north were higher.

I can't sense a thing toward Arles. The ridges are too high, Morgon said in the *aethereal*.

It was worth a try, Gabriel shot back, and then they turned slowly, and Ariosto took them north and west into the high valleys of the mountains of eastern Arles. The moon rose as they flew, first, disconcertingly, appearing below them, as if they were indeed in the *aethereal* beyond the world of air. An hour's flying, with no sound but the rush of air, no feeling but the steady thump of the great wings. The darkness was so intense that Gabriel had to look up into the star-filled void to get a sense of himself; to look down at the valley below was to become disoriented.

Gabriel concentrated on flying. Now that they were past the first valley and into the Arles mountains, he let Ariosto fly lower, where the air was "thicker" and the great avian had more power and more breath as well. And, at least as far as he and Morgon understood, the lower they were, the harder they would be to detect.

Ariosto rode a warm current of air up out of the last of three great valleys, rising toward the notch of light that marked a high pass. It was too high for the army. Gabriel tried to breathe deeply, but his chest was tight and his arms felt without strength.

He was deeply afraid.

Look, Morgon said.

Gabriel rested his hands on his thighs so that Ariosto would not receive the wrong message and went *into his palace. From there, he ducked into Morgon's labyrinth.*

Look! the magister said.

He had rigged a dark mirror of his own thought, and on it, a spot glowed a deep, matte black.

There he is. They are. Whatever abomination they have become. Morgon nodded.

And we are now visible to them? Gabriel asked.

No, Morgon shot back, pettishly. I explained this. Unless we work ops, *we cannot be seen.*

I will stay low anyway, Gabriel said.

I will watch them, Morgon said. They are . . . fascinating.

In the real, Gabriel landed just south of the top of the pass, with a mass of hundreds of paces of solid rock and ice between him and his adversaries. He wished he could build a fire, and he was astounded to find that his canteen had frozen.

Moving, Morgon said.

Gabriel's heart gave a great beat, as if it were going to leap from his chest. He *went back to Morgon's palace and stood on the black-and-white chessboard as the magister moved his pieces.*

I cannot tell if they are two or three, Morgon said. *But one is moving this way.*

Gabriel felt reality flicker around him. His fear rose to choke him, and he, veteran of fear, master of fear, almost lost his concentration. "How can they see us?" *he asked.*

Morgon shrugged. "Perhaps they can and perhaps not. Perhaps even the tiny trickle of ops we use to maintain our palaces is visible to a magister as puissant as the Necromancer."

Gabriel wondered if this was how Sauce felt when he made a pronouncement and was wrong. He took a deep breath and counted to three. He could only manage three.

"Can you use mathmetika to estimate its speed?" *he asked.*

Morgon fiddled a moment. "An excellent thought. Yes. It moves…" *He paused.* "Very fast. A hundred fifty leagues in an hour, perhaps."

"Nothing is that fast," *Gabriel said.*

"Dragons are that fast," *Morgon said.*

The word dragon *hung between them in the* aethereal, *as if, in this case, naming surely called.*

"The missing dragon," *Gabriel said.* "The sorcerer, the Odine, and a dragon. A man, a dragon, and a nest of Wyrms. The black carrion thing that followed Kronmir and the duchess. Crap. And we thought we were the first to make alliance with the Wild." *He frowned.* Master Smythe. I have found the missing traitor, Rhun."

Morgon stroked his beard, which was a better, more elegant beard in the aethereal *than his somewhat thin beard was in the real.* "No point in running," *he said.*

"Damn," *Gabriel said.* "Although Bad Tom wants to kill a dragon."

But even as he thought it, his nerves died away. He surfaced into the real and put a hand on Ariosto.

Ready? he asked. We have to fight.

The griffon turned and its eyes glittered in the starlight. *Fight?* it asked with relish. *You said this would be hard!*

It will be, Gabriel said.

449

*

No talking of any kind. No memory palace, no hermetical detection. Nothing.

They rose into the jeweled sky and Ariosto took them higher on the slope of the mountain that rose above them, until they were at the snow line, looking east and north. And then the great avian began to fly long, lazy spirals.

Gabriel felt a new tension rising in him, connected to the ring on his finger and the golden cord of light that tied him to Amicia a continent away. Somewhere far to the west, something was happening.

He did not dare check. He did not dare to send a pulse of power along the golden cord, or to try to find her walking on the wind.

It was dark, and cold, and even as they turned again, so the moon began to come into his visor, and an icy, wind-driven rain began to fall on them.

Doubt, the enemy of ambush, began to gnaw at Gabriel. The dragon—if there was a dragon—could be anywhere; above them, behind them...

So powerful was his own fear that he whirled in his saddle to look behind. There was nothing there but cold air and the rush of endless darkness. Cold rocks and ice awaited him two thousand feet below, and the dull sky spat rain and a little snow on the last scrubby tall pines off Ariosto's left wingtip.

Arrgggh!

AAAAARRGGGHHH!

The great scream roared through the aethereal *like the first gust of a hurricane, and the second was louder and longer; not agony but rage and defiance.*

Gabriel found the source. Instantly. And left before he could get entangled.

Whatever had just bellowed in the *aethereal* was less than ten miles away, and lower, somewhere to the west. Gabriel reached back and pinched Morgon's unarmoured thigh, and then pointed.

Morgon tapped his helmet, perhaps a little too hard.

Using his legs and hands, Gabriel turned Ariosto west and the great wings beat harder. Then, for the first time, Gabriel was fully in command of his mount, and he turned them a little north of west and passed between two of the great towering spires, keeping the western-most between himself and the adversary.

ArrggghhhhhhhhhAAGRRGGGFFFGGG!

Gabriel felt the blast reverberate off the hillsides. Had it been sound, snow might have fallen, but in the *aethereal*, only hermetical things were rattled. Along with his nerves.

It was the scream Ash had given when he turned to face Master Smythe. And Gabriel knew what it was for.

It was not defiance or not solely so. It was a scream meant to echo; it was an attempt to locate the foe in the sky. Or so Gabriel guessed, and with that guess came a second.

Their foe expected to face another dragon.

Of course.

He banked Ariosto a little to the north, and then more, following a very high valley, a ripple in the up-thrust mantle of the earth. Mountains flew by each wingtip in a rush of air and a roaring silence.

AARARAGGKKUS—

There it was. Black as coal, ragged, and rising beneath them, its scream was directed west into the mountains.

Ariosto opened his beak and gave a shriek of joy and terror in the real.

Now Gabriel spat in a timeless moment as the griffon's talons reached for its monstrous adversary.

He tugged at the reins and they rolled north toward the thing's endless tail, a whipping, rotting rope of black. Even in the high cold air, Gabriel could smell the decay.

A line of fire struck the black dragon high on its back and began to walk forward along its spine and Gabriel turned Ariosto again, now coming across the aerial leviathan from above and behind.

His griffon had its own ideas. Like an angry cat, Ariosto's talons went in every direction as the griffon slashed down into a black wing from above and behind, and despite the disparity in size, the griffon shredded yards of rotten, scaled flesh as it plunged *through* the dragon's wing. Morgon's line of fire burned steadily away.

The dragon seemed to fold in half.

The long, sinuous neck reached, and the jaws opened—a tortured stench flowed over the Red Knight as he banked, but Ariosto ignored his piloting and folded his wings and dropped even as the air exploded in a black-lit rage of malevolence that left a dark stain in the *aethereal*.

They tumbled away, trading altitude for speed.

Gabriel looked up into the wind and threw a single white bolt of lightning from his prepared store and then, *entering his palace fully and trusting Ariosto, he summoned* ops *and cast from scratch, a long process.*

"Net, Pru. A big net of ops." *He waved at the symbols and she chanted with him, reinforcing his will. He* emerged to cast and then pulled the golden shield over all of them even as three black bolts struck back and the titanic dragon dove straight at them, following them down.

Down was an impossible depth beneath them, and there was no moon to tell Gabriel how close death was.

You know what you are doing? Gabriel asked his mount.

Do you? Ariosto spat back.

All the weight of the world began to settle on Gabriel's shoulders and hips.

He was completely disoriented; his sense of up and down was lost, and only a chance sighting of starlight on an ancient glacier to his right told him that he was upside down and his gallant mount was in a loop, racing destruction and the ground. Behind him the dragon blew through the *aethereal* net and there was a concussion in the real as the whole thing gave way all together, and every peak sprouted an avalanche, as if the mountains themselves were weeping.

Ariosto leveled his dive and rolled south around a spire of rock, and the dragon, mere seconds behind, carried straight on, snapping the spire off cleanly fifty feet above its base and sending tons of rock plunging down the hillside.

A huge talon reached out, a predator reaching for prey.

Morgon loosed from his whole right hand five separate emanations all worked simultaneously. The talon was incinerated and the monster roared. Stone split.

Ariosto turned again, but the wall of the ridge was rising up before them and there was almost no more room to turn.

"Too heavy!" the gallant griffon sighed. He turned again...

...and Morgon Mortirmir rolled over the back of the saddle...and was gone.

"No!" Gabriel screamed, but Ariosto had already turned; lighter by one whole rider, the griffon rode the dragon's own wave front, surfing across the pulse of displaced air along a wing, mere inches from destruction, and Gabriel, desperate, hacked with the *ghiaverina* and had the satisfaction of watching the blade strike effortlessly through the great bone that supported the rotten structure of the wing.

The head turned.

The great black eye...

...was empty...

No malevolence burned in it. No enmity raged.

No one was there, in that head.

The black dragon's left wing began to fold where he'd cut it. It seemed to happen in a dreamlike stillness; the rush of air drowned all sound, the cold seemed to blanket his perception, and he watched as the dragon lost whatever it was that allowed it to fly.

And still the head came around, its focus total. In the same dream-speed, even as the long-dead carcass began to plunge toward the glacier two thousand feet below, and dimly lit by the emergent moon, the black jaws cracked open, and the head tracked them.

Gabriel stood in Ariosto's stirrups and threw the *ghiaverina* straight down into the opening mouth.

Almost directly under him, the dragon's jaws opened wide—

White light exploded all around the dragon's head and body. A red fire burned at its heart and lit the foul stuff of the dragon's breath deep inside it, or perhaps some other deadly gases long penned in the pools of bile and corruption.

Gabriel, granted a fraction of a second, threw all three of his precious shields between himself and the dragon like a farmer sowing grain into the wind...

But whatever last strike the mastering will deep inside the dead dragon planned, the flesh was too weak. The red and white fires burned; the *ghiaverina* fell like a meteor through the corpse and burst in a halo of fire from the underside as, flaming, the not-dead dragon fell, burning, a slow meteor in a black sky. The stars towered above its fall, and its fall was very slow. The undamaged wing still beat, so that the not-dead beast fell like a fluttering leaf, shedding fire. Twice, gouts of black *ops* emerged from the corpse. The first detonated on Prudentia's glowing shield and subsumed it. The second ate through Gabriel's inner shield like a new fire consumes dry wood.

Aspis! he called, and drew *potentia* like a drowning man drawing breath. He threw in his reserve, and all of Pru's and then, unthinking, he drew power through the golden thread that bound him.

And power came. There was a blinding flash of it and for a moment, in the real, the whole world seemed to blink.

Four thousand miles to the west, in the great Abbey of Lissen Carak, Amicia was singing her praises to God with her sisters. In their praises was all their trust, and love; a hymn of protection and keeping and holding. Because in the air above the ancient fortress hovered another dragon, and he was trying their defences from the air.

Ash had come.

And Ash was old, even as dragons reckoned age. The workings of Thorn had been nothing to Ash's workings, and every flick of his talons sent another volley; fire, ice, raw *ops*, subtle counterenchantment, sullen fury and straight power.

Amicia was kneeling with her sisters: seventy women, some ordinary and some extraordinary, who together made a choir. And their polyphony rose to heaven, and their workings buttressed, reinforced, enabled, repaired. They unleashed no torrents of fire; they worked no glowing crystals of *ops*-redolent ice.

They endured.

And in the midst of their choir, Amicia stood. Her brown-gold hair and her white veil alone stood out among her sisters, and she began to glow gold—pure gold, as if she were herself cast of the stuff, except that the glow suggested that she might be molten gold.

Miriam stood. "Sing!" she commanded as the mighty *Agnus Dei* faltered.

Amicia spread her arms. The golden *ops* flowed through her so fast that gouts of it fell away from her to shower the other sisters, and those who knew how gathered it and flung it into the net of workings that protected the fortress.

Amicia began to rise.

For a moment, she turned and looked down at Miriam.

"Good-bye," she said.

And then she rose to the chapel's roof-trees. Just short of the roof itself, she spread her arms as wide as they would go, and said one word aloud.

Fiat.

And then she was gone, leaving only a lingering perfume; the thought of roses, the odour of veneration and carefully tended altars, and the scent of love.

Every magister in the world felt it. Every irk, every man and woman, every shaman, every wight and warden and the fish in the sea, and each and every dragon felt it.

Morgon Mortirmir lost control of his descent and crashed into a tree.

Harmodius, in midworking in an orphanage in Harndon, watched the prepared *ops* in his hand go out like a candle in the wind, unaccountably drawn elsewhere with the scent of pine and rose.

Lord Kerak, an island of fire in a sea of bogglins, received all unlooked-for a gout of worked *ops* tinged in gold and roses, and his body seemed to emit light as once more he rained fire on his foes, no longer beyond hope.

Tamsin, shielding N'gara with all her might, felt power like the march of a relieving army flood her ancient bones.

Gavin Muriens watched as helpless fury gave way to joy; as his beaten army, poised on the edge of massacre, seemed to take a breath; as every one of his potent magisters gathered new strength that seemed, in the same breath, to rob their adversaries of theirs.

It was not victory. But in one breath the balance shifted, and massacre became mere defeat. Ash's multitude of westerners paused, as if struck with awe.

And Ash hesitated, turned in the air over Lissen Carak, and fled. There was no laughter in him, and he was, for once, afraid.

Ruin's last emanation burned; the black fire raged through Gabriel's shield, and then . . .

For a moment, there was . . .

nothing . . .

But a sense of roses in spring, and the distant scent of pines, and perhaps a trace of orange, as if it were a late-spring night in the courtyard of the great fortress.

good-bye she said.

And the black dragon struck the icy glacier to break into a thousand worm-infested shreds on the ice far below.

Weeping, for he knew what must have happened, Gabriel nonetheless reached out and spoke one word in Archaic, and the *ghiavarina* rose out of the depths to his hand as Ariosto turned to avoid joining the dragon in death, or a second death, in the clutches of a glacier as old as the world.

Together they turned, and Gabriel's tears flowed, and froze against his face.

good-bye

Morgon Mortirmir was high in a mighty tall pine, and only his pride was injured; pride, and a series of lacerations on both arms that would in other circumstances have warranted a different response than Gabriel's laughter.

"It's not funny. I had everything correct except..."

Ariosto fetched the magister with one practiced claw.

"By God," Gabriel said, and threw his arms around the magister.

Morgon Mortirmir burst into tears. "We..." He paused. "Where did all the power come from?"

"Amicia. She's gone. And we are not done," Gabriel managed.

"We slew a *dragon*," Mortirmir said. "Oh, my lord. I miscalculated grievously there. I did not expect that."

"You and me both." Gabriel shook his head. "And now the Odine know we're coming."

Ariosto required an hour's rest. Morgon spent the time muttering anxiously and watching the sky, but there was nothing to be done. The great griffon was tired—so tired he wanted to sleep, and the mountainside was so cold...

"Light a fire," Gabriel said. He had been watching the black streaks that were the ruin of the dead dragon on the next ridge. "The Odine know we put the dragon down. They must."

"What will they do?" Morgon said. "What would you do?" he asked, curious. "For a moment, there was no world," he said. "Oh, what I have just learned."

"No world..." Gabriel paused.

Gabriel had known for a long time that Amicia was...leaving. But he found the truth very difficult to endure, and worse, he saw that she had pushed him away to make this moment easier. He thought of Blanche. He thought of what he must, in the end, do to Blanche.

And then, with an effort of will his mother would have approved of, he pushed it all away. He concentrated on the night, the icy air, the tired griffon, and the Odine.

"Negotiate?" Gabriel said. "If I were them and someone killed my dragon, I'd negotiate." He managed a weak smile. Using *ops... he was full of it, now...* he got a fire lit and managed some warm water for the three of them, which was fine provender compared to a cold night at high altitude. "I'm perfectly serious, Morgon. If I were on the receiving end of the destruction of my dead necromantic pet dragon, I'd negotiate." He looked at the young magister. "And if they live in the *aethereal*, as Al Rashidi said..."

Mortirmir looked out over the dark woods. No light showed. There was not a single person to light a candle in fifty miles of plains. It was *very dark*.

"This is what the world must have been like, before man came," Mortirmir said.

Gabriel nodded and shivered.

"I don't think that they can negotiate," Mortirmir said. "They can only conquer or die."

"What a terrible flaw," Gabriel said.

The night was passing, and all three of them experienced cramps, and the sweat inside Gabriel's furs was all but frozen. The fire couldn't seem to reach his bones. He tried to wall off his sorrow. He wanted Blanche.

"Dark humour to die here of exposure after that fight," he said.

Morgon nodded. "If Ariosto will bear us, let us get this thing done." He smiled. "It is a mad thing, my lord, and yet I understand it. In one bolt, you free us from having to wade in the blood of all these poor souls."

Gabriel shrugged. "Yes," he said. "Except the dragon was rotten, Morgon. What does that tell you?"

"That the Odine can keep them after death," Mortirmir said.

"The taken, not-dead villagers may already have starved to death," Gabriel said bitterly.

Morgon paused, looking out over the sparkling stars that seemed close enough to touch, and the dark woods that seemed like a carpet of velvet under their feet. "We will know in an hour," he said.

"Ariosto is tired," Gabriel said.

"You said we only have one chance at this. It's not really true. We could go back to camp. But *if* the Odine think like strategists; *if* they know what happened here…"

"They must," Gabriel said.

"Don't interrupt. I'm thinking…" Mortirmir shot back.

Gabriel laughed.

Even in the starlit darkness, the magister's look of annoyance was palpable, followed instantly by a look of sheepish embarrassment. "I'm doing it again, am I?"

Gabriel was just getting feeling in his fingers. "Well, one of us is the emperor. And it is not you, my friend."

Mortirmir laughed. "That's true."

"But I agree, nonetheless. They'd disperse. This must all have happened before; the working Al Rashidi built; it's the twin of the one I saw Master Smythe employ. If the Odine remember, then they have responses to it, even if…" He shook his head. "We have to try. There's fifty thousand people out there, and I will not tell my lady I failed to save them because I was too cold."

Mortirmir smiled. "You can be funny, too," he said. "But come, let us be heroes."

"Ariosto will be the hero of this piece. *Comrade, can you bear us?* Gabriel asked.

Can you build a fire on my saddle? But yes. I am so filled with… the thing? The thing when you crush your enemy and you are the one with the most power? I will fly to Albinkirk if you like. Only…

Speak to me. Only what? Gabriel asked.

Only… I am very tired and very hungry.

Thirty miles. Gabriel tried to show the griffon an image of the distance.

Whatever that is?

From the Tower of Albinkirk to the nice farm with all the maidens. And back, Gabriel said.

Perhaps, the griffon said. For a monster of almost unlimited puissance, he sounded very unsure.

Gabriel didn't like the sound of that. *If we were in Albinkirk, could you fly to Mistress Helewise's farm? And land there?*

Yes.

Gabriel looked at Morgon. "Change of plans," he said.

*

When Ariosto leapt into the air, night was passing, and indeed, the sky was just slightly brighter. It was the false dawn; the time when old people die, when hopes fail, and when ambuscades lose their nerve, when men call out and wives comfort them.

They flew low, because even a modicum of surprise was better than none, and they did not communicate. Mortirmir cast a complex working on one of his rings to indicate direction. The rest was left to guesswork.

It was very cold. Even in furs, even inside the hermetical protection of his helmet, Gabriel was not sure he had ever been as cold, and as the sky grew pale in the east, their proximity to the ground began to wear on him. Ariosto rode low, skimming across fields like a skate skimming the ocean bottom, and rising only to clear trees by the barest margin.

By their calculations, the trip from the Range of Arles should have taken no more than a third of an hour.

It seemed to take forever. And they flew, alone, over abandoned fields and along valley floors, and the wind bit into them, and Gabriel knew fear, terror, despair.

But he had known them since youth.

And far out to the east, the sun was rising over the deserts of Hatti. The sky was becoming pale.

Dawn was coming amid the Darkness.

"Day will come again," he whispered to the rushing air.

At some point he began to recognize that he was seeing people. There were fields of them, tens of thousands, standing in groups, or alone, or packed in huddles, most walking. A few lay on the ground, and not just people, but deer, and bears, and mules and cattle and sheep, as far as he could see. They were a blur under Ariosto's wings, close enough that he might have thrown his dagger and hit them.

Most were moving.

Not a head turned at the rush of Ariosto's wings.

Gabriel turned to look at Morgon, who was leaning over, clearly very cold, hunched in a near ball, his eyes on his ring.

He tapped Gabriel. And held up his hand. Even as Gabriel watched, a finger went down.

Four.

Gabriel reached out for his griffon. *Ready? High as you can.*

Ready. Very tired.

Last stop. I promise.

From Morgon's hand. *Three.*

Where can I land?

I'm working on that. Gabriel felt Ariosto's fatigue and sorrow.

Two.

Here we go. High as you can.

I will give you everything I have.

One.

Now, Ariosto.

Since the count began, the great griffon had begun to fly faster, the red and green and gold wings sweeping up and down, the freezing air passing over them, the rush become a hurricane.

And now Ariosto's head came up in a snap on the word *now*. And with his head his body, and his wings beat like a cavalry charge, and a surge of power lifted them up.

And as they rose, the sun crested the mountains far to the east. One single warm ray like a lance of light caught Ariosto's wings so that he seemed to catch fire.

Below them, every head on every not-dead creature swiveled. Every head.

And still Ariosto raced up into the heavens, burning like a phoenix rising from its own ashes.

Not there yet, Morgon said. *Higher.*

Trying!

As far as Gabriel could see, there were not-dead. And every one of them seemed to raise an arm in salute; there was a ripple in the aethereal.

Aspis.

Hoplon.

Scutum.

Greatly daring, Gabriel angled his shields.

In the emotional safety of Morgon's chessboard, the magister uncrossed his legs. "Oh, very good indeed," he said.

The first strike of the Odine was fire. Every not-dead raised a spark, like a choir of discordant sound that nonetheless makes music, and the fire rose in a magnificent ball. A human sorcerer's effort, cast by the Odine.

Gabriel angled his shields and took the fire as heat, deflected and contained it, and Morgon helped him, and the inferno became propulsion, and they rose suddenly.

Ariosto let forth a scream, whether of pain or triumph Gabriel didn't know, and rode the sudden updraft.

Higher. We can take anything they can throw. Mortirmir now sounded like himself. Certain.

We have been wrong so many times.

Higher. One time pays for all.

A second time the chorus of Odine sent fire, and again Ariosto rode it.

Now it will change tactics. Too late.

Morgon Mortirmir's voice had the hard sound of fate.

A little higher.

I am very tired, friends.

Everything, my love. This is for everything.

Hah! Take this then! called the gallant griffon, and his wings beat, and beat again, like a giant hummingbird.

And they went higher. The people in the fields below were no longer visible as people, or even a mass of people, but only as colours. And the fields and high passes of Arles spread under them like a carpet, and the massing of all the slaves of the Odine was like a stain, spreading even as they watched.

There, Morgon said.

He raised his hand. Gabriel turned to watch.

"To cast fire upon the earth," Morgon said, and with those words, his working unfolded like dye in water, or smoke from a new fire.

First he held a fire in his hand, and then an uncountable multitude of tiny dots of intense red light fell away from his hand, exploding into the darkness below, falling and yet flying, spiraling, a fountain of light and fire and gold and green and red exploding outward and away.

The myriad of light fell away into the Darkness at the speed of thought, and yet had presence and colour, so that trails of light burned in their retinas, a thousand, ten thousand, a hundred thousand.

They raced to the earth for as long as a man might draw five breaths. So long, that Gabriel began to fear...

And in one long breath, the Odine flinched. There was a ripple of Darkness, a sort of purple effervescence across ten miles of fields. And yet in that moment, Gabriel had the impression that the Odine had found some limitation; that their choir could not access *potentia* as they expected.

The black wave rippled through the Darkness.

The world took a shuddering breath.

And every pinpoint of red and gold and green blew through the black and struck its target.

There was a flare, a flicker of light.

I must go down now, Ariosto said.

Can you glide? Gabriel asked.

For a little while, I suppose. Ariosto turned. *That was glorious. Did we . . . win? Did we subsume our prey?*

Gabriel was looking at the ground. *I don't know*, he said. And then he rushed to Morgon's palace.

We need to help him get down, he said. *I assume you know how to fly.*

Morgon laughed. *Fly is a little extreme*, he said.

They came to rest in a field a few hundred paces from the great citadel of Arles, which showed in its fabric the attempts of the last two months to take it. The citadel had mighty protections that rose hundreds of feet in the air, and neither Morgon nor Ariosto had the energy to spare to flutter weakly against the great shields for admittance.

And Ariosto, game to the end, managed to bring them to rest against the slightly rotten remains of a hayrick. The griffon could not stand; in fact, he simply toppled over as soon as he came to rest, and Gabriel, having survived a black dragon and the Odine, was only saved from a particularly nasty broken leg by cutting his harness straps with his dagger.

He rose, cut Morgon free before the griffon could roll on him, and then spent a moment cutting the saddle away too.

Morgon Mortirmir was on his knees.

Gabriel thought of Amicia and joined him. He said his first prayer in ten years.

Morgon spat and got to his feet.

"Hear that?" he said.

Gabriel pulled the helmet from his head. Sound rushed in, normal sound, the background noise of life.

A baby was crying. Two ragged and very hungry sheep were *baaaing* for all they were worth.

There were people moving with the ragged imprecision of people. Many lay still in the unmown hay, but others were moving, crying, laughing, embracing. Falling to their knees.

Morgon extended one puissant hand. He lifted the two sheep from the warm grass and moved the two astounded creatures through the air and dropped them at Ariosto's beak.

"Some eggs have to be broken," Morgon muttered.

With painful deliberation, the griffon looked at the sheep, and then, in one careful lunge, it had one, and began to pull it apart with all the finesse of a predator. And eat.

Gabriel smiled at his mount. "Indeed," he said to Morgon. He was looking out over the fields of Arles, where thousands of peasants, and survivors of various armies, and all the souls held captive by the Odine had become a mass of panicked, hungry people. "Fewer eggs than I expected. I think I'm on the side of the smallest negative outcome. For once."

"And you have a plan for fifty thousand refugees?" Mortirmir asked.

"Yes," Gabriel said. He shrugged. "Sort of."

"You have a plan for saving N'gara and beating Ash?" Mortirmir asked.

"I do now," Gabriel said.

Mortirmir smiled. "I like it when you sound confident. What do we do now?"

The Red Knight pointed at the citadel of Arles. "We get inside that fortress," he said.

Morgon nodded. "How do we get in?" he asked.

Gabriel pointed at the gates. "Clarissa de Sartres comes and lets us in. And then..." He smiled. "And then the hard part starts."

"So you keep saying."

The gates to the fortress were, indeed, opening. Ariosto opened one eye, and a taloned foot shot out, and the second sheep died.

"Arles holds a master gate. In twenty-three days, all the gates will be aligned in seven spheres. Ash thinks he's lured us to this point with his Odine allies, whom he wanted destroyed anyway, so that while we were focused on Antica Terra, he could take Lissen Carak, control the gates, and win the game. And since we've just put the Odine down, they won't be waiting at the other master gate as rivals."

Morgon ran his fingers through his beard. There was a streak of grey in his beard, and a flash of white at each temple. The night had aged him. "Ash is very clever."

There was a young woman on a white horse, in armour, emerging from the fortress and riding toward them. A hundred men-at-arms followed her, and Gabriel could detect not one but two magisters with her.

Gabriel twirled his mustache. Seated his sword where he wanted it, and put his dagger back in its sheath.

"Since you are your usual cocky self, I assume you have something in mind," Morgon said.

"I am betting everything...a pretty large everything...on Ash having forgotten that gates swing both ways," Gabriel said. "After we defeat the Patriarch and stabilize all the starving people, we march to Lissen Carak. Through all seven spheres."

Morgon began to laugh.

"Oh," he snorted. "Oh God. That's...beautiful."

"Tom Lachlan thinks so, too," the Red Knight said.

The woman in armour was coming closer, and her knights were pointing at the griffon, and two were riding toward the vast crowd of people in the valley at their feet.

Gabriel waved to Clarissa. "As promised, I've come back," he called.

THE TYRANT

SERIES

by CHRISTIAN CAMERON

Opening in the setting sun of Alexander the Great's legendary life, follow the adventures of Athenian cavalry officer Kineas and his family. When Alexander dies, the struggle for power between his generals throws Kineas's world into uproar. He must fight if he is to hold on to what is his . . .

Available now from Orion Books

THE LONG WAR
SERIES

by CHRISTIAN CAMERON

Arimnestos of Plataea is just a young boy
when he is forced to swap the ploughshare
for the shield wall and is plunged into the fires
of battle for the first time. As the Greek world
comes under threat from the might of the
Persian Empire, Arimnestos must take up his
spear to preserve his entire way of life.

Available now from Orion Books